SOME
SOME
SOMETHI
SOMETHING BLUE

CONTENTS

SOMETHING OLD, SOMETHING NEW, SOMETHING BORROWED, SOMETHING BLUE

BY
MARY LYONS
VALERIE PARV
MIRANDA LEE
EMMA GOLDRICK

MILLS & BOON LIMITED
ETON HOUSE   18-24 PARADISE ROAD
RICHMOND   SURREY   TW9 1SR

*First published in Great Britain 1992
by Mills & Boon Limited*

© Mary Lyons 1992
© Valerie Parv 1992
© Miranda Lee 1992
© Emma Goldrick 1992

*Australian copyright 1992
Philippine copyright 1992
This edition 1992*

ISBN 0 263 77717 0

*Set in Times Roman 10½ on 12 pt.
98-9207-102468 C*

Made and printed in Great Britain

SOMETHING OLD
Mary Lyons

CHAPTER ONE

'I PUBLISH the Banns of Marriage between Serena Jane Harding of this parish and Archibald Leonard Fox of the city of Westminster. If any of you know cause, or just impediment, why these two persons should not be joined together in holy Matrimony, ye are to declare it. This is the first time of asking.

'If the congregation would now please stand?' the vicar continued. 'We will sing the hymn, "Love Divine, All Loves Excelling".'

Embarrassed to feel a flush spreading over her pale cheeks as various friends and neighbours turned their heads to smile at her, Serena frowned at her younger sister, Jenny, who was dramatically rolling her eyes and giving Serena a wide toothy grin.

'*Archibald*? Who is Arch-i-bald . . .?' the girl whispered with a stifled giggle. 'I thought that "Mr Terrific" was called Damian?'

'He is—well, most of the time, anyway. And will you *please* stop calling him by that stupid name!' Serena hissed back out of the corner of her mouth.

She was very fond of Jenny, but there were times when her young sister could be a real pain! And why the girl, who prided herself on being a trendy fourteen-year-old, should have taken such an aversion to her fiancé, Serena had absolutely no idea. Her mother, for instance, had been amazed and thrilled that her eldest daughter—who'd decided on leaving university to become a freelance researcher into historical re-

7

cords—should have become engaged to the well-
known TV and film producer, Damian Fox.

'Wasn't it lucky that it was *you* the TV company
hired for that programme about rich Americans being
able to buy themselves a title?' her mother had
enthused. But, although Serena had tried to explain
that they weren't *real* titles, with a seat in the House
of Lords, Mrs Harding hadn't been interested.

'That's not the point, dear,' she'd said firmly. 'I'm
just so pleased that your job—which I always thought
so tedious and boring—should have brought you into
contact with dear Damian. *Such* an interesting man—
and all my friends are *so* envious that I'm going to
be his mother-in-law!' she'd added with a beaming
smile.

However, Jenny, far from being dazzled by her
sister's marriage, had been highly critical of the
forthcoming nuptials.

'Do you *really* want to marry someone who keeps
saying "terrific, wonderful!" every five minutes?'
Jenny had demanded as Damian's smart red sports
car had driven off down the drive, after his first and
only visit to her family home.

'But I thought you liked his programmes?' Serena
looked at her in surprise.

Jenny had shrugged, staring glumly down at the
ground. 'Yes, I do. But I didn't like the way he hardly
took any notice of you,' she'd muttered. 'I mean, he
was all over Mum and Dad—everything they said was
"absolutely terrific!"—but he was ordering you
around as if you were a slave! I know he's famous,
and all that,' the girl had added, her cheeks growing
pink as she raised her eyes towards her much older

sister, 'but are you absolutely *sure* that Damian is going to make you happy?'

'Don't be so silly—of course he is,' she had laughed dismissively.

But that had been some weeks ago, and Serena was no longer quite so sure that she was going to live happily ever after. In fact, she wasn't at all sure about *anything* any more.

Serena stared at the heavy stone columns, which supported the hammer-beam arched roof of the old Norman church, rising above the nave and chancel far below. And as the high treble voices of the small choirboys soared up to the rafters, filling the church with such a pure and angelic sound, she was startled to find her eyes filling with tears.

It was only pre-wedding nerves, as well as the increasing tension of living at home, she told herself firmly. After the freedom of sharing a flat in London with her old school-friend, Claire, she was finding it difficult to readjust to family life. She loved her mother, of course, but the feverish activity produced by Vera Harding, as she'd thrown herself into a frenzy of organisation for her eldest daughter's wedding, had left the whole family reeling with exhaustion. Her father, a partner in a firm of local solicitors, hardly ever seemed to be at home these days, escaping from the house to spend most of his time on the local golf course.

Since her mother was chairman of goodness knows how many charitable organisations, Serena had assumed that arranging her daughter's marriage would hardly cause a ripple in Mrs Harding's busy life. But how wrong she'd been! Did every bride feel as if she was a mere accessory at her own wedding? And was she always the *last* person to be consulted about the arrangements?

Happily immersed in vital decisions regarding the church service and the reception afterwards, her mother had not only insisted on the two bridesmaids, Jenny and Claire, wearing a particularly revolting shade of muddy pink—'It will blend so well with my fuchsia-coloured silk outfit, dear'—but, unfortunately, she had also chosen the wedding dress.

Serena, gazing longingly at a simple, classical dress in heavy ivory satin, had been firmly redirected towards her mother's choice. Her green eyes widening, she'd stared in horror at the frothy creation, whose wide crinoline skirt was covered with tier upon tier of brilliant white net flounces, edged with *diamanté* and pearls. With garlands of large pink roses running riot over the low, off-the-shoulder bodice, around the waist and on down over the skirt, she had no doubt that the dress would have looked absolutely wonderful on Scarlett O'Hara!

But, as Serena had tried to point out to her mother, she was *not* a dark-haired, petite southern belle. And she knew that with her pale ash-blonde hair, and equally pale alabaster skin, that particular dress on her tall and slender figure was going to be a *total* disaster!

If only she wasn't so weak! If only she could find the courage to tell her mother that she simply *dreaded* having to wear a garment that was not only completely wrong for her style and colouring, but also guaranteed to make her look like a tall fairy on top of a Christmas tree!

A sharp dig from her mother broke into her distracted thoughts, and she realised that the hymn had ended, the congregation settling themselves back down in the pews as the vicar began mounting the pulpit to give his sermon. But as she tried to concentrate on the elderly man's measured words of wisdom Serena couldn't seem to keep at bay the questions which had been constantly surfacing in her mind during the past few weeks.

She was finding it harder and harder to remember exactly *why* she'd agreed to marry Damian—or why, indeed, he appeared to be so keen to marry her...? Was she merely responding to some sort of tribal pressure? Most of her female friends were already married, happily giving up their careers to concentrate on their small babies. So, was it her longing for children of her own that had finally tipped the balance in Damian's favour? If so, she might have been making a grave mistake. Because it was only last week that Damian had firmly stated his views on that subject.

'Really, darling!' he had laughed scornfully, when she'd pointed out that his one-bedroomed apartment in the Barbican—to which he was insisting that she move after their marriage—would hardly leave room for a child. 'I don't feel that the patter of tiny feet is exactly *me*, somehow! Besides, I want you all to myself. To wipe my fevered brow; to act as a ministering angel, after I've had to deal with all the super-ego trips of those boring, *boring* actors. Surely that's why we agreed you weren't going to work after you got married—remember? I want you spending all your time concentrating on *moi*!' he'd added with a querulous note in his voice.

Hastily reassuring her fiancé that she was looking forward to living in his penthouse suite in the

Barbican, and no, she wasn't serious about wanting to have babies, Serena now realised that she hadn't been speaking the truth.

Maybe it was something about this timeless old building, the sense of peace and serenity embodied in its age-old stone and timbers, but for the first time she was able to acknowledge to herself that she hated the Barbican. That grim, fortress-like complex in the City of London, with its harsh modern architecture, seemed to throw a chill on her spirits every time she went there. In fact, she couldn't think of anything she wanted more than to live quietly in the country, surrounded by children of her own. If *only* she had time to think. To have a few hours away from the never-ending wedding preparations, then maybe...

It wasn't until she received another quick jab in the ribs from her mother that Serena realised she hadn't heard one word of the vicar's sermon, and that the service was drawing to a close.

'For goodness' sake do try and concentrate, dear,' her mother sighed impatiently. 'And don't forget to thank Mrs Wilkins for her lovely vase.'

'But it's absolutely hideous!'

'Nonsense—it's a very kind thought,' her mother retorted crushingly. 'And since Alice Wilkins is giving me a large donation for the Red Cross, I hope you'll send her a fulsome letter of thanks. And *do* try and look more cheerful, dear,' she whispered fiercely with exasperation, before hurrying off to have an urgent word with the bell-ringers, who had already been hired for the wedding.

Walking slowly back down the aisle towards the front door of the church, where the vicar was shaking hands and saying goodbye to his parishioners, Serena gazed around her at the ancient stained-glass windows and the memorial tablets on the walls of the old building. The church was full of such commemorative panels, their pious verses all recording the passing of various members of the Raven family, who had been the biggest land owners in the district—and lords of the manor of Ravenswood—since medieval times.

It was some years since Serena, living and working in London, had attended a service in the village church, where she'd been christened almost twenty-six years ago. So, maybe it was the unexpected sight of a new memorial tablet, recording the passing of the last members of the Raven family, which caused her stomach to give such a sudden, sickening lurch?

She had been abroad—taking a year off and working for a charitable trust in Indonesia, before going to University—when she'd heard in a letter from her mother that Paul, the eldest and favourite son of old Sir Thomas and Lady Raven, who'd been driving his parents down to stay with friends in the South of France, had been involved in a car accident, in which all three members of the Raven family had been instantly killed.

Over the year she was away from England, her mother's occasional letters had kept her informed of all the local news, including details of the forced sale of the huge old Georgian mansion, and its surrounding parkland, which had been bought for a modern housing development. The sale had been insisted on by the trustees of the estate, heavily burdened by huge debts and death duties. This was a particularly sore point with Vera Harding, since, once the old house had been demolished, there was now only a small playing field between the end of their garden and the new housing estate, on which work had already begun by the time Serena returned from abroad.

Thoroughly annoyed by the relentless march of progress, Mrs Harding placed the blame firmly on the shoulders of Giles Raven—the wild, uncontrollable and wayward younger son.

'It's all Giles Raven's fault!' her mother had declared furiously. 'I know he tried to stop the sale, but if that young man hadn't been so wild and completely irresponsible—causing his parents nothing but grief with his *scandalous* love-affairs, and running up all those *wicked* gambling debts which his father had to settle—maybe the estate could have been saved.'

Ignoring Serena's protest that the multiple car crash—resulting in massive death duties—had probably more to do with the sale than a few gambling debts, Mrs Harding had refused to listen to reason.

'Giles Raven is going to come to a bad end—just you mark my words!' her mother had said furiously, before insisting that her husband have the house double-glazed to mask the noise from the bulldozers laying out the foundations for the new housing estate.

That had been the last of Ravenswood Manor and of the Raven family, as far as the village was concerned. And there had been a total silence on the eventual fate of the remaining son, Giles Raven.

'It's good riddance to bad rubbish!' Vera Harding had proclaimed loudly. But Serena, although she'd kept silent all these years, had known—and loved—quite a different person.

No! No... you *mustn't* think about him, and certainly not *now*—not when you're about to marry another man in three weeks' time! Serena told herself fiercely, quickly averting her eyes from the memorial tablet and hurrying out of the cool church, into the warm sunshine outside.

But there was little she could do to control her increasingly disturbed, tortuous dreams about her all too brief, passionate relationship with Giles, which she'd kept secret for so long. As the days passed, she completely lost her appetite and began looking so pale and drawn that even her mother had become worried.

'Really, Serena—you're becoming as thin as a rake! If you don't try and eat something, your lovely wedding gown will be far too loose.'

Since she already knew that she was going to look hideous in the elaborate dress, her mother's warning had little effect. Serena had merely shrugged and returned to writing bright, happy 'thank-you' letters for the mountain of wedding presents, which had been arriving at the house over the past month. Some hours later, as she was struggling to compose a suitable letter to Mrs Wilkins, thanking her for her gift of the ugly vase, Serena looked up as Jenny bounced into the room.

'It's lover-boy on the phone for you,' her sister announced with a grin.

'Why on earth can't you call him Damian, like everyone else?' Serena sighed, putting down her pen and rising from her chair.

'Because it's not his name,' her sister pointed out with devastating logic. 'Mind you, I have to admit that if I was christened Arch-i-bald...' she grimaced

'... I expect that I'd want to be called something else, too!'

Serena's wide brow was creased in a worried frown as she went into the hall. Jenny definitely seemed to be going through a difficult stage of adolescence. Maybe she ought to try to have a long talk with her sister before the wedding day in just over three weeks' time?

'Ah, Serena—I've got a job for you,' Damian said quickly as she picked up the phone. 'I'm in a tearing hurry, so just take down the details and you can tell me all about it on your way back from East Anglia.'

'On my way back from—where?' she queried, wondering if she'd heard him correctly as she picked up a pad and a pencil.

Damian gave a heavy sigh, clearly audible down the phone. 'This is *not* the moment to be dim, darling! I'm in the middle of a walk-through rehearsal for a new TV play, so just listen and do as I say, hmm?' he added with unlover-like impatience.

As he continued to rattle off his instructions, Serena's green eyes widened with apprehension. 'My mother isn't going to be at all happy about me swanning off like this,' she told him, when she managed to get a word in edgeways. 'And I've still got a mountain of letters to write to people, thanking them for their gifts. Not to mention——'

'For God's sake!' Damian exploded angrily. 'Here I am, up to my ears in work. But when I ask one— just *one*—small favour all I get is a mass of negative vibes!'

Serena flinched at the cold, harsh note in his voice. 'I'm not trying to be difficult, Damian, honestly I'm not,' she muttered unhappily.

'So—just get on and see to it, ducky!' he snapped before loudly slamming down the phone.

Serena tried to feel remorse about leaving her mother to cope with everything, but the sense of relief at her release from the hectic atmosphere of the wedding preparations was enormous. Winding down the window of her little car, she couldn't help relishing the heat of the midday sun, shining down from an almost cloudless blue sky.

Unfortunately she'd left home rather later than she had planned, mostly because of the need to complete some jobs for her mother, who'd taken grave exception to her daughter's sudden announcement that she was going to be away from home for a day.

'It's *very* inconvenient,' Vera Harding had snapped. 'You know that I want you to be at home to answer the phone for me. And it's only because darling Damian needs your help that I'm prepared to let you go,' she'd added grudgingly.

'Darling Damian' could obviously do no wrong! Serena found herself thinking sourly, and then was ashamed of such a disloyal thought about her future husband. She knew that she ought to be glad, happy that her mother was clearly over the moon at having a minor celebrity for a son-in-law.

Driving along winding lanes deep in the Kentish countryside, she had time to savour the scents and colours of rural life. Summer was rapidly taking over from spring, and the clumps of cow-parsley and rose-bay willow-herb were competing with wild roses in the hedgerows. Through the open window of the car she was disturbingly aware of the fresh, entrancing smell of new-mown hay. How could she bear to leave all this behind her, to live in the heart of a concrete jungle?

As she left the countryside behind her, driving through the built-up areas either side of the motorway leading to the Dartford Tunnel, Serena was too busy concentrating on the heavy traffic to indulge in any more such treasonable thoughts. But when she found herself virtually at a standstill, stuck in a three-mile queue waiting to go through the tunnel, she had plenty of time to think about Damian's request.

Of course she was, as he'd so firmly pointed out, uniquely qualified to help him. In fact, as an experienced, professional freelance researcher, specialising in the history of manorial records, the task was right up her street.

'The fact is, ducky, I've got an opportunity to buy the Lordship of the Manor of Foxwell—before anyone else gets wind of it,' Damian had rattled out over the phone yesterday. 'But I want to make sure that everything's on the up-and-up. So, get up there, *tout de suite*, and check it out for me. OK?'

It wasn't the examination of the ancient documents, many of which would be handwritten in ancient script or in Latin, which was bothering her. It was, after all, an area in which she'd had many years' experience, and which had led to her original meeting with Damian.

Appointed by the TV company to provide the basic research for a programme on the sales of Lordships of Manors—a subject which seemed to fascinate the general public—she'd been surprised and pleased by the keen interest taken in the subject by the producer of the programme, Damian Fox. He'd also decided to feature her in the programme to explain some of the technicalities involved.

As she'd pointed out, these Lordships carried no *legal* title to be known as 'Lord so-and-so', although the purchaser was entitled to describe himself as the Lord of the Manor of Richmond, for instance, and could also use the title on stationery, silverplate, legal documents, and even have the title entered on a British passport.

However, as her relationship with Damian had developed, she'd realised that his fascination for the subject came in part from his deprived inner-city childhood. Very much a self-made man, Damian hadn't just changed his name to one more in keeping with his new image of himself. He had also clearly become obsessed by the idea of being able to buy what he called 'instant aristocracy'. It wasn't a notion that she found appealing, since her interest lay in the ancient deeds themselves, which generally included Court Rolls, Chancery Deeds and ancient maps of the original land holdings of the manor.

Although she knew she ought to be more understanding, Serena couldn't help thinking that Damian was now indulging himself in some form of ridiculous snobbery. It seemed madness to spend many thousands of pounds buying the Lordship of Foxwell from some unknown millionaire City financier, who apparently lived at a place called Southey Hall in a remote area of East Anglia.

Since she was absorbed in her thoughts, it was some time before Serena became aware that the bright summer day had been overtaken by dark, lowering clouds, with alarming streaks of lightning occasionally flashing across the sky. As the distant rumbles

of thunder drew closer, accompanied by heavy drops
of rain which rapidly became a thick, impenetrable
deluge, it became harder and harder to see where she
was going. Getting lost several times, and having to
get out of the car to ask the way, she was drenched
and shivering with cold in her light summer dress by
the time she drew near to Southey Island.

Her teeth chattering with cold, Serena drove slowly
and carefully along a winding track, through a pair
of high wrought-iron gates, and brought her small car
to a halt outside a large Victorian house.

Damian hadn't said anything about Southey Hall's
being on an island in the middle of a river. And she
had to admit that it didn't *look* like an island, although
it was difficult to see very much in the murky darkness
of the thunderstorm. However, with any luck, she'd
be offered a hot cup of tea while she checked the
documents, and then she could be on her way back
home. If the weather got any worse, she could always
spend the night at her old flat in London. Claire
wouldn't mind, and, since her friend was also going
to be one of her bridesmaids, it might be useful to
sort out any last-minute details.

Gathering up her handbag and briefcase, she took
a deep breath before opening the car door and dashing
through the heavy rain towards the shelter of a large
porch.

Almost drenched to the skin and shivering with cold
in her thin dress, Serena yanked down on the heavy
iron bell-pull. The loud chimes seemed to echo forever
before the large oak door was slowly opened, and she
found herself gazing down into the friendly brown
eyes of an elderly woman, who looked vaguely
familiar.

'Hurry up and get inside, Miss Serena; it's raining cats and dogs out there!' the woman told her with a slight laugh.

Serena frowned in the dimly lit hall. 'It's...it's Mrs Davies...isn't it?' she asked hesitantly.

'Yes, that's right, dear,' the woman nodded, her bright eyes twinkling up at the tall girl. 'I wasn't sure whether you would remember me and my Fred, seeing as how it's been such a long time since we both had to leave the old house. How is your mother these days?'

'Oh, she's—er—she's fine,' Serena murmured, feeling totally confused at meeting someone she hadn't seen for almost ten years. What an extraordinary co-incidence! How *amazing* that Meg Davies—who'd been the housekeeper at Ravenswood Manor, before it had been sold and demolished—should be working here, in such a remote area of the country!

But her initial surprise slowly gave way to a strange, numb feeling that there was something very odd going on. And her increasing apprehension was instantly and alarmingly confirmed as she followed the elderly woman across the wide hall.

'Come along, dear. I'll make you a nice cup of tea, presently, but we don't want to keep Sir Giles waiting, do we?'

CHAPTER TWO

'RIGHT, Sir Giles, the tea-tray is all laid ready, and dinner is in the oven,' the housekeeper said as she followed Serena into the book-lined study. 'So I'll just pop off home now. All right?'

'Yes, that's fine, Meg. I'll see you in the morning,' a deep male voice answered before Mrs Davies added a bright, 'Cheerio!', and bustled from the room.

The receding clatter of the housekeeper's shoes across the stone floor of the hall, and the occasional crackle of the wood logs burning in the large fireplace, were the only sounds to disturb the long, heavy silence as Serena stared across the room at Giles Raven. She was shaking like a leaf, her green eyes glazed with shock and consternation at meeting the man she hadn't seen for so many years, and it was some time before she could begin to try to pull her distraught mind together.

'Hello, Serena,' Giles drawled before slowly rising to his feet from behind the far side of a large mahogany desk.

Managing to open her mouth at last, Serena found she couldn't utter any words, just a hoarse croaking sound. She quickly cleared her throat and tried again.

'Er—hello Giles,' she murmured huskily. And then, even as she realised that it was an idiotic question, she found herself adding, 'What on earth are *you* doing here?'

He obviously found the remark equally stupid. Giving a dismissive shrug of his shoulders, he walked slowly across the room to the fireplace.

'This island—and the house too, of course—was left to me by an aged aunt, over five years ago,' he told her smoothly.

Still feeling faint with shock, Serena momentarily closed her eyes. Oh, *pray God*, this was all a ghastly nightmare, or some awful figment of her deranged mind...? But as she opened her eyes, gazing across at the lean, tanned face and those clear, all-too familiar grey eyes, she realised that she was, unfortunately, both in her right mind and wide awake.

Quickly clutching hold of the back of a nearby chair to support her trembling legs, which felt as though they were going to collapse any moment, she heard him say, 'It's been a long time since we met.'

'Er—yes, it must be almost nine years,' she agreed breathlessly.

'Really?' he murmured. 'It seems only yesterday that you were a small, scrubby schoolgirl with her hair in long plaits. How time flies!'

Surely he *can't* have forgotten everything that happened between us? Serena's knuckles whitened as she endeavoured to bring her chaotic thoughts and emotions under some kind of control. To suddenly meet again—without any warning—the man who had once meant so much to her, and from whom she had heard nothing from that day to this, was almost more than she could cope with.

And why on earth had Meg Davies called him 'Sir Giles'? she asked herself wildly, unable even to begin thinking about the many far more important questions, which were rapidly multiplying in her dazed mind. It was a few blank moments before she found the simple answer; that, as the sole remaining member of his family, he must have inherited his father's baronetcy.

'My dear girl—you're absolutely soaked!' he exclaimed as he gazed at her shivering figure. 'I was expecting you to arrive for lunch, but it now looks as though you could do with a hot cup of tea. First of all, however, I think we'd better get you into some dry clothes.'

'There's no need to bother...'

'There's every need!' Giles told her sternly, crossing the room to take hold of her trembling arm, before firmly steering her out of the room.

Almost jumping out of her skin at the electric shock of his warm fingers on her bare flesh, Serena shivered with tension as Giles led her up a wide mahogany staircase. As she glanced nervously through her eyelashes at his tall figure, it seemed that, despite a long lapse of time, the passing years had done little to change Giles's outward appearance.

All the members of his family had been as dark as their surname, and his hair still possessed that blue-black sheen, normally only found on ravens' wings—even if now there seemed to be a few silver strands among the black hair at his temples.

'There should be some dry clothes in the guest room,' Giles remarked before leading her into a large, beautifully decorated bedroom with an adjoining bathroom.

'There's no need...'

'Don't be stupid, Serena. I certainly don't want to be responsible for you catching pneumonia!' he retorted harshly, opening a large cupboard in the far corner of the room. 'I often have friends to stay and,

as you can see, a few of them appear to have left
some items of clothing behind. I suggest that you help
yourself from this cupboard, and there are some warm
sweaters in there——' He gestured towards an elegant
Chippendale chest of drawers.

'So, if you bring your wet clothes downstairs with
you, we can put them in the drier while you have a
warm cup of tea,' he added, his grey eyes sweeping
over the girl's trembling figure before he turned and
left the room.

The moment he had gone Serena collapsed down
on to the wide double bed, burying her face in her
shaking hands and trying to control the frantic, wild
thumping of her heart.

It was almost nine years since she'd last seen Giles,
but of course she'd known him all her life. His elderly
father, Sir Thomas Raven, had been old-fashioned
enough to still believe in the principle of *noblesse
oblige*, and had regularly opened Ravenswood Manor
and its large garden to the public, on behalf of any
number of charitable good causes. His sons, too, had
been encouraged to participate in village affairs, and
Serena couldn't remember a time when she hadn't
been wildly and foolishly in love with the youngest
son, Giles Raven. And ever since he'd carelessly pulled
one of her long blonde plaits at the village fête, and
with equal, careless charm had drawled, 'You must
promise to wait for me, little Serena—because, in a
few years' time, I reckon that you're going to be a
raving beauty!' she'd worshipped him with blind
adoration.

That had been when she was thirteen, and he a tall
twenty-year-old, already away at university and beginning to sow his wild oats. In fact, it was probably

his reputation for wild behaviour—and the thrilling
reports of the wickedly dangerous, lethal damage he
was causing to female hearts—which had added to his
romantic attraction. Viewing Giles as a modern-day
reincarnation of Lord Byron—'mad, bad and
dangerous to know'—and daydreaming for hours
about how she would rescue him from a life of sin
and debauchery—which he would, of course, reward
with a chaste kiss on her brow—Serena had been
content to worship him from afar.

Maybe if her parents and Jenny hadn't gone abroad
to Italy one summer, leaving her to look after the
house while waiting to hear her A level results, their
adult company might have dissolved some of her
overheated, romantic fantasies about Giles; or she
might have been more receptive to her mother's dire
warnings about his wild lifestyle. But, knowing the
Raven family were also away during that hot summer,
she'd taken to wandering about the deserted park and
garden of the old manor house—sometimes even il-
licitly using the large outdoor swimming-pool, when
the heat of the day became unbearable.

And it was there that Giles, returning unexpectedly
from a trip to the United States, had discovered her
floating silently in the pool. As he'd told Serena later,
he had been mesmerised by the sight of her long
strands of pale blonde hair, glinting in the sunlight
as they drifted and swirled about her slim, naked
figure—as if she were an ethereal, mysterious water-
nymph.

Serena hadn't been aware of his tall, dark presence
as she floated dreamily in the water. When he suddenly surfaced beside her in the pool, it had all seemed
part of her continuing fantasy, as he'd drawn her

slowly towards him. And when he had gently possessed her lips, as he'd done so often before in her
imagination, it had seemed the most natural thing in
the world to press her bare, slim figure against his
own naked form; to respond without thought to the
increasing passion of his kiss. As she floated mind-
lessly in the cool water, with the hot sun blazing down
from a cloudless sky, it had been as though she were
drifting weightlessly in time and space. Even Giles's
helpless groan and the arms tightening fiercely about
her slim form had not disturbed her mindless, dreamy
state. Lost in their mutual desire, she had hardly been
aware of him carrying her up the shallow steps out
of the pool, and into a nearby secluded summer-house.

It was only when he had placed her gently down
on the small sofa-bed that he'd clearly begun to realise what he was doing, attempting to withdraw from
the slim arms clasped so tightly about his neck.

'No, Serena,' he whispered as she pressed herself
closer to him. 'We mustn't do this. You're far too
young... and far too innocent!' Opening her dazed
eyes, she could see a vein beating wildly at his temple,
and feel his body trembling violently against hers as
he fought for control.

'Don't let me go... I love you with all my heart!'
she breathed, her senses reeling out of control a she
moved her body against him with an innocent provo-
cation that produced an answering deep groan. His
arms closed convulsively about her slender form, her
lips parting beneath his with a small moan of satisfaction as a shudder ran through his strong body at
the enticing, yielding warmth of her naked flesh.

Serena knew that she had no one to blame but
herself for his helpless, overwhelming loss of control.

But despite the raging excitement of his kisses, and the thrilling caress of his hands, he had shown restraint and infinite tenderness as he'd gently led her inexperienced body from one delight to another, raising her to peaks of delirious ecstasy which she could never have believed possible.

In the two weeks that followed they had spent every possible moment together. And, with Giles's vows of love and devotion filling her whole existence, that hot summer had seemed bathed in a magical enchantment. Heedless of the passage of time, Serena had found it a shock to receive a telephone call from her parents, announcing their imminent return from Italy—a reminder that she, too, would be going abroad in just over a week's time.

It had been an even greater shock—and one which had left her totally devastated—to arrive at Ravenswood Manor the next day, and find the old Georgian house completely empty and deserted. Giles had never contacted her to explain his sudden disappearance, nor had he been in touch either by letter or phone, from that day to this. And now, as she looked back down the years, Serena realised that helping to care for and feed the starving orphans during her year abroad must have helped to save her sanity. When she had returned to England to go to university, she'd been able to bury herself in the academic work necessary to gain a good degree.

For the past nine years she'd managed to push far down into the deep, subconscious recesses of her mind the all too brief, fleeting moments of total happiness which she'd experienced that summer. But now...now that by some strange accident of fate they'd met, once again, those memories were rising again to haunt her.

Stop it! You mustn't think about it! Serena screamed silently at herself, quickly clamping her clenched fists against her closed eyelids as she rocked desperately back and forth on the bed.

Suddenly realising that Giles might well be a married man by now, Serena jumped quickly to her feet. Feeling sick, she staggered into the bathroom on legs that felt as though they were made of cotton wool. Splashing cold water on her face didn't seem to help her state of blind panic; nor her horror and dismay that, after all these years, they should meet again when she was looking so awful—just like a drowned rat! And there was very little she could do to make herself look more presentable. Having rushed out of the house in such a hurry this morning, Serena knew that she hadn't even put a lipstick in her handbag, let alone a brush and comb.

She knew that she couldn't stay in the guest-bedroom suite forever, so she forced herself to go and explore the contents of the cupboard. And it soon became apparent that the 'friends' Giles had referred to had been strictly female.

So—it didn't look as if he was married, after all. Although I bet he's got simply thousands of girl-friends, she told herself savagely, grimly recalling that Giles's wild reputation in the past had, after all, been the result of so many women finding him fatally attractive. Unfortunately it looked as though his taste now ran to females who were small and petite, since most of the clothes on the hangers were designed for those much smaller and shorter than her own tall figure.

There was nothing here that was even remotely suitable, she thought glumly. But she was going to have to find something, because Giles had been quite right. She *was* soaked—right down to and including her underwear.

After hunting through the cupboard and chest of drawers, Serena hurriedly put on all she could find: a brief pair of pants, slim designer jeans and a pale-blue cashmere sweater. Unfortunately none of the lacy bras left behind by Giles's girlfriends had fitted her. Despite being tall and slender, Serena had always bemoaned the fact that she had such large, firm breasts—the cause of much embarrassment and unhappiness as a young teenager.

However, it didn't look as if the various girls who'd stayed here had suffered from her problem—not if the tiny wisps of frothy nylon and lace were anything to go by. And, while it felt most peculiar not to be wearing anything under the warm cashmere sweater, Serena realised that she had no choice in the matter.

Going over to the large mirror by the window, she flinched at the cruel reflection of her lank, damp hair and the dark shadows beneath her dazed green eyes. Nor could she ignore the obvious fact that her make-up hadn't survived the day's journey.

'I *can't* face him looking like this,' she moaned helplessly out loud to herself. 'I look absolutely *dreadful*!'

Her panic-stricken hands were shaking so much that she could hardly remove the combs which held the heavy coil of pale, ash-blonde hair at the nape of her neck. Damian had insisted on her long hair being caught back like this to expose what he called her 'delicate and swan-like' neck. But as she scowled nervously at herself in the mirror she suddenly realised that the severity of the style did nothing for her; that she appeared plain and ugly—like a very strict, old-fashioned schoolmistress.

She tried letting down her hair, but the damp kinky strands made her look even worse, and with a helpless sigh of resignation and defeat she rewound it back into her usual style.

Despite hunting high and low in the drawers, she could find nothing to offset the pallor of her complexion. While Giles's girlfriends might suggestively have left some of their underwear behind, they'd removed every scrap of make-up, except a small stick of brown mascara. And it was in the certain knowledge that she looked more like a corpse than a human being that Serena slowly and very reluctantly left the room, and began making her way downstairs.

'Come and have some tea by the fire,' Giles said as she nervously entered the study. 'You're looking marginally better than you did when you arrived,' he added in a sardonic drawl, gesturing to an armchair opposite his own, beside the fire.

But only *marginally*, Serena thought glumly, before remembering her manners. 'I—er—thank you for lending me these clothes,' she muttered, very conscious of what an absolute shambles she must look, especially when compared to all his glamorous girlfriends.

'What have you done with your dress?'

'Oh, goodness—I completely forgot.' She gazed at him in dismay. 'I...I'm afraid I left it in the bathroom, upstairs.' She jumped nervously to her feet.

'For heaven's sake—sit down, and have something to eat! You look as if you could do with a decent square meal,' he told her roughly, cutting a large slice of dark fruit cake.

'I couldn't possibly manage all that,' she muttered, sinking back down into her chair. She was already feeling quite sick with nerves, and quite unable to face the thought of any food.

'You're nothing but skin and bone! In fact, I can hardly believe just how thin and stringy you've become,' he said brusquely, his grey eyes sweeping over her face and trembling body. His gaze, lingering for a moment on her unconfined breasts, brought a hectic flush to her pale cheeks.

I just *knew* that this sweater was too tight! Serena told herself bitterly, unable to prevent her hands from shaking as she lifted the cup of tea to her lips, and desperately wishing she had the courage to chuck the contents at his handsome, tanned face. If only she could think of a good reason to leave this house—as quickly as possible. But there seemed nothing she could do to escape his ruthless grey eyes, nor their continuing hard and determined appraisal.

'You used to be such a lovely, fresh and sparkling young girl. But, if you'll forgive me for saying so, you now look almost old enough to be your own mother,' Giles said bluntly before glancing quickly down at his wristwatch. 'What on earth has happened to you, Serena?'

'I'm just tired, that's all,' she muttered, telling herself that there was no reason why she should have to sit here, meekly listening to this awful man pulling her to pieces. But there didn't seem anything she could do, when she knew that she was looking so bedraggled and such a mess in these borrowed clothes.

Especially when compared to the beautifully cut Savile Row suit covering his elegant, tall figure.

It all seemed so desperately *unfair*! Giles had virtually accused her of looking like an old hag, while he—the swine!—was still one of the most devastatingly attractive-looking men she'd ever seen. Maybe the lines about his firm, determined mouth might be more deeply etched now, and possibly there was a more authoritative air to his movements, a more commanding stance to his tall figure. However, Giles still seemed to possess that unconscious glittering aura, a sinister stillness and self-control which, despite his 'wild' reputation, had always marked him out as being very different from his friends and contemporaries. And it now looked as if that original promise of outstanding ability had been fulfilled. Because Serena had no doubt that she was in the presence of a very strong, powerful and ruthless personality.

'And speaking of your mother——' his voice broke into her sombre, unhappy thoughts '—how is the old dragon?'

Before she could protest about his unkind, if possibly true description of her mother, he added drily, 'I imagine she must be in her element at the moment. Is she driving everyone up the wall with her arrangements for your wedding?'

Serena raised her startled green eyes. 'You know about...?' She flushed. 'I mean, I didn't realise that you knew I was getting married.'

'But surely that's why you're here?' Giles raised a dark eyebrow. 'To cast a professional eye over Mr Damian Fox's wedding present to himself.'

'Yes—yes, of course,' she agreed hurriedly. 'It was just that I didn't know... Have you met my fiancé?'

she queried helplessly, and when he nodded she wondered why Damian hadn't mentioned the fact over the phone yesterday.

'Oh, yes. Indeed I have,' Giles murmured sardonically before casting another quick glance down at his watch.

He obviously finds me totally boring and insipid, she thought desparingly. 'I . . . I really must go and put my clothes in the drier,' she muttered, putting her empty cup back down on the tray before quickly getting to her feet. 'If you'll just tell me how to find the kitchen——?'

Her words were interrupted by the loud clanging of the doorbell as it reverberated through the house, and a moment later a yellow whirlwind seemed to flash into the room.

'*Darling*! I'm *so* sorry to be late!' a female voice exclaimed, dramatically throwing aside a yellow oilskin cape to reveal a beautiful young girl, clothed in a low-cut, figure-hugging red linen dress which left nothing to the imagination.

'What ghastly weather!' the girl declared before joyfully throwing herself into Giles's arms. 'Naughty me for being so late! But I was having a liquid lunch with Gerry and his friends, and the champagne simply went to my head—you know how it is?' she pouted up at him prettily.

'Yes, I know exactly how it is!' Giles laughed, smiling down into the upturned, amazingly beautiful face of the girl in his embrace. 'Oh, by the way, Tamsin—I don't think you've met Serena Harding? She's here to research some old documents of mine.'

'No, I don't think I have.' The girl turned her head to glance at Serena, her dark eyes quickly sweeping over the other girl before giving her a brief, dismissive smile as she turned back to face Giles.

'I can only stay a moment—you know what the tides are like around here! And I have to get back home for a dinner party that Mummy's giving tonight. But you haven't forgotten that you promised to take me to Paris next week?' she asked in a childish, wheedling tone of voice.

Serena didn't catch his reply as she stared at the tiny dark vision in his arms. The glowing perfection of the other girl's face, the warm golden skin and midnight-black hair, arranged in loose curls over a perfect pocket-Venus figure, was guaranteed to make any red-blooded male drool at the mouth. And clearly Giles was *no* exception!

Standing rooted to the floor, unable to tear her eyes away from his tall figure looking fondly down at the girl, who was gazing adoringly up into his face as she nestled within his arms, Serena was shattered by her own reaction to the sight in front of her. It was no good trying to fool herself. She knew, without the shadow of a doubt, that the emotions tearing at her heart with such sharp, venomous claws could be nothing other than an overwhelming surge of blind green jealousy.

Feeling faint and almost sick, she turned back to stare blindly at the fire as she struggled to control herself. Like a wounded animal, she wanted only to escape into some deep, dark place where she could lick her wounds in secret. Her agitated thoughts were interrupted as she heard Tamsin give a high, shrill peal of laughter.

'I wish I could stay—but I really *must* go, darling! I'll see you soon,' the beautiful dark girl promised him confidently, winding her arms about Giles's neck, and giving him a long, lingering kiss which brought an embarrassed flush to Serena's face.

'Tamsin is—er—very beautiful,' she said as Giles came back into the room after seeing his girlfriend to the front door.

'Yes, she certainly is!'

Stung to the quick by his enthusiastic tone, Serena could feel the blood draining from her face. There was a long, agonising pause before she heard herself asking, 'Are you thinking of getting married?'

'Oh, yes—I'm definitely thinking about it,' he told her with a brief smile.

'Well, I . . . I hope you'll both be very happy,' she muttered, suddenly feeling devastated by the note of determination and purpose in his voice.

Unable to bring herself to meet his eyes, she stared fixedly at the width of his strong shoulder, suddenly swept by a mad, crazy desire to lean her weary head against its broad strength.

With an almost superhuman effort, she managed to pull herself together. 'I really must go, too,' she told him, barely able to articulate the words, her lips and face feeling numb and frozen as if she'd just visited the dentist.

'But you still haven't looked at the documents, have you?'

Serena stared at him, wildly trying to think of a good and valid reason why she *must* immediately leave this house. But Giles gave her no time to come up with a convenient excuse.

'I suggest that you sit down now, and study the memorial records,' he said, but it was clearly more of a demand than a suggestion as he firmly grasped her arm, leading her reluctant figure across the glowing Turkish carpet towards a window, beneath which lay a long table covered in documents.

'And while you are doing that,' he added crisply as he pulled out a chair, 'I will see to your clothes.'

Left alone in the empty study, Serena gave a heavy sigh as she lowered her tired body down into the chair. It really had been one *hell* of a day! she thought, reaching forward to switch on the pair of small reading-lamps set at either end of the table. Although it was only early evening, the sky outside the large window was dark and threatening, occasionally lit by startling neon-like flashes of forked lightning, while the thunder of the summer storm was still rumbling and crashing overhead. It must have been continuing to do so throughout the afternoon, she realised, but she'd been so overwhelmed by her traumatic meeting with Giles that she simply hadn't noticed.

Serena stared blindly down at the documents in front of her, finding it almost impossible to concentrate on the intricacies of the Court Rolls and Feet of Fines of the Lordship of Foxwell. All she could think about was the sight of that exquisitely beautiful girl, Tamsin, clasped in Giles's arms.

She must stop being so stupid, Serena told herself desperately, suddenly burying her face in her shaking hands. She was getting married in three weeks' time. So how could it possibly matter to her *who* Giles did or did not marry?

But, of course, it did. And Serena was totally shattered as she realised that her deep, emotional response to him hadn't changed. But he obviously didn't feel anything for her. And why should he? Not only had Giles become a very rich and powerful City financier, but he'd also made it very clear that he now found her both unattractive and boring.

CHAPTER THREE

SERENA leaned back in her chair, and stretched her weary body. There didn't seem to be anything wrong with the documents spread out before her. In fact, the Lordship of Foxwell Manor, which had been owned by the same family since the Norman Conquest, had proved to contain some interesting historical records. Passing through various generations, often down the female line, the last owner had been a Mrs Edith Beauchamp—who was, presumably, the aged aunt to whom Giles had referred.

Leaning forward to look more closely at an old map, Serena wasn't too alarmed when all the lights in the room suddenly went out. With the thunder crashing and banging directly overhead, the lamps on the table had been flickering on and off for some time, obviously responding to the streaks of forked lightning flashing through the dark sky. So it was clearly just a case of waiting for a few moments before the electricity came back on again once more.

However, it was only after she'd been sitting in the darkness for some time that she heard the door of the study being opened. Turning, she saw, through the dim, flickering light, the tall figure of Giles entering the room.

'I'm afraid it looks as though we've got a power cut,' he said, placing a branched candlestick down on the table beside her.

Gazing up at him, Serena wasn't able to think of anything except how desperately attractive he looked in the flickering light. The strong shadows thrown over his handsome features were highlighting his prominent cheekbones, and the sensual curve of his mouth. He also seemed to have found the time to change out of his smart city suit, since he was now wearing a cream Aran sweater over an open-necked, dark brown shirt and a pair of casual tan cords.

'I have a stand-by generator, of course,' he told her. 'But it may be some time before we can get it going.'

Quickly pulling herself together, Serena realised that the cut in the electricity supply gave her the perfect excuse to leave Southey Hall. It was a heaven-sent opportunity for her to escape from this embarrassing situation with a few sheds of dignity intact.

'As far as I can see, these documents look quite all right,' she forced herself to say briskly. 'I'm sorry about the power cut, of course. But it's getting late, and I really must go.'

Giles gave a low, mocking laugh which sent shivers feathering up and down her spine. 'I'm afraid it doesn't look as if you're going anywhere!'

'What...what do you mean?'

He smiled down at her in silence for a moment as the sound of her shrill, panic-stricken voice seemed to echo around the large room.

'First of all, I'm afraid that, with no electricity, your clothes are still lying wet in the drier. And secondly...' Giles shrugged his broad shoulders '...this is the season of high spring tides, when the causeway running from the island to the other side of the river is completely covered with water for hours at a time. In fact,' he added, looking down at his watch, 'with high tide this evening at eight o'clock, you haven't a chance of leaving here—not until at least half-past ten tonight, at the earliest.'

She gazed at him, aghast. 'I don't believe it! Your girlfriend, Tamsin, was here not long ago, and *she* managed to leave the island. So why can't I?'

He shook his head. 'That was almost an hour ago, and Tamsin was driving a Range Rover. Your small car would be completely submerged if you tried to leave now.'

'I just *don't* believe it!' she repeated helplessly, almost unable to comprehend what he was saying: that, with her dress still lying wet in the drier, and this island apparently totally cut off from the mainland, she was well and truly stuck!

His next words, echoed her own thoughts. 'I'm sorry to say that I think you have no alternative but to spend the night here.'

He doesn't look at all sorry, Serena thought, glaring up into his handsome face. In fact, despite his apologetic words and bland expression, she was almost sure, from the fleeting glint of laughter in his eyes, that the damned man was thoroughly amused by her awful predicament!

'If you don't believe me—and if you don't mind getting drenched to the skin yet again—I suggest that you go outside and take a look for yourself,' he said drily.

Serena bit her lip with indecision. He probably *was* telling the truth about the height of the tides around the island. And she really didn't feel brave enough to face up to going outside in the midst of all that thunder and lightning.

'It doesn't seem as though I've got any choice,' she sighed with glum resignation.

He grinned down at her dejected figure. 'Cheer up! It's not the end of the world! You'll feel a good deal better with a strong whisky inside you. After I've contacted Meg's husband, Fred, with any luck we'll soon have the generator working. And we can then see what Meg has left us to eat for dinner.'

Although she hadn't believed that it was possible to 'cheer up', as he'd put it, Serena had to admit that with a stiff drink flowing through her veins, and the sheer comfort of a hot meal inside her, she was feeling much better by the time he was pouring them both a cup of after-dinner coffee.

The fact that she was feeling far more relaxed was entirely due to Giles. Keeping well away from any awkward subjects, he'd concentrated on telling her about Southey Island, and about his successful career in the financial world of the City of London.

As related by Giles, his swift rise to fame and fortune had appeared to be a series of lucky accidents. But Serena suspected that once he'd 'got his act together', as he put it, it was solely thanks to Giles's own entrepreneurial and ruthless business sense which had enabled him to cut such a swath through the City. Building on the very small amount of capital which had been left from the sale of Ravenswood Manor, he had now amassed a considerable number of companies, including a large and prestigious city bank.

'It isn't all beer and skittles, of course,' he told her with a shrug. 'For instance, there is one take-over which I'm planning at the moment—but unfortunately I may have left it just a little too late.'

It was only then that Serena realised she ought to let her mother know that she wouldn't be returning home until tomorrow. 'And I—er—I would like to phone my—er—fiancé, if you don't mind?' she muttered, a flush spreading over her cheeks.

'My dear girl—why on earth should I mind whom you telephone?' he drawled smoothly before picking up some candlesticks and leading the way into the study.

The telephone calls proved to be painfully embarrassing. Giles seemed determined to turn a deaf ear to her heavy hints that she'd like to be left alone. Ignoring him as best she could, Serena first dialled Damian's flat in London. Careful to avoid mentioning the fact that she wasn't at home, she concentrated on giving her fiancé the good news about the documents—and that there was nothing to stop him becoming the Lord of the Manor of Foxwell.

Anxious to avoid a row with her mother—whose temper was on a short fuse these days—Serena merely emphasised the bad weather, and casually implied that she was spending the night with an old friend, before returning home early tomorrow.

'You never were any good at telling lies!' Giles drawled mockingly from where he'd been lounging back in a comfortable chair beside the fire in the study, while she'd been using the phone. 'Although it's probably just as well that you didn't give her the name of your "friend"—especially since she's always actively disliked me.'

'You can't blame her—you always had a *terrible* reputation!' Serena retorted curtly, quite sure that she'd never felt so mentally exhausted as she did at this moment! Trying to talk to Damian with Giles sitting only a few feet away—a man with whom she'd once had a wild, torrid affair—clearly required a degree of worldly finesse and sophistication which she simply *didn't* possess! And Giles's obvious amusement at her embarrassment had just made the whole thing ten times worse!

'Yes, my reputation wasn't too good—although I can assure you that I'm a reformed man nowadays,' Giles said coolly. 'But your dear mother only really took against me when she learned about our summer romance.'

'That's absolute nonsense!' Serena retorted angrily, almost welcoming the opportunity to release some of her pent-up, long-suppressed feelings of rage and fury about the way this man had treated her. 'My mother was away on holiday that summer—remember? And I definitely never made the mistake of telling her *just* what a stupid fool I'd been!'

'Oh, no—I was the fool! Certainly as far as *you* were concerned!' Giles ground out bitterly, all trace of amusement having vanished completely from his face. 'When I think how often I tried to get in touch with you—the letters I wrote, and the phone calls that——'

'*What rubbish!* You know very well that you did no such thing!' Serena exploded, jumping to her feet and rounding on him in fury. 'And after all these years what's the point in suddenly coming up with these feeble excuses for your lousy behaviour?'

'I'm telling you the truth!' he rasped. 'And if you didn't get my letters or messages, then there's only *one* person to blame—your damned interfering mother!' he added savagely.

'Don't you dare talk about her like that!' she lashed back angrily. 'She'd *never* hide letters or messages from me!'

'Oh, no?' he sneered.

'No! And, in any case, what possible reason could she have for doing so?'

'For the simple reason that she knew I was deeply in love with her precious daughter!'

Serena gave a shrill cry of scornful laughter. 'Do me a favour! The whole world knows that you could never keep your hands off any woman. I was just one in a long, *long* line of conquests—just another notch on your bloody bedpost!'

'That's not true!' he ground out through clenched teeth, swiftly rising to his feet and covering the distance between them in two long strides. Gripping her shoulders, he gave her an angry shake. 'You know very well that I was crazy about you!'

'So you may have been—for a few short weeks,' she retorted bitterly, raising her chin defiantly as he stared down at her with a grim expression. 'But that was years ago, and as far as I'm concerned the whole episode is dead and buried!'

'Serena! You must let me explain...'

'There's no "must" about it—and I don't want to listen to any explanations, either! I'm going to bed now. And don't try to follow me, because I intend to make sure my door is firmly locked!' she shouted at him before quickly wriggling free of his hands, seizing hold of a candlestick and storming out of the room.

On reaching the guest room, and quickly locking the door behind her, Serena furiously stripped off her clothes and slipped into the bed—which, luckily, was already made up—before blowing out the candle.

Despite the heat of her anger, she was shivering with cold and nervous tension as she lay wide awake, staring up into the darkness above her head. However, as the minutes ticked slowly by, and Giles had made no move to follow her, the rage slowly drained out of her chilled, numb body to be replaced by almost unbearable pain—a pain as fresh today as it had been nine years ago.

When Giles had suddenly disappeared from her life, and she had never heard from him again, she'd firmly stored her heart away in the deep-freeze, concentrating on her studies and her career. It had taken her years to get over him, but she'd remained cautious, careful not to get involved with any of the men—and there were many—who'd made it plain they were interested in her. None of them had even come near to touching her heart, since they'd all appeared to be merely cardboard cut-outs, when compared to Giles's blazing, dynamic and vital personality.

The meeting with Damian, and the collaboration between them on the TV programme, had come at a time when her mother had been conducting a fierce campaign to persuade her daughter to get married. Constantly nagging Serena about the fact that she was rapidly becoming an old maid, and continually moaning that she, herself, was never likely to be a grandmother, Mrs Harding had finally begun to wear down her daughter's resistance with her complaints.

While Damian had been impressed first by Serena's professional grasp of her subject, and then with her fragile beauty, he'd become intrigued by her apparent indifference to his fame and reputation—so different from the frantic competitiveness of his own world. Bombarded with flowers and invitations, she had

eventually agreed to go out with him, and without
any conscious decision on her part it had somehow
been agreed, after they had been seeing each other for
some months, that they would get married.

While she knew that she didn't love Damian, Serena
had persuaded herself that a marriage based on warm
friendship and respect was likely to lead to a more
lasting relationship than her violently sensual, tu-
multuous feelings for Giles, which had so quickly led
to the torture and agony of his desertion. And, having
once experienced the desperate misery of an unhappy
love-affair, she'd been determined that it was not going
to happen to her a second time....

It was at some point during the night that Serena
was aroused from a restless sleep to find her face and
pillow damp with tears. As she lay, staring up into
the unfamiliar darkness, she slowly realised that the
sounds which had awoken her had been her own desperate sobbing. She couldn't remember ever shedding
such miserably helpless tears—not since her life, and
her heart, had been so irrevocably shattered by Giles,
all those years ago.

After managing to fall asleep at last—a restless
slumber disturbed by nameless hideous dreams—
Serena woke to find the early morning sun flooding
in through the open window.

Wincing at the bright light, and feeling like death
warmed up after her disturbed night, she closed her
eyes and buried her face in the pillows. If *only* she
could go back to sleep and then—like the fairy-story
of *Sleeping Beauty*—not wake up for a hundred years!

Momentarily carried away by the thought of not
having to be present at her own wedding, Serena
couldn't help indulging herself in the delicious luxury

of a crazy daydream: one in which she didn't have to wear that totally unsuitable wedding dress, chosen by her mother, not be followed up the aisle by her young sister and Claire—both of whom were sure to be in a bad temper, since they hated the style and colour of their bridesmaids' dresses. Neither would she have to witness the sight of her mother, squeezed into her fuchsia outfit, riding roughshod over everyone as she insisted on producing the wedding that *she* wanted— and not the far more simple, quiet ceremony which her eldest daughter would have preferred.

However, like all daydreams, it gradually faded away, and Serena was ashamed that she could have been even *thinking* of such a disloyal, inconsiderate idea. How could she possibly begin to contemplate letting her parents down—not to mention Damian, and all the hordes of friends and relatives due to attend the wedding?

Besides which, she knew that she simply didn't have whatever it took to call off the proceedings at such a late date. Just thinking about her mother's incandescent rage and fury was enough to make her shudder—and everyone would think she was totally mad to turn down the chance of being Damian's wife!

For almost the first time since she'd become engaged to him, when she'd been amazed that anyone so well-known and famous should want to marry her, Serena found herself wondering exactly *why* Damian had chosen her. Despite Jenny's remark about him treating her as a 'slave', Damian's increasing success in the world of show business had attracted any number of beautiful actresses and starlets, anxious to be seen out and about with the 'trendy' blond-haired man—a man, moreover, who could so dramatically affect their careers. But when she'd given hesitant voice to such questions in the past Damian had merely laughed and told her not to be so silly. He'd assured her that he was looking for a quiet, stable relationship and that he knew they would be very happy together.

As her confused mind see-sawed back and forth, Serena realised that it was far too late for her to admit any doubts about her forthcoming marriage. She *must* be sensible. It was just the sudden and totally unexpected reappearance of Giles in her life which was causing her to ask such difficult and uncomfortable questions. All she had to do was leave this house. Get away from the disturbing presence of a man with whom she'd once been so foolishly in love, and back to the sane, down-to-earth if possibly boring existence which lay ahead of her.

Yes, it was definitely time she started being sensible, Serena told herself firmly. Her shocked response to Giles's presence, yesterday, and the deeply buried emotions which had so startlingly swept up to the surface, had merely been the pathetic remnants of her past feelings for him. Everyone said that you never forgot the first man with whom you fell in love. So that must be it. That *must* be the reason why she felt so sick and ill and yet excited, all at one and the same time, whenever Giles came anywhere near her.

Determined to bury any disloyal thoughts about Damian and their forthcoming marriage, Serena leapt out of bed and went over to the open window, her tired green eyes blinking at the bright morning sunlight. Outside, the garden of the old house looked fresh and green after yesterday's deluge, a clump of tall chestnut trees, covered in pink and white candles, nodding in the light breeze. But despite the lovely scene in front of her she couldn't seem to throw off a feeling of deep depression.

Her mood of glum despondency was deepened as she realised that she couldn't leave this house—not without having to see Giles again. The thought of their forthcoming encounter, especially after her angry words last night, was enough to make her feel distinctly ill. What on earth could she say to him? While she had to agree that her mother *was* very difficult at times, Serena found it almost impossible to believe that the older woman would have deliberately withheld any letters or messages from Giles. Wasn't it far more likely that Mrs Harding—a great believer in frank speech—would have hit the roof, before forbidding her daughter to have anything to do with such a 'bad character' as Giles Raven...?

Leaving the window, Serena nearly cried out in horror as she caught sight of herself in a mirror. She couldn't *possibly* face Giles when she was looking so deathly pale, and with such dark shadows beneath her troubled green eyes—clearly the result of her tears last night. As for her hair...!

Half an hour later, after having a shower and finding some shampoo with which to wash her hair, Serena was feeling a good deal more presentable by the time she left the bedroom. Luckily it seemed that the electricity had been restored, which meant that she'd been able to use a small hairdrier which she'd found in the bathroom. There hadn't been anything she could do about her lack of make-up, of course. But at least her pale gold hair was squeaky clean, and floating like a shimmering cloud down past her slim shoulders, over a black polo-necked sweater from the chest of drawers.

The large, old Victorian house seemed to be empty, until she tracked down Meg Davies, happily humming away to herself in the kitchen.

Serena hesitated for a moment in the doorway before saying casually. 'I—er—I'm afraid I got caught by the tide last night. I didn't realise that this island can be so cut off at times.'

Meg turned her head to smile at the girl. 'Yes, it can be a pesky nuisance. Especially when we has these high tides. And so I warned Sir Giles, when we knew you was coming yesterday. I told him straight: "You just watch out. Otherwise poor Miss Serena will be stuck here on the island, for goodness knows how long." But would he listen? Not he!' she added with a rumble of indulgent laughter.

Serena's lips tightened as she realised that Giles *had* known that she was likely to be trapped here, on the island! And that would explain the fresh sheets and towels in the guest room. The man was a total *rat*! she fumed silently to herself. Although why he should want to keep her here, on Southey Island, she had absolutely no idea.

'Yes, well . . . it's been lovely to see you again, Meg, but I really must leave as soon as possible, especially if I want to get home by lunchtime.'

'You haven't a hope, deary,' the housekeeper told her cheerfully. 'That causeway won't be fit to drive across until well after ten-thirty this morning— probably nearer eleven o'clock, if you ask me.'

Serena stared at her in dismay. 'But surely . . . ? Doesn't the tide *ever* go down?'

'We has a high tide just about every twelve hours,' Meg told her. 'So you could have got across the river in the middle of the night, if you'd a mind to. But we've got them spring tides now, seeing as how it's the full moon. So why don't you go and have a nice cooked breakfast?' she added, casting a critical eye over Serena's slim figure. 'It looks to me as if you could do with a good square meal.'

With a heavy sigh, and realising that there was nothing she could do about the situation, Serena made her way into the large dining-room. Despite its size, the room was cosy and comfortable, with a deep red carpet and walls covered in dark pine panelling.

She was feeling far too nervous to face anything other than a cup of coffee, and the entry of Giles into the dining-room caused her heart to begin thudding painfully in her chest. Although she'd braced herself for an awkward interview, after their angry quarrel last night, she was taken aback when he merely expressed a hope that she'd slept well, before asking what she was intending to do that day.

'I'm going to leave here—just as soon as I can get off the island!' Serena muttered before taking a deep breath and adding accusingly, 'Meg Davies says that she warned you I might get stuck here last night.'

'Did she?' Giles murmured blandly before helping himself to some scrambled eggs and sitting down at the far end of the table.

Silently regarding the man whose dark attraction had been the chief cause of her sleepless night, Serena found herself desperately wishing that she could leave—right this minute! Because if she'd hoped that the cold light of day would reduce or weaken the disastrous effect that he appeared to have on her nervous system, she'd been very much mistaken. Even now, watching the man who was so carelessly dressed in casual country clothes, she could feel the same sick

longing in the pit of her stomach, the same shivering
excitement flooding through her veins, that she'd felt
on first seeing him yesterday.

'Shouldn't you be doing something ruthless in the
City? Or do you run your business according to the
tides on this river?' she asked, the nervous tension
causing her voice to sound more sharp and shrill than
she had intended.

But Giles didn't appear to notice the jagged note
in her voice, or the slight flush which had swept over
her pale cheeks.

'The answer to both your questions is no,' he told
her smoothly. 'I commute by helicopter to the City.
It's a much faster method of travel, and it has the
great virtue of cutting out any problem with the tides.
As for today...?' He paused while he poured himself
another cup of coffee. 'It will be some time before
the tide goes down, so I thought you might like a conducted tour of the island? A few hours in the fresh
air, before waltzing down the aisle, and going off to
live in a small, poky flat in London.'

Serena's lips tightened at the hard, sardonic note
in his voice. How does he know about Damian's plan
for us to live in his apartment, in the Barbican? she
asked herself wildly. But she wasn't going to give Giles
the satisfaction of asking how he'd come by that piece
of information. He seemed to know *far* too much
about her as it was, and, if she was going to get out
of here with her heart in one piece, the less intimate
discussions they had, the better.

'Come on,' Giles said, throwing down his napkin
and rising from the table. 'Let's see if we can find
you a pair of wellington boots, because the ground is
still very wet from the storm last night.'

'But...but I'm sure I ought to look at the documents again,' she protested.

'Nonsense! They're perfectly all right,' he said impatiently, not giving her any further opportunity to argue the point, as he grasped hold of her arm and led her reluctant figure from the room.

Over an hour later, as they both stood leaning over a gate and watching the half-grown lambs gambolling among a herd of ewes in the field, Serena was glad that Giles had persuaded her out into the fresh air. The whole island didn't amount to more than two hundred acres, of which a hundred and fifty formed part of a working farm. It was never going to pay for itself, but after a day spent in the City he found it very restful to get back into the fresh air of the countryside, he confessed with a slight smile, before suggesting that they climb up a low rise to admire the view on the other side of the river channel.

Sitting down on Giles's waxed green jacket, which he'd spread out on the damp grass, Serena stared blindly across the sparkling water towards the far river-bank.

'You're right,' she murmured. 'It really is lovely and peaceful on this island. I can easily see why it must be worth the trouble of commuting back and forth every day.'

When Giles didn't answer her, she slowly turned to find him regarding her with a cool, mocking smile on his face.

'Make the most of it, Serena. It looks as though it's going to be a long, long time before you'll be able to enjoy the peace and quiet of the countryside again,' he drawled sardonically.

'I don't know what you mean,' she retorted quickly—far too quickly, she realised, as his mocking grin widened. Although there seemed to be no spark of humour in his hard, eyes.

'Because, my dear girl,' he told her with grim menace, 'your future husband is clearly intending to lock you up within the claustrophobic, dungeon-like walls of the Barbican—and throw away the key!'

CHAPTER FOUR

THE harsh, grating cry of a sea-gull circling overhead in the light breeze was the only noise to disturb the sudden silence. Serena's green eyes grew apprehensive as she stared warily at Giles.

'You don't know what you're talking about!' she protested, her heart pounding at the chilly, grim expression on his face.

'No?' he drawled with hard irony.

'No!' she breathed huskily. 'It's just...well, it makes sense for me to move into Damian's flat in London—especially since he works such difficult hours. Whatever gave you the crazy idea that he's intending to "lock me up"?' she demanded. 'Why on earth would he want to do that?'

Giles shrugged. 'Maybe you ought to ask yourself, first of all, just *why* he wants to marry you. Especially since he clearly isn't making you happy.'

'Of course I'm happy! *Very* happy,' she added defensively as he lifted a dark, sardonic eyebrow. 'And...and why shouldn't he want to marry me, anyway? I'm not all that bad-looking, and...'

'Nonsense!' he growled, and she knew a moment's deep despair that the man who'd once declared her the loveliest girl he had ever seen should now find her so plain and ugly.

And then, as if hurtling along on a switch-back ride, her spirits immediately soared again as he said, 'You are a *very* beautiful girl. So, OK—you're looking somewhat tired and exhausted at the moment. Mostly, I imagine, from having to live with your over-organised mother. But that's not the problem,' he added firmly, taking hold of her limp hand, and holding it securely within his own. 'Your problem, Serena, is that you seem to have so little self-confidence, so little belief in yourself.'

'I don't know what you mean,' she whispered breathlessly, unable to prevent her hand trembling within his warm clasp.

'I mean that you've always been totally dominated by your mother. And you are now exchanging her domination for that of Damian,' Giles told her sternly. 'As far as I can see, your fiancé seems to think he's found the perfect wife: a lovely, complacent slave! A slave who will not only be extremely decorative, but will give him very little trouble, run his life and—possibly the most important, as far as he's con-cerned—accept his every word as gospel truth! *That's* why he wants to marry you. But what I want to know,' Giles added harshly, 'is exactly why *you* want to marry him?'

'Because . . . because I love him—that's why!' she cried, unable to meet his eyes as she struggled to tear her hand away from his firm grip.

Giles was right! She'd never been any good at telling lies, and his sudden verbal attack had thrown her badly off balance. Where on earth had he got hold of his weird ideas about her future life with Damian? Of course she wasn't going to be dominated by him—the whole idea was simply too ridiculous! Giles had no idea of what he was talking about. Except . . . well, she couldn't help remembering that, only a few days ago, Jenny had also mentioned something about

Damian treating her like a slave. But her sister was only fourteen, for heaven's sake!

'I don't know why you're marrying the man—but I suspect it has a lot to do with your mother,' Giles was saying grimly. 'In fact, I'm willing to bet that the old dragon has convinced you that you're on the shelf! Right?'

'You're quite wrong!' Serena mumbled, avoiding his intense gaze as she desperately tried to think of some reason—something which would convince Giles that she was deeply in love with Damian. But the warmth of his hand and the nearness of his strong, tall body was playing havoc with her senses. She felt almost faint and dizzy, unable to stem the flooding tide of weakness flowing through her veins.

'Please let me go,' she begged nervously, and when he didn't release her she tried to push him away with her other hand. But trying to match her puny strength against his was laughable. In fact, Giles *was* laughing at her—his shoulders shaking with amusement as he gazed down with a disturbing gleam in his grey eyes.

It was suddenly all too much! After their row yesterday, her sleepless night, and the shock of finding herself trapped on this island, her badly frayed nerves simply couldn't take any more.

'I'm fed up with this nonsense!' she stormed. 'I'm leaving now—even if I have to swim for it!—and I'm never——' But whatever else she might have been going to say was lost as she found herself jerked swiftly forward into his arms.

For a few brief moments she felt his breath fanning her hair, her nostrils filled with the distinctive male scent of his aftershave, before his arms closed about her slim body like a vice, and he lowered his dark head.

The mouth that possessed hers was hard and forceful, and though she beat her fists against his broad shoulders it made not a scrap of difference. Keeping one of his hands firmly pressed to her spine, he swiftly raised the other to bury his fingers in her cloud of long hair, holding her head firmly beneath him.

Weak and breathless, Serena slowly realised that his lips had softened, caressing hers with a warm, experienced sensuality that sent liquid fire racing through her veins, her heartbeat pounding out of control.

Desperately trying to tell herself that she wasn't a gullible teenager any longer didn't seem to make a scrap of difference. With her now mature vision, she knew that he was using his masterly skill as a weapon—one which he was wielding with deadly effect—in a deliberate seduction of her senses. But it was nine long years since this man had held her in his arms, and his deepening kiss was tearing down all her carefully erected barriers, arousing a response that she was unable to control as a treacherous heat began to invade her trembling limbs. The erotic warmth of his tongue, ravaging the inner softness of her mouth, sent her senses spinning completely out of control. Her body was blindly overriding the frantic danger signals from her brain, arching instinctively against him as he slowly ran a hand down over the soft curve of her breast.

Caught up in a dense mist of need and desire, she couldn't prevent herself from giving a small, faint moan of regret when he at last lifted his dark head.

His glittering eyes burned with an intensity which sent a torrent of heat flooding across her pale skin, her body shivering as he gently ran a finger over her swollen lips.

'I told you last night that you were a hopeless liar,' he murmured softly. 'And after your response to my kiss, just now, I'm quite sure that you're *not* in love with that creep Damian Fox!'

'Damian is not a creep!' she panted breathlessly. 'You know nothing about him—nothing at all!'

'On the contrary. I've had the misfortune to meet Damian—alias Archibald Fox!—several times since he suddenly decided to become a "Lord of the Manor".' Giles's voice was heavy with scorn. 'And I must say, I've totally failed to discover what you see in the awful, boring man.'

'Damian is not awful!' she lashed back furiously. 'And he's certainly *not* boring!'

'Oh, yes, he is!' Giles drawled with a mocking smile. 'Anyone who comes to see me in my city office, wearing a black shirt, a white tie to match his oh, so trendy tight white trousers, and is also wearing a gold bracelet and several gold rings, is *definitely* awful! And when he insisted on wearing dark glasses indoors, and addressing me as "ducky", I realised that he was also *extremely* boring as well!'

'You're just a damned snob! Full of nothing but narrow-minded, old-fashioned prejudice!' Serena ground out angrily. 'I'll have you know that Damian is famous and talented and—um—and . . .' Her voice trailed away as her mind seemed to go completely blank.

'It's difficult to think of anything else, isn't it?' Giles murmured drily. 'However, I might be slightly more impressed if you'd mentioned a few sterling virtues such as kindness, tolerance and generosity.'

Serena could feel a deep tide of crimson flooding over her face, her heart thumping in angry panic. Why couldn't he leave her alone? So, OK—she wasn't 'in love' with Damian, but there was no reason why they couldn't have had a reasonably happy marriage. And until she'd found herself here, on Southey Island, she'd been quite content with the life which lay ahead of her. But now...? Now that she'd met Giles again, and he seemed so determined to tear down her defences, all her hopes and plans for a happy married life with Damian were now proving to be nothing but a flimsy house of cards.

For a few moments the sheer hopelessness of her situation almost overwhelmed her, before anger and fury came to her aid. Just who did Giles think he was, lecturing her like this? What right had he to be so revoltingly smug and holier-than-thou—when he clearly had no intention of practising what he preached? She fumed as she recalled Giles's words about his forthcoming marriage to Tamsin. Was *he* intending to marry the beautiful girl for her 'sterling virtues'? Not bloody likely!

Scrambling to her feet, Serena scowled down at his handsome, mocking face, her slender figure almost shaking with rage. 'I've had just about enough of your nonsense!' she cried bitterly.

'Now calm down, Serena!'

'I'm perfectly calm!' she screamed at him, her temper by now well out of control. 'I didn't want to come to this beastly island in the first place, and I'm not prepared to stay here one minute longer! How *dare* you try to rubbish my fiancé, when *you* are planning to marry that simpering nincompoop Tamsin? And don't try and tell me that you're in love with her wonderful *mind*—because it's as plain as the nose on my face that you can't keep your hands off her sexy *body*!' Serena yelled defiantly before taking to her heels and dashing back down the small incline, across the meadow towards the house.

Unfortunately, despite running as fast as she could, Serena was having difficulty in managing the heavy green wellington boots. And, turning her head, just to make sure that Giles wasn't following her, she didn't notice the large stone boulder lying directly in her path. One moment she was racing across the meadow, and the next she found herself lying on the ground, moaning helplessly as she clasped a trembling hand to her ankle.

Serena sighed heavily, lying back on the sofa as Giles escorted the doctor to the front door. Trying to make herself more comfortable, she winced at the attempt to move her left foot, which was propped up on a cushion.

What an incredibly stupid thing to do! If only she'd had the sense to look where she was going, none of this would have happened. She raised her head to glare at her aching, throbbing ankle. Nothing had changed. Instead of being well on her way back to Kent, she was *still* forcibly trapped here, on Southey Island.

With another heavy sigh, she slumped back on the cushions, staring gloomily up at the intricate plaster-work on the study ceiling. It was one thing to have a massive loss of temper with someone, and say some highly embarrassing things—especially when you never intended to see that person again. It was *quite* another to be forced to continue living cheek-by-jowl with them for the next two days! How on earth was she going to cope with the situation?

Unfortunately it was no good blaming Giles, she told herself glumly. Although it had been his disturbing embrace and unkind words from which she had been fleeing, it was her own stupid fault not to have seen the large stone boulder in her way. And, lying moaning on the ground, she'd been in no position to argue when Giles had quickly scooped her up in his arms, and carried her carefully across the field to the house. Although she *had* argued fiercely, through teeth clenched with pain, that there was no need for his expressed intention of immediately flying her by helicopter to the nearest hospital.

'I'm quite all right—I've just twisted my ankle, that's all,' she'd told him as firmly as she could, quailing at the thought of the tremendous disruption likely to be caused by such an unconventional arrival at the local hospital. However, obviously deeply concerned about her injury, Giles had insisted on calling upon the services of a local doctor, who had, luckily, agreed with Serena's own diagnosis.

'You're a lucky girl,' he'd told her, deftly cutting the lower seam of her jeans before examining her foot. 'It looks as though you've only twisted your ankle. Just try not to put any weight on that foot for the next forty-eight hours,' he'd ordered with a slight smile, before turning to Giles. 'Your wife's looking a bit tired and peaky, so it might be a good idea to see that she gets plenty of bed rest.'

Giles had nodded gravely. 'Yes, I'll make sure of that,' he'd told the doctor blandly. Only Serena—who was blushing furiously at the doctor's mistake—

caught the low note of sardonic amusement underlying Giles's smooth reply.

I *really* hate him! she'd told herself viciously. But
now, as she wondered why it was taking Giles so long
to see the doctor off the premises, she knew that all
her troubles stemmed from the fact that she *didn't*
hate him. Remembering how, despite the pain of her
throbbing foot, she had trembled with longing in
Giles's arms, as he had carried her into the house, she
knew she was in deep, deep trouble. Even now, recalling the steady beat of his heart and the comforting
warmth of the hard body pressed so closely to her
own was enough to make her stomach ache with
desire. And telling herself that it was only the memory
of their past love-affair which was causing such
breathless hunger and need didn't seem to make any
difference. There was only one solution: somehow—
despite her twisted ankle—she simply *must* find a way
to leave this island!

Unfortunately, Serena had only been able to think
of some totally unpractical, wild plans of escape when
Giles came back into the room.

'How are you feeling now?' he asked, coming over
to stand looking down at her with concern.

'Awful!' she muttered, closing her eyes against the
sight of his handsome, tanned face poised above her,
and knowing that it wasn't just the pain in her foot
which was causing her so much anguish.

'You'll feel better when you've taken some pain-
killers,' she heard him say cheerfully before adding,
'I've just been phoning your home, and——'

'Oh, no!' Serena gasped, the colour draining from
her cheeks as she struggled to sit up.

'Calm down. There's no need to get so excited.'

'No—you don't understand!' she exclaimed. 'I was supposed to be going home today. And when I don't arrive my mother will be absolutely furious!'

'No, she won't,' Giles drawled coolly. 'I've just telephoned your home, and had a few words with your sister Jenny. Now there's a lively young girl!' he grinned.

'You . . . you didn't tell her that . . .'

'No. I did *not* go into long explanations about what had happened to you. I merely asked Jenny to tell your mother that you were still, unfortunately, involved in the long and very difficult task of researching the manorial deeds for "dear Damian",' he added smoothly, ignoring Serena's muffled groan of exasperation. 'Your sister doesn't approve of your fiancé any more than I do!'

'Why don't you try minding your own damn business?' she snapped irritably. She knew that she was behaving childishly, but the whole situation seemed to be getting *completely* out of control!

'I'm sure that dear Damian will be equally understanding,' Giles continued calmly, clearly unruffled by her brief flash of temper.

'Oh, no!' Serena gazed at him in dismay. 'You didn't ring him as well?'

'Of course I did,' he told her blandly, only the amusement dancing in his grey eyes betraying how much he was enjoying baiting her—the swine!

'I knew that he would be anxious about you. Unfortunately, he wasn't at home. So I left a message on his answer-phone, explaining that a problem had arisen over the documents. Nothing too disastrous, of course, but just enough to keep you involved here for a day or two.'

'You *have* been a busy little bee, haven't you?' Serena ground out through clenched teeth. 'Are there any other major rearrangements of my life that I ought to know about?' she added sarcastically.

Giles shook his dark head. 'No, I don't think so,' he drawled coolly before swiftly bending down and lifting her up from the sofa.

'Hey!' she protested as she found herself being carried across the room. 'What do you think you're doing? Put me down—at once!'

'I'm merely following orders. The good doctor recommended bed rest—and that's exactly what you are going to have!' he told her with a low rumble of laughter, ignoring the wildly struggling figure in his arms as he strode across the hall. 'And if I don't carry you, how do you imagine that you're going to get upstairs to your bedroom?'

'Oh—all right,' she sighed, realising that it was useless to protest any further as she hid her flushed face in his shoulder. She closed her eyes as he carried her lightly up the stairs, and her nostrils were again assailed by the aromatic fragrance of his aftershave, mingling with the fresh, musky scent of his hard male body. For one crazy, fleeting moment Serena found herself wishing that she could remain safely held by these strong, firm arms forever, and then the fantasy faded quickly as she felt herself being lowered down on to a bed.

'But...but this isn't my bedroom!' she cried, opening her eyes and gazing about her in confusion.

'No, of course not. It's mine,' Giles told her calmly before suddenly disappearing into the adjoining dressing-room and bathroom.

'You'll be far more comfortable in here,' he added as he returned, carrying a glass in one hand, and some clothes in the other. 'It's a much larger room than you were in last night. And with a TV to watch and plenty of books to read—if you have to stay in bed for the next two days—at least you'll be more comfortable.'

'I only have to rest my foot—not my body!'

'That's not what the doctor said,' Giles retorted, sitting down on the bed and handing her some aspirins.

'This is too silly—I'm perfectly all right,' she grumbled, taking the glass from his hand and swallowing down the pills.

'Of course you are,' he agreed patiently, as if talking to fractious five-year-old. 'Now, I think it's time we got those jeans off you.'

'"We"...?' She gazed at him in alarm. 'I don't know what game you think you're playing,' she began nervously, 'but there's no way——'

'Come on, Serena, let's not have any more nonsense! Undo your zip.'

'I won't do anything of the sort! I——'

'Then I'll have to do it for you!' he growled threateningly.

'You wouldn't dare!' she whispered huskily.

'Oh, wouldn't I?'

As he leaned menacingly towards her, she was deeply aware of the hard, muscled thigh so close to her own, and of the strong hands placed so firmly either side of her trembling body. She could almost feel the physical tension in his tense figure, and, from the sudden hardening of his sensual mouth, she knew that he was quite capable of doing *anything*!

'Unless you're intending to spend the next two days in those jeans, they've got to come off.' And as she still hesitated he added with heavy irony, 'There's no need to worry about preserving your modesty. I've got umpteen pairs of pyjamas, which I never wear, and they're all guaranteed to act as passion-killers!' He gestured towards the pile of navy blue and deep red garments which he had brought from the dressing-room.

Lying flat on the bed and gazing up at his determined, forceful expression, Serena reluctantly did as she was told, arching her back to enable him to slowly and carefully remove the tight designer jeans. Blushing furiously as she looked down at her long legs, only topped now by a scanty pair of briefs, her embarrassment deepened as she caught sight of the mocking gleam in his slate-grey eyes.

'I'm glad you seem to think this is so damn funny!' she ground out savagely.

'Well, I must confess that I do find your maidenly, virginal blushes somewhat amusing,' he drawled sardonically. 'Especially since I can recall once having seen a great deal more of your flesh, and——'

'OK—OK,' she muttered quickly, her cheeks flushing hectically, as she tried not to think about their lovemaking in the past. 'If you'll just give me those pyjamas, I can do the rest myself.'

'Are you sure?' he teased, bending down to pick them up from the end of the bed.

'Yes, I am!' she hissed furiously, ignoring the throb in her ankle as she quickly sat up and tired to grab them from his hands.

'Relax!' he murmured, sitting down on the bed once more, and pushing her firmly back against the pile of soft pillows. 'There's no need to get so upset,' he added, gently brushing away a tangled lock of hair from her brow. 'You're quite safe with me.'

Oh, no, I'm not! she wanted to scream, her heart beginning to beat rapidly at his close proximity, and the warm touch of his fingers as they began to move slowly down her cheek. She felt quite faint as the overpowering masculinity of his strong, powerful figure assailed her senses. What was it about this man? How was it that he could—even after so many years— still cause her to tremble like a leaf in the wind? Just the way he was now gently toying with a coil of her long fair hair, and the disturbing gleam in his grey eyes, was enough to send the blood racing frantically through her body.

For a moment she could hardly breathe as the heat of treacherous desire and overwhelming need swept like a fire through her veins. 'I—er—I can manage to change my clothes . . . on my own,' she muttered desperately, moistening her lips, which had suddenly become dry and parched.

'Are you sure?'

'Yes, of course, I'm perfectly capable . . .' Her breathless, husky voice trailed away as he gave a low laugh, his eyes gleaming with amusement at her obvious confusion.

'Poor Serena!' he mocked softly, bending forward to brush his mouth across her trembling lips. It was only a light sensual caress, but her body began shaking as if he'd lit a match and sent her flaming out of control. Against her will she began to respond, the driving need and desire of her own emotions proving irresistible. Almost without knowing it, she gave a small sigh of wanton languor against his mouth, her hands creeping about his neck to bury themselves in his hair. She felt rather than heard his quick intake of breath, and then his kiss deepened, his lips and tongue moving over hers with a sensuous, erotic expertise that melted away all resistance as he held her captive against his hard chest, and she could feel the heavy slam of his heartbeat against her own.

It seemed as though she was slipping into a dark, sweet oblivion in which she could neither move nor even think clearly, only instinctively respond to the mounting excitement of his embrace. Time seemed to have no meaning, and she was totally unaware of anything other than the sweeping sensations of the moment, until he slowly and gently released her.

After gazing at him with dazed eyes for a moment, Serena turned to burying her flaming face in the pillow. How *could* she be behaving like this? She—who was going to marry another man in two weeks' time? Unfortunately it seemed as though Giles was more than capable of reading her mind.

'I'm sure your fiancé will forgive me for stealing one kiss,' he murmured softly as he rose smoothly from the bed. 'Especially since it's obvious, however extraordinary it might seem, that he's never made love to you!'

'Oh, yes, he has!' she cried, scrambling to sit up and angrily brushing the tangled hair from her brow as he strode across the room towards the door. 'He's made love to me hundreds and hundreds of times!' she yelled defiantly, enraged to see from Giles's mocking smile, as he turned to open the door, that he knew she was lying. 'And what would you know about anything, you . . . you lecherous seducer?'

'Ah—it's just because I *was* a "lecherous seducer" when I was young and foolish that I now know what I'm talking about,' he told her quietly before silently closing the door behind him.

By the time Serena had managed to change out of her clothes and into the huge pair of pyjamas, which completely dwarfed her, she was feeling totally exhausted. Although maybe the fact that she'd been weeping her heart out had something to do with it, she told herself helplessly as she finally managed to crawl beneath the sheets of the huge bed. There must be something wrong with her, because all she wanted to do was cry and cry until she had no more tears left to shed. If only... if only she hadn't got engaged to Damian; if only Giles wasn't going to marry Tamsin; if only...

'Too late... too late!' The cry of a wood pigeon in a nearby clump of trees seemed to be echoing the mournful cry in her heart. With her marriage to Damian due to take place so soon, it was far, *far* too late to suddenly realise that she was still deeply in love with Giles—the man she had loved and lost all those years ago.

CHAPTER FIVE

TOTALLY worn out, Serena eventually lapsed into a deep and heavy sleep. At some point she was dimly aware of Meg Davies setting down a tray of food beside the bed. But, although with part of her drowsy mind she knew that she ought to be concerned about the housekeeper finding her in Giles's bedroom, she was simply too exhausted to do anything—other than to give the older woman a dazed and sleepy smile before lapsing back once more into a dark void.

When she eventually awoke, the tray had been removed and curtains drawn across the windows. A pair of bedside lamps were throwing a soft glow, through their rose-coloured shades, over the gleaming, highly polished furniture, and the slim gold frames of the watercolour paintings on the walls. The darkly sombre, masculine decoration of the room was echoed by the dark blue silk curtains—the same material used for a thick quilt that was lying across the bottom of the enormous bed.

It was some moments before her sleepy mind absorbed the fact that she was still in Giles's bedroom. And, alerted by a small sound, she turned her head to see him standing in the open doorway which led to the en-suite bathroom.

'The good doctor was quite right—you were obviously totally exhausted,' he said, walking slowly across the dark Turkish carpet towards her.

Still feeling semi-drugged from her deep sleep, Serena slowly realised that he must have recently had a shower, since his black hair was still damp, and he was wearing nothing but a short towel about his slim hips.

The glow from a bedside light threw gleaming shadows on his tall, lithe figure, illuminating the smooth, tanned skin rippling over the muscles of his arms and broad shoulders, the mat of dark curly hair covering his deep chest.

It seemed to Serena—briefly frozen in a moment of time—as though the past nine years had done nothing to change his powerful, masculine figure, nor the shivering response that gripped her stomach as she blinked nervously up at him. It might have been yesterday that this man had stood looking down at her so intently in the summer-house, at Ravenswood Manor, the first time they'd made love together. But it was only now, when he moved to sit down on the bed beside her, that alarm bells began to clang loudly in her brain, breaking through the sleepy mists of her mind with a clamorous, strident urgency.

'What—er—what time is it?' she muttered, desperately trying to break free from the paralysis which had momentarily imprisoned her.

'It's about eleven o'clock at night. You've been dead to the world for the past twelve hours!' He smiled down at the girl lying back on the pillows. Her long, pale gold hair swirled in a tousled cloud about her head, and she was clearly still far too sleepy to realise that the buttons of the pyjama-top—which dwarfed her slender figure—had become undone while she slept.

'I didn't realise I'd been asleep for such a long time,' she frowned.

'It's not so long—not when you clearly needed a good rest,' he said firmly. 'How does your ankle feel?'

'It . . . it must be OK because it isn't throbbing any more,' she murmured before remembering that the housekeeper had been in the bedroom earlier in the day. 'What on earth did Meg Davies say about my being in here? I hope she didn't think . . .'

'I'm not interested in Meg's views one way or the other,' he drawled arrogantly. 'However, if you're worried about the propriety of the situation, I can assure you that Meg fully agreed with both myself and the doctor: that you were obviously in dire need of a good, long sleep. She's quite determined to make sure that you stay in bed tomorrow as well,' he added with a warm smile.

'Yes, well . . .'

'In fact, Meg and I are in total agreement with one another on this subject. We're both convinced that what you need are large amounts of TLC. That stands for Tender Loving Care,' he added as she gazed bemusedly up at him.

Serena's nerves began to tingle at the soft emphasis he'd placed on his explanation, a flush slowly creeping over her pale cheeks at the unmistakable message carried by his gleaming grey eyes.

'I was quite wrong about my pyjamas being passion-killers,' he murmured, with a low rumble of sardonic laughter. 'On you, my darling Serena, they are clearly designed to promote rampaging lust!'

For one long moment she didn't understand what he was talking about. And then, as he unashamedly feasted his eyes on the silky sheen of her pale alabaster skin, gleaming in the warm glow of the lamplight, and the sight of her breasts, full and round, bared erotically to his sight through the wide-open pyjama-top, she gave a muffled shriek of horror. Her trembling hands hurriedly pulled the edges of the garment together, the flush on her cheeks deepening to a dark crimson of overwhelming embarrassment.

'There's no need to hide your loveliness from me,' he told her softly, raising a hand to toy idly with a tendril of her long blonde hair.

'Oh, yes, there is!' she muttered, unable to prevent a nervous tremor fluttering through her body as his hand moved to gently stroke the long, sinuous line of her neck.

'I—er—I'm obviously much better...so I ought...I really should go...go back to my own room,' she babbled helplessly, trying to inch away from his tall, dominant figure.

'You aren't going anywhere!'

There was a hard, determined edge to his voice that sent the blood racing through her body. Her breath quickened, a pulse throbbed frantically in her throat and she swallowed hard, clamping her eyes tightly shut for a moment.

'Please... please don't do this to me, Giles...' she begged huskily, unable to prevent a tell-tale quiver of sexual response from vibrating through her trembling body at the soft, velvety touch of his fingers slipping erotically down over her skin. When he gently touched the throbbing pulse at her throat, she jumped as if it had been a live switch.

'Oh, Serena!' he murmured sardonically. 'We both know that you want me to make love to you.'

She caught her breath at the hard note of certainty in his deep voice, heat flooding over her face and body as she bitterly acknowledged to herself the truth of his words.

'No!' she gasped, her husky, breathless denial seeming to echo eerily around the still, quiet room. And in the deafening silence which stretched out between them the mounting tension appeared to increase, moment by moment, until Serena was certain that she could feel it battering hard up against her skull. Desperately trying to break free of the dense mist of sensual excitement, which seemed to be paralysing her mind, she couldn't tear her eyes away from the almost hypnotic gleam in his eyes—an intense, searching gaze with which he appeared to be invading her very soul.

'Stop trying to fool yourself—or me,' he said thickly. 'I've been in love with you for most of my adult life, and I'm damned certain you feel the same way about me!'

He was right—that was the trouble, she thought helplessly, weakly closing her eyes as his hand moved on down over her shoulder. She *did* want him. She was being almost torn apart by fierce longing and desire—so fierce that she was shaking with it, unable even to begin to think clearly, when her whole existence was concentrated on the man leaning over her, and the aching need pulsating through her body. Unresisting, she quivered and shuddered helplessly as he gently pulled down the open pyjama-top to fully expose her bare, glowing flesh.

'For God's sake, darling!' he groaned. 'It's been nine long years since I've had you lying naked in my arms like this. I can't believe that you don't want me—every bit as much as I want you!'

Serena couldn't say anything. She was totally breathless, her stomach clenching in sudden tension as he trailed his fingers slowly and erotically down over her quivering flesh towards the deep valley between her breasts.

'I...we...we mustn't do this! It's quite...quite wrong!' she managed to gasp helplessly as he leaned over her, her whole body burning with a frantic heat, her nostrils absorbing the male, musky scent of the powerful body so close to her own. The normally calm expression on his face had vanished, wiped away as though it had never existed. There was now a hard sexual angle to his handsome features, the tanned skin seeming to be stretched more tautly over his cheekbones, his eyes glittering with desire and rising passion as he stared hungrily down at her trembling lips.

Despite the fact that she wanted his kiss so much that it was almost a physical pain, Serena used her last reserves of strength to try to bring them both back to reality.

'No—we can't do this!' she cried wildly. 'You're going to marry Tamsin, and I...' she gulped, tears filling her eyes '...I'm getting married to another man in just a few days' time!'

'My sweet, lovely Serena. I don't love Tamsin, and you don't love Damian.' Giles's voice was thick and hoarse as he pulled her roughly to him. 'But *I* love you—and I'm *damned* if I'm going to lose you again.'

'Don't...we can't!' she breathed against his skin, held captive by the strong, hard arms clasping her tightly to him. The peaks of her bare breasts were crushed against the thick mat of dark, curly hair on his chest, and she could feel the pounding beat of his heart against her own.

'Oh, yes, we can!' he said softly, lowering her back against the pillows and gently pressing his lips to her eyelids, the corners of her mouth and her throat, before lowering his head to kiss the burgeoning softness of her breasts. 'And we will!' he added in a low, thrilling whisper as his mouth closed over the swollen rosy tip of one breast, taut and aching for his touch.

'Giles...!' she gasped as his tongue brushed against her nipple, her body on fire at the seductive warmth, her senses reeling out of control as she writhed helplessly beneath him.

'Believe me, darling—everything else in your life may be wrong, but this... *this* is right!' he told her, and she knew from the harsh, rasping note in his voice and his sudden, sharp intake of breath that his caress was giving him as much pleasure as it did her.

With a helpless sigh of surrender, she wound her slim arms about him, pressing her lips to his black hair and burying her face in its thick, dark texture. Her longing for him was so intense that there was no more room for denial. And then, as his hands and mouth moved down over her body, she was lost.

Blindly she arched her body in mute invitation towards him, the lamplight throwing rosy shadows over her soft flesh, and excitement danced across her skin as he slowly and carefully removed her last vestige of clothing.

'You're so lovely—your skin is as soft as pure silk,' he breathed huskily against her flesh, his lips almost burning her skin as he trailed his mouth and hands

down the length of her body, which seemed on fire
from his erotic touch.

A low, husky moan broke from her throat as he
caressed her trembling thighs, trailing his lips over her
quivering flesh to her soft female core, his intimate
caress making her whimper and cry out with pleasure
before his hands swept up to firmly cup her aching
breasts. His lips and tongue tormented their hard,
swollen points, her ever-increasing, incoherent cries
and pleas seeming to incite his own ardour until,
shaking as if with a fever, he pulled her tightly up
against his hips, letting her feel the full extent of his
hard arousal.

'Tell me that you want me! Tell me that you love
me, Serena,' he demanded hoarsely, pressing his lips
to the pulse beating frantically at the base of her
throat.

'Yes . . . yes, I want you!' she whispered, clinging
dizzily to his wide, powerful shoulders. His skin was
damply hot beneath her palms, the heat and power
of his body almost overwhelming her for a moment
as he gripped her so closely to his body, and she could
feel the rhythmic urgency within him.

'I want you . . .' she breathed, her hands running
down his back, feeling the rippling muscles contract
beneath the soft touch of her fingertips. 'I love you—
I love you with all my heart!'

It was as if she had suddenly turned a key, un-
locking a previously hidden door. A deep shudder vibrated through his tall frame at her softly whispered
words, and their burning mutual desire seemed to
burst into flames, a scorching heat which swiftly de-
voured them both. She was only barely aware of his
raw, savage growl, too lost in ecstasy to hear the cries

that broke from her own throat as their bodies merged in the wild, unleashed hunger of their overpowering need for each other. She was only conscious of the surging power of his thrusting possession, and her own joyous abandonment.

Her response to him was without all inhibition. It was deep and wild, and the cool, quietly serene personality, which she had assumed and presented to the world for the last nine years, was discarded forever as he rekindled the deep, slumbering fires of passion and desire which had been buried for so long within her.

Flying higher and higher until, within the same split-second, they reached a mutual ecstasy, she and Giles were no longer two separate entities, but one. Serena only slowly became aware of her own cries, and that her face was wet with tears. He softly kissed them away, murmuring tender words of love and devotion until she lay quiescent within the warmth and security of his strong arms.

Much later, as they lay entwined together in the darkness, he murmured, 'You must break it off with Damian. You really must give him up—he's no good for you.'

'Yes, I know,' she sighed heavily. 'I expect it's cowardly of me, but I'm not sure I can face the awful rows and arguments, or the fact that I will have upset so many people. And as for what my mother is likely to say...' She shuddered.

'Darling one, you can't let other people tell you what to do, or to try and dominate your life,' he murmured sleepily as he tucked her head comfortably in the curve of his broad shoulder. 'I'm going to take care of you, so there's no need to worry about the future. And if you want to continue working I can always find you lots of interesting jobs,' he added softly before drifting off to sleep.

But Serena wasn't so fortunate. Lying wide awake and staring blindly up at the ceiling, Giles's quiet, rhythmic breathing seemed to act as a counterpoint to her increasingly distraught thoughts.

He had said he loved her, and they'd made wonderful, glorious love together, but... but at no point had he said anything about their future life together. Giles might have urged her to break off her forthcoming marriage to Damian—but there had been no suggestion of her marrying him instead. Indeed, the more she thought about what he'd said, the more it became obvious to her that, although he didn't love the beautiful girl, he was still intending to marry Tamsin—undoubtedly the perfect, decorative wife for an international businessman.

Almost fainting with pain at the thought of Giles making love to the other girl, Serena suddenly realised what she must do. Inching slowly away from beneath his arms, she carefully eased herself off the bed. Equally carefully she limped to the door, opening and closing it silently behind her as she made her way down the corridor to the guest room, where the clothes in which she had arrived were lying in a neat, tidy and freshly ironed pile on the bed.

Having pulled into a motorway café, where she'd spent the early hours of the morning drinking innumerable cups of coffee to keep herself awake, Serena had thought hard and long about the problems of her situation. And so she was in a fatalistic mood when

she at last reached London, and drove into the under-
ground car park of the Barbican.

However, it still took her some minutes, as she sat
staring blindly through the windscreen, before she
could summon up enough courage to open the car
door.

It was the sudden realisation that she had automatic gears in her car which had prompted her hasty
flight from Southey Island. Even with her left foot
out of action she would still be able to drive the car,
and as the tide was almost at its lowest point there
had been nothing to impede her escape from the
island—and Giles.

Before leaving, she'd wasted a precious half-hour
down in the study, staring blankly at a pad of paper
as she tried to think what on earth she could say to
Giles. And, after several abortive attempts to try to
express her deep, emotional feelings, she'd eventually
given up the hopeless task. There seemed no way she
could even begin to explain that it was simply because
she loved him so much that she realised she'd no
alternative but to put as much distance between them,
as soon as possible.

By the very fact of what he *didn't* say, Giles had
made it clear that there would be no permanent place
for her in his life. He was obviously determined to
marry Tamsin, and every fibre of Serena's being
shuddered at the thought of becoming the 'other
woman' in some dreadful marital triangle. If Giles
didn't want her as his wife, then she didn't want anything to do with him, she told herself firmly. But,
despite the hard common sense of her arguments,
there seemed nothing she could do about the flood
of tears which kept blinding her eyes, and which had

caused her to pull into the side of the road so many times on her journey back to London.

Negotiating all the locked gates, designed to keep the inmates of the Barbican protected from the outside world, Serena eventually found herself sitting, with her foot propped up on a plate-glass coffee-table, in the severely modern sitting-room of Damian's apartment.

That Damian himself was definitely *not* pleased by her sudden appearance was obvious. Indeed, his first words of greeting had been neither lover-like nor encouraging.

'I don't know why you're here, but I'm afraid I can't stop, ducky. I've got a *frightfully* hectic schedule today,' he'd told her, not bothering to hide his irritation at her unexpected appearance.

'Well, I'm sorry about that,' she'd retorted firmly, 'but I'm afraid your "frightfully" important meeting will just have to wait!'

Clearly unaccustomed to her using an even faintly sardonic tone when addressing him, Damian had gazed at her with astonishment—as if he couldn't believe his ears—before shrugging his shoulders and asking her to sit down while he sorted out some business paperwork.

And now, as she sat back in the leather armchair, Serena surveyed the room, realising that she never could have have lived happily within these stark white walls. Damian was very proud of what he considered his instinctively good, modern taste, but to her eyes the glass and chrome furniture and black leather armchairs were singularly unwelcoming. It was only the floor-to-ceiling windows, offering a wonderful panoramic view of the city of London, which redeemed the apartment in any way.

The next ten minutes, following Damian's return to the room, were predictably every bit as fraught and difficult as she had feared. Initially, convinced that Serena was obviously in a highly over-emotional state and suffering from wedding nerves, Damian hadn't taken her decision to call off the wedding too seriously. And when he *did* realise that she was firmly determined on her course of action he shook his head with incredulity.

'You must be totally out of your mind!' he told her flatly. 'Quite apart from making me look a complete and utter fool, how do you suppose I can possibly concentrate on producing a very avant-garde, exciting modern play, with all this sort of nonsense on my mind? And what about the Lordship of the Manor of Foxwell?' he added petulantly. 'You *know* how much that meant to me. Instead of coming back here with the documents, all I get is this aggravation!' His querulous voice rose in fury and astonishment.

'I'm sorry to have upset you, Damian,' Serena murmured.

'I simply fail to understand why you don't want to marry me,' he continued, ignoring her words as he paced up and down the room. 'How can you turn me down—*me* ... who plucked you from total obscurity, and introduced you to such a wonderful new world?'

He's completely preoccupied with himself. He hasn't even bothered to think or worry about how *I* feel, Serena thought grimly, gazing silently at her ex-fiancé as he struck a dramatic pose of outraged dignity. Although, with a fresh and clear vision, she noted that he wasn't able to resist his eyes straying towards a full-length mirror on the wall, obviously checking on his 'performance'.

Giles had been absolutely right. Damian was a one-hundred-per-cent *creep*!

'I suggest you go home and have a long, serious talk to yourself about this crazy decision,' Damian told her as she rose to her feet, and he grimaced with distaste as she limped gingerly back towards the front door. 'And *when* you come to your senses I also suggest that you'd better do something about that foot. I don't want my smart friends laughing at my bride as she hobbles down the aisle beside me,' he added spitefully.

Realising that it was her fault, for having become engaged to him in the first place, Serena kept her temper and her composure.

'I'm very sorry about this, Damian,' she said quietly. 'However, I can promise you that I *won't* change my mind,' she added firmly before he peevishly slammed the door shut loudly behind her.

CHAPTER SIX

WHEN Serena eventually arrived back at the family home, in Kent, it was obvious that Damian had taken a churlish, sulky revenge for her temerity in turning him down.

Barely had her small car driven up to the front door before her mother rushed out of the house, almost wrenching the car door off its hinges.

'You stupid girl!' she cried. 'What *have* you done to poor Damian? I've had the dear boy on the telephone for most of the morning, and he's very, *very* upset!'

'I'll tell you all about it in a minute,' Serena muttered, trying to get out of the car past the bulky figure of her mother.

'You must be out of your mind, turning down a chance to marry an exciting man like Damian! No one else is going to look at you... and what are you going to do when you're an old maid and on the shelf? That's what I want to know,' her mother thundered angrily.

But for once the older woman's invective and caustic tongue-lashing didn't upset Serena, who was still feeling totally numb and frozen from the effort of forcing herself to walk away from the only man she'd ever loved.

'And don't think I don't know what you've been up to!' Mrs Harding cried as her daughter limped past her into the house. 'I didn't tell dear Damian, of course—not while there's a slight chance I can still persuade him that you're suffering from a temporary derangement! But *I'm* well aware that that wicked rogue, Giles Raven, is behind all this nonsense!' the older woman added hysterically. 'As soon as Damian told me where you'd been staying, and the name of the man who owned the house, I just *knew* what had happened.'

'Nothing has happened. I've just decided that I don't want to marry Damian, that's all.' Serena sighed wearily.

But Mrs Harding clearly wasn't prepared to listen, continuing to rant and rave loudly at her daughter's outrageous behaviour.

'As I told your father, that awful man has no morals—none at all! And, although I managed to put a stop to his nonsense some years ago, I can see that——'

'So you really *did* prevent his letters and messages from reaching me!' Serena exclaimed, her words cutting off Mrs Harding in full flow.

The older woman flushed, not quite able to meet her daughter's eyes. 'Well...what if I did?' she blustered.

'Oh, Mother...!' Serena sighed helplessly, sinking down into a chair. 'I was so certain that you'd *never* do such an awful thing! Don't you realise just how much unhappiness you've caused me?'

At the sight of her daughter's abject misery, Vera Harding took out a handkerchief and dabbed her eyes before loudly blowing her nose.

'I only did what I thought was best for you,' she sniffed. 'Giles had been called away unexpectedly from Ravenswood Manor because of the sudden death of his brother and parents in that terrible car accident. And when he came back—after spending days sorting out matters with the French authorities—you'd already gone abroad,' her mother explained. 'So, you see ... well, it just seemed best if I didn't pass on his letters. I mean ... he's at least seven or eight years older than you, Serena. And with his *terrible* reputation—so wild, so unsteady—I knew that he would cause you nothing but grief. I really was just trying to protect you, darling ...' she added lamely, blowing her nose fiercely once again.

Faced by the totally unfamiliar sight of her strong, dominant mother now reduced to tears, Serena's warm heart softened. The older woman clearly couldn't help being over-protective, and it was obvious that, although gravely mistaken, she really had acted from the very best motives.

'Don't worry, Mother,' she said with a heavy sigh. 'You were probably right. It looks as though things would never have worked out between us.'

'So why not tell Damian that you've made a mistake?' her mother murmured hopefully, her face falling as Serena stubbornly shook her head.

'No,' she said firmly. 'He was totally wrong for me, and I should have known that right from the beginning,' she added before getting up and limping quietly out of the room.

It was clearly too much of a miracle for Serena to expect her mother to change her character overnight. And there were many times in the succeeding days when the older woman couldn't resist giving way to her exasperated feelings. Even her easygoing father was upset—the speech he'd been carefully preparing for the wedding reception now being totally useless.

In fact—amid all the ghastly business of having to tell the vicar the wedding was off, the hours spent on the telephone trying to contact all friends and relations, and the dreadful chore of having to pack up and return all the wedding presents—Serena's only friend in the house seemed to be her young sister, Jenny.

Bouncing happily around in all the gloom and doom, Jenny was obviously delighted that 'Mr Terrific' wasn't going to become her brother-in-law.

'You're well out of *that* relationship!' she told Serena cheerfully as she offered to help parcel up the last remaining wedding presents. 'Damian would have made you terribly unhappy, you know.'

'Yes, I do know. That's why I called off the marriage,' Serena muttered, bitterly aware that she had behaved appallingly, and upset just about everyone. But all she could think about was Giles, and their wonderful, earth-shattering night of passion. Even when she lay wide awake in her cold single bed there seemed to be nothing she could do to prevent the memory of his lovemaking from searing the insides of her closed eyelids. And trying to fill her days with small, boring routine tasks didn't succeed in keeping his handsome image at bay. She was filled with the unhappy knowledge that she would never love or care for anyone else with the same strong, overwhelming emotional intensity which she felt for Giles. So it looked as if her mother was right, after all. She was going to spend the rest of her days as a sour old maid. It clearly wasn't an enviable life which stretched ahead of her—but to settle for second best would be a far worse fate.

'Mother was telling me about your old boyfriend.' Jenny's voice interrupted her distraught thoughts. 'Do you still love him *very* much?'

'Yes,' Serena sighed helplessly, feeling too low and miserable even to attempt to prevaricate.

However, as the days passed, and she continued to drift like a wraith about the house—deeply alarming her mother at how thin and drawn she was looking— even she began to find her sister's suppressed air of excitement, and persistent interest in Serena's romance with Giles Raven, to be almost more than she could bear.

'For heaven's sake, Jenny! Do stop going on about the man,' she snapped one day. 'And I'm fed up with being practically knocked down by you rushing to answer the phone every time it rings! What's so important that you have to insist on taking all the calls?'

'Oh, nothing much,' her sister told her airily. 'Er— I've just entered a competition to meet a famous pop star, that's all.'

I wish my life was centred on the manifold attractions of a pop star, and not on the unattainable, tall, dark figure of Giles Raven, Serena told herself unhappily as she was helping her mother to prepare lunch two days later.

'This should have been your wedding day!' Mrs. Harding sniffed tearfully, scraping angrily away at a potato until there was practically nothing left. 'I still can't bring myself to see Alice Wilkins. She was apparently *very* upset at the return of her lovely vase.'

'I'm not surprised. I expect she's been trying for years to get rid of the hideous thing!' Serena muttered caustically under her breath as her mother continued to complain about the embarrassing situation.

'I don't think I'll ever be able to look Alice Wilkins in the eye, after what's happened,' Mrs Harding moaned. 'And your father dreads going to the golf club these days. The vicar has been very kind and understanding, of course, but... Whatever is that noise?' she demanded as the air seemed filled with an increasingly loud roaring sound.

As she peered out of the window, the older woman's eyes grew wide with astonishment at the sight of a green helicopter landing in the field which lay on the other side of the garden hedge.

Preoccupied by the amazing sight, she totally missed hearing her elder daughter's shocked gasp of surprise. It was only when Serena gave a loud cry, and rushed past her to the kitchen door, before dashing down the garden path as fast as her weakened ankle would allow, that she began to have a faint inkling of what was happening.

Laughing and crying at one and the same time, Serena wrestled impatiently with the latch on the garden gate, which led out into the field behind the house. A moment later she had released it, and, not caring about the jabbing pain in her ankle, she raced across the turf towards the tall figure climbing out of the aircraft.

'Oh, Giles!' she cried, throwing herself into the open arms which were waiting for her. 'I've missed you *so* much... I've been so *desperately* unhappy! I really don't care if you don't want to marry me... I'd be happy to be just your mistress, or whatever you want...'

'I don't want a mistress—I want a wife!' Giles laughed as his strong arms closed protectively about her slender figure, and he put a quick stop to her babbled, incoherent words with a hard, firm and thoroughly satisfactory kiss.

'I'm not having any more nonsense,' he told her grimly, when they both came up for air. 'You and I are going to get married—at the first possible moment. Right?' he demanded fiercely.

'Oh, yes!' she breathed ecstatically, stars in her eyes as she gazed mistily up at his handsome face. 'Absolutely right!'

'Darling one, I'm desperately sorry that I didn't manage to get here before now. Unfortunately I was abroad on a business deal, and I only got Jenny's phone call the day before yesterday.'

'Jenny's phone call...?' Serena repeated, gazing at him in bewilderment.

'She's been trying to contact me for the past few days to tell me that you were *not* going to marry that arch-creep "Mr Terrific"!'

'I had no idea Jenny was interfering in my life like this,' Serena muttered crossly.

'I can only thank God that she did!' Giles said fervently. 'I was absolutely shattered when I woke up, after the wonderful night we'd spent together, to find that you'd just silently slipped away from the island. I was certain that you must have decided to marry your awful fiancé, after all.' He sighed and shook his dark head. 'I did my best to try and stop you making such a terrible mistake, but when you disappeared into thin air I was certain that I'd failed.'

'Do... do you mind if I sit down?' she gasped, the full magnitude of everything that had happened in the last five minutes suddenly causing her to feel weak and feeble, her legs trembling as if they were made of jelly.

'I'm sorry, darling—I've completely forgotten about your poor ankle,' he muttered, lifting her up in his arms and carrying her over to a patch of long, fragrant meadow grass. 'I understand from Jenny that your mother has been going completely over the top about the cancellation of the wedding?' he added, lowering her gently down on to the ground.

Serena gave a shaky laugh. 'I think that's probably the understatement of the year.'

'Then we'd better stay right here. I always was a lily-livered coward—especially as far as your mother was concerned!' he grinned, sitting down beside her and gathering her once again in his arms.

He possessed her lips in a long, lingering kiss, and it was some moments before they realised they were no longer alone.

'I don't want to play gooseberry, or interrupt the path of true love...!' Jenny grinned down at her sister, who was obviously quite dotty about the handsome, dark-haired man whose arms were so tightly clasped about her slim figure. 'But I think I'd better tell you that Mummy is going completely bananas—and even Daddy isn't looking *too* happy!'

Giles gave her a broad smile. 'Ah—you must be that great girl Jenny. I owe you a deep debt of gratitude, since it's entirely thanks to you that I'm at last going to possess the wife of my dreams!'

The young girl gave him a toothy grin. 'Well, I don't mind being a bridesmaid if *you're* going to marry Serena, but I absolutely refuse to wear a horrible pink dress!'

'I don't blame you. Pink is definitely out of fashion this year!' Giles agreed smoothly before reaching inside his jacket. 'Here, you'd better give this to your mother. It might help to calm her down.'

Jenny gave a slight shrug as she took the thick, folded document. 'OK, but I don't think *anything* is going to make a scrap of difference. When I last saw Mummy she was absolutely trembling with rage!'

'I think you'll find that document will achieve quite dramatic results,' he drawled sardonically as Jenny shrugged again before going off to find her mother.

'I can't believe that I'm so happy!' Serena breathed huskily. 'It wasn't until the other day that I learned you were quite right. Mother *did* stop all your letters, and never passed on any messages to me when I was abroad,' she told him sorrowfully. 'And I also now know why you suddenly disappeared from Ravenswood that summer. But I didn't hear about your family's terrible car accident until I'd been abroad for some time. My mother isn't a very good letter-writer, you see, and so...'

'Darling—that's all in the past,' Giles murmured, clasping her tightly in his arms once more.

Serena leaned her head against the comforting strength of his broad shoulder. 'You're right, of course. But just think—if it hadn't been for the *amazing* coincidence of Damian wanting to buy a Lordship which you owned, we'd never have met again.'

'That was no coincidence.' Giles smiled down at her. 'I saw you on the TV, during that programme of Damian's, and, as you were introduced as *Miss* Serena Harding, I realised that you hadn't married anyone else, despite becoming even more beautiful than I remembered. And then——' he sighed heavily '—then I discovered that you were engaged to a TV producer,

and about to get married any day. I didn't know what
to do—he *might* have been the man of your dreams,
for all I knew. But the more enquiries I made, the
more awful the man sounded. And, since I'd discovered his maniac desire to become a pseudo-
aristocrat, I had the bright idea of dangling the
Lordship of Foxwell before his nose. Of course, when
I did eventually meet him, I immediately knew that
he was totally wrong for you.'

'But...but what about Tamsin?' Serena muttered
accusingly. 'You said you were going to marry her.'

'No...I was very careful not to specify exactly *who*
I was intending to marry. And in any case——' he
gave her a sheepish grin '—Tamsin was just a piece
of window-dressing.'

'What on earth do you mean?'

'Oh, come on, Serena!' he laughed. 'I had to keep
my own end up, didn't I? So I asked the most beautiful
girl I knew to come to lunch. Luckily you were both
late, or I'd have spent the whole day being bored to
death by Tamsin. However, although she didn't stay
very long, I felt far more optimistic about my
chances—especially when I saw how intensely jealous
you were!'

'No, I wasn't!'

'You're always going to be a rotten liar!' He laughed
again at the flush rising over her cheeks. 'Although
I reckon I ought to be insulted by your thinking I
might marry such a totally feather-brained, stupid girl.
She'd have driven me mad inside a week!

'And in any case,' he continued quickly, as his beloved seemed reluctant to let go of the subject of
Tamsin, 'I'm far more interested in *us*. That document

I gave Jenny was a special licence. I hope we can get married as soon as possible.'

'Oh, yes—yes, *please!*' she whispered huskily.

'And you'll come and live with me, on Southey Island?'

'Of course I will,' she told him simply before suddenly being struck by a deeply important point. 'We are going to have some children of our own, aren't we?' she asked anxiously.

'Absolutely—and the more, the merrier!' he told her expansively before gathering her once more into his arms, his mouth possessing her lips in a warm, passionate kiss of total commitment.

Inside the house, Jenny and her father were apprehensively eyeing Mrs Harding, who had briefly interrupted a full-blown fit of screaming hysterics to study the piece of paper which Jenny had placed in her trembling hands.

The heavy silence was at last broken by a loud exclamation as the woman, who had, only moments before, been screaming the house down, suddenly gave a peal of happy laughter.

'How extraordinary! I can't think *why* it never occurred to me ...' she murmured, sinking down into a chair, and pulling a pad of paper towards her. 'I must make some more lists, of course, and then ...'

'For goodness' sake, Vera—what's going on?' her husband demanded, gazing in bewilderment at his wife.

His wife gave him a beaming smile. 'Serena is now going to marry Giles Raven—isn't it wonderful news?'

'But I thought you didn't like him?' Jenny said tactlessly.

'Nonsense! I always knew that Damian wasn't quite right for Serena. And, of course, now that my darling daughter is going to be a real Lady—and I can't wait to tell Alice Wilkins *that* piece of news!—everything has just worked out perfectly, hasn't it?'

'What on earth are you talking about?' her sorely tried husband demanded brusquely.

'Well...I did make just a small, rather foolish error,' his wife admitted. 'You see, I never realised that, when both his father and older brother were killed, Giles was bound to inherit the baronetcy. And that means my darling Serena will soon be Lady Raven!'

'Wow—that's really cool!' Jenny giggled.

'Yes,' her mother murmured, leaning back in her chair with a happy sigh. 'He might have been just a tiny bit wild in the past, but I *always* knew that dear Giles would be the perfect husband for Serena...'

SOMETHING
NEW
Valerie Parv

For Nan Bennett, civil marriage celebrant,
with love and thanks for letting me use
some of your exquisitely chosen words.

At times it seems that to love and be loved
is the only purpose of human existence

Nan Bennett

CHAPTER ONE

THERE it was. *Sunseeker*. Nicole Webber's eyes widened as she took in the futuristic lines of the cruiser with its jet-propelled hull and superstructure so white it dazzled her. It dwarfed the other private vessels tied up at the Cleveland Bay wharf. Bill's friend must be worth a fortune to own such a vessel, and he had offered to lend it to Bill and Diane for their honeymoon. Lucky Bill and Diane!

Nicole smiled as she caught sight of them on the after-deck, talking to another man whose face was in shadow. How happy her friends looked. They stood so close together that a credit card wouldn't have slipped between them. Nicole felt privileged to share their happiness but couldn't help contrasting it with her own single state. Then she shook herself mentally. At twenty-seven she had plenty of time yet.

The third man must be Bill's friend, she thought as her steps brought her closer. Diane had said he would brief them on the running of the vessel before they cruised to Crystal Island on the Barrier Reef where Bill was the resident ranger and where the wedding was to take place.

Suddenly, the man shifted into the sunlight and Nicole froze, shock rippling through her, as recognition came. It couldn't be. Fate wouldn't do this to her.

But Diane would.

Suspicion flooded her mind. Diane was so starry-eyed about her own romance that she probably thought she was doing Nicole a favour by throwing her together with Mark Kingston again.

Another thought made her falter. If Mark was Bill's friend, then he was also to be best man at the wedding, at which Nicole was to officiate in her role as a civil marriage celebrant.

'Oh, Diane, how could you do this to me?' she groaned aloud, fighting the urge to turn and flee. She might have survived a couple of hours' cruising with Mark if she had to, but how could she stand in front of him and recite marriage vows which they had nearly shared themselves?

Her gaze darted about, seeking escape, but Diane spotted her and waved from the cruiser. 'Come aboard, Nicole. We've been waiting for you.'

With sinking heart she did as bidden, passing Bill her overnight case and document folder before accepting his hand to board the cruiser. Immediately Diane swept her up in an exuberant hug. 'Now we're all here. Just think, by this time tomorrow I'll be Mrs William Foster.'

'Hello, Nicole.'

Mark's honeyed tones sent a shiver down Nicole's spine and she looked away from his sea-green gaze, although she could feel it levelled at her from under her lowered lashes. Her voice came out husky with strain. 'Hello, Mark. I didn't expect to see you here.'

'So I gather.' The irony in his tone said he didn't think she would have come if she'd known. He didn't seem nearly so taken aback, so Diane must have told him who was conducting the ceremony. In spite of

herself, she wondered whether he was annoyed or
pleased. Or did he no longer care either way?

She wished she could claim indifference, but whatever else she felt she was never indifferent to Mark.
Already her senses were quivering with awareness of
him. In the ten months since their parting she'd
blocked out the memory of his effect on her. Now
she felt like a lightning conductor in an electrical
storm, waiting for the next strike.

'You're looking well,' he said with what she felt
sure was mere politeness.

Appearances had never counted for much with
Mark, who was more interested in her feelings and
opinions. Still, she was pleased to know she looked
her best. She was a few pounds lighter than when
they'd parted and it suited her. Her hair was longer
now, too, the honey-coloured strands curling on to
her shoulders. If Mark was affected by the sight of
her, he gave no sign.

Nicole was relieved when Diane came between them.
'Champagne, anyone?'

Mark shook his head. 'I never mix sailing and al-
cohol, especially when there's a storm brewing.' He
glanced at the impossibly blue sky which was feathered
with fragile cirrus clouds. It was hard to believe they
presaged any sort of bad weather.

'It won't stop us getting to the island, will it?' Diane
asked uneasily. Like the others, she had lived in North
Queensland long enough to know that, in April,
tropical storms could blow up with surprising
suddenness.

'It shouldn't,' Mark assured her. '*Sunseeker* can
outrun most storms. And this one is heading out to

sea. But I'll keep a listening watch on the radio in case it changes course.'

Nicole had also heard the storm warnings this morning, wondering then if it would interfere with her friends' wedding plans. The rest of the guests were to arrive by boat next morning. With luck, the storm would have blown itself out in mid-Pacific by then.

For one uncharitable moment she wished the storm would prevent them from going to the island. Then she wouldn't be thrust into Mark's company and forced to deal with feelings she had tried desperately to bury. They threatened to bubble to the surface with the force of a long-dormant volcano coming abruptly back to life.

Mark was showing Bill how to cast off from the wharf and she used the moment to study him covertly. Try as she might to find fault, she was forced to admire the sculpted lines of his athletic body, outlined to perfection in cream drill trousers and a white knitted shirt. He considered good health a business asset, she recalled, investing in his fitness as meticulously as he poured money into his property development projects.

As he moved smoothly around the deck, his hair rippled in the breeze and he pushed it out of his eyes with a gesture so familiar that her eyes misted, forcing her to blink hard. How often she'd pushed it back for him; her fingers tingled with the remembered sensation of those russet strands against her palm.

'You're not angry, are you?' Diane asked hesitantly, following her gaze.

Nicole returned to the present with an effort. 'Why should I be angry?'

'Because Mark is Bill's best man,' she rushed on. 'They're diving buddies, and since Bill has no brothers . . .'

'It's all right, really,' Nicole assured her. 'It would have been easier if I'd been forewarned, though.'

Diane wrapped her arms around herself. 'Be honest. Would you have agreed to conduct the wedding if you'd known?' Nicole's silence spoke volumes. 'I knew it, you'd have run like a rabbit.'

'I would not!' Laughter eased some of her tension. 'All right, I probably would have. But not because I'm scared of Mark.'

'More likely you're scared of falling for him all over again,' Diane countered.

Nicole sighed. 'You can take those stars out of your eyes, because it isn't going to happen.'

'It almost did once.'

'Until we came to our senses.'

'*We*, Nicole?'

She jumped a foot, not realising he had moved up behind her. 'We—we both agreed that marriage wasn't right for us,' she stammered as hot colour flooded her usually creamy complexion.

'You make it sound like a mutual decision,' he murmured, earning a curious look from Diane.

'This is hardly the time to discuss it. If we're going to talk about weddings, it should be Diane and Bill's.'

'Quite right,' he agreed smoothly, his smile switching to Diane. The flash of evenly spaced white teeth in his tanned face, with the laughter lines fanning out from either side of his wide mouth, made Nicole's insides cramp in protest. It was such a kissable mouth; it took no effort at all to imagine the impact on her own lips.

Her fingers brushed her mouth in imitation of the gesture until she realised what she was doing and dropped her hands. But not before he had seen the movement, she realised. His satisfied look taunted her as he turned to Bill and announced that they could get under way.

'Join me for coffee?' Diane suggested when the two men moved up to the flying-bridge.

'Why not?' She didn't really want coffee, but she needed time to gather her turbulent thoughts, away from Mark's distracting presence.

While Diane made the coffee Nicole admired the gleaming interior. The cruiser was new since she'd known Mark. It was typical of him to choose state-of-the-art, although she had to admit that the high ceilings and cane furnishings gave the boat a pleasantly tropical atmosphere.

The colours ranged from white to buttery cream, punctuated by a Matisse-inspired print upholstery and hand-painted silk wall coverings. Everything was custom designed right down to the door-handles.

Diane saw her studying the interior. 'Fantastic, isn't it? I can't believe it's going to be our honeymoon suite.'

'Mark can be generous when it suits him,' Nicole observed drily. With everything but his time, she added inwardly.

'You two met at a wedding, didn't you?'

'The bride was his secretary and I was the celebrant,' Nicole admitted.

Diane smiled. 'Wasn't Mark rumoured to be marrying that same secretary?'

'The rumours were wrong. Mark was already married to his work.'

Diane caught the bitterness edging her tone. 'Was that what went wrong between you two?'

'Probably.' Even to her friend, she hated to admit how futile it felt to compete with telephones and fax machines for crumbs of Mark's attention. Even picnics in the country weren't sacred, thanks to the cellular telephone. How could any woman compete with the demands of a corporation?

To change the subject, she asked, 'When do I get to see your dress?'

Diane's eyes sparkled. 'Now, while the men are safely occupied.'

A carpeted passageway led to the master suite, which fairly took Nicole's breath away with its opulence. Then her whole attention was riveted on the gown which Diane spilled across the king-sized bed. 'Diane, it's gorgeous!'

'Not too much for an island wedding?'

'It's perfect.' With a sigh of wonderment, Nicole traced the fine beadwork on the guipure lace bodice. Below a narrow waist the silk fanned out to knee-length, then flowed into a floor-length train at the back. A head-dress of crystal and pearls sparkled beside the dress. Impulsively, she hugged her friend, her eyes misting. 'You'll look sensational.'

Diane began to gather the dress and return it to its protective covering when the cruiser suddenly lurched, flinging them both off balance. Diane's alarmed look met Nicole's. 'The sea's getting rougher.'

'It's probably the fringes of Cyclone Eddy. The radio said it's two hundred miles out to sea, so I wouldn't worry.'

At the same time, Nicole was aware that a cyclone could travel two hundred miles in a day, but there was no point mentioning it to Diane. She was already on edge, wanting everything to be perfect. 'Have you decided what verse you want me to include in the ceremony?' she asked, to divert her friend.

'I like the passage from Sir Walter Scott.'

'"Love rules the court, the camp, the grove, And men below, and saints above; For love is heaven, and heaven is love."' Nicole quoted. 'I'm glad you chose that one. What does Bill think?'

'He doesn't care if we recite the grocery list as long as we're together.'

'And he's right,' Nicole conceded. Something very like envy racked her. How would it feel to be as secure in her love as Diane was with Bill? She had never felt it with Mark, who was forever juggling a dozen priorities, of which she was but one. In the end, leaving had seemed less painful than waiting her turn for his attention. Seeing him again today had eroded that certainty.

Her work as a marriage celebrant, which she supplemented by selling her paintings when she could, gave her plenty of opportunity to meet people socially but none of the men she had dated lately could hold a candle to Mark. Or was it the attraction of forbidden fruit, wanting what she couldn't have? She wished she knew the answer.

Below deck, the boat's movement had become much more noticeable. Venturing up on deck, they were shocked to see how much the weather had changed. It was still intensely hot and sultry but a stiff breeze had sprung up. The feathery clouds were giving way to sullen sheets of darker clouds extending towards the horizon. Instinctively, Nicole moved closer to Mark. 'Have you heard anything new on the radio?'

His jaw was set in a grim line. 'The cyclone's turned back this way. Islands offshore of Townsville have been warned to batten down. Even if it doesn't touch us, it could get rough.'

'Maybe we should turn back.'

Mark's frown deepened. 'We've come too far. It's better to get into the lee of the island. The ranger's quarters are built to withstand a cyclone, so we'll be as safe there as anywhere.'

'When is the cyclone expected to hit?' Nicole asked.

'Impossible to predict. It's like trying to plot the course of a spinning-top.'

From somewhere, Nicole recalled that the word 'cyclone' came from the Greek for 'coil of a snake'. She shivered, suddenly glad that Mark was with her. 'What about the rest of the wedding party?' she asked. 'They won't be able to get to the island, will they?'

'The coastguard has warned all vessels to remain in port for twenty-four hours,' Mark said, lowering his voice.

Diane clutched Bill's arm, her face paling. Nicole wished there was something she could say which would help, but there was nothing.

By the time they reached the island, the sea had changed from shining silver to a sheet of dull pewter. The wind whipped away their words and the sky was filled with an iron-grey mass of rain clouds.

As the low, forested island appeared, the sea changed to yellow-green, showing that they were over coral reefs. On the right, a line of coral marked rocks thrown up by previous storms. Between those rocks and the shore was a reef-flat where the sea life flourished.

Near the jetty, shoals of sardines massed near the sand. Once, Nicole had swum underwater in the middle of the small silver fish, a living, circling wall which moved fascinatingly as one creature.

Now she hardly noticed them as she stared in awe at the pandanus palms lining the beach. They were bent almost double, their fronds streaming like mermaid's tresses in the strengthening wind.

The rain forest looked like a raging sea as the wind blew waves across the springy undergrowth. Gulls, egrets and herons coasted on the wind and tiny silvereyes huddled in the branches, too fragile to battle the gusts.

At the jetty, Mark snapped out orders with a crispness which reminded Nicole uncomfortably of their earlier relationship.

Even as she appreciated the need for leadership, she was irrationally angered by his take-charge behaviour. Bill was a ranger. He could run things equally well, couldn't he? Why did Mark always have to be the one in charge?

But Bill seemed happy to let Mark take over, unloading stores and helping to secure the vessel without protest. When the cruiser was secure in a sheltered mooring, they hurried up the coral path.

The safest place in a cyclone was a high, sheltered building. Built of mud-bricks, Bill's house, which doubled as the ranger station, was ideal. While they settled in, he and Mark secured tape across the windows to prevent them shattering, then opened a window on the side away from the wind to reduce pressure inside the building.

The preparations looked incongruous alongside those which had already been made for the wedding ceremony. Tropical flowers were massed in corners and rows of folding chairs were set out in the spacious living-room. The kitchen bulged with food and drink for the guests.

'We had put you in the guest cabin, Nicole,' Diane told her.

'I think Nicole would rather be under the main roof tonight, if you have room,' Mark intervened.

About to suggest the same thing, Nicole's jaw clamped shut. He always knew what was best for her, didn't he? 'I'll be fine in the guest cabin,' she said, glaring at him.

Diane chewed her lip. 'Mark's right. You shouldn't be on your own in this. I'll put you in the room my sister was going to use.'

Why did everyone automatically take Mark's side in an argument? Couldn't he see that his need to run everything was the reason they had split up in the first place? It left him no time for anything—or anyone—else. Resignedly, she picked up her case, but he lifted it from her fingers.

'I'll carry this.'

'I can manage,' she said through clenched teeth.

'Stubborn as ever,' he murmured, but relinquished his hold on the case.

It was a small victory and gave her no pleasure. It seemed as if nothing had changed. She was still fighting with Mark for control of the small details of her life. If they were still together, it would be the same as before. He would run everything with terrifying efficiency because he was simply so darned *good* at everything. And she would be left following in his wake, remembered during the brief breathing spaces in his life.

She had made the right decision to call a halt, she saw now. If only it didn't hurt so much to be reminded of what they could have had, if he had learned to let go a little.

Diane followed her into the bedroom. Seeing her friend's stricken expression, Nicole was ashamed of dwelling on her own problems. 'What is it? Is there more bad news?'

Diane sank on to the bed and covered her face with her hands. When she looked up, her tawny eyes were brimming. 'Mark just got the latest forecast. The storm's getting worse. Nobody will be able to come for days. Oh, Nicole, I wanted everything to be perfect and now it's ruined. It's an omen, I know it is.'

Nicole sat down beside her and dropped an arm around her friend's shaking shoulders. 'It's nothing of the sort. You're a Queenslander, you know these things happen.'

Diane's turned a white face to her. 'I was in a cyclone when I was a child. It destroyed our house, all but the bathroom we were sheltering in.'

Nicole's protest was torn from her. 'That's why you're so upset, isn't it?'

'I never told anyone before, but tropical storms terrify me. I turn to jelly.'

'Well, not this time.' Nicole stood up, her thoughts whirling. 'We're going to go ahead and have this wedding anyway.'

'It isn't fair to joke about something so important.'

'I'm not. We have everything we need right here. I have the paperwork in my briefcase and the authority to solemnise the wedding. The groom is here. We even have the best man.'

'Did I hear my name taken in vain?'

Nicole's heart somersaulted as Mark lounged in the doorway, his nearly six-foot height dwarfing the small room.

'Nicole has a crazy idea about going ahead with the wedding anyway,' Diane said with a tearful smile.

'It's not crazy. We came here for a wedding. Let's have one.'

A faint smile teased the corners of Diane's mouth. 'Do you really think we could?'

'I know it. All we need is one more witness to make it legal.'

'Jack Harman,' Mark said.

'Who?'

'The lighthouse keeper. At least he was until the new automated one was built in 1973. He and his wife are retired but still live in the keeper's cottage across the ridge.'

'Betty Harman is visiting her sister on the mainland this week,' Diane put in. 'I found out when we invited them to the wedding.'

'What about Jack?'

Mark gave a chuckle. 'He says the only way they'll get him back to the mainland is feet first. He'll be there, no doubt battening down like everyone else. I'll go and fetch him.'

Nicole followed him to the front door. 'Will you be all right crossing the ridge in this wind?'

His dark gaze searched her soul. 'Do you care?'

'Of course I care.' She had always cared about him. The problem was, he hadn't cared enough about her to put her ahead of his work.

'I believe you mean it,' he said thoughtfully. 'Maybe there's hope for us yet.'

Unexpectedly, he touched her cheek with the back of his hand, the fleeting contact sending fiery signals all through her body. 'Don't,' she pleaded, not quite sure what she was asking him not to do. 'There's no point.'

He regarded her for a long, agonising moment. 'Isn't there? You were always honest with me, Nicole. Can you look at me now and swear that you feel nothing for me?'

Why did he have to ask such a question? 'No,' she whispered, the admission torn from her like the leaves on the windswept trees. 'No, I can't.'

Although she tried to resist, curiosity overcame her and she snapped open the jewel case, gasping when she saw what lay inside.

On a bed of indigo velvet lay a polished gold and diamond heart-shaped pendant on a smooth, flat-linked chain. Matching earrings set with diamonds nestled beside the necklet. It was perfect and she loved it, just as he had known she would. With a strangled cry, she hurried back inside and thrust the case into her overnight bag, determined to return it to Mark as soon as she possibly could.

She found Diane in a flurry of preparations, her lovely gown sheathing her trim figure. She glanced over her shoulder at Nicole. 'Could you fasten this for me? I'm a bit short of bridesmaids.'

'All the same, you look gorgeous,' Nicole assured her, fastening the gown and arranging the train in graceful folds. Diane had brushed her long hair into a French pleat and coiled the ends into a bun, entwined with flowers. The crystal head-dress hugged her head.

A wistful expression darkened her features. 'This wasn't quite how I dreamed my wedding would be.' Then she forced a smile. 'But I'm glad you're here. At least Bill and I can be married, which is the important part.'

'You can always have a party later for your friends and family.'

Diane nodded. 'It isn't as if I have parents who'll be disappointed. My sister's the only one who'll be sad to miss the ceremony. She was looking forward to being my bridesmaid. And Bill's mother is too frail to travel down from Cairns, so we aren't letting anyone down.'

'Stop talking about letting people down,' Nicole said firmly. 'This is your day, no one else's. Look at it this way. How many brides do you know who get married in the middle of a cyclone?'

She was relieved when Diane laughed. 'You're right. It will be something to tell our grandchildren about.'

The thought sent a pang through Nicole, but she dismissed it. This was Diane's day. Her own problems could wait until after the wedding.

The sky was as dark as evening by the time she changed into her own outfit of cap-sleeved top and full skirt banded with cut-out embroidery and lace. A wide belt of the same shell-coloured fabric cinched her waist. She knew the outfit flattered her creamy skin-tone and pale, heart-shaped face and the colour complemented her honey-coloured hair. But it was carefully chosen not to overshadow the bride, whose right it was to have all eyes upon her.

'Will I do?' she asked Diane, swirling the full skirt around her stockinged legs.

'You look great,' Diane said, then bit her lower lip. 'Are you sure you have all the paperwork? We did give you the blue form?'

'One month and a day before the ceremony, as legally required,' Nicole confirmed with a laugh. 'Relax, I have done this before, you know.'

'I know. I'm just nervous, what with the storm coming.'

'All brides are nervous. It's traditional.'

There was a knock on the door and Bill's voice reached them through the timber. 'Is everything all right, you two?'

'Don't come in. It's bad luck to see the bride before the ceremony,' Nicole cautioned.

'I know. I wanted to tell you that Mark's back with Jack Harman. He says he's happy to help out.'

Relief made Nicole's knees buckle and she sat on the edge of the bed. Mark was back safely. It shouldn't matter to her, but it did. Seeing him go off into the teeth of the wind had alarmed her more than she realised. Now he was safe and she could breathe again.

How he would laugh if he knew she'd been worried on his account. He'd put another chalk mark on his wall chart or move another of those little flags he used to chart corporate progress. For she was sure that was what she represented to him: a challenge yet to be met. Knowing it didn't lessen her relief that he was back safely.

She became aware that Diane was muttering to herself and looking agitated. 'What's the matter?' Nicole asked.

Diane twisted her hands together. 'I knew it. This isn't going to work.'

'Of course it is. Tell me what's bothering you.'

She ticked the points off on her fingers. 'I have my grandmother's antique lace slip for something old, Bill's blue silk handkerchief for something blue, and my sister's lace garter as something borrowed. But I don't have something new.'

'What about your dress?'

'I don't think it counts.'

'Wait here. I have an idea.' Nicole went to her room and returned carrying the leather jewel-case. 'This should do. It's brand new, I promise.'

Diane opened the case and her eyes flew wide when she saw what was inside. 'It's magnificent, but it looks like a love token. Are you sure you want me to wear it?'

'Better than that. I want you to keep it as a gift from me.'

For emphasis, she clasped the stunning necklet around her friend's throat where it winked in the electric light like a galaxy of tiny stars. It nestled in the V of her neckline as if it belonged there. Seeing it, Nicole felt an irrational urge to snatch it back. But Diane was right, it *was* a love token, and it represented more pain than she was prepared to endure again in a lifetime.

She pressed the earrings into Diane's palm. 'You'd better put these on as well. Then we'll have to get started. If this wind gets much stronger we won't be able to hear a word of the ceremony.'

Although it was only mid-afternoon, darkness had come early and the horizon was lit with flashes of distant lightning. The nearest clouds seemed yellow, as if illuminated from within, and the sun looked oddly haloed, before it disappeared altogether behind a dark line of nimbostratus clouds. Through the trees Nicole could see white caps crowning the waves. 'Any news?' she asked Bill, who was leaning over the radio.

'It looks as if the cyclone will pass far enough to the north that we won't get the brunt of it. But we'll know it's there, I'm afraid.'

Mark frowned. 'Hadn't we better get started?'

'I'm about to.' She answered more sharply than she intended, annoyed that he was once again ahead of her. She was also annoyed with herself for noticing every little detail about him. It was a long time since she'd seen him in a formal suit. She'd forgotten how the tailored lines emphasised his broad shoulders and narrow waist and hips. The black fabric contrasted starkly with the whiteness of his dress shirt under a brocade waistcoat which fitted him like a second skin.

Irresistibly, her eyes travelled upwards to the velvet bow-tie at his throat. It was ever so slightly crooked and she itched to straighten it for him. But the wifely gesture suggested an intimacy they no longer shared and she kept her hands at her sides.

Bill, who had also changed into formal clothes, left the radio and crossed to a stereo player in a corner of the living-room. Moments later, the introduction to the bridal march soared above the wind's devil yell. Bill took his place beside Mark, and Nicole stood in front of them, her eyes straying to Mark's although she tried to avoid it.

His sea-green eyes danced with amusement, as if he knew the effect he was having on her. It was as if he were the groom and she the bride. For a moment she forgot her opening remarks, her brain turning to cotton wool in the warmth of his gaze.

She was saved when Diane emerged from her room, looking every inch the blushing bride in her designer gown, native orchids and ferns trailing from her hands. Nicole knew that her sister was supposed to bring the bouquets, so Mark must have collected the flowers when he went to pick up Jack Harman. Why couldn't he always be so thoughtful?

With an effort, she collected her thoughts and smiled reassuringly at Diane. Maybe if she didn't look at Mark during the ceremony she could get through this without making some awful blunder.

'Good afternoon,' she began, forgoing the usual introduction because everyone in the small group knew who she was.

'I am duly authorised to solemnise marriages according to the law,' she said formally. 'I have been asked by you, Diane Margaret Gould, and you, William John Foster, to conduct for you a ceremony which will join you in marriage.'

Normally at this juncture she would point out how fortunate the couple were to be surrounded by family and friends on this occasion. Instead, she went straight to the part where she was bound to remind the couple of the serious and binding nature of the commitment they were about to enter.

Diane and Bill looked solemn, but shot shy glances at each other as Nicole described marriage as a voluntary union for life, to the exclusion of all others. Judging from their expressions, it was fine with Diane and Bill.

She was required to hear them say publicly that they took each other in marriage. The responses were firm and clear from them both, despite the efforts of the rising wind to drown them out.

Since marriage celebrants wrote their own wedding ceremony, Nicole had added a few words about the joys and responsibilities of partnership where 'the partners are no longer alone—where both physically and emotionally they can touch and be touched by another—where they can unreservedly open their hearts to another.'

Now she felt choked as she recited them, wondering what it would be like to commit to such a relationship with Mark. She already knew how wonderful it felt to touch and he touched by him. Her body and mind vividly recalled the wonder of his caresses and the precious feeling of being held in his arms. But had he ever unreservedly opened his heart to her? She had opened hers to him, but on his side there was always a wall she couldn't breach, a sense that he was keeping part of himself beyond her reach.

But what *would* it be like if the wall crumbled, and they opened to each other as fully as Bill and Diane were doing? Somehow, as she called upon the bride and groom to join hands and make their vows, she saw herself in Diane's place and heard her own voice say dreamily, I, Nicole Denise Webber, take thee, Mark Walter David Kingston, to be my lawfully wedded husband, to have and to hold from this day forward . . .

For better, for worse . . .

For richer, for poorer . . .

To love, honour and cherish . . .

A crash of thunder banished the vision and Nicole's eyes clouded as she realised how impossible it was. All the same, her voice shook with emotion as she called upon Mark to pass Bill the ring. He placed it on Diane's finger with the time-honoured promise, which she repeated with a ring for him.

'I now pronounce you man and wife,' Nicole declared, inviting Bill to confirm his vows by kissing his bride. This he did with obvious enthusiasm, while Jack Harman applauded in the background. There remained only the signing of the register, when Diane wrote her single name for the last time. The signing was duly witnessed by Mark and Jack, who claimed their right to kiss Diane and shake Bill's hand.

Nicole completed her duties by signing the certificate of marriage, which she passed to the couple with a flourish. 'Congratulations, Mr and Mrs Foster.'

Diane blushed. 'Thank you, Nicole. It was a beautiful ceremony.'

'Beautiful,' Mark echoed, resting a hand on Nicole's shoulder. It burned through the light fabric of her dress like a brand. Had he guessed what she was thinking as she recited the vows? It was her turn to blush as she hoped not.

'Champagne, anyone?'

Bill came around with a tray of brimming glasses. 'At least we aren't short of food and drink. There's enough here for a dozen people.'

They toasted the happy couple and ate some of the canapés which had been prepared for the next day. Diane seemed to have forgotten her nervousness over the storm, for which Nicole was glad, although she noticed that her friend kept an arm linked through her new husband's.

'They go well together, don't they?' Mark said at her elbow.

She jumped. 'I wish you wouldn't do that.'

He took a sip of champagne, the sparkling liquid beading his upper lip. 'Do what?'

'Sneak up on me.'

'With only five of us on the island, it isn't hard to establish my whereabouts. I can hardly be accused of sneaking.'

Sighing, she sipped her own champagne. 'At least the wedding went well.'

'I agree. Despite the cyclone, the bride looks radiant. Her jewellery is stunning.'

Nicole swallowed hard. When she gave Diane the necklet and earrings as the 'something new' to ease her distress, she hadn't considered Mark's reaction. Judging by the tightness in his jaw and the dark shadows in his eyes, he was furious. 'I wanted you to have those,' he said, his voice dangerously vibrant.

'And what you want, you always get,' she said on a sigh. 'Didn't it occur to you that I might want something different from you?'

'You know you can have anything that it's in my power to give you.'

There was the rub. He wasn't exaggerating when he said he would give her anything which was in his power to give. The one thing she wanted—his undivided attention—was not part of the bargain and she'd known it for a long time.

All through the ceremony the wind had been strengthening, making the buildings creak and groan. Occasional crashes told them that bits of trees had been torn off and carried into the boiling sea.

As Mark proposed a toast to the happy couple, dazzling forks of lightning lit the island in a blue glare and an ear-splitting crash of thunder shook the house.

Instinctively Nicole moved closer to Mark. Jack put down his glass. 'I'd better get back to the cottage. Wait till I tell Betty I was a witness at the wedding. She'll never forgive me for leaving her out.'

'Tell her it was the cyclone's fault,' Mark said over the howls of wind.

Jack grinned. 'She'll find a way to blame me for the weather if she can.'

Noting the fondness in his voice which belied the criticism, Nicole asked, 'How long have you two been married?'

'Forty-eight years,' he said with pride. 'Betty was my first and only love, but don't let on I said so.'

Nicole had the feeling that Betty knew how much she was loved, although, like Jack, she would probably make jokes about it, saving the tenderness for private moments. Thinking of Jack and his Betty, and now Bill and Diane, she felt achingly lonely, as if all the world was paired off except her. She knew it was foolishness, but the feeling persisted all the same.

'Won't you be safer staying here?' Nicole asked, wincing as a flash of lightning lit the cottage in its electric glare.

'I've been through worse. Betty will never forgive me if I don't keep an eye on things while she's away.'

'Will he be all right?' she asked Mark as the old man ventured out into the wind. He waved, then was swallowed up by the gathering darkness.

'He's lived on this island for most of his life. He knows what he's doing.'

There was a discreet cough behind them and they turned. 'Diane and I should be going, too.'

'Going where?' Nicole asked, not thinking. Then she felt herself redden. 'Of course. This is your wedding night.'

Bill smiled fondly at his bride. 'We thought, since you aren't using the guest cottage, we'll spend our first night there.'

'Is it safe?'

Diane giggled and Nicole frowned. 'I didn't mean . . . oh, I was talking about the storm.' She knew it was the idea of being left alone with Mark which troubled her.

'I know. It's built of the same materials as this place so it should be just as safe. We'll batten down securely.'

'And we have each other,' Diane added, snuggling close to Bill.

'What about the radio?' Nicole asked, clutching at straws.

'Everything's drowning in static. There won't be any messages in or out until this is over. Besides, Mark knows how to use it. He'll call us if we're needed.'

There was nothing more she could say to delay them. They were entitled to their wedding night, she accepted, cyclone or no cyclone. She only wished it didn't mean she would be left alone with Mark.

Diane's 'going-away' outfit consisted of shorts, a T-shirt and vast yellow waterproof cape. She looked down at herself. 'Not what I planned to wear for my honeymoon.'

'*Sunseeker* will be waiting when the weather clears,' Mark reminded her, and earned a smile of gratitude.

'Thanks for everything, you two.'

While they were changing, Nicole had toyed with the idea of using flower petals as confetti, but she abandoned the notion when they opened the door and the wind gusted through it, full strength. With a squeal, Diane darted out into the storm, pulled along by Bill's tight grip on her hand. The guest cottage was a stroll away under a covered walkway, although it was more of a forced march against the gusts. Moments later, the cottage door slammed and the newlyweds were safe in their improvised love-nest.

Mark struggled to close the door. Righting chairs which had been blown over while the door stood open, Nicole felt his gaze on her like a laser beam threading through the gloom. She kept her eyes averted.

He secured the door then crossed to the bar. There was an almighty crash of thunder and the lights dimmed, brightened, then went out. 'It's all right, we've got plenty of candles,' his voice assured her through the darkness.

'Maybe we should check on the others.'

A strong hand grasped her elbow and guided her to a chair. 'They'll tell us if they need anything. Right now, they probably want nothing so much as to be alone.'

Her voice came out scratchy with emotion. 'You're right. I didn't mean——'

Like a whipcrack, his response cut in. 'Yes, you did, Nicole. I'm well aware that you'll go to any lengths to avoid being alone with me. But this time you aren't going to get your wish.'

CHAPTER THREE

IT WAS an effort to keep her voice steady. 'What makes you think I have a problem being alone with you?' Nicole was glad he couldn't hear the tremor in it over the wind singing crazily through the trees.

He rested against the door, his arms folded, as amusement flickered in his dark eyes. 'Maybe it's the way you're attacking those plates. No one's coming, you know. The housekeeping can wait.'

He was right. She *was* nervous. Tidying up the remains of the impromptu reception was her way of dispelling her tension. She thrust the pile of plates into the kitchen sink. 'They must be done sooner or later.'

He slid behind her and took the plate from her hands. 'What's wrong with later?'

She regarded him uneasily. 'But you're the one who hates putting things off.' He'd never, ever put anything off to be with her, she recalled, particularly if it concerned business.

He shrugged. 'People can change.'

Was he trying to tell her that *he'd* changed? A silver thread of hope wound itself around her heart until she shook it off. Mark was a workaholic like her father, and he hadn't changed, devoting every waking hour to his insurance business until a heart attack had claimed him at fifty-two. He'd insisted he was working for Nicole and her mother, but they'd both known he loved the cut and thrust of corporate life. She's seen the same signs in Mark and left for fear it would kill him, too.

Methodically, she filled the sink with soapy water and began to wash the dishes. Wordlessly, he picked up a tea-towel and dried them as she washed. If it hadn't been a ploy to keep herself busy, she would have found the scene companionable.

The dishes were soon done, however, and she looked around for something else to occupy her. They would need an evening meal, she decided, opening cupboards and staring blindly at their contents.

He was aware of her tactics, she saw when he closed the cupboard door firmly and spun her towards the living-room. 'I guessed the power would go out, so I brought a picnic up from *Sunseeker*. All we need are plates and wine glasses.'

Despair assailed her. He was doing it again, taking charge and assuming he knew what was best for her. Her cry came from the heart. 'Don't do this to me.'

His face was a study in innocence. 'Do what? All I've done is arrange some food for us.'

Her hands fluttered in the air. '*You've* done! *You've* arranged! Can't you stop arranging for one minute and listen to my needs?'

It was the argument they should have had when she'd walked out. She had never dreamed they would have it here, now. But the words were out and he demanded an explanation.

'I don't think I want to talk about it now.'

His gesture took in the storm-tossed island beyond the windows. 'We'll never have a better opportunity. And I'm entitled to know why you took off without a word of explanation. I had no idea anything was wrong.'

Her sharp intake of breath rattled in her throat. 'Which is precisely my point. If you hadn't been so wrapped up in your work, you'd have noticed how unhappy I was. I didn't enjoy waiting around to pick up the crumbs of your attention when you could spare the time.'

His finely chiselled features were set in an expression of impatience. 'For Pete's sake! I was fending off a hostile take-over of my company. What did you expect me to do? Let it happen?'

Tears clustered in her eyes and she brushed them away. 'Of course not. I know the company is your life, but I didn't think that equal time was too much to expect.'

Tension crackled in the air between them. 'You have my undivided attention now.'

Nicole stared at him, noticing how his tall, spare form was haloed by lightning as he stood with his back to the window. How she had longed to hear him say those words. To be completely alone with him, away from telephones and assistants. Now the moment was here, she was suddenly nervous, like a teenager waiting for her first date. Did she want to start this all over again?

Frustration threatened to choke her. 'It's too late.'

He moved closer, his steps muffled by the rising wind. 'Is it, Nicole? There hasn't been anyone else since me, has there?'

How could he possibly know, unless... 'You've been watching me, haven't you?'

His hand drifted towards her hair, one finger teasing a strand loose. 'Let's say I made it my business to know what you were doing.'

The intimate gesture almost robbed her of her voice. 'But why? It's over between us.'

His hand trailed down the side of her face, sending a fiery sensation along every nerve-ending. 'It isn't over and you know it. What we had—have—is special, "till death do us part", as the lady said this afternoon.'

'But we aren't married.' Her hoarse whisper was barely audible against the storm's devil voice.

'Tell me you weren't seeing yourself in Diane's place this afternoon.'

He *had* divined her thoughts. 'I . . .'

'I saw myself there, taking those vows,' he said.

The admission was torn from her. 'So did I.'

The hand which had been caressing the side of her face suddenly found the nape of her neck and pulled her closer. Too stunned to resist, she felt panic coil through her as his mouth found and explored hers.

Caught against his hard-muscled chest, she was torn between the need to escape and the desire to lose herself in the mind-numbing passion his kiss aroused. For a moment, passion won, until some vestige of remaining sanity made her pound against his chest.

He released her, amusement and desire warring with each other in his sea-green gaze. Knowing how much she wanted him, he was toying with her like a cat with a mouse, waiting for her to beg him to kiss her again. Her self-control wavered. Begging wasn't so hard, was it? In the candle-light she caught the gleam of satisfaction in his gaze and knew that he was aware of her struggle.

'Let's eat,' he said unexpectedly.

Gratitude surged through her. He hadn't pushed his advantage, as well he might. Even as her anger and confusion receded, she wondered if it was what he'd had in mind. Letting her win this round might make his victory all the sweeter when it came.

Except that it wasn't going to come, she vowed, fighting the disappointment which accompanied the thought. What was the matter with her? She wanted him, yet she feared the involvement. Which was it to be?

Stiffly, she moved to the couch where he had set out their picnic on the coffee-table. Her appetite wasn't for food, yet the sight of the cold cuts of chicken, smoked salmon, dark Continental bread and glistening tropical fruits stirred her taste-buds, and she licked her lips. 'This looks good.'

Outside the sky was a solid mass of molten clouds. The horizon was almost black, lit by flares of lightning which flooded the room with ghostly light. He saw her flinch. 'It will rain soon, maybe five or ten inches in the next twenty-four hours.'

'And this is only the fringe of the cyclone,' she said shakily. 'What must it be like to be in the middle?'

He handed her a slice of dark bread, folding a slice of smoked salmon on top of it. 'Strangely calm. I've been through a cyclone in Torres Strait. You live through about eight hours of absolute hell then it all just stops. You're in the eye.'

The salty tang of the salmon teased her tongue. 'How long does the calm last?'

'An hour or so. Then you get another ten hours of raging storm from the opposite direction.'

'I wonder how many people think it's over and come out of hiding, to be devastated when it starts up again?' She was referring to the storm but it also applied to them, she thought, taking a sip of champagne. They were in the eye of their relationship now.

If she made the mistake of thinking it was reality, she risked being blown away when the raging storm returned.

'If you know cyclones, you don't make that mistake,' he said and helped himself to a golden chicken drumstick.

Watching the methodical way he stripped the flesh away with his even white teeth, she shivered. She knew cyclones but could still see herself making the elemental mistake of regarding the eye of the storm as the true calm.

She closed her eyes, trying to shut out the sight of him to give herself time to think. But his image flared behind her closed lids, solid and compelling. Focus on the past, she told herself. Remember the times when you needed him and he wasn't there.

He sat back and she felt his arm slide along the couch behind her shoulders. Automatically she stiffened, her eyes flying wide. But he didn't touch her. A sidelong glance showed him relaxed and at ease, his hooded eyes unreadable. How could he relax when she felt tense enough to jump out of her skin?

The reason for her tension hit her like a tidal wave. She wanted him to touch her, to feel his arm heavy across her shoulders and his mouth warm and demanding on hers. Common sense was being edged out by the primeval need to touch and be touched by him.

'Yes.' The softly spoken word was barely audible above the howl of the wind, but he heard it and moved closer, his arm finally encircling her.

Her anger seeped away, replaced by relief at finally nestling into his embrace. 'Oh, yes,' she whispered as she bent her head into the curve of his neck.

Whether it was the romantic aura cast by the wedding, or the heady effects of the champagne, she wasn't sure. She felt suddenly dizzy with need for him. Being in his arms felt right, in spite of everything.

On the fringes of awareness, her anger hovered, just out of reach. She stiffened, trying not to respond to the hectic sensations aroused by his touch. She didn't want to go through this again, to let herself love him, only to be cast aside when he had more pressing concerns. Still his lips roved over her heated skin as if he sensed that her control was no more than surface-deep.

Her self-control was slipping fast, submerged in a chaos of needs and desires such as only Mark could arouse. She tried one last time. 'This isn't why we came.'

'It's why I came,' he murmured, his mouth soft and pliant against her throat.

'You couldn't know about the storm.'

'Couldn't I?'

Confusion roiled through her. They did amazing things with satellites these days. Could he have known they would be marooned here by the cyclone? No, even Mark couldn't exercise that much control over events. But the doubts lingered, shaded by a persistent, *Why*? Would he really go so far to have her back? Pleasure spiralled through her at the idea of being so cherished.

It was enough to demolish her remaining self-control. He felt her surrender as surely as if she'd spoken, and his hold tightened. His kisses trailed across her closed eyes and the soft zephyr of his breath caressed her cheeks.

Her anger evaporated in a rush of memories. She had forgotten so much, like the lingering male scent of him which assailed her now, and the sandpapery feel of his skin where his morning shave was wearing off. She ran the back of her hand along his jawline, feeling a rasping sensation.

He turned his head, nipping her fingers between sharp teeth, then nibbled on the ends until barbs of sensation speared deep inside her.

A fierce crash of thunder made her cower against him and she heard his murmured reassurance as a throaty sound. Words were not needed, even if they could be heard above the roar of the storm. It didn't matter. She was safe in his arms. The only storm which mattered was the whirlwind of need spiralling inside her.

Without breaking the kiss, he slid his hands across her shoulders and eased her dress down so the material fell in soft folds around her waist. The bra was dealt with just as swiftly. Shock-waves eddied through her as he caressed her, bringing her to the brink of ecstasy with his sweetly tormenting touch.

At last she was free to touch the velvet tie at his throat, releasing it and tossing it aside to play with the buttons on his dress shirt. When they were all undone, she ran her hands across the rough-textured wall of his chest, aware of his indrawn gasp of pleasure, telegraphed through her fingers.

The cries of the wind spoke for her as he shed his remaining clothes, then helped her to undress with an urgency which was like a fever. His skin felt heated under her hands. They were both on fire. 'I love you,' she cried, finally free to say it, knowing he couldn't hear above the storm.

On the fringes of her awareness, she heard the wind strengthening to a gale, whipping away branches and leaves off trees, stripping the foreshore bare. Sand washed against the windows in gritty clouds, as if a lover were throwing tokens to his beloved from beneath the window.

Then the first heavy drops of rain smashed against the roof, so violently that Nicole mistook it for hail at first. Soon all sound was lost in the roar of the storm. There was no need for words, only touch and movement. It was more than enough. Words would have spoiled the pure communication of Mark's hands, superbly athletic body and tantalising mouth.

When touch was no longer enough, he came to her, his strength filling the empty places in her heart until she cried aloud for the sheer beauty of it.

With him, she rode the wind. The lightning crackled across the sky and the thunder roared, barely keeping pace with her storm-driven feelings. Up and up she spiralled on the wings of the cyclone until at last they reached the eye, the well of calm in the midst of turmoil.

Cradling her in his arms, Mark held her tightly until their heartbeats slowed. When her breathing became less ragged, she found his mouth and kissed him gently, a wordless thank-you for the precious gift of his love. What awaited them on the other side of the eye, she would deal with in time. For now, she felt cocooned in his embrace.

She knew something was wrong as soon as her eyes fluttered open. Where was she? Then it came back. She was coiled on the couch, fitting into Mark's sleeping form like two pieces of a jigsaw puzzle. They had made love at the height of last night's storm.

How could she have done something so stupid?

She had even confessed to loving him, although the wind had whipped her words away before he heard them. Heaven help her, it was still the truth. She *did* love him, even though in the cold light of day she knew that it was as futile as ever.

She bit her lip, tasting salt carried on the wind. The air was laden with it. All these months she had been fooling herself. She had never stopped loving Mark. She had simply accepted that she needed a larger place in his life, a place he wasn't going to make for her.

Last night he had hinted at changes. She hardly dared hope that it was possible. Balance was all she wanted. A fair division between his work and home life. If it came to that, she had her own work both as a painter and a marriage celebrant and she wouldn't give up either one. And still they left her room to love. Why was it so hard for him?

The rain had eased to a wind-driven mist. The calm seemed unnatural after the express-train roar of last night's storm. Carefully she eased herself off the couch, colouring at the sight of her clothes scattered across the floor. Mark's dress shirt lay on top of her skirt and she draped it over a chair. The tangled clothes were an awkward reminder of her abandoned behaviour the night before.

Her limbs ached from sleeping on the couch and she eased them under a hot shower. At least the power was back on. Less than half an hour had elapsed by the time she emerged dressed in jeans and a white silk shirt, her celebrant's clothes wadded into her suitcase. She wondered if she would be able to wear them again without remembering this night.

The aroma of coffee greeted her as she stepped into the kitchen. Mark was up and she froze at the sight of him, ruggedly attractive in nothing but the trousers from his dress suit. His bare chest glinted golden in the morning light. Her hands clenched, remembering the feel of it under fingers.

Even his bare feet tantalised her with their aggressive masculinity. Why hadn't she noticed before what beautifully shaped feet he had, long and lean with every toe elegantly defined, like Michelangelo's statue of David? She dragged her gaze upwards. 'Good morning.'

'Good morning. Like some coffee?'

'Yes, thank you.' A weight lifted from her chest as she realised he wasn't going to mention last night, even though the couch still bore the imprint of their tangled bodies. They were back to being polite strangers.

'Did you sleep well?'

She accepted the steaming cup he held out to her and sipped it, burning her throat. 'Not too badly,' she admitted carefully. 'Although I think I drank a bit too much champagne.' There, let him think her response was due to the wine, rather than to his effect on her. 'Is the storm over?' she asked, anxious to change the subject.

'It blew itself out during the night. Judging from what I've seen outside, the island didn't fare too badly.'

'What about Bill and Diane?'

'I checked their cottage while you were showering. It's still in one piece so I didn't disturb them. I doubt if they'll want to see anyone for a few hours.'

Which meant she still had to endure the morning in his company. 'When do you think we can leave the island?'

'You haven't enjoyed your stay?'

The irony in his question wasn't lost on her. 'The whole thing was a colossal mistake,' she ground out. Thrusting the coffee-cup back at him, she turned on her heel and escaped into the rain-soaked morning.

CHAPTER FOUR

THE wind plucked at Nicole as she headed down the coral path towards the seashore. The island steamed in the morning air, moisture dripping from every tree branch. Signs of the storm's fury greeted her everywhere.

Soft green plants had been uprooted from the soil and carried away on the wind. Beneath the tougher grasses, the ground had dissolved, leaving them bare-rooted and forlorn. Broken fronds of pandanus palms littered the beach, tangling in the morning glory vines which sprawled across the sand.

The devastation mirrored the bleakness in her heart as she walked across the spiky grey beach rocks, watching the white surf break across the rim of the reef. The surface was loose and treacherous. She walked with care.

If only she'd been more careful last night. But the truth came back to her as inexorably as the waves beating against the rocks. She still loved Mark. No wonder no other man could hold her attention. As long as she remained in his orbit, she had no chance of finding someone else. Maybe she should get away, leave Townsville where there was always a chance of running into Mark.

It was tempting but impracticable. Her work was here. She was just starting to become known as a marriage celebrant and her specialised paintings of sea life and underwater scenery were beginning to sell.

Local galleries now showed her work. Leaving simply wasn't an option.

'Penny for them.'

She started as the object of her thoughts loomed close behind her, his broad profile blotting out the sun. He had changed into linen trousers and an open-necked shirt and the mere sight of him threw her thoughts into chaos. 'I doubt if they're even worth that much.'

'You undervalue yourself. Your painting of butterfly cod among the anemones is magnificent.'

'It was my wedding present to Bill and Diane,' she said. A lot of herself had gone into that painting. For hours she had swum among the jungles of the reef, using only mask and snorkel to avoid frightening the delicate fish she wished to capture in her painting.

Meticulously, she had noted the types of coral, weed and rocks in which the fish lived and their characteristic poses. The results, painted in oils on canvas, had surpassed even her own expectations. She was unaccountably glad that he had seen and appreciated it.

'I'm going to check on Jack at the lighthouse cottage,' he said. 'Come with me.'

Rebellion welled inside her. He was still trying to organise her in the way he thought best. This time he was wrong. She was resigned to sharing the island with him until the seas abated enough to let them leave, but she didn't have to spend the day in his company if she didn't want to, although she avoided examining her reasons too closely.

Seeing the stubborn set of her jaw, he gave an impatient sigh. 'I didn't mean it to sound like an order. I'd like you to come.'

'Do you think something's happened to Jack?'

'Probably not, but I can't raise him on the radio so I'm going over to check.'

'In that case, I'll come with you.'

Taking two steps to each long stride of his, she accompanied him towards the ridge which divided the island nearly into two. Their path was shaded by towering umbrella trees, flame trees and paperbarks, their trunks wound around with Fern of God and leafy clusters of native orchids.

Now and again she caught the azure flash of a Ulysses butterfly as it climbed swiftly then dropped to settle on a tropical flower. How had such delicate creatures survived last night's turmoil? she wondered.

'Who's running things back in Townsville while you're here?' she asked Mark on a sudden impulse. Not so long ago, he would have been fuming with impatience at being cut off from the mainland like this, yet today he actually seemed to be enjoying the enforced isolation.

'I have a good management team,' he said.

She flashed him a startled look. 'You're actually delegating some of your work?'

'I do it quite often these days. It gives me more time out on *Sunseeker*.'

The cruiser had been nagging at her. In a city where most of the population were either fishermen or boating enthusiasts, Mark had shown no interest in either. The only time they'd gone out on a boat, it had belonged to one of Mark's business associates. He and Mark had spent the entire cruise in the saloon, poring over balance sheets.

'Do you still live in your flat above the shop?' she asked, wondering what else had changed.

He laughed, the warm sound reaching out to her like a caress. 'Only you could call a three-million-dollar penthouse above an office tower "a flat above the shop". And yes, I still live there. But not for long. I've started building a house.'

She stopped in her tracks. 'You have? Where?'

'Not far from Castle Rock. The views are breathtaking.'

Mark, building a house? Putting down roots? It seemed inconceivable. Then she realised it would probably be linked to his corporate headquarters by every kind of fax machine and phone line possible. Still, she was curious. 'What is the house like?'

If he heard the astonishment in her voice, he chose to ignore it. 'Perhaps you should see it for yourself some time. There was a formal palm plantation on the site, which I'm using for inspiration. The design is styled along the lines of a traditional high-set Queensland house, adapted to a more formal scale. When the gardens are finished, there will be a different colour and scent at every corner. At sunset, with flares flickering among the plants, it should be quite striking.'

And incredibly romantic, she thought, finding it easy to imagine. It was more difficult to picture Mark taking the time to enjoy such a setting. Could she have been wrong about him after all?

No. The denial screamed through her mind. It wasn't possible for a leopard to change his spots so completely. Mark hated to lose. Changing his image would be a small price to pay to win her back. Unconsciously, she quickened her steps.

He caught up with her in three strides, catching her arm and spinning her around to face him. 'Slow down a moment, Nicole. Can't you hear what I'm telling you?'

She clamped her hands over her ears, the gesture childish but effective. 'I don't want to hear it.'

Inexorably, he forced her hands down and held them at her sides, his gaze meeting hers with steely resolve. 'Well, you're going to. I know what happened to your father and I know why you were so frightened for me, wanting me to slow down, take time off. It all makes sense now.'

'How did you find out?' The question was a hoarse whisper. She had avoided telling him about her father, feeling sure he would dismiss her fears as foolish.

'Your mother told me. I went to see her after you left. She wouldn't give me your new address, of course, but she did help me to understand a few things.'

Her eyes brimmed. 'You had no right to go to her. Why won't you accept that it's over between us?'

'Because it isn't. What I don't understand is why you didn't tell me why you were so frightened for me. I thought you were jealous of my work.'

'I suppose I was afraid to tell you in case...' Her voice tailed off as she regarded him with huge, uncertain eyes.

'Go on.'

'In case it didn't make any difference.' She had finally confessed to him her deepest fear. Now she wished the ground would open up and swallow her. She had never felt so raw and vulnerable before.

He gave her a slight shake. 'But it *is* making a difference.'

If he only knew how she ached to believe him. 'I thought you were—how would you put it?—redefining your marketing profile to increase your sales appeal,' she said flatly.

'Stop it, Nicole, it's nothing of the sort.' He turned away then swung back, his eyes brightly accusing. 'Unless you're clinging to your notion of me as a workaholic to justify your own behaviour.'

'I might have known it would somehow turn out to be my fault.'

'You are the most impossible, stubborn, beautiful, bewitching woman I have ever known.'

His face loomed so close that she could feel every breath he took. His hands tightened on her arms, pulling her close and she closed her eyes. Then his mouth was on hers, smothering her protests until none were left. There was only the driving need to taste him and touch him, to be a part of him. She moaned softly against his lips as she gave herself up to the ecstasy of the kiss.

Recalling why she had left him became more and more difficult as his hands slid around her waist, under her shirt. The heat of his touch seared her and she swayed against him, wanting him with every fibre of her being.

He felt it, too, because his hands slid up the column of her back then around to her breasts. Her heartbeat raced as the kiss deepened.

'This is crazy. We belong together. ''One man and one woman to the exclusion of all others'',' he quoted her own words back at her.

Panic flared through her. 'It's not that simple.'

He thrust stiff fingers through his hair. 'Damn it, why isn't it simple? The only thing which matters is...'

Before she could find out what it was, they became aware of a faint cry. 'It's coming from Jack's cottage,' Mark said, a frown creasing his forehead. 'Come on.'

Tugging her with him, he sprinted the last few yards through the undergrowth. Suddenly the trees gave way to an open, rocky area and ahead was the modern lighthouse.

In its shadow was Jack's cottage, the front obscured by a massive flame tree which lay askew across its roof, the giant roots hanging in the air. Nicole felt a stab of fear. 'Oh, no! If he's under that...'

'Jack, keep calling so we can locate you.' Mark's clear, ringing tones carried around the foreshore.

'I'm not under the tree. It's jammed me in so I can't get out of my hallway.'

Nicole gave a relieved sigh. 'Thank goodness!'

Mark began heaving away the tangle of boulders and tree debris from the cottage door. When he had cleared a triangle-shaped section of the door, he called, 'Do you have an axe anywhere?'

'In my shed behind the house.'

He disappeared and came back moments later carrying a stout-looking woodsman's axe. 'Stand back from the door. I'll try and break through it,' he instructed.

The cottage was strongly built and it took many blows from Mark's axe before the wood began to splinter. Nicole watched him with a feeling of awe. He was a city businessman but he swung the axe as if he had been born to it. His muscles strained the fabric of his shirt and perspiration beaded his face. But he didn't stop until he had blasted an opening in the door large enough for a man to crawl through.

Jack's grinning face appeared in the opening. 'Just as well you two happened by,' he said.

They helped him to his feet. 'We came because Mark couldn't raise you on the radio,' Nicole explained.

'I heard the call but couldn't get to the set. That old tree had me coralled in one tiny corner of my hallway.'

'Are you sure you're all right?'

Jack flexed his muscles to demonstrate. 'Fit as a fiddle. But I'll need to get the chain-saw out to deal with this monster.' He patted the fallen tree almost with affection. 'I've been meaning to take it down for a while, but I hate to kill trees.'

'It looks as if nature's done the job for you,' Mark put in. 'I'll stay and help with the cutting if you like.'

'You've done enough getting me out of there. If you come around the back, I'll make you some tea. Had breakfast yet?'

Nicole was about to demur but Mark said, 'Tea would be great, thanks.'

Jack led the way around the side of the cottage but Nicole held back, pulling on Mark's sleeve to gain his attention. 'We shouldn't stay. Jack has more than enough to cope with.'

'He's stubborn and proud,' Mark said in an undertone, glancing at Jack to make sure he couldn't hear. 'Do you think he would tell us if he was hurt?'

She might have known he had a reason for staying when common sense dictated they should leave. She felt small, wishing she'd thought of the ploy herself.

It seemed Jack was being honest with them. Apart from some superficial bruises where he'd tried to fight his way past the tree, he was uninjured. He whistled as he made tea for them. Over their protests, he made a pile of hot buttered toast and set it between them. Spreading dark-coloured Queensland honey on a slice, Nicole found that she *was* hungry. Jack and Mark's conversation flowed past her as she ate—she was lost in thought.

Suddenly something Jack was saying snapped her back to the here and now. 'What was that about a resort?' she demanded, setting her coffee-cup down and leaning forward.

'The one Mark's going to build on the freehold land between here and the ranger station,' Jack said. His tone said he expected her to know all about it.

This was the first she'd heard of it. 'You mean you own all the freehold land on this island?' she asked Mark.

'I have done for some time.'

She felt the ground crumble beneath her. So he had come here because of her, had he? Fool that she was, she had believed him. Worse, she had let him make love to her as if what they once shared could be re-kindled. 'What sort of resort are you planning?' she asked in a choked voice.

'It won't be a resort, as much as a retreat,' he explained. 'The units will be low-rise, designed in harmony with the island environment so people can come here to relax and recharge their batteries.'

Her tone was bleak. 'You've thought it all out, haven't you?'

'We've been working on Crystal Cay for months now. I want to be sure I get it just right.'

Which was about the time he became Bill's diving buddy, she thought grimly. She wouldn't put it past him to befriend Bill in order to gain his co-operation.

Wasn't Mark the one who said you caught more bees with honey than with vinegar?

'Does Bill know about this?' she asked.

'He knows I own the land, but the plans have been kept under wraps until now. I don't want extremists coming here and objecting until I can show them that my plans will help the environment, not harm it. Jack knows because he owned a parcel of the land.'

'Young Mark has some fine ideas for rebuilding the island's bird population,' Jack said. 'He wants me to show visitors the lighthouse, explain how it works and such, and show them my collection of photos from the days before the light was automated.'

Mark was a master of manipulation, she had to concede. He had totally won over Jack Harman by the simple expedient of making him feel useful again. She hadn't the heart to tell him he was being used by Mark, just as she had been used by him from the moment she'd stepped aboard his cruiser.

Suddenly she was thankful she had given the pendant to Diane. Wearing Mark's gift would have choked her after this. As it was, she would give anything to have last night to live over again. There was no way she would allow Mark to charm her into letting him make love to her. He might well have decided to pursue her to salve his hurt pride, but it wasn't the reason why he was on Crystal Island. She doubted whether the wedding was the main reason either. This conversation proved he was here on business. As always, everything else came second, including her.

She was hardly aware of excusing herself and stumbling out of the cottage by the back door. Mark's puzzled query followed her but she didn't bother to reply as she hurried around the side of the cottage past the fallen tree, and plunged across the shimmering coral sands.

At low tide it was possible to walk right around the island on the coral sands. On the windy south side, the delicate casuarinas were sparse and distorted by the strong winds, unlike the sheltered northern side where the trees flourished. She was aware of the casuarinas only as obstacles in her path and hardly saw the grey and white reef herons stalking through the shallows ahead of her, their sharp beaks darting down as they fished.

She only knew she had to put some distance between herself and Mark. How could he do this to her? All his talk about building a house and delegating work had almost convinced her he had changed. Now the truth was doubly hard to bear.

'Nicole, wait.'

Although she broke into a jog, he soon caught up with her. His expression was perplexed as he slid around in front of her, forcing her to a halt. 'What's the hurry?'

'I don't feel well,' she told him with more than a grain of truth.

'This is sudden, isn't it?'

'So was the news about the resort you're planning to build.'

'So that's what this is all about. You're upset because I didn't tell you my plans.'

Put like that it sounded petty and childish, she knew, but if she told him the real reason he would try to talk his way out of it. After last night there was every chance he would succeed, and she had learned her lesson. 'I'm worried about Bill's job and the future of the island,' she said instead. Both were legitimate concerns, after all.

'I've told you the island's future is assured,' he said with exaggerated patience. 'This was precisely the kind of reaction I feared, although not from you, Nicole. I thought you knew me better.'

She could say the same of him, she thought mutinously. 'What about Bill?' she asked.

'He will still be the ranger here, although I'd prefer him to work for me, managing the resort's wildlife conservation programme. Perhaps when he hears our terms he'll consider it.'

And what about me—where do I fit in? she wanted to cry out. But she was afraid she already knew the answers. As far as he was concerned, she had been unfinished business. He had won her back, or so he thought, so there were no more loose ends in the relationship. Thinking of how close he had come to succeeding, she shuddered.

He misinterpreted the reaction. 'You're cold. Let's get out of this wind and I'll tell you the rest of my plans.'

'There's no need,' she said icily. 'I'll hear them along with everyone else when you make them public.' Before he could stop her, she dodged around him and sprinted across the sand. She wanted to put as much distance between them as possible before she broke down completely. She wasn't going to give him that satisfaction.

CHAPTER FIVE

NICOLE worked furiously, her fingers spotted with orange paint to her elbows and speckling the man's business shirt which she wore like a smock. Pushing her hair back from her eyes, she left an orange streak across one cheek. She hardly noticed, focusing all her attention on the vast canvas in front of her.

When the doorbell rang she frowned and debated whether to ignore it, then she heard Diane's voice through the timber. 'I know you're in there. The window's open.'

She tore herself away from the canvas and opened the door, smiling at her visitor. 'The honeymooner returns at last!'

'I hope I'm not interrupting anything.' Diane breezed into the room like one sure of her welcome. She came to a halt in front of the canvas. 'Good lord, this is amazing! It's like looking through the windows of an underwater observatory.'

Some of the tension seeped out of Nicole and she flexed her tired shoulders. 'I take it you approve.'

'Approve? You must know this is the best thing you've ever done.'

'I hoped it was. It's part of a special commission—the chance of a lifetime, you might say.'

Diane dropped her bag on the floor and headed for the kitchen, where she helped herself to a cold drink. 'I can see you're in the throes, so carry on and we'll talk when you're finished. OK?'

153

Anyone else would have distracted Nicole but Diane possessed a reassuring stillness. Her silences were soothing and companionable rather than disturbing. Nicole had no difficulty in carrying on.

In any case, the painting was almost finished. A few more strokes of vivid white and the clown fish came to life amid a field of sea anemones, their orange and fawn tentacles seeming to undulate softly in the submarine currents.

The big anemones and the tiny orange and white striped fish fascinated Nicole. No other fish could swim safely among the tentacles which would capture and poison other kinds of fish. Even the clown fish had to go through a process of making longer and longer forays into the tentacle forest until they could hide there safely and share their food with the anemones.

Her marine paintings were Nicole's way of celebrating her joy at the beauty and wonder of the Barrier Reef. Her spirits soared at the thought of where her painting would be displayed. 'There, it's finished,' she said, reaching for a rag to smudge the paint from her hands.

Diane handed her a lemon drink, the glass dewed with moisture from the generous amount of ice she'd added. 'Now tell me what this is all about.'

'When I returned from Crystal Island, there was a message on my answering machine from Peter Valentine about a commission for the foyer of a new high-rise building opening soon on the Strand.'

'Reef Towers. I read about it.' Diane raised her glass. 'Congratulations, you deserve the recognition.'

Nicole pressed her glass against her forehead, enjoying the coolness against her heated skin. 'Thanks.

I only wish I had more time to complete the job. They want three large canvases by the opening date.'

Diane whistled softly. 'No wonder you're hard pressed.' She reached for her bag. 'I'd better get out of your way.'

'Not so fast. This is the first break I've taken all day and I'm enjoying it, so sit down and tell me all about your honeymoon. The bits for public consumption, anyway,' she added.

Diane looked dubious but relaxed. 'Well, I won't stay long.' She went on to describe the glorious cruise she and Bill had taken through the Whitsunday Passage as far as Cairns. 'Everyone should travel aboard a vessel like *Sunseeker* at least once in their lives,' she said rapturously.

Sunseeker. The name conjured up a vision of Nicole's last journey aboard the cruiser in the company of its charismatic owner.

Somehow, they'd got through another day and night on the island before the seas became calm enough to return to the mainland. It helped that the newlyweds had emerged from their quarters long enough to play a rousing game of Scrabble, which had saved Nicole from having to make polite conversation with Mark. She'd doubted whether she could anyway, when her instincts inclined more towards scratching his eyes out.

How could he have let her believe she was the reason he came to Crystal Island when he was actually there on business? The thought of their lovemaking still sent a *frisson* of unwonted pleasure down her spine although she tried to suppress it. Pure chemistry, she told herself. It wasn't enough to build a future on.

She roused herself in time to hear Diane say, 'I have the most wonderful news about Bill.'

Noting her friend's sparkling eyes, Nicole guessed the news had something to do with Mark's job plans for Bill. She kept her face impassive. 'What is it?'

'Mark is building a luxury retreat on the island and he wants Bill to manage the wildlife side of things.'

'How does Bill feel about it?' Nicole asked, managing to keep her reaction under control. So Mark had won Bill over already. Why was she even surprised?

'He loves the idea. He'll be sorry to leave the wildlife service, of course, but he'll have more scope to develop his own ideas working for Mark.'

'It sounds wonderful. I'm delighted for you both,' Nicole said in all sincerity. It did please her to see Diane so obviously happy. 'What about your work here?'

'Mark's asked me to be the resort's public relations manager, so we can live at the resort full-time.' She sighed. 'Just think, Bill and I will be living and working together all the time.'

'It sounds like every newlywed's dream,' Nicole said with a teasing smile.

Diane coloured prettily. 'It is, I suppose. Which reminds me: will I be hearing more wedding bells any time soon?'

Nicole stared at the ice bobbing in her glass. 'I shouldn't think so.'

'You can't blame me for trying, can you?'

'I don't blame you. But Mark and I are just too different. His work will always come first.'

'Pardon me, but look who's talking.' Diane's expansive gesture took in the canvas occupying most of the living-room floor-space. Around it were other paintings in various stages of completion as well as a jumble of oil paints, cleaning rags and brushes standing in jars of turpentine.

'This is different,' Nicole protested. 'This is my living.'

'Maybe Mark feels the same. Hundreds of people depend on his company.' She drained her glass and swung her long legs off the chair. 'But, speaking of work, I'd better let you get on with it.'

At the door, she looked back. 'By the way, the belated wedding reception is set down for two weeks' time on the island. We're counting on you.'

'Mum mentioned your invitation. We'll both be there,' Nicole assured her. Her heart sank at the prospect of seeing Mark again, but it couldn't be avoided. Diane was right about her work being important to her, but she wasn't about to become another Mark, letting it dominate her social life as well.

She was putting the finishing touches to another large panel, a companion to the anemone piece, when the doorbell rang again. Had Diane forgotten something?

Snatching up a rag, she wiped the paint off her fingers and opened the door, stunned to find Mark standing there. He must have come from his office, because he was impeccably dressed in a white shirt and tailored trousers, the charcoal grey etched with a chalk stripe so that he looked every inch the prosperous businessman. As a concession to the heat he had loosened the knot of his silk tie, and his suit jacket swung raffishly from two fingers as he leaned against the door-frame. 'Hello, Nicole.'

She swallowed hard. He was the last person she had expected to find on her doorstep. 'What are you doing here?'

'Visiting you.' He glanced over her shoulder. 'Unless you already have company.'

Did he think she was entertaining another man? 'No, I was working. Would you like to come in?'

She half hoped he would refuse, but he strolled past her and dropped his jacket on to the nearest chair. She hoped it wouldn't get paint on it. The dry-cleaning bills alone must be enormous, although he didn't seem to care.

Her heart, which had begun beating double-time as soon as she'd seen him on the doorstep, settled to a faster than normal rhythm, and her palms felt moist. When was she going to be able to relax around him? 'You didn't answer any of my calls,' he said, regarding her from under hooded lids.

She looked away, twisting the paint rag between nerveless fingers. 'I've been busy lately.'

'Too busy to pick up the messages on your answering machine?' He walked over to the machine and flicked it on, running the tape backwards. When he stopped it, his honeyed tones filled the room. 'Please give me a call, Nicole. We have to talk.' Then he gave the date and time when he would be at home. He didn't have to play the rest of the tape. They both knew it was the first of several such messages he'd left for her since they returned from Crystal Island. 'We do have to talk,' he said softly.

'I told you on the island, we have nothing to talk about,' she protested. 'You have your work, and I . . .' Her fluttering gesture indicated the unfinished painting. 'I have mine.'

'And never the twain shall meet, is that it?' He moved to the painting and studied it for several heart-tearing minutes.

She couldn't help herself. 'What do you think of it?'

'It's magnificent,' he said, as if stating an obvious fact. She became aware that she was holding her breath, and released it, annoyed with herself for caring so much about his opinion. Then he spun around. 'But I didn't come here to discuss art. I want to know why you're dodging my calls.'

What could she say that hadn't already been said a dozen times? 'I don't have time for this,' she protested. 'I'm on a deadline with this series of paintings. They have to be finished by——'

'The Reef Towers opening, I know.'

'Then you also know I don't have much time to finish them.'

One eyebrow lifted in a gesture she should have recognised as dangerous but didn't until he closed the trap. 'So I'm supposed to respect your deadline and not care if you don't bother to return my calls?'

An icy despair washed over her. How often had she accused him of doing the same thing? 'It isn't like that,' she defended herself. 'This project's important to me.'

'As important as my projects are to me,' he reminded her with chilling conviction.

'But my work provides my living.' She grasped for the same argument she'd used with Diane.

'And mine doesn't?' His eyes blazed. 'How in the name of glory do you think I got to where I am today? I wasn't born with any silver spoon in my mouth. My parents were miners at Mount Isa and my grandparents were penniless immigrants before that. Everything I have now I owe to sheer hard work, with little time taken for anything else.'

It was the reason why he had never married, she recalled from late-night conversations they'd had in the past. 'I'm sorry, I didn't mean to imply that your work isn't important,' she said in a low voice. 'I know a lot of people depend on you for their living.' She saw his eyes glitter as she seized on Diane's argument.

'Including you.'

'I beg your pardon?'

'Peter Valentine and I are partners in the Reef Towers project.'

Her knees weakened and she sank on to a stool, the makeshift smock bunching around her legs. 'You're part-owner of Reef Towers? The papers didn't mention anything about it.'

'I'm a silent partner. Peter plans to buy me out as soon as he's able.'

Her throat felt arid and it was an effort to summon her voice. 'Then this project is—what? A grace-and-favour thing?' Desolation threatened to engulf her. She'd been so proud of the commission, so sure that this was the recognition she'd dreamed of for so long.

His harsh gesture cut through her growing despair. 'It's nothing of the sort. Peter saw some of your work in a Townsville gallery and recommended it to the board as a sound investment. I voted in favour, but mine was only one of the votes.'

Pleasure spiralled through her as she imagined him voting in favour of her work, then doubt began to creep back. 'You're not saying it just to make me feel better?'

He raised a hand with two fingers held close together. 'Scout's honour. You earned this commission and, from the look of these panels, the board is getting a top investment.'

Tears began to slide down her cheeks. He saw them and came to her, brushing them away with the back of his hand. 'What's this?'

'I don't know. For a moment I thought you were behind the commission. Now I find you're not and they really do like my work. It's all too much.'

'Sounds more like the symptoms of overwork to me, my girl,' he said sternly. 'You must have worked like a slave to get this far since Valentine called you.'

Dumbly she nodded, wishing her insides would stop doing somersaults at such trivial things as hearing him call her 'my girl'. She wasn't his girl any more. Didn't the last few minutes prove how incompatible they were?

All the same she stayed in his arms, enjoying the feel of them around her shoulders, until she realised she must be getting paint all over him and tried to push him away. His hold tightened.

'Oh, Nicole, it feels so good to hold you again. There must be a way we can work this thing out.'

It was what she wanted too, but not at the expense of her peace of mind. It had taken her too long to recover the last time. 'I don't know,' she said diffidently.

His lips skimmed her hairline, sending electric quivers of sensation along her scalp and down her spine. 'Well, I do. As the saying goes, I'm taking you away from all this. We're going out to dinner.'

A crazy sense of unreality overtook Nicole. She was dreaming; she must be. Overwork was finally making her give in to fantasies. A throaty chuckle escaped her as she looked down at her paint-streaked clothing. 'Like this?'

He lifted her to her feet, his warm hands lingering around her waist before he gave her a small shove in the direction of the bedroom. 'You have ten minutes to change.'

Removing the paint from her face and arms took eight of the ten minutes, leaving her with little time to choose something to wear. It doesn't matter, doesn't matter, doesn't matter, she recited to herself. This wasn't a date, more an act of kindness on his part. Still, her hand hovered over her wardrobe as she agonised over her choices.

Finally she selected a lace tunic petalled in a flutter of partially cut-out embroidered flowers over a simple underdress, both in her favourite coral colour. Her hair she twisted into a simple chignon. Her face glowed from working at the easel all day—or was it from knowing that Mark was waiting for her in the living room? So she sketched in eye-liner and a dash of misty grey shadow, outlined her lips in coral lipstick and grimaced at herself in the mirror.

Ten minutes might be enough to change herself outwardly, but it wasn't nearly enough to adjust herself inwardly to the idea of going out with Mark again.

When she emerged, he was studying the unfinished painting. His transparently appreciative look warmed her even as she cautioned herself not to respond. 'You look lovely. Except for one detail.'

He stepped forward and she tensed reflexively as he loomed over her but it was only to flick out an immaculate white handkerchief and blot a last speck of orange paint from her hairline. 'Better, much better.'

The fleeting contact set her senses reeling. This wasn't going to work, she told herself. If he could reawaken her feelings for him with a touch, what chance did she have of resisting him for a whole evening? 'Maybe this isn't such a good idea,' she began.

He silenced her with a gesture. 'It's an excellent idea.'

'But the paintings...'

'Remember what you told me about all work and no play?'

'Nobody could ever accuse you of being dull,' she said with a sigh.

Her words weren't meant to be audible, but he heard her and his lopsided grin pierced her to her core. 'Now we're getting somewhere,' he said, opening her front door to escort her downstairs.

He took her to a seafood restaurant on the banks of Ross Creek, not far from the casino. Quite a few people greeted him as they were shown to the best table, but for once Mark merely returned their greetings and kept his hand on her arm as they threaded their way across the room. The last time they'd come here, she recalled, it had taken him half an hour to cross the room. A tiny flickering flame sprang up inside her which she refused to recognise as hope. Could things really be different this time?

The hope was fuelled when she saw him lightly touch the *maître 'd*'s hand. Presumably some money had changed hands. 'No telephone calls this evening, thank you, Giuseppe.'

The man smiled. 'No problem, Mr Kingston. I will see that you and Miss Webber are not disturbed.'

He was as good as his word, Nicole noticed, flattered that the man had remembered her name as well. Not only were they not interrupted by a single phone call, but several times she saw Giuseppe intercept people on the way to their table. After a few obviously discreet words, they returned to their own tables.

They quickly agreed on their choices of oysters with shallot and basil vinaigrette, followed by John Dory fillets for Mark and scallop *quenelles* with a vermouth and chive sauce for Nicole. While Mark studied the wine list, Nicole studied him.

It was hard to believe that not only was she spending the evening with him, but they were gloriously alone, even in the busy restaurant. A few months ago she wouldn't have believed it was possible. Looking at his dark head bent over the leather-covered menu, she fought to suppress a thrill of pleasure. There was a long way to go before she could accept that the change was a lasting one.

He gave his order to the wine waiter, then turned to her. 'Glad you decided to come?'

'Yes,' she said.

He heard the note of doubt in her voice. 'But?'

'No buts,' she said emphatically. Even if it didn't last, this night was a gift and she intended to enjoy it to the full. 'Diane came to see me today,' she informed him. 'She's thrilled about the job you offered Bill.'

'Did she tell you I offered her a job at Crystal Cay as well?'

She nodded. 'As public relations manager. It was kind of you to arrange it so they could work together.'

His jaw tightened. 'There was no kindness involved. Diane is skilled at PR work. The mainland hotel where she works now will be damned sorry to lose her. But it's my gain. Both she and Bill will be assets to the resort.'

Hearing Mark speak of their friends in such a calculating way reminded her uncomfortably of the Mark Kingston of old. It was hard to remember her vow to take the evening at face value when every instinct warned her that it couldn't last. After she'd been working so hard to convince herself she was over him, it came as a shock to realise that she wanted it to last more than anything in the world.

CHAPTER SIX

IT WAS late by the time they returned to Nicole's flat.
The evening had flown as they had caught up on ten
months of separation, and Nicole couldn't remember
when she had enjoyed herself more. The note of
caution had stopped sounding in her head hours ago,
dulled no doubt by the excellent champagne Mark had
ordered with dinner.

It wasn't only the champagne, she acknowledged
to herself. It was being the focus of his undivided attention which had gone to her head like wine. It was
a new and dizzying experience.

Mark came around to her door and opened it. 'I'll
see you safely inside.' Her heart sang as she realised
the night didn't have to end here.

'Would you like to come in for coffee?' she asked
when they reached her front door.

He took her key and opened the door then rested
his arm on the door-jamb over her shoulder, effectively trapping her in the circle of his body. 'I know
what I'd like to come in for.'

A shiver of desire shook her. 'Oh, Mark.'

'Nicole.' The way he said her name made it sound
like an endearment. His sea-green eyes met her blue
gaze and she felt herself drowning. She was barely
aware of offering her mouth to him until he accepted
the invitation and swept her away on a tidal wave of
such longing that she was shaken.

Dizzily she linked her hands behind his neck, stretching to her full height until her body melded with his. His heartbeat felt fast and strong through her dress, so she was sure he must feel hers against his chest.

I love you, she thought, the words sizzling through her mind like a brand. Somehow she managed not to say them aloud, lord knew how. If she did he would never let her go again, and she wasn't at all sure whether tonight was an ending or a new beginning.

She couldn't go back to the way things used to be between them, yet it was too soon to know if things had really changed. So she put all her love into the embrace, telling him with her body what she was afraid to put into words.

Whether he guessed her secret or not, she didn't know, but there was no mistaking the fire which she had ignited in him. The stirring of his passion set the blood pulsing hotly through her veins. A longing for him so strong that it was like a hunger gnawing at her.

Knowing she was exciting Mark gave Nicole a dizzying sense of power, as if, in this one moment, he was utterly and completely hers. Her fingers dug deep into his back and he made a throaty sound of encouragement.

'Let's go inside,' she implored. What had begun as a goodnight kiss had become a plundering of her senses and she wanted more, much more.

His eyes blazed like hot coals as he dragged his gaze to her face, his hands holding her inches away from him. 'No,' he ground out as if the single word cost him a great effort.

Confusion dulled her eyes. 'What is it? Is something the matter, Mark?'

Releasing her, he raked taut fingers through his hair. 'I meant to do this slowly, one step at a time, to avoid frightening you away again.'

'I'm not frightened.'

'All the same, you've had a hard day with another one ahead of you tomorrow. You need your rest.'

Rest was the last thing on her mind. 'You didn't worry about frightening me away when we were on the island,' she said. In spite of his reasons, she felt a numbing sense of rejection. Was she the only one to feel the magic between them? The passion in his response made it hard to believe.

'On the island we were affected by the wedding and the cyclone. With the romance of one and the chaos of the other, it's no wonder we couldn't think straight.'

And now they could. With a resounding thump she came back to earth. This was more like the Mark Kingston she knew, pragmatic to the core. It was a shame she couldn't be so coldly logical on cue, then perhaps they might be better suited to one another.

As it was, she felt bruised by his logic, as if he had beaten her with fists instead of words. What had happened to the magic of the evening? Reality has stepped in, she reminded herself. Maybe it was better late than never.

'Then I'll say goodnight,' she said, holding on to her self-control by the thinnest of threads.

He touched her chin with the back of his hand, wincing as she shied away from his touch. 'It's for the best, Nicole.'

The best for whom? she wondered, but held her tongue. Mark always knew what was best for her, or had she forgotten so soon? Blind fool that she was, she had managed to believe that tonight signalled the start of a new phase in their relationship, when it was really the old one being replayed endlessly. They would meet as and when he thought best, even make love when he thought it appropriate.

His gesture of refusing calls and visitors while they dined no longer seemed quite so charming. Was it another example of his high-handed manipulation? Disappointment made her voice ragged as she summoned the polite phrase. 'Thank you for a pleasant evening.'

As she moved to close the door he forestalled her, looking genuinely baffled. 'This isn't easy for me either, you know.'

Her sigh rippled between them. 'I'm glad we agree on something.'

'I want us to agree on a lot of things.'

Tiredly she pushed a strand of hair away from her eyes. Maybe he was right. It had been a hard day and she was exhausted. Perhaps it wasn't the best time to decide the future of a relationship. 'I'll see you at the Donovan wedding, won't I?' she asked.

He frowned. 'I'll be there because Alec Donovan runs our accounting department. But I assumed you wouldn't be conducting any weddings while you have your hands full with the Reef Towers commission.'

For once, she had outguessed him, she saw with a rush of satisfaction. There were some parts of her life under her own control after all. 'Then you guessed wrong,' she said lightly. 'I love my work as a marriage celebrant. I wouldn't dream of putting anyone off just because I'm busy otherwise.'

He seemed about to criticise her stance then thought better of it. 'The change of scene might be what you need after spending long hours at the easel.'

'I think so.'

His hand grazed the side of her face. 'So long as you don't overdo it.'

'I won't.'

'Then I'll see you at the wedding on Saturday.'

'Not before then?' Try as she might, she couldn't keep the disappointment out of her voice.

'I have to fly to Cairns tomorrow,' he explained. 'A site amalgamation I've been after for months has finally come good. If you weren't so busy you could have come with me.'

And do what? Sit in a luxury hotel room eating room-service food by herself while he met with his colleagues? The thought echoed her bitter experience. She might have known he would have business commitments which would keep them apart until Saturday. What else was new?

What did surprise her was the depth of anger she felt over it. She had thought she was over all that months ago. Evidently tonight *had* been a mistake. 'Goodnight, Mark,' she said, shutting her door before he could say anything else.

Fortunately the painting kept her busy until Saturday, and by then she was more than ready to wash the paint out of her hair and dress up to perform the marriage ceremony for Alec Donovan and his pretty young fiancée, Amanda Fiorelli.

At least Mark's role in this wedding would be minor, she was relieved to think. Alec's brother was to be best man. Mark was simply an invited guest.

The ceremony was held at the Reef World aquarium where Amanda worked. Nicole was totally in favour of the unusual venue. As a diver herself, and lover of the undersea world of the Barrier Reef, she never tired of meandering through the vast walk-through aquarium, feasting her eyes on the brilliantly coloured fish and corals, shells and starfish.

Part of the aquarium had been roped off for the ceremony and a number of guests were already assembled by the time Nicole arrived. Alec Donovan paced nervously up and down.

'Relax. You're about to be married, not eaten by one of those predators,' Nicole teased him.

Then she tensed as an all too familiar figure strode on to the scene. Nicole had dived with sharks and felt completely at ease, but now she felt distinctly threatened as the crowd parted for him and he came up to her. He shook Alec's hand and murmured his good wishes before turning to her. 'I'd like to see you after the wedding, Nicole.'

Anger flared inside her. His business in Cairns was finished and he was available, therefore she should be prepared to fit in with his schedule. Just like old times. 'I'll be attending the reception afterwards, so I don't know when I'll be free,' she dissembled.

'You won't mind sharing her with me after the ceremony, will you, Alec?' Mark asked in a smooth aside to the groom.

Alec, she recalled, worked for Mark. 'Of course not,' he said with a grin.

'There, you see? All fixed.'

She drew him away from Alec. 'How could you? You know Alec is hardly in a position to say no.'

'I have something to show you,' he persisted.

He was impossible, first assuming that she would want to leave the reception early to be with him, and then using his position as Alec's boss to get his own way. In spite of herself, her curiosity was piqued. What could he want to show her which justified such tactics?

Before she could press for more information, the matron of honour signalled that the bride was ready. Music spilled through the chamber and the ceremony began.

Although Mark wasn't standing in front of her this time, he might as well have been. Every time she lifted her head to lead the couple in a line of the ceremony, his dark gaze was fixed on her. It was crazy but she felt as if they were the only two people in the aquarium.

The burbling sounds of the water and the lazy movements of the fish made a tranquil, beautiful backdrop to a moving ceremony. Despite the awareness of Mark which vibrated through her like whale song, Nicole managed to get through the proceedings perfectly. With relief she asked Alec to seal his vows by kissing Amanda, which he did with touching enthusiasm.

She had already asked the guests to remain in place while the couple moved to a prepared table to sign the register. After they did so, the guests surrounded the couple and congratulated them. Nicole knew the instant Mark came to her side, so strong was the awareness of him.

'Nice. Very nice,' he murmured. She looked up to find his gaze fixed on her again.

'Do I have a speck on my nose or something?' she asked.

He touched a finger lightly to the end of her nose, the fleeting contact sending fiery sensations surging through her. 'There's nothing wrong with how you look. The opposite, in fact.'

She felt inordinately pleased. Her dress was new and the flutter-sleeves looked soft and feminine in floral georgette set off with an embroidered lace collar. Telling herself that he had nothing to do with her choice of dress, she was nevertheless pleased that he liked it. Then she shook herself mentally. When would she stop caring what he thought?

The reception was to be held at Amanda's home a short drive out of Townsville, and cars had been arranged to transport the guests. 'Ours is over here,' Mark told her when they emerged into the sunlight.

After the dimness of the aquarium the daylight was dazzling. Wishing she'd brought sunglasses, Nicole allowed Mark to escort her to the last in a row of white Mercedes limousines. When he opened the back door, she slid across the seat, expecting him to join her. But he moved around to the driver's seat. They had pulled out into the traffic by the time she noticed that the other cars all had uniformed drivers.

Apprehension rippled through her. 'Whose car is this?'

'Mine.'

Suddenly she realised they were heading along the scenic drive which led to Castle Hill, the spectacular red mountain in the middle of Townsville. The other cars were nowhere in sight. 'What are you doing?' she asked.

Reflected in the driving mirror, his eyes danced with amusement. 'I told you I had something to show you after the wedding. Don't worry, the bride and groom know where we are.'

'But everyone will think that you and I...that we...' She couldn't go on. 'How could you? Quite a few of those people are friends of mine!'

'They'll think it's all terribly romantic,' he said, unperturbed by her anger. Then he added, 'I gather you don't include me among your friends.'

She lapsed into a brooding silence. Whatever he was to her, he could never be a friend. Whether they were at war with each other or celebrating a turbulent peace, there could never be anything as tame as mere liking between them.

Distractedly she noticed that they had turned off the main road. The city was spread out beneath them. 'Where are we going?' she asked, curious in spite of herself.

He brought the car to a halt outside a house which took her breath away with its magnificence. Contemporary in design, it nevertheless had a presence usually associated with more traditional homes. This must be the house Mark had said he was building.

He gave her time to study the exterior. 'What do you think?'

Knowing her fondness for modern design, he must guess her response. 'I love it.'

'Would you like to see the inside?'

Her annoyance at being virtually kidnapped vanished in her eagerness to see it all. 'Yes, please.'

The entrance was via an impressive sandstone staircase. Inside, the clever plan of the house became obvious. It was designed so that the fabulous views could be appreciated from its many levels. White Carrara marble predominated and everything was flooded with natural light.

By the time he had led her through the gallery and entertaining areas, a master suite with separate fitted dressing-room and en-suite bathroom, and a kitchen which would be a dream to work in, she could hardly speak for the lump in her throat.

Just once, they had talked about their dream houses. The hour had been late and, for once, they were uninterrupted by business demands. She had indulged her fantasy to the full, describing every detail of the house she would build if she could.

Now she was standing in it.

'I can't believe it,' she said, her voice cracking with emotion. 'You remembered every detail.'

'There's more,' he told her. His eyes gleamed with a satisfaction which told her she hadn't disappointed him.

He opened yet another door to a huge room which was flooded with natural light. Built-in cupboards filled one wall and the other opened on to a covered patio leading to a pool area. 'This would be wonderful for weddings,' she said, clasping her hands together in delight.

He studied her carefully. 'Actually I had it in mind for a studio.'

Her bright gaze met his. 'Of course, it would be ideal for...' Her voice tailed away as she realised what he meant. 'Oh, Mark, you did this for me, didn't you?' Confusion welled up inside her as he nodded, muscles working in his jawline. 'I don't know what to say.'

'Then don't say anything until we've finished the guided tour.' There were more bedrooms, each with its own bathroom, and a rumpus-room where she could easily imagine a handful of children playing contentedly. Then he led her out to the pool and spa, which, he informed her, were solar-heated.

Under an Italian market umbrella, a table was set for two. With a flourish, he removed covers from plates of fresh seafood salad and melon cocktails on beds of crushed ice. Moisture dewed a bottle of champagne nestling in a silver ice bucket.

He uncorked the wine while she sat down at the table, too astonished to remember that she hadn't wanted to be here with him. Her gesture encompassed the table.

'This is amazing! How on earth did you manage it?'

The cork slid out with a satisfying pop and he filled their glasses before he answered. 'My magician is a catering service.'

She didn't know of any catering service in Townsville which would conjure up a feast such as this on top of a mountain. Were there no limits to Mark's resourcefulness? She took a sip of the chilled champagne and the bubbles teased her throat. 'I feel as if I'm asleep and dreaming.'

'It's no dream, Nicole. I built this house for you. If you won't live in it with me, I'll have it taken apart stone by stone.'

It was the most romantic thing anyone had ever done for her, and the realisation went to her head more surely than the wine, drowning out the alarm bells which rang in her head.

He was manipulating her again, knowing that she wouldn't want to see the magnificent house destroyed. But her resistance had never been about possessions, and it wasn't now. 'Oh, Mark, it's the most wonderful thing anyone's ever done for me,' she said, her tone wistful and blurred with tears.

'You needn't give me your answer yet. Take all the time you need to think it over.'

Nodding, she gave her attention to the seafood so that he wouldn't see the tears clustered in her eyes. If he knew how close he was to victory at this moment, nothing would stop him pressing her for an answer. And she wasn't at all sure what the right one was yet.

After the light meal, they rested on the terrace, enjoying the glorious views. Yet they had total privacy, she realised now. There wasn't another house in sight.

'Would you like a swim?' he asked, breaking into her reverie.

Colour rushed into her cheeks. 'I don't have a swimsuit with me.'

'Who needs one up here? The pool is heated. And you're dying to try it.'

How well he knew her. The pool looked inviting and a swim might clear her turbulent thoughts. Still she hesitated. She had never swum without a costume before.

'I'll turn my back until you're in the water,' he said, guessing the reason for her hesitation.

'All right.'

He was as good as his word, not looking until she had shed her clothes and slid into the water, which closed around her like a satin cocoon. Her eyes went round with delight. Why hadn't anyone told her how wonderful the water felt, lapping against her skin? Moving her arms lazily, she drifted just beneath the surface of the water, floating on her back, her eyes closed in ecstasy.

Her tranquillity was shattered when she heard a splash as he joined her in the pool. Why hadn't she anticipated it? There was no graceful way to climb out so she stayed where she was. With sure strokes, he swam up to her and hooked an arm around the edge of the pool. Drops of water glistened on his chest like diamonds. She stared at them, mesmerised.

When he scooped her into his arms it felt so inevitable that she didn't resist, resting her damp head against his chest. She heard his indrawn breath and it dawned on her that he had been expecting resistance.

His mouth was hungry on hers and she returned the kiss with all the pent-up passion inside her. The house must have cast a spell on her, because she felt suddenly as if she was in the right place—the only place—for her to be.

'Say you'll marry me and be mistress of our dream house,' he urged, his lips moving seductively against her throat.

Her thoughts spun crazily. By bringing her here he was trying to tell her something. The man who built it must have time for something other than work. Was that the message? If so, it removed the last barrier between them.

'Yes, I will,' she said, setting off an explosion of joy around her heart which told her it was the right decision. Trust had to start somewhere, and where better than in the home they would make together? Her vision of children playing in the family-room sprang vividly to mind. Their children would play here. And much too soon if she didn't get out of this pool.

He offered no resistance as she swam out of his arms. Now he had her answer he seemed content. She watched as he dived to the bottom and swam underwater, dolphin-like, giving her time to climb out and swathe herself in the towel he'd provided.

She was dressed and towelling her hair dry when he emerged from the water and began to do the same. There was a stillness about him she hadn't seen before, as if he had found his centre. It seemed unbelievable that she could have caused the change.

'It seems wrong to be driving away,' she said as they pulled out of the circular driveway. Mark had said he would drive her home after dropping some documents off at his corporate headquarters downtown.

'Soon we'll be coming back to stay,' he said. 'When would you like to be married?'

'Soon,' she said. Now that the decision was made, there seemed no reason to delay. 'Can we visit my mother tomorrow and tell her our news?'

'Of course,' he agreed. 'I'll pick you up at ten and we'll drive out to her place.'

During the remainder of the drive her thoughts were busy with plans. There was so much to do. She hardly noticed they'd stopped until Mark began to get out of the car. 'I'll come with you,' she said, wanting to prolong every moment with him.

Although it was a Saturday, she was surprised how busy his offices were. 'You've hired a lot more people since I was here last,' she noticed.

He favoured her with a wink. 'It gives me more time for the things I want to do.'

So he really was delegating more work, she thought with a feeling of satisfaction. She settled on to a chair in his office to wait for him. Added to the discovery of the house, it was almost too good to be true.

The minutes ticked by and she grew uneasy. What was keeping Mark? Going in search of him, she found him huddled with several assistants around the boardroom table. 'What is it, Mark?' she asked, looking in.

'There's a major hitch with the site amalgamation in Cairns,' he said shortly. 'Unless I can sort it out, we won't be able to settle on Monday.'

Unless I can sort it out... Her heart sank as she heard his words. His promise to visit her mother tomorrow already seemed forgotten. 'You're going to Cairns,' she said flatly.

'I have no choice. This has to be done at the highest level.'

No choice. Highest level. No one else. The words hammered at her like blows. He was surrounded by highly paid staff. Surely he wasn't the only one who could go to Cairns at short notice?

Then she really looked at Mark. His shirt-sleeves were pushed up to his elbows as he leaned over the boardroom table. His eyes blazed with a fire which hadn't been there until they came to the office.

This was his world. What was she doing, trying to come between him and the work he loved? How long would it be before he resented her, perhaps hated her, for taking him away from all this?

None of the men looked up when she slipped quietly out of the office.

CHAPTER SEVEN

FOR the next few days Nicole was too busy finishing the Reef Tower paintings to think about her decision, although it haunted her whenever she put down her brush.

She couldn't rid herself of the image of Mark in the boardroom, firing off instructions to his staff and taking command like a general of an army. He was in his element, she accepted, and expecting him to change would eventually destroy the love he felt for her now.

'You're crazy,' Diane told her when she dropped in to see how the paintings were going. The visits would become fewer once Diane went to work at Crystal Cay with Bill, so they had an unspoken agreement to make the most of them now.

Nicole shook her head. 'You didn't see him the way I did. He was only half alive until that crisis hit. He couldn't wait to get to Cairns and sort it all out.'

'He sounds like Bill when he discovers a new species of plant life,' Diane observed drily. 'It's the modern equivalent of the hunting instinct. They Tarzan. We Jane.'

Nicole dropped her brush into a jar of turpentine and reached for a paint rag, then faced Diane, her expression bleak. 'How many dates with you has Bill broken because of his work?'

'A few, when it's an emergency.'

Nicole spread her hands wide. 'A few I could live with. But not every second date. Business even took precedence over telling my mother we were engaged.'

Diane nodded. 'I see your problem. What did Mark say about your decision?'

Nicole lowered her eyes. 'We haven't discussed it.'

'You mean you haven't spoken to him since you walked out of his office? Hasn't he tried to contact you?'

'Yes.' Her answering machine was choked with messages from him which she hadn't returned. When he'd arrived on her doorstep, she had pretended to be out. 'I know exactly what he'll say,' she cut in when Diane started to protest. 'He'll apologise for letting me down and swear that it won't happen again. But it will. And if it doesn't, it will be even worse.'

'Now I'm really confused.'

Nicole gave a sigh of despair. 'I can't live with his work and he can't live without it. Impasse.'

'So what are you going to do?'

Go crazy. Cry herself to sleep every night. Wonder what he was doing and who he was with. She'd done them all in the last few days, but she didn't say so. 'I'll carry on, I suppose.'

Diane nodded. 'We always do, don't we?'

Nicole looked at the painting, which only needed the addition of her signature to be finished. 'I'm lucky to have my own work,' she said. 'I might move to Brisbane and try for more corporate commissions like this one.'

'Reef Towers should be a great advertisement for you,' Diane agreed, then looked wistful. 'I'll miss you, though. I was counting on you to be godmother to our first child.'

A pang shot through Nicole. She could hardly believe that jealousy could hurt so much. She fought the feeling. 'Brisbane isn't far away. I'll fly back whenever you need me.'

'It'll have to do, I suppose.' Diane gathered her things. 'I'd better be going. Bill's in town on business and we have a hot lunch date.'

How lucky she was, Nicole thought. She didn't grudge her friend a moment of her happiness, but it highlighted her own loneliness. Was she doing the right thing in cutting herself off from Mark? Maybe she should have gone with him to Cairns. But, recalling how absorbed he'd been when she left, she knew it wouldn't help. She didn't doubt that he cared. The house was a living testament to his devotion. But she couldn't spend her life in a dream house, waiting for him to come home when he could spare the time.

Diane hugged her. 'Good luck with Reef Towers. Not that you'll need it. Mr Valentine is going to love what you've done.'

'I hope so,' Nicole said. It was all she had left.

'I'll want to hear every detail at the reception on Saturday,' Diane warned her.

'You will,' Nicole agreed, although she dreaded the thought of the gathering where she would have to see Mark again.

Diane hesitated, then reached into her handbag. 'I brought this for you.' In her outstretched palm was the heart-shaped locket Nicole had given her as the 'something new' to wear at her wedding.

Nicole's startled gaze went from the pendant to her friend's face. 'It was a gift for you to keep.'

'When you look inside it, you'll see why I can't.' Diane pressed the pendant into Nicole's hand and closed her fingers around it, then slipped out of the door.

Slowly Nicole uncurled her fingers and looked at the pendant. She hadn't realised it was meant to open because the hinge was cleverly concealed in the scrollwork around the edges. Opening it, she saw what Diane meant. It contained a miniature portrait of Nicole and Mark together, copied from a photograph taken almost a year before.

At the sight of their heads close together her eyes brimmed. Was she never to be free of this aching sense of loneliness?

She knew she should hide the pendant in her jewellery case but somehow her fingers fumbled open the clasp and she fastened it around her neck, dropping the heart inside her blouse. It was too valuable to leave lying around, she reasoned. It wasn't because it meant anything to her.

'The board asked me to congratulate you on a fine effort,' Peter Valentine said warmly.

She sat in his office, sipping an excellent cup of coffee and trying to feel proud and pleased that her work had been accepted with such enthusiasm. A cheque for her fee nestled in her handbag. She should feel on top of the world. Instead she felt empty inside. 'Thank you for thinking of me,' she said. 'It was a tremendous opportunity.'

Peter Valentine stood up, extending his hand to indicate that the meeting was over. 'You have more than justified my faith in you. It isn't often that the board is unanimous about accepting works of art.'

Her throat went dry. 'Everyone liked them?'

'Absolutely. You have a real champion in Mark Kingston, by the way. He was your staunchest supporter.' He regarded her keenly. 'I know you two are friends. I don't suppose you have any idea where he's disappeared to?'

Bewilderment clouded her eyes. 'He's disappeared?'

'Dropped right out of sight. His staff are going crazy but no one knows where to get hold of him. I thought you might have some idea.'

She shook her head. 'No, I don't.'

Peter Valentine laughed. 'If I didn't know better, I'd say he was suffering from a broken heart.'

It was more probably frustration because he hadn't got his own way, she thought uncharitably. Suppressing a surge of fear for him, she told herself it was probably for the best. If he was away, he might miss Diane's reception and she would be able to go, free of the shadow of his presence.

Still she felt uneasy as she prepared for the trip to Crystal Island the following Saturday. There were no new messages from Mark on her answering machine. To her astonishment, she missed turning it on and hearing his voice.

Once, she had tried telephoning his office, but had been told that he was out of town and no, his secretary had no idea when he would be back. She had replaced the phone feeling anxious. It wasn't like Mark to go away without notifying his office of his whereabouts. It had been a source of annoyance to her once. Now she was alarmed at the apparent aberration.

'Maybe he cares more than you think,' Diane theorised as they boarded the charter vessel taking the party to Crystal Island. At first Nicole was disappointed not to find *Sunseeker* riding at anchor at the end of the wharf. Mark was probably out on the cruiser somewhere; working, if she knew him.

'I hardly think he'd let my leaving interfere with business,' Nicole said but felt a prickle of unease. *Could* she have affected him more than she'd thought possible?

She remembered his vow to destroy the new house if she wouldn't share it with him. She didn't really think he would go to such lengths, and yet . . . he was a man of great passions. And he was also a man of his word.

Stewards came around with trays of food and drinks and Nicole accepted a soft drink, her thoughts distracted. Several of the other guests spoke to her and she murmured automatic replies, only coming back to reality when one of the guests made a noise of irritation. 'Oh, hello, Mum, I didn't realise it was you,' she said, recognising her mother belatedly. Jean Webber had been Diane's surrogate mother since the death of her friend's real mother five years before, so Nicole had expected to see her here.

'I was beginning to think I should introduce myself,' Jean Webber said, smiling to soften the criticism. 'You were miles away.'

Nicole sipped her drink. 'I have a lot on my mind.'

'A lot like Mark Kingston?' Reading Nicole's startled reaction, she nodded. 'I knew it. He isn't the sort of man to give up easily when he sets his sights on something.'

'It isn't like that,' Nicole protested. 'I've seen him a few times, but there's nothing more to it.'

'Then why do you look as if they'd abolished Christmas?' her mother asked, regarding her daughter through narrowed eyes.

'I'm probably working too hard. But I'll take some time off now the Reef Towers commission is finished.'

A frown creased her mother's forehead. 'Make sure that you do. If your father had taken more time off...'

Nicole saw the shadow darken her mother's eyes and touched her hand. 'Thanks for worrying about me, but it's all right, really.' She took a deep breath. 'I've never understood why you stayed with Dad when he was so wrapped up in his work.'

Her mother's expression softened. 'Nobody understands a marriage except the two people involved. I loved your father. His zest for life strengthened me even when we were apart, which was a lot of the time, I admit. But I wouldn't trade a minute of what we shared for lifetime with someone else.'

Pain made Nicole's voice ragged. 'I think I understand. Thank you for telling me, Mum.'

She sipped her drink in silence. Was it so simple? She loved Mark. Surely she could accept every part of him unconditionally, as her mother had done with her father? A tremendous sense of optimism crept over her. It was all she had to do.

Picturing him out on the ocean in *Sunseeker*, she fervently hoped it wasn't too late. Wait for me, Mark, she implored silently. She felt imprisoned aboard the chartered cruiser, as if it was taking her further and further away from the man she loved.

She had no choice but to continue the journey to the island for the delayed wedding reception. At least they were returning at sunset, she consoled herself. Mark was unlikely to return to Townsville himself before then.

For Diane's sake she made an effort to enjoy the party, although her heart was back in Townsville, waiting for Mark to return. The food was plentiful and excellent although she only picked at the seafood buffet. There were the usual speeches and jokes about newlyweds, which were amusing despite the delay between wedding and reception. Diane positively glowed, and Nicole began to suspect there could be another reason besides the party.

'Yes, I'm fairly sure I'm pregnant,' she confided to Nicole a short time later.

'That's wonderful. But what about your new job?'

Diane grinned. 'It being a live-in position will let me combine work and motherhood. Crystal Cay will get double their value.'

'How is the resort coming along?' Nicole asked.

'Why don't you walk over and see for yourself? Most of the buildings are being prefabricated on the mainland and brought here by boat. You'll be amazed at the progress since your last visit.'

Nicole hesitated. Visiting the site would be like trespassing in Mark's domain. But it was the closest she could be to him until they returned to the mainland. 'I think I will,' she said.

When last she'd come this way, Mark had been by her side, she remembered, conjuring up his tall, athletic form pacing the path beside her. She had to blink to clear her gaze of the vision. Knowing she had walked out on him, not once but twice, she would be lucky if he wanted to see her again.

She found the resort easily enough. Already several partly completed guest cabins were scattered around the skeleton of a central building. The low structures nestled into the contours of the land, so they barely disturbed the groves of lush rain forest around them.

A spectacular pool wound its way between stands of melaleucas overhung with fragrant orchids and ferns. Although it was empty, she could imagine birds swooping down to drink from its surface. When it was finished, Crystal Cay would be an Eden, and she envied the people who would stay here.

'What are you doing here?'

The harsh challenge halted her steps and she dragged in a sharp breath as she saw who was barring her path. 'I—I came to look at the site,' she stammered, her heart constricting at the sight of the man she loved. His jaw was shadowed by several days' growth of beard, and lines of fatigue radiated around his eyes.

Under his cut-off jeans and shirt, his body was deeply tanned as if he had been working outdoors for some time. 'This is where you've been?' she asked in a strangled voice. Too late, she noticed *Sunseeker* riding at anchor in the lagoon below the site.

'I started out in construction work. I still pick up some tools when I feel the need.'

The lesson was clear. She had betrayed him and he had come here to work off his anger. Even now, it radiated out from him like an aura, and she flinched from its ferocity. But she couldn't leave him like this. 'I owe you an apology.'

'You don't owe me a thing. Now, if you'll excuse me, I have work to do.'

As he tried to brush past her, she caught his arm, marvelling at the raw strength of muscle and sinew beneath taut skin. 'Wait, please. Even if you never speak to me again, you must let me say this. I was wrong.'

'Wrong to say you'd marry me? I worked that out for myself.'

'No, wrong to set conditions on love. I realise it's probably too late, but I don't expect you to choose between work and me. I love you, Mark, as you are. You must believe me.'

He massaged his chin with a work-roughened hand. 'Oddly enough, I do believe you.' His voice became deep and husky. 'Maybe because it's what I want to believe.'

'Oh, Mark, do you mean it? There's still a chance for us?'

'There always was. If you'd stayed in the boardroom for five more minutes, you'd have heard me hand over the Cairns crisis to my assistant. When I started taking over, I saw what I was doing and immediately changed tactics. But you'd already gone and I couldn't get in touch with you to tell you.'

'I panicked,' she said in a low voice. 'I thought you were like my father all over again, working yourself to death. If you knew how afraid I was . . .'

Suddenly, magically, she was in his arms, her tears leaving red trails through the dust clinging to his shirt. 'It's all right,' he murmured, stroking her hair. 'It's all right, you're with me now.'

She lifted her head. 'Diane sent me to look at the site. Does she know you're here?'

'Diane, Bill and Jack are the only ones. I didn't even tell my office where I was going.'

She sighed. 'I know. I tried to call you there.'

'You did?' He sounded pleased. 'What else have I missed, playing Robinson Crusoe?'

Her answer was in her shy gaze as her hands crept up around his neck. His hold tightened and she felt his answering stir of excitement. It was going to be all right; it had to be. Still, he hadn't said that he loved her.

'Mark,' she said, apprehension making her voice vibrant, 'can you ever forgive me?'

'For caring enough to be frightened for me?' He shook his head. 'I don't ever want you to stop caring that much.'

Her lashes fluttered down. 'I care much more, Mark. You're my life.'

Her startled cry echoed through the rain forest as he scooped her into his arms. 'Where are you taking me?'

'You came to see the resort. We'll start with my private retreat.'

He carried her across the threshold of a Polynesian-styled *bure* set apart in a fern-filled grove. The cedar building had a high peaked ceiling and cool terracotta flooring. It was unfinished and the only furnishing was a king-sized pine bedstead in one corner. He placed her on it and stood looking down at her as if he could never get enough of the sight. 'Say you'll marry me,' he urged. 'You'll always come first in my life.'

'I know, as you'll always come first with me,' she vowed. 'The answer is yes, with all my heart.'

He knelt beside her, his breathing fast and shallow, as he leaned across and brushed her mouth with his lips.

The butterfly touch set her senses reeling and she clasped her hands across his broad back, feeling the heat from him radiating along her fingertips. Eagerly her lips sought his and he kissed her back with a fierceness which promised wonders in the nights and years ahead. 'I've missed you so,' she said when she could speak again.

He rained kisses along the slim column of her neck until he reached the sensitive valley between her breasts and she arched her back in pleasure. 'What made you change your mind?' he asked.

'Something my mother said about a minute of life with my father being preferable to a lifetime with someone else,' she said.

He nuzzled her gently. 'Wise woman, your mother. Clever, too, producing a daughter like you.'

Her laughter pealed in his ear. 'No wonder she's your best supporter. She warned me you wouldn't give up.'

His fingers worked at the top buttons of her blouse then he stopped as he encountered the heart-shaped pendant. 'I thought you gave this away.'

'I couldn't when I saw what was inside. I haven't taken it off since Diane returned it to me.'

'And now it's brought you back to me.' He pressed a kiss to the golden heart then another to the cleft between her breasts. 'Promise me you'll never leave me again.'

Music floated on the air, teasing at her memory, and she sat up. 'I may have to for a little while. Bill's tuning up the Bridal March. We were going to re-enact their wedding ceremony.'

'They'll have to go on without you,' he said, clasping her to him. 'The next wedding you attend is going to be ours.'

'I suppose nobody's indispensable,' she agreed.

'Not even me.'

'Except to me,' she said, her hands wandering over his chest. She wanted to touch and taste and know this man so much that it almost hurt. 'I hope we find another marriage celebrant quickly.'

'The sooner, the better,' he agreed. 'Because next time you say "I will", there's no going back.'

Her heart swelled with joy and pride. She didn't want to go back. From this day forward, she thought, floating on a cloud of sheer happiness. Were there any more beautiful words in the whole of language?

Except, perhaps, the ones he whispered next. 'I love you.'

SOMETHING BORROWED
Miranda Lee

CHAPTER ONE

'JAMES hasn't seen your dress, has he?' Kate asked, glancing at the magnificent satin and lace bridal gown hanging on the wardrobe door. 'You know that's considered unlucky.'

Ashleigh put down her mascara and smiled at her chief bridesmaid in the dressing-table mirror. 'No, Miss Tradition. He hasn't. Not that it would worry me if he had,' she added with a light laugh. 'You know I don't believe in superstitions. *Or* fate. *Or* luck. People make their own luck in life.'

Kate rolled her eyes. 'You've become annoyingly pragmatic over the years, do you know that? Where's your sense of romance gone?'

It was killed, came the unwanted and bitter thought. A lifetime ago...

Ashleigh felt a deep tremor of old pain, but hid it well, keeping her mascara wand steady with an iron will as she went on with her make-up.

'Just look at you,' Kate accused. 'It's your wedding-day and you're not even nervous. If I were the bride my hand would be shaking like a leaf.'

'What is there to be nervous about? Everything is going to go off like clockwork. You know how organised James's mother is.'

'I wasn't talking about the wedding. Or the reception. I was talking about afterwards... You know...'

197

'For heaven's sake, Kate,' Ashleigh said quite sharply. 'It's not as though I'm some trembling young virgin. I'm almost thirty years old, and a qualified doctor to boot. My wedding-night is not looming as some terrifying ordeal.'

Oh, really? an insidious voice whispered at the back of her mind.

Ashleigh stiffened before making a conscious effort to relax, letting out a ragged sigh. 'I'm sorry,' she apologised. 'I shouldn't have snapped at you like that.'

'You *are* nervous,' her friend decided smugly. 'And you know what? I think it's sweet. James is a real nice man. Much nicer than...' Kate bit her bottom lip and darted Ashleigh a stricken look. 'Oh, I... I'm sorry. I didn't mean... I...'

'It's all right,' Ashleigh soothed. 'I won't collapse in a screaming heap if you mention his name.'

'Do you... ever think of him?' Kate asked, eyes glittering with curiosity.

Too damned often, came the immediate and possibly crushing thought.

But Ashleigh gathered herself quickly, refusing to allow Jake—even in memory form—to mar her wedding-day.

'Jake's as good as dead as far as I'm concerned,' she stated quite firmly. 'As far as *everyone* in Glenbrook is concerned. Even his mother doesn't speak of him any more.'

'What about James?' the other girl asked. 'I mean... he and Jake are twins. Doesn't he ever talk about his brother?'

'Never.''

Kate frowned. 'I wonder what Jake would think of his quieter half marrying his old girlfriend. Does he know, do you think? They say some twins, especially identical ones, have a sort of telepathy between them.'

Ashleigh's fine grey eyes did their best to stay calm as she turned to face her old school-friend. 'Jake and James never did. As far as Jake knowing . . .' She gave a seemingly offhand shrug. 'He might. His mother insisted on sending him a wedding invitation. God knows why, since she doesn't even know where he's living now. She posted it to his old solicitor in Thailand, who once promised to pass on any mail. Naturally, she didn't receive a reply.'

Ashleigh sucked in a deep breath, then let it out slowly, hoping to ease the constriction in her chest. 'Jake wouldn't give a damn about my marrying James, anyway,' she finished. 'Now . . . perhaps we'd better get on with my hair. Time's getting away.'

Kate remained blessedly silent while she brushed then wound Ashleigh's shoulder-length blonde hair into the style they'd both decided on the previous day. Even though Ashleigh appeared to be watching her hairdresser friend's efficient fingers, her mind was elsewhere, remembering things she shouldn't be re-membering on the day she was marrying James.

Jake . . . holding her close, kissing her.

Jake . . . undressing her slowly.

Jake . . . his magnificent male body in superb control as he took her with him to a physical ecstasy, the like of which she doubted she would ever experience again.

A shiver reverberated through her.

'You're not cold, are you?' Kate asked, frowning.

Ashleigh tried to smile. 'No . . . Someone must have walked over my grave.'

Her friend laughed. 'I thought you didn't believe in stuff like that. You know what, Ashleigh? I think you're a big fibber. I think you believe in fate and superstitions and all those old wives' tales as much as the next person. And I'll prove it to you before this day is out. But, for now, sit perfectly still while I get these pins safely in. I don't want to spear you in the ear.'

Ashleigh was only too happy to sit still, her whole insides in knots as a ghastly suspicion began to take hold. Was she marrying James simply because of his physical likeness to Jake? Could she be indulging some secret hope that, when James took her to bed tonight, her body would automatically respond the same way it had to his brother?

She hadn't thought so when she'd accepted James's proposal. Ashleigh believed she was marrying him because he was the only man she'd met in years who seemed genuinely to love her, whom *she* liked enough to marry, and who wanted what she was suddenly wanting so very badly: a family of her own. Sex had not seemed such an important issue.

Now... with her wedding-night at hand... it had suddenly become one.

Perhaps she should have let James make love to her the night he'd asked her to marry him. At least then she would have known the truth. Looking back to that occasion, she had undoubtedly been stirred by his unexpectedly fierce kisses. Why, then, had she pulled back and asked him to wait? Why? What had she been afraid of? As she'd said to Kate... she was hardly a trembling virgin.

Ashleigh mentally shook her head, swiftly dismissing the possibility that her body—or her subconscious—*might* find one brother interchangeable with the other. She had *never* confused James with Jake in the past. Others had, but never herself. The two were totally different in her eyes, regardless of their identical features.

They'd been in the same class at school since kindergarten, she and Jake and James, though the boys were almost a year older than her. The three had been great mates always, spending all their spare time together. It wasn't till the end of primary school that their relationship had undergone a drastic change. The three of them had seemed to shoot up overnight, Jake and James into lithe, handsome lads, and Ashleigh into a lovely young woman with a figure the envy of every girl in Glenbrook.

By the time they had finished their first year in high school the more extroverted, aggressive Jake had staked a decidedly sexual though still relatively innocent claim on Ashleigh. She'd become his 'steady', and from then on James had taken a back seat in her life, even though she had always been subtly aware that he was equally attracted to her, and would have dearly liked to be in his brother's shoes.

But she'd had eyes only for Jake.

How they had lasted till their graduation from high school before consummating their relationship was a minor miracle. Oh, they'd argued about 'going all the way' often enough, with Jake sometimes becoming furious with her adamant refusal to let him. But she had seen the way other teenage boys talked about girls who gave sex freely, and had always been determined not to give in till Jake had proved he wanted her for herself, not her nubile young body.

Ashleigh almost smiled as she remembered the first time Jake had made real love to her, the day after her eighteenth birthday, two weeks after they'd graduated. What an anticlimax their first effort had been. Jake had been furious with himself, knowing he'd been too eager, too anxious.

'Too damned arrogant and ignorant,' were *his* words.

Jake had gone out then and there and bought a very modern and very progressive love-making manual, then quickly became the most breathtakingly skilful lover that any mortal male could become, mastering superb control over his own urgent young body, thrilling to the way he'd eventually learnt to give the girl he loved such incredible pleasure.

Or so Ashleigh had romantically imagined at the time. She should have known that it was just Jake being his typical obsessive self. She certainly should have begun to doubt the depth of Jake's love when he announced in the New Year that he was going overseas—*alone*—for a couple of months. She'd stupidly believed his story about his rich Aunt Aggie's giving him the holiday as a reward for his great exam results and insisting he go immediately, saying it would broaden his mind for his future writing career. He'd promised Ashleigh faithfully to be back in time to go to university with her in March.

But by March Jake had been in prison in Bangkok, awaiting trial for drug trafficking and possession, after trying to board a plane home with heroin in his luggage. Though greatly distressed, Ashleigh had flown over to support her boyfriend, certain he was innocent. The penny hadn't dropped till after Jake had been found guilty and given a life sentence. He had looked her straight in the eye from behind those filthy bars and told her quite brutally that *of course* he was guilty. What in hell did she think he'd really come over for?

But it had been his subsequent personal tirade against her that had shattered Ashleigh completely. His cruelly telling her that he had grown out of their puppy love during his weeks abroad; that he found her blind faith during his trial suffocatingly laughable; that she was boring compared to the *real* women he'd enjoyed since leaving home and that he didn't want to see her pathetic face again, let alone receive any more of her drippy, mushy love letters.

Ashleigh had returned home to Australia in a state of deep despair and disillusionment, having had to defer her entry into medical school till the following year due to her emotional state. In truth, she had almost succumbed to a nervous breakdown over Jake. Yet still some mad, futile hope had made her keep on writing to him. Not love letters. Just words of forgiveness and encouragement. Every day she had gone out to the mail box, hoping against hope for a letter back.

It had never come.

In the end, she'd crawled out of her crippling depression and gone on without Jake.

But the scars left behind from her disastrous teenage romance had plagued her personal life, spoiling every relationship she'd tried to have. Always she'd compared the man with Jake. His looks, his personality, his drive, his lovemaking . . .

They'd all failed to measure up. Which was crazy! For what had Jake done to her? Let her down. Let his family down. Let *everyone* down.

'What made you come home to Glenbrook to practise medicine?' Kate asked all of a sudden, startling Ashleigh from her reverie. 'From what you've told me, you were doing well down in Sydney.'

'Very well,' Ashleigh agreed. 'But the city can be a lonely place, Kate, without your family or someone special to share your life. I remember I spent my twenty-ninth birthday all alone, and suddenly I was homesick. Within a week I was back here in Glenbrook.'

'And in no time you found James. God, life's strange. There you were in Sydney for years, where there must be hordes of handsome, eligible men, and what do you do? Come home and find your future hubby in good old Glenbrook.'

'Yes...' Ashleigh recalled the night she'd answered an emergency call from the Hargraves home where Mr Hargraves senior had unfortunately suffered a fatal heart attack. It had been James who'd opened the door...

'I suppose there's no hope of you-know-who coming back to town, is there?' Kate probed carefully.

'I wouldn't think so. It's been over three years now.'

Three years since the Thailand government had unexpectedly pardoned a few foreign prisoners during a national celebration—one of them being Jake—and Ashleigh had still foolishly started hoping he'd come home to her.

Well, he had come home all right. For less than a day, apparently, his visit only to ask for money before he went back to the very country that had almost destroyed him! He hadn't come to see her, even though she'd been home at the time.

One would have thought that such callous indifference should have made it much easier for Ashleigh to see other men in a more favourable light. But somehow...it hadn't.

A type of guilt assailed Ashleigh. James deserved better than a bride who spent her wedding-day thinking about another man, especially his own brother.

She gave herself another mental shake. She wouldn't do it any more. Not for a second! And if tonight there were fleeting memories of another time, and another lover, she would steadfastly ignore them.

I will be a good wife, she vowed. The very best. Even if I have to resort to faking things a little...

'Well, what do you think?' Kate asked after one last spurt of hair-spray.

Ashleigh swallowed, then glanced in the mirror at the way her wayward blonde hair was now neatly encased in a sleek French roll. 'That's great,' she praised. 'Oh, you're so clever!'

'*You're* the clever one, Dr O'Neil,' came her friend's laughing reply.

A hurried tap, tap, tap on the bedroom door had both women glancing around. The door opened immediately and Nancy Hargraves, James's mother, hurried into the room.

'Goodness, what are you doing here, Nancy?' Ashleigh exclaimed, getting to her feet. 'Has something gone wrong? Don't tell me it's raining down at the park!'

The actual ceremony was to take place in a picturesque park down by the river, James having vetoed his mother's suggestion they have the wedding at a church neither of them attended. Ashleigh had happily gone along with his idea of a marriage celebrant and an open-air wedding, choosing the local memorial park as a setting. Nancy, though not pleased, had acquiesced, warning them at the time that if it rained it would be their own stupid fault!

'No, no, nothing like that,' she muttered now in an agitated fashion.

Ashleigh was surprised at how upset James's ultra-cool and composed mother seemed to be. Her hands were twisting nervously together and she could hardly look Ashleigh in the face.

'Could I speak privately to Ashleigh for a minute or two?' she asked Kate with a stiff smile.

'Sure. I'll go along and check that the others are nearly ready.' The others being Alison and Suzie, Ashleigh's cousins—the second bridesmaid and flower girl respectively.

'Thank you,' Mrs Hargraves said curtly.

Kate flashed Ashleigh an eyebrow-raised glance before leaving the room, being careful not to catch the voluminous skirt of her burgundy satin bridesmaid's dress as she closed the door behind her.

Ashleigh eyed her future mother-in-law with both curiosity and concern. It wasn't like Nancy to be so flustered. When she'd offered to help with the wedding arrangements Ashleigh had very gratefully accepted, her own mother having died several years before. She imagined not many women could have smoothly put together a full-scale wedding in the eight weeks that had elapsed since the night she'd accepted James's proposal. But Nancy Hargraves had for many years been Glenbrook's top social hostess, and all had been achieved without a ruffle.

Ashleigh got slowly to her feet, taken aback to detect red-rimmed eyes behind the woman's glasses.

'What's happened?' she said with a lurch in her stomach.

'I...I've heard from Jake,' came the blurted-out admission.

Ashleigh felt the blood drain from her face. She clutched her dressing-gown around her chest and sank slowly down on to the stool again. It was several seconds before she looked up and spoke. 'I presume he rang,' she said in a hard, tight voice. 'There's no mail on a Saturday.'

The other woman shook her head. 'He sent me a letter through a courier service. It arrived a short while ago.'

'What...what did he say?' she asked thickly.

'Apparently the wedding invitation only just reached him,' Nancy said with the brusqueness of emotional distress. 'He...he sends his apologies that he can't attend. He...he also sent this and specifically asked me to give it back to you today *before* the wedding.'

Ashleigh stared at the silver locket and chain dangling from the woman's shaking fingers. Her own hand trembled as she reached out to take it, a vivid memory flashing into her mind.

'What's this?' Jake had asked when she'd held the heart-shaped locket out between the bars of his cell the night before the verdict had come down.

Her smile had been pathetically thin. 'My heart,' she'd said. 'Keep it with you while you're in here. You can give it back to me when you get out, when you come to claim the real thing.'

'I could be here for years, Leigh,' had come his rough warning. Jake always called her Leigh, never Ashleigh.

'I'll wait . . . I'll wait for you forever.'

'Forever is a long time,' he'd bitten out in reply. But he'd taken her offering and shoved it in the breast pocket of the shabby shirt he'd been wearing.

Now she stared down at the heart-shaped locket for a long, long moment, then crushed it in her hand, her eyes closing against the threatened rush of tears.

'I'm sorry to have upset you, Ashleigh,' Nancy said in a strained voice. 'I know what Jake once meant to you. But believe me when I say I wanted nothing more than to see you and James happily married today. I did not want to come here with this. But I had to do what my son asked. I just *had* to. I . . .'

She broke off, and Ashleigh's wet lashes fluttered open to see a Nancy Hargraves she'd never encountered before. The woman looked grey, and ill.

Anger against Jake flooded through her, washing the pain from her heart, leaving a bitter hardness instead. How dared he do this, *today*, of all days? How *dared* he?

Ashleigh pulled herself together and stood up, the locket tightly clasped within her right hand. 'It's all right, Nancy,' she stated firmly. '*I'm* all right. I have no intention of letting Jake spoil my wedding-day. Or my marriage. You haven't told James about the letter, have you?'

Nancy's blue eyes widened, perhaps at the steel in Ashleigh's voice. 'N . . . no . . .'

'Then everything's all right, isn't it? I certainly won't be mentioning it. By tonight, James and I will be driving off on our honeymoon and he'll be none the wiser.'

She was shocked when her future mother-in-law uttered a choked sob and fled from the room.

CHAPTER TWO

ASHLEIGH stood there for a few moments in stunned silence, her thoughts in disarray. But she soon gathered her wits, renewing her resolve not to let Jake spoil her marriage to James. No doubt Nancy would soon collect herself as well and present a composed face at the ceremony in little over half an hour's time.

'Mrs Hargraves gone, I see?' Kate said as she breezed back into Ashleigh's bedroom. 'What on earth did she want? She looked rather uptight.'

'Yes, she did, didn't she?' Ashleigh agreed with a deliberately carefree air. Kate was a dear friend but an inveterate gossip, the very last person one would tell about the correspondence from Jake. Everyone in Glenbrook would know about it within a week, with suitable embellishments. It had been Kate who had furnished Ashleigh with the news of Jake's fleeting visit over three years before, the information gleaned from Nancy Hargraves's cook, a talkative lady who had her hair done at Kate's salon every week.

Ashleigh smiled disarmingly at her friend. 'It proves that even someone like James's mother can be nervous with the right occasion. I thought something must have gone wrong there for a moment. But she just called in to give me this to wear today.' And she held up the locket and chain. 'Must be one of your mob, Kate. An upholder of old traditions. This is to be my *something borrowed*.'

The irony of her excuse struck Ashleigh immediately, but she bravely ignored the contraction in her chest. She'd lent Jake her heart, and now he'd given it back to her.

Good, she decided staunchly. I'll entrust it to James. He'll take much better care of it, I'm sure.

With a surge of something like defiance, she slipped the chain around her neck. 'Do this up for me, will you?' she asked her chief bridesmaid.

'Will do. But what are you going to do for the something old, something new and something blue?'

'No trouble,' Ashleigh tossed off. 'My pearl earrings are old, my dress is new, and my bra has a blue bow on it.'

'Spoil-sport,' Kate complained. 'I had a blue garter all lined up for you.'

'OK. I'll wear that too. Now help me climb into this monstrosity of a dress, will you? The photographer's due here in ten minutes.'

'You're suitably late now, Miss O'Neil,' the chauffeur of the hire-car informed. 'Shall I head for the park?'

'God, yes,' her father grumbled from his seat beside her. 'If we go round this damned block one more time I'll be in danger of being car-sick for the first time in my life!'

'Kate insisted I be at least ten minutes late,' Ashleigh defended, feeling more than a little churned up in the stomach herself. But it wasn't car-sickness. Much as she had maintained a cool exterior since the perturbing encounter with Nancy, inside she was a mess. And it was all Jake's fault. The whole catastrophe of her personal life so far had been Jake's fault!

But no longer, she decided ruefully. She was going to marry James and be happy if it killed her!

She slanted her father a sideways glance, thinking wryly that he was far from comfortable in his role as father of the bride. He was a good doctor, but an antisocial man, whose bedside manner left a lot to be desired.

Ashleigh believed she'd contributed a lot to his practice since joining it, always being willing to lend a sympathetic ear, especially to women patients. They certainly asked for her first. She planned to continue working, at least part-time, even if she did get pregnant straight away, which was her and James's hope.

Thinking about having a baby, however, brought her mind back to the intimate side of marriage, and the night ahead of her. Another attack of nerves besieged her stomach. Dear heaven, she groaned silently. She hadn't realised that going to bed with James would loom as such an ordeal.

Her hand fluttered up unconsciously to touch the locket lying in the deep valley between her breasts.

Any worry over her wedding-night was distracted, however, when the park came into view. Oh, my God, she thought as her eyes ran over what Nancy had arranged for her favourite son's wedding.

A rueful smile crossed Ashleigh's lips. James's vetoing a church service clearly hadn't stopped his mother's resolve to have a traditional and very public ceremony. Right in the middle of the park under an attractive clump of trees sat a flower-garlanded dais, with an enormous strip of red carpet leading up to it, on either side of which were rows and rows of seats, all full of guests. But the *pièce de résistance* was the electric organ beside the dais, which seemed to have a hundred extension leads running from it away to a van on which two loud speakers were placed.

Ashleigh shook her head in drily amused resignation. Serve herself right for giving James's mother *carte blanche* with the arrangements.

'Trust Nancy Hargraves to turn this wedding into a social circus,' her father muttered crossly as the white Fairlane pulled up next to the stone archway that marked the entrance to the park. A fair crowd of onlookers were waiting there for the bride's arrival, not to mention several photographers and a video cameraman. 'Thank God I've only got one daughter. I wouldn't want to go through all this again.'

Ashleigh felt a surge of irritation towards her father. Why did he always have to make her feel that her being female was a bother to him?

If only Mum were still alive, she thought with a pang of sadness. She would have so loved today. Not for the first time Ashleigh wondered how such a soft, sentimental woman had married a man like her father.

People always claimed she took after her mother. She certainly hoped so.

'I've been thinking,' Edgar O'Neil went on curtly while they sat there waiting for the chauffeur to make his way round to Ashleigh's door. 'It's as well Stuart will be joining the practice next year. You're going to be too busy having babies and dinner parties to be bothered with doctoring. And rightly so. A woman's place is in the home.'

Ashleigh was too flabbergasted to say a word. She had always known that her father was one of the old brigade at heart. Also that her younger brother would be joining the practice after he finished his residency.

But her father spoke as if her services would be summarily dispensed with!

As for her giving dinner parties...Nancy Hargraves and her late husband might have been the hub of Glenbrook's social life, the Hargraves family owning the logging company and timber mill which were the economic mainstays of the town. But James was not a social animal in the least, and Ashleigh didn't anticipate their married life would contain too much entertaining.

She had planned to go on working, babies or not. Or at least she *had*...till her father had dropped his bombshell just now. Her heart turned over with a mixture of disappointment and dismay, though quickly replaced by a prickly resolve. She would just have to start up a practice of her own, then, wouldn't she?

Alighting from the car, Ashleigh had to make a conscious effort to put a relaxed, smiling face on for the photographers and all the people avidly watching her every move. Heavens, but it looked as if the whole town had turned out to see their only lady doctor getting married.

Or was there a measure of black curiosity, came the insidious thought, over her marrying the wrong brother?

Stop it! she breathed to herself fiercely. Now just you stop it!

'Doesn't she look beautiful?' someone whispered as she made her way carefully up the stone steps and through the archway, her skirt hitched up slightly so she didn't trip.

'Like a fairy princess,' was another comment.

Ashleigh felt warmed by their compliments, though she knew any woman would look good in what she was wearing. The dress and veil combined had cost a fortune, Nancy having insisted she have the very best. Personally she had thought the *Gone With The Wind* style gown, with its heavy beading, low-cut neck, flounced sleeves and huge layered skirt, far too elaborate for her own simpler tastes. But Nancy had been insistent.

'It's expected of my daughter-in-law to wear something extra-special,' she had said in that haughty manner which could have been aggravating if one let it. But Ashleigh accepted the woman for what she was. A harmless snob. James had a bit of it in him too, but less offensively so.

Jake had been just the opposite, refusing to conform to his mother's rather stiff social conventions, always going his own way. Not for him a short back and sides haircut. Or suits. Or liking classical music. Jake had been all long, wavy hair, way-out clothes and hard-rock bands. Only in his grades had he lived up to his parental expectations, being top of the school.

Irritation at how her mind kept drifting to Jake sent a scowl to her face.

'Smile, Doc,' the photographer from the local paper urged. 'You're going to be married, not massacred.'

Ashleigh stopped to throw a beaming smile the photographer's way. 'This better?'

'Much!'

'Come, Ashleigh,' her father insisted, taking her elbow and shepherding her across the small expanse of lawn to where the imitation aisle of red carpet started and her attendants were waiting. 'We're late enough as it is.'

Her chief bridesmaid thought so too, it appeared. 'Now that's taking tradition a bit too far for my liking,' Kate grumbled. 'I was beginning to think you'd got cold feet and done a flit.'

'Never,' Ashleigh laughed.

'Well, stranger things have happened. But all's well that ends well. I'll just give the nod for the music to start and the men to get ready. I think they're all hiding behind the dais. Still nervous?' she whispered while she straightened her friend's veil.

'Terrified,' Ashleigh said truthfully, a lump gathering in her throat as all the guests stood up, blocking out any view of the three men walking round to stand at the base of the dais steps.

'Good. Nothing like a nervous bride. Nerves make them look even more beautiful, though God knows I don't know how anyone could look any more beautiful than you do today, dear friend. James is going to melt when he sees you.'

'Will you two females stop gasbagging?' the father of the bride interrupted peevishly.

'Keep your shirt on, Dr O'Neil,' Kate returned, not one to ever be hassled by a man, even a respected physician of fifty-five. Which could explain why, at thirty, she'd never been a bride herself. 'We'll be ready when we're ready and not a moment before. Your father's a right pain in the neck, do you know that, Ashleigh?'

'Yes,' came the sighing reply.

The organ started up.

Kate grinned. 'Knock 'em dead, love.'

'You make this sound like the opening night of a show,' Ashleigh returned in an exasperated voice.

Kate lifted expressive eyebrows, then laughed softly. 'Well, it is, in a way, isn't it?'

Heat zoomed into Ashleigh's cheeks.

'Aah,' the other girl smiled. 'That's what I wanted to see. The bridal blush. She's ready now, Dr O'Neil.'

As ready as I'll ever be, Ashleigh thought with a nervous swallow.

The long walk up the red carpet on her father's arm was a blur. The music played. Countless faces smiled at her. It felt almost as if she were in a dream. She was walking on clouds and everything seemed fuzzy around the edges of her field of vision.

Only one face stood out at her. Nancy's, still looking a little tense, and oddly watchful, as though expecting Ashleigh to turn tail and run at any moment.

And then the men came into view . . .

First came James, looking tall and darkly handsome in a black tuxedo, his thick, wavy hair slicked back neatly from his well-shaped head. And next to him was . . .

Ashleigh faltered for a moment.

For the best man *wasn't* Peter Reynolds, the new accountant at Hargraves Pty Ltd and James's friend since college, but a perfect stranger!

Her father must have noticed at the same time. 'Who the hell's that standing next to James?' he muttered under his breath to her.

'I have no idea . . .' The man was about thirty with rather messy blond hair, an interesting face and intelligent dark eyes. After a long second look Ashleigh knew she'd never seen him before in her life.

Her eyes skated down to the other groomsman. Stuart, her brother. He smiled back reassuringly, after which she swung her gaze back to James. Their eyes

locked and for one crashing second Ashleigh literally
did go weak at the knees. For James was looking at
her as if she were a vision, an apparition that he could
scarcely believe was real, as if he couldn't tear his eyes
away from her.

All thought of mysterious best men fled, her breath
catching at the undeniable love and passion encompassed within James's intense stare. He'd never looked
at her like that before, even when he'd said she was
the only woman he'd ever loved, the only woman he
could bear marrying. His stunningly smouldering gaze
touched her heart, moved her soul. *And* her body.

Ashleigh was startled to find that suddenly the night
ahead did not present itself as such an ordeal after
all. Her eyes moved slowly over her husband-to-be
and her heart began to race, her stomach tightening,
a flood of sensual heat sweeping all over her skin.

The raw sexuality of her response shocked her. She
hadn't felt such arousal since...since...

Quite involuntarily one trembling hand left her
bouquet to once again touch the locket.

James's deeply set blue eyes zeroed in on the
movement—and the locket—and her hand retreated
with guilty speed. Surely he didn't know anything
about the locket, did he? Surely Nancy hadn't told
him about it, and the letter from Jake?

James was frowning now, all desire gone from his
gaze.

'Keep moving, Ashleigh,' her father ordered in an
impatient whisper.

Haltingly she took the remaining few steps that drew
her level with the still frowning James. For a second
she didn't know what to do, where to look, but as she
gazed up into James's face she was distracted from

her emotional confusion by the dark circles under his eyes. She peered at him intently through her veil, and saw how tired and strained he looked, as though he hadn't had much sleep the night before.

A possible solution to the mystery of the missing best man catapulted into her mind. Peter had taken James out on a stag night last night, *against* everyone's advice. Maybe they'd really tied one on and something had happened to Peter in the process. A severe hangover, perhaps?

James reached out his left hand towards Ashleigh. Still rattled, she almost took it without first handing her bouquet over to Kate. Turning to do so, she caught a glimpse of Kate and the others, staring and frowning, first at the strange best man, then at her. Ashleigh shrugged, handed the bouquet to Kate then turned back to place her hand in James's. When his right hand moved to cover it she looked down and almost died, her mouth falling open as she stared down at the bruised knuckles, the badly grazed skin.

Her eyes flew to his. 'James,' she husked. 'What happened to your hand? What——?'

'Ssssh,' he hushed. 'Afterwards... The celebrant's ready to start.' And he urged her up on to the wide step, where they would be in full view of the guests.

'We are gathered here today to celebrate the marriage of...'

Ashleigh found it hard to concentrate on the ceremony, her head whirling with questions. The image of James in a physical fight was so out of character that she couldn't even think of what possible reason there could be for it. And whom had he been fighting with, anyway? Surely not Peter?

Peter was even less physically inclined than James, being older and much slighter in build, as well as a connoisseur of the finer things in life. Art... the theatre...fine wines... Ashleigh often wondered what he was doing in a small timber town like Glenbrook. He didn't appear to like the place any more than he liked *her*.

Not that he ever said as much openly. But she had seen the coldness in his eyes when he looked her way, and he rarely let an opportunity go by to slip in a mildly sarcastic comment about women in general, even though Ashleigh knew they were really directed at one woman in particular. Namely herself.

In fact, Peter Reynolds was the one dark cloud on the horizon of her future with James, one made all the darker because she hadn't been quite able to pin down the reason for his antagonism towards her. Usually she got on well with men on a social level. Better than with women, who seemed threatened by her being a doctor.

Except for Kate, of course, Ashleigh thought warmly. Kate was never threatened by anything.

'Till death us do part.'

'A tight squeeze on her fingers snapped Ashleigh back to the present.

'I... I do,' she said shakily, and flashed James an equally shaky smile.

He didn't smile back.

Ashleigh stared. At his grim mouth; his hooded eyes; his clenched jaw.

It was at that moment she realised something was dreadfully wrong. James had not been involved in some silly male spat with Peter after drinking too

much. It was something much more serious than that.
Not only serious. But somehow dangerous.

    To her . . .

CHAPTER THREE

PANIC clutched at Ashleigh's insides, making her heart-rate triple and her thoughts whirl.

But not for long. Ashleigh was a logical thinker and she quickly calmed down, accepting that she was being ridiculous and fanciful. The events of the day so far had clearly unnerved her.

James would *never* do anything to hurt her, or cause her to be in any danger. She was mad to even think so. He was too kind, too caring, too gentle. As for his having been in a physical brawl with Peter... The very idea was ludicrous! There had to be some other reason for his damaged hand. Certainly something *had* happened to Peter, but probably no more than the hangover she'd first envisaged. Meanwhile she refused to let her imagination run away with her.

Lifting her chin slightly, she turned her eyes to the front. But, despite all her inner lectures, an uneasy churning remained in her stomach.

A long shuddering breath of self-exasperation trickled from her lungs, which brought a sharp glance from the groom, *and* the celebrant, who was about to start James's vow.

She let her eyes drop away from both of them, staring uncomfortably at the floor while the celebrant's deep male voice rolled on.

'Do you, John James Hargraves, take...?'

Ashleigh's eyes jerked up, her lips parting in protest. For John James was what *Jake* had been christened, the exact reverse of James's names.

But as the celebrant continued, loud and clear, she reconciled herself to the mistake and shut her mouth again. Why make a fuss? These things happened all the time at weddings. Nevertheless, she hoped James didn't mind the mix-up.

Apparently not, for his 'I do' at the end was strong, even if there was a decided raspiness in his voice.

The doctor in Ashleigh automatically diagnosed that he was getting a cold—the result, no doubt, of a heavy night out and whatever else James had been up to last night.

Truly, she thought somewhat irritably, never being at her sympathetic best when it came to male drinking bouts, let alone indulging in one the night before getting married.

Ashleigh was mulling over this uncharacteristic lack of consideration in her husband-to-be when James reached out and abruptly took her left hand, almost crushing her fingers within his as he drew it across her towards him. Her eyes flew up in startled alarm, meeting his steely blue gaze with a definite contraction in her chest.

This was a side of James she had certainly never seen before—a tougher, harder, much more macho side. It came to her astonished self that perhaps he was more like Jake than she'd realised.

And why wouldn't he be? inserted the voice of ruthless reason. They were identical twins, weren't they? They had probably started out with identical natures, till the stronger of the two personalities stamped his presence more loudly, forcing the other to adopt a more passive, compromising role. Maybe, once Jake had gone from the Hargraveses' household, James had been able to crawl out from under the shell his brother's dominance had forced around him, even though the gentle, less assertive manner he'd adopted over the years had by then become a habit.

Today, however, the pressure of the wedding and the mishap over Peter was probably bringing his basic male aggression to the fore.

To be frank, Ashleigh wasn't sure if she liked this more masterful James or not. Perhaps she didn't want to be faced with the prospect of his becoming more and more like Jake. Perhaps she was more comfortable with their remaining totally different.

'The ring?' the celebrant asked of the best man.

The stranger with the fair hair and dark eyes extracted the ring from his pocket and handed it over. Only the one ring. James had resisted Ashleigh's attempts to make him wear one, saying he didn't like to wear jewellery of any kind. Which was quite true.

Lifting her hand, he began sliding the wide gold band on to her ring finger, saying the traditional words as he did so. 'With my body I thee worship...'

Ashleigh's heart caught at the fierce emotion James was putting into his vow. Unless, of course, it was the oncoming cold bringing that huskily thickened quality to his voice.

Her eyes lifted to his and she knew instantly that that was not so. The earlier steel had melted to a swirling blue sea of desire, drawing her gaze into its eddying depths, seducing her with the silent promise of a passion she had never dreamt James capable of. But it was there in the eyes holding hers, in the hand wrapped securely around her fingers, in the chemical electricity which was surging from his hand to hers.

'And with all my worldly goods I thee endow,' he concluded, his eyes dropping to caress first her softly parted lips, and then her lush cleavage.

Ashleigh was shocked, a shaming heat stealing into her cheeks. Surely this was not the right moment for open seduction?

Flustered, she yanked her hand away from James's disturbing touch, not daring to look at him in the process. Instead, she concentrated her regard on the celebrant, who cleared his throat and announced pompously, 'I pronounce that they be Man and Wife together.' Beaming widely at them both, he added, 'And now, Mr Hargraves, you may kiss your lovely bride.'

Oh, God, Ashleigh thought with a flip-over of both her stomach and heart. Instant nerves had her holding her breath as James turned her to face him before slowly lifting the thin layer of netting back over her head. Quite deliberately she didn't look up into his eyes, focusing her attention on his chin. But slowly and inexorably her eyes were drawn upwards till they were right on his mouth. She watched, heart pounding, as those well-shaped lips opened slightly.

And then he was bending his head.

Ashleigh froze till contact was made, suppressing a gasp of dismay to find that his lips were oddly cold and lifeless on hers. Somehow, after his smouldering scrutiny, she'd been expecting—no, *hoping*—for more. A possessive, hungry kiss. An explosion of passion. A sample of what was to come.

But when James's mouth lifted from hers she was left feeling desolate, a jagged sigh of disappointment wafting from her lungs.

The sigh brought another incisive glance from her brand-new husband. This time Ashleigh wasn't quick enough to avoid returning his look.

There was no longer any promise of seduction in his silent stare, only an unreadable implacability that sent a deep shiver reverberating through her. For, though the expression in his eyes seemed impassive on the surface, there was a razor's edge lurking within those cool blue depths. One got the impression of suppressed violence, of wild forces, barely tamed behind a civilised façade.

Ashleigh had a vivid mental picture of James to-night, ripping her clothes from her then taking her with a savagery bordering on rape. She sucked in a startled breath, her glossed lips gasping apart, her breasts rising and falling in a bemused agitation, caused as much by her own reaction to such a vision as the vision itself.

Was she appalled, or aroused?

If the latter, how could that be? She had never been a woman to indulge in rape fantasies. She had consistently shrunk from sexually aggressive men over the years. They reminded her too forcibly of Jake, who, though never violent, had exploited her own sexual vulnerability towards him with a frightening ruthlessness.

Would James turn out to be of the same ilk?

Her agitation was just about to rocket into fully fledged panic when the dangerous light disappeared from his gaze and he was turning away from her to accept his best man's congratulations, leaving Ashleigh wondering if she was imagining things again.

Of course you are, her high degree of common sense argued, seemingly for the umpteenth time that day. James is a gentleman. A *gentle* man. Now you stop this nonsense this very second!

But it still crossed Ashleigh's mind as the celebrant led the wedding party up on to the dais for the signing of the marriage certificate that not once, so far this afternoon, had James smiled at her.

Now that wasn't like him at all!

While the adolescent James had been a shy, sensitive lad who didn't make friends all that easily, especially with girls, maturity had developed in him a more relaxed, easygoing personality which was quietly successful with women. In fact, there wasn't an attractive girl in Glenbrook who hadn't at some stage been dated by the very eligible and handsome James Hargraves.

He had, however, gained a reputation for being a bit fickle, never staying with one girl for too long. It had also been rumoured that he had a mistress stashed away somewhere, accounting for his many weekends spent away from the town, probably in Brisbane or the Gold Coast. Though Glenbrook was in New South Wales, it wasn't far across the Queensland border, and only a couple of hours' drive to that state's capital and the nearby tourist Mecca of Surfer's Paradise.

But the weekends away had lessened with the added responsibility that fell on James's shoulders after his father's death, and Ashleigh hadn't given James's supposed mistress—or his sex-life—a single worrying thought.

Till now...

Could he still be seeing this woman occasionally? Was that why he had almost meekly accepted her wish not to make love before their marriage?

Unsettling doubts besieged her, but she quickly brushed them aside. Any reason James had for seeing another woman would no longer be valid after tonight. She would make sure of that! Meanwhile, she *did* need to have explained some of the things that had bothered her this afternoon. Peter's absence and James's hand, as well as his swinging moods.

'James,' she whispered as they sat down side by side at the special signing table. 'You must tell me what's going on.'

'Regarding what?' he said slowly, turning an annoyingly bland face her way.

'What happened to Peter, for one thing?' she went on agitatedly.

Now James smiled, a sardonic grimace that did nothing to ease Ashleigh's peace of mind. 'You might say Mr Reynolds and I didn't see eye to eye on a particular subject,' he muttered.

'You mean me, don't you?'

He nodded. 'I found it necessary to impress on him quite forcibly that it would be in his best interests to leave Glenbrook forthwith.'

Ashleigh's mouth fell open. 'Then you did . . . hit him?'

James's smile showed great satisfaction. 'Several times.'

'Oh, my goodness . . . Oh, James . . . I'm so sorry.'

'Don't be. I enjoyed it.'

'You . . . *enjoyed* it?'

James must have seen her shock, for his hand moved swiftly to cover hers, his eyes holding hers with the first real warmth and affection he'd bestowed on her since she'd arrived today. 'Forget Peter. He's not worth thinking about.'

She jumped when Kate touched her on the shoulder. 'You're supposed to be signing,' her friend said with a teasing laugh, 'not having an intimate little tête-à-tête. Keep that for later.'

James flashed Kate a smile that was more like his usual self, and Ashleigh let out a long-held breath.

'Whatever you say, Kate,' James agreed. 'Has Rhys explained about Peter's sudden attack of appendicitis?'

Ashleigh only just managed to stifle her astonished gasp at this cool delivery of the obviously pre-arranged excuse. Goodness, but James was constantly surprising her today. Who would have thought so many faces were hiding behind his usually bland façade?

'Yes. It was a real shame, wasn't it?' Kate returned with blithe indifference. Peter Reynolds was not one of her favourite people, either. 'You were lucky to have someone else to step in at the last minute who could fit into Peter's clothes.'

'You're so right. Well, let's get on with this.' And, picking up the pen, he started to sign.

Ashleigh stared down over his shoulder with a peculiar feeling of tension invading her chest. When she saw the words 'James John Hargraves' form in James's usual conservative hand an unmistakable wave of relief flowed through her, bringing a measure of exasperation. For heaven's sakes! What had she been expecting?

'Smile, Mrs Hargraves,' Nancy's hired photographer said, crouching down in front of the desk and snapping away. 'Now one while you're signing . . .'

Finally she was finished, and settled back in her chair to watch both Kate and this Rhys person sign, happy for her heartbeat to get back to normal.

It was impossible to mind Peter's not being one of their witnesses, as she was only then realising how much she'd despised the man. Still, she couldn't imagine what he'd said or done to turn James against him so vehemently. They'd been such close friends for so long. But, whatever it was, she sure as heck hoped James had smacked him one right on his supercilious moosh.

Yes, now that she'd had time to mull it over, she wasn't at all upset by this turn of events.

The substitute witness finished signing, startling her with a surprisingly warm smile as he turned to step away from the desk. She got the oddest feeling he knew a darned sight more about her than she did about him. When the celebrant also stepped up to put his name to the official documentation of her marriage Ashleigh glanced down at the best man's signature. Rhys Stevenson . . .

A jab of recognition tickled her brain. The name was familiar. But why? She glanced over her shoulder to where he was standing, talking very amiably to Kate. No, she didn't recognise him at all, yet the name still rang a vague bell.

'I'm sorry I have to dash away,' the celebrant was saying, a widely apologetic smile on his face. 'But I have another engagement this evening and you were— er—a little late getting here. My hearty congratulations, and I hope everything turns out very well. Might

I say you both did splendidly? No one would have guessed that——'

'All finished here?' Rhys interrupted, leaving Ashleigh wondering what it was no one would have guessed. 'You have to go now, don't you, Mr Johnson?' he directed at the celebrant. 'You did a great job. A really great job.' He pumped the man's hand then pressed an envelope into it, which no doubt contained the prearranged fee. A big one, judging by Mr Johnson's huge grin as he departed.

A triumphant wedding march suddenly burst forth from the nearby speakers.

'Shall we go, darling?' James said, getting to his feet. Smiling, he picked her bouquet up from where it was lying on the table and handed it towards her.

Ashleigh took it with a trembling hand, his calling her darling leaving her unexpectedly breathless. It was not an endearment James had ever used with her before, but, goodness, the word had sent a ripple of sexual response quivering down her spine.

And what's wrong with that? came the voice of logic. He's your husband now. And, after tonight, your lover...

With a little shiver she hooked her arm through his offered elbow and allowed herself to be propelled down the dais steps and along the red strip of carpet to the clapping and congratulations of the guests.

Ashleigh would have liked to dive straight into the waiting Fairlane, but she was obliged to go through the motions of posing for photographs in various locations around the park, all the while hotly aware of her new husband beside her, of his hand taking her hand, of his arms encircling her waist, his eyes on hers every now and then.

Yet every time she felt her pulse-rate leap it was accompanied by the most peculiar stab of dismay. For with this new and unexpected desire for James she was irrevocably and finally abandoning what she'd once felt for Jake. For how could she pretend to herself that she still treasured her teenage love while she yearned for his brother's body?

She couldn't, she finally accepted. This would be the end of Jake. The real end. Once she physically surrendered herself to James, there would be no going back, even in her mind.

The thought depressed, then confused her. But then...a lot of things had confused her today. Maybe that was the prerogative of nervous brides.

But she gave voice to one of her minor confusions as soon as they were semi-alone in the back of the hire-car and on the way to James's house for the reception. 'Who is this man Rhys Stevenson? I have the strangest feeling I should know him.'

'He's an up-and-coming Australian film director. You've probably seen his name on the screen, or on television, and absorbed it subconsciously.'

'But how did you meet him and what was he doing at our wedding?' she persisted, not entirely satisfied. 'Don't tell me he was invited, because I saw the list of guests and he wasn't on it.'

'I asked him personally, only a couple of days ago. Lucky I did, as it turned out,' he finished drily.

'Well, yes, but——'

'Are you going to talk about Rhys all the way to the house?' James interrupted, startling her by disposing of her bouquet on to the floor then sliding an arm around her waist and pulling her close. 'I'd much rather tell you that you're the most stunningly beautiful woman God ever put breath into,' he rasped, 'and then do this.'

There was nothing cold and lifeless about his kiss this time. Far from it . . .

Ashleigh found it difficult, however, to forget the chauffeur behind the wheel, who was possibly watching then in the rear-view mirror. She squirmed under the hot possession of her husband's mouth and hands, an embarrassed heat flushing her cheeks.

Squirming, however, was not the best activity for a woman in the close embrace of a man she'd been becoming more sexually aware of all day. Her chest rubbed against his dinner-suit jacket, a button scraping harshly over one already hardening nipple.

Her lips fell open in a silent gasp, and immediately James's probing tongue found its mark, filling her mouth with a hungry thrust that sent the blood whirling in her head. Dazed, she clung to the lapels of his dinner-jacket, and all thoughts of chauffeurs vanished. There was only that ravenous mouth crushed to hers, and its insatiable tongue, feeding on the sweetness it found behind her own panting lips.

When James finally abandoned her mouth it was to kiss her neck, to mutter unintelligible words against her flushing skin. Ashleigh's head tipped back in a raw response, her whole body drowning in a flood of warmth and heat. The drum-beat of desire began pounding in her heart, and her head, making her oblivious to her surroundings, making her a willing victim to her husband's passion. Already James's mouth was back on hers, taking her down deeper and deeper into maelstrom of need and yearning.

'Damn it,' he rasped when the car turned the corner that led up the hill to his home. 'We won't be staying at this reception late,' he growled. 'I've already waited too long for this night. Far too long.'

Ashleigh shivered at the darkly intense resolve in James's voice and face. But it was a shiver of excitement, not fear. She wanted him as much as, if not more than, she'd ever wanted Jake. Such a realisation ripped through all her preconceived ideas on what she felt for the two brothers. Before it had been love and desire for one. Liking and respect for the other. Now Ashleigh was forced to accept this wasn't so any longer. She had *never* felt this kind of desire before without love. That was why no man had ever reached her since Jake, simply because she'd never loved any of them.

She lifted a trembling hand to James's face and held it there, tears swimming in her eyes. 'I love you, James,' she whispered. 'I really, really love you.'

His head jerked back and he stared at her. For a second Ashleigh was taken aback, unsure if the frozen mask on his face meant he was appalled, or merely deeply sceptical. With a sigh of understanding she realised it had to be the latter.

'I know I said I didn't love you when I agreed to marry you,' she rushed on in a low whisper as the car pulled into the long driveway that led up to the Hargraveses' house. 'To be brutally honest, I thought that, underneath, I was still in love with Jake.'

She felt the muscles in his jaw flinch, though his eyes didn't waver.

'There's been no one else, you see, and I always believed...' Her hand trembled against his skin. 'But, when you kissed me just now and I responded the way I did, I knew it had to be true love.'

There was no doubting the relief that zoomed into those blue eyes, or the emotion behind the husky, 'I knew it. I *knew* it!'

And he kissed her again, deeply and hungrily.

He only released her when the car pulled up at the house. 'Just as well,' she murmured with an embarrassed laugh. 'If we keep this up I'll get your cold.'

'My...cold?' His puzzlement was only momentary. 'Oh, you mean my raspy voice. Don't concern yourself, my darling. It's not a cold. Let's say I—er—did a fair bit of shouting last night and it affected my vocal chords. Now, take that frown off your lovely face and don't let that bastard Reynolds spoil things for us.'

Ashleigh blinked her amazement. That bastard Reynolds? Astonishing. Only last week James had been telling her what a wonderful friend Peter had always been and how grateful he had been for his help with the financial side of the company since his father's death.

She might have liked to take the discussion further—such as exactly what Peter had said to cause the blow-up between them—but the chauffeur's opening the back door for her to get out put paid to that. Putting her hand in the chauffeur's, and a blush of lingering embarrassment on her face, she alighted at the base of the wide steps, glancing up at the house where she would have to live for a while till she and James found something suitable around Glenbrook in which to set up their own home. Perhaps something with enough room for her to have a small attached practice, she thought, since Nancy would hardly let her turn any of the Hargraveses' home into a surgery.

Two-storeyed and in a Cape Cod design, the house had a setting suited to the family's status in Glenbrook, grandly overlooking the town from the crest of a hill. Tall English trees stood in elegant clumps of shade over the surrounding lawns, upon which a large marquee had been erected for the reception.

The guests had not yet arrived, but soon the nearby area would be full of parked cars. Even the photographer hadn't made it yet, having stayed behind to snap some more pictures of the bridesmaids and guests.

All of a sudden Ashleigh recalled what James had said to her in the car, about how they would leave the reception early. She turned to watch him stride around the white Fairlane to join her, a splendid male figure in his tuxedo, his well-tailored clothes highlighting his wide-shouldered, lean-hipped frame.

He caught her staring at him, and an amazingly confident smile caressed his mouth. It jolted her. For there had only ever been one male who'd been so sexually sure of himself with her. Only one...

'Jake,' she whispered on a breathless note, and her fingers fluttered up to the locket.

But the man beside her wasn't Jake. It was his brother, his brother who had finally taken Jake's place in every possible way...

James had stiffened at her uttering his brother's name. He stared down at her, then at the locket, the muscles twitching in his strong jaw. Ashleigh stopped breathing, certain now that he suspected the locket had something to do with Jake. Which was why he had stared at it earlier on.

She opened her mouth to try to explain why she'd chosen to wear the thing today, but he cut her off.

'Do not speak that name again,' he rasped, 'or I won't be responsible for what happens.'

He drew in then expelled a ragged breath.

'Now,' he went on sternly, 'go inside and replace your lipstick. The others will be here soon and it wouldn't do for everyone to think I'd been ravaging you already. My mother, particularly, might find that thought...unnerving. She isn't quite herself today, as I'm sure you've already realised.'

It was at that precise moment that Ashleigh realised James knew not only about the locket, but Jake's letter as well.

CHAPTER FOUR

'You know, don't you?' Ashleigh confronted James. 'About Jake's writing to your mother, about his sending me back this locket?'

James's blue eyes grew watchful beneath a dark frown. 'I am acquainted with my mother's visit to you before the wedding,' he admitted slowly.

'Good God!' Ashleigh gasped. 'Why did she have to tell you? What point was there?' She shook her head in agitation. 'I suppose you think I wore this damned thing because I was still pining for Jake. I wasn't. I wore it in defiance of his rotten arrogance and lack of tact in wanting me to have it on the very day I was marrying his brother!'

'I see,' James said somewhat drily. 'To be honest, I would not have thought of that reason.'

'It's the truth.'

'I don't doubt you.'

'You did believe me when I said I loved you, didn't you, James?'

There was no mistaking the flash of painful irony in his eyes. 'I think you might be a touch confused, my dear, in these unusual circumstances. But I'm a patient man. I know I can win your love, even if it takes me the rest of my life.'

Ashleigh was distressed at the bleak intensity behind his words.

'Leave me now, Ashleigh,' he went on brusquely. 'There are cars coming up the hill. I'll stay out here and greet the guests and organise things for the photographs while you fix your face. Someone will be up shortly to collect you.'

Ashleigh didn't want to leave him. She wanted to go on explaining, reassuring. Oh, how she'd hated seeing the hurt in his face, hated feeling the withdrawal in his manner towards her. But she could hardly stand there arguing with him in front of other people, especially with smudged make-up. Reluctantly she turned and made her way up the front steps and in through the open double doors, holding her skirt up as she made her way slowly up to the bedrooms Nancy had set aside for her as a changing-room.

The door was already open and Ashleigh walked in, her mind still on James and the unhappy thought that he didn't believe she really loved him. But she did. She was sure of it! How could she convince him?

Tonight, she decided breathlessly. Tonight she would leave him in no doubt that she both loved and wanted him as she had wanted no other man, not even Jake.

Damn Jake, she thought angrily. Damn him to hell!

With an abrupt movement her hand swept up under her veil and behind her neck, where she fumbled to unclasp the now hated locket. It stubbornly refused to yield, and in the end she reefed it from her neck with a savage yank, the locket spilling on to the parquet floor and sliding under the double bed.

And that was where she left it, tossing the silver chain on to a chest of drawers.

'Something borrowed,' she scorned out loud. 'Something *buried* would be more like it!'

Ashleigh counted to ten till her breathing was back to normal, then quite deliberately turned her back on the chain and gazed with satisfaction at her going-away outfit, all laid out ready for her on the double bed, complete with shoes and handbag.

It was an elegantly simple suit in emerald-green silk, which hugged her tall, shapely figure and proclaimed to the world that she was all woman. James would like it, she was sure. And in the packed suitcase of clothes already in the boot of James's Jaguar, awaiting their honeymoon, was an ivory satin négligé set that would make any man sit up and take notice, let alone the man who already loved her.

Picking up the black leather handbag, she carried it over to the corner dressing-table, where she opened it and drew out the make-up she'd put in there. First she touched up her foundation, then replenished her blusher and lipstick. She was just applying some perfume when Kate knocked on the open door and breezed in.

'There you are, Ashleigh. James sent me to get you. Hmmm, perhaps I could do with some more lipstick too. May I?'

'Be my guest.'

'The photographer wants to take a few shots in the garden,' Kate explained as she applied the deep pink shade to her wide mouth. 'He spied that clump of rhododendrons and thinks they'll make a splendid backdrop. There . . . all done . . .' She looked at herself critically in the mirror, then shrugged. 'Oh, well, we can't all be gorgeous. Come, oh, beautiful bride,' she said, and linked arms with her friend's. 'Your panting groom awaits!'

Laughing, the two friends made their way down the sweeping staircase and out into the mild autumn air, Ashleigh immediately expressing her gratitude that all the guests seemed to have disappeared into the marquee, and weren't waiting to besiege her on the front lawn.

'You have James to thank for that,' Kate informed her. 'I also heard him sneakily instructing the drink waiters to ply everyone with as much liquor as they could handle to keep them out of our way while the official photographs were being finished. By the time we make our grand entrance they'll be high as kites on sherry and a quite lethal fruit punch. I know: I sampled it.'

'I could do with a shot of something lethal myself,' Ashleigh said drily. Kate's ebullience hadn't totally distracted her from how she had left James a little earlier. Neither could she forget that in a couple of hours she would be driving off on her honeymoon with a husband who didn't really believe his bride loved him.

'I could do with sitting down as well,' she continued with a sigh. 'I didn't exactly have a chance to break in these shoes before today, and they're killing me.'

'Ditto repeato,' Kate groaned expressively.

Both girls looked at each other and laughed again.

'Just as well we didn't decide to become models, eh, Kate?'

Kate made a face. 'Well, I didn't have much option on that count, being five feet two and having a face that *didn't* launch a thousand ships.'

'You have a *great* face,' Ashleigh insisted, stopping to look at her friend. And she did, all her big, bold features combining well to present an arresting, vivacious image.

Kate beamed with pleasure at the compliment. 'You are so good for my self-esteem, do you know that?'

'Will you two giggling Gerties mind shaking a leg?' James called over from where the rest of the bridal group were waiting impatiently beside the pink rhododendrons. 'We're all dying of dehydration and hunger here.'

Ashleigh was astonished and relieved to see that James was actually smiling at her. Gone was his earlier scowl, his look of pained anguish. He was a totally different man, confident and positive in his manner. She heaved a happy sigh. Everything was going to be all right after all.

Walking quickly over, she slipped a loving arm through his, smiling up into his face. Clearly her gesture startled him, for he stared back down at her for a second before expelling an exasperated though good-natured sigh.

'Right,' the photographer announced. 'Everyone facing front and smiling.'

'Wait!' Kate shouted, making everyone jump. She rushed over and started straightening Ashleigh's veil where it had caught slightly on some beading on her shoulder. Suddenly she stopped and frowned down at Ashleigh's bare neckline. 'What happened to the locket?' she asked.

Ashleigh groaned silently. Trust Kate to notice and comment. She opened her mouth to voice an excuse, but nothing came to mind, and she was left looking like a flapping flounder.

'It broke,' James said coolly from beside her. 'In the car.'

'Oh, what a pity!'

'Not to worry, Kate,' Ashleigh inserted swiftly, having regathered her wits. 'I still have your garter, which was borrowed as well as blue.'

'A garter?' The new best man perked up. 'How quaint. Can I see it?'

'Certainly not while it's on,' James intervened firmly.

Rhys laughed. 'How possessive you are! But rightly so. Your bride is as lovely as you described to me. I fully understand you now, dear friend. Some things are worth any sacrifice.'

Flattered and flustered, Ashleigh lifted startled eyes to her husband, catching the end of a harsh glare thrown his best man's way.

'Do you think we could get on with this, folks?' the photographer sighed.

The session seemed interminable, as was having to keep on smiling. By the time it drew to an end Ashleigh's mouth was aching. She was also harbouring the beginnings of a headache.

'Something wrong, darling?' James murmured from her side when she put a hand to her temple.

'Only a very small headache,' she smiled softly, thinking that she did so like his calling her that.

'I'll get you something for it. Kate! Take Ashleigh over to that garden seat there while I rustle up some aspirin. Or do you need something stronger?' he directed back at his bride.

'Well . . . panadol is kinder to the stomach.'

His mouth curved into a wry smile. 'Of course. Doctor knows best.'

She flinched, knowing how men didn't like to be corrected, or told things by a woman. She could never tell her father or brother anything—even about medicine—without earning a reproachful glare or a sarcastic remark. 'Sorry,' she murmured.

'Don't be. I'm proud of your being a doctor. Kate? The seat, please. Be back shortly.' And, flashing them a parting smile, he strode off.

'I didn't realise James could be so masterful,' Kate remarked as she led Ashleigh in the direction of the shaded seat. 'It's very attractive on him, isn't it? I mean, being nice is all very well, but a man shouldn't be too, *too* nice. If he is people walk all over him, including his wife, and then he might lose her respect, don't you agree?'

Ashleigh did.

'Rhys is a very interesting man too,' Kate raved on. 'I could talk to him all day. The places he's been and the people he's met! Fantastic!'

'Don't tell me you've finally met a man you didn't want to put solidly in his place,' Ashleigh said, amazement in her voice.

'I can't imagine anyone putting Rhys Stevenson in his place.'

'Kate! I do believe you're smitten.'

'Not at all. Just jealous.'

'Of what?'

'Of his lifestyle.'

'Well, we can't all be movie directors!'

'Why not, if that's what we'd like to be?' she said quite aggressively.

Ashleigh stopped and stared at her friend.

'Now don't go giving me one of those looks of yours,' Kate huffed.

'What looks?'

'Oh, your "one must keep one's feet firmly on the ground" looks. Life is meant to be lived, Ashleigh.

And I'm not so sure I want to live the rest of mine in good old Glenbrook! Oh, forget it,' she grumbled. 'You wouldn't understand. Not only do you have a rewarding career, but you've just married a great bloke whom it's quite clear you're mad about—and who's mad about you—so what would you know about frustration?'

Suddenly she smiled, a sort of brave, sad smile that caught at Ashleigh's heart. She hadn't realised her dear friend was so unhappy. One would never have guessed. She so wished there was something she could do.

'Just listen to me,' Kate laughed, but it had a brittle edge to it. 'As if this is the right moment to be pouring out all my worries and woes. Now come along and sit down before I get into trouble for not doing as his lord and master commanded. Heavens, if I didn't know different I might have thought it was Jake telling me what to do. Remember how he used to boss us around at school?'

'Yes, Kate,' Ashleigh said stiffly. 'I haven't forgotten. But I'm *trying* to.'

'Oh...oh, sorry, love. God, me and my big mouth. Is your headache very bad? I guess I haven't made it any better by my whingeing then bringing up ancient history. Truly, Ashleigh, I'm a real clot. Forgive me?'

Ashleigh patted her friend's hand. 'Of course, but I would rather you not talk about Jake, especially in front of James. It's rather a sore point between us, I'm afraid.'

'I won't, believe me. The James I'm seeing today might just bite my head off. Aah...here he is now...'

'Nurse Hargraves to the rescue,' he said mockingly, and pressed the glass of iced water he was carrying into her free hand. 'Now...give me that infernal bouquet and hold out your other hand,' he commanded.

She did, and he dropped two white tablets into her palm.

'Swallow them up straight away. I know you medical people. Great at dosing others but rotten at taking things yourself. Gone? Good. Look, I'm sorry, but we'll have to make an appearance in the marquee. Mother is making unhappy noises.'

Ashleigh was surprised to find she quite enjoyed the feeling of being cosseted, not having had that experience since her mother died. Leaving the empty glass behind on the garden seat, she allowed James to walk herself and Kate over to the marquee, a lovely, warm sensation spreading in the pit of her stomach at having his solicitous arm around her waist.

If this was what being married to James was going to be like then she was all for it. Being married to *her* seemed to be good for him too. As Kate had rightly observed, James wasn't usually so quick to take control of situations, to taking the role of leader. Yes, he certainly was coming out from under the shadow of his brother and being his own man. And suddenly Ashleigh no longer minded.

'Oh-oh,' James whispered in her ear. 'Brace yourself. Here come the aunts and uncles and various assorted cousins to tell you how beautiful you are and how lucky I am. You'll have to kiss the men too. Convention, you know. And we must uphold all the social conventions,' he added quite testily. 'Mother would have a seizure if we didn't!'

It wasn't till they'd finally taken their adjoining seats at the main bridal table under the huge tent that a puzzling thought struck Ashleigh. James never called his mother 'Mother'. He always called her Nancy. Neither was he in the habit of using that caustic, almost cutting tone when speaking about her foibles.

A deep frown settled on to her high, wide forehead as she tried to fathom out why she was so bothered by that, since the reason for it was clear enough. Mother and son had clearly had an argument that morning about Jake's letter—hence Nancy's agitation and tears—and James was taking his anger out on her by being disdainful and aloof.

Yet it *did* bother her. Quite considerably. Perhaps because she wanted her wedding-day to be a really happy occasion.

'James,' she whispered, and he leant her way, pressing his whole side against hers.

A shivery charge zoomed through her body. 'Please don't be cross with your mother,' she said thickly.

The muscles along his arm stiffened. 'What makes you think I'm cross with her?'

'You don't usually call her "Mother" like that, for one thing. And you were...well, you were sarcastic when talking about her. That's not like you.'

'I see,' he murmured thoughtfully. 'And what would you like me to do about it?'

'Go and talk to her and make up. She looks so unhappy.' Which the woman did, not a smile having passing Nancy's thinnish lips all day.

'Mmmm...well, we can't have that, can we?' he muttered in a voice that didn't sound as conciliatory as Ashleigh might have hoped.

He got to his feet and strode off in the direction of his mother, leaving Ashleigh feeling oddly perturbed.

'God, it *is* good to be sitting down,' Kate pronounced from her right-hand side. 'Where's James off to?'

'Has to see his mother about something,' came her suitably vague answer.

'I have to give Mrs Hargraves credit where credit it due,' Kate said. 'This is all top-drawer stuff. Genuine lace tablecloths, real silver cutlery, candelabras, the finest crystal glasses. We might be out under a circus tent—if you can recognise canvas through the decorations—but it could well be a king's banquet table, judging by the accoutrements.'

Ashleigh agreed that Nancy had pulled out all stops in making sure that her son's wedding had no equal in the history of Glenbrook. Right at this moment two hundred happy, suitably intoxicated guests were busy finding their silver-embossed place-names at one of the twenty lace-covered tables, while a small orchestra played subtle wedding music and silver, white and burgundy streamers and balloons fluttered over their heads. A four-tier wedding cake stood proudly on its own table to one side, patiently awaiting its part in the celebration that was about to start. The caterers were hovering, clearly wanting to serve the first course of the meal.

Ashleigh was still glancing around when her eyes landed on James talking to his mother in a far corner. They were too far away for her to see the expressions in their eyes, but their body language reeked of a barely controlled anger, Nancy making sharp movements with her head and hands while she spoke. James's fists were balled at his side, his broad shoulders held stiffly while he stood silently and listened. Suddenly James launched into speech, and

Nancy's head rocked back, as though his words were like a physical blow. She stared back at him while he raved on, her face frozen.

At last he finished speaking and they simply stood there, eyeing each other, both still obviously livid, each one seemingly waiting for the other to break first.

It wasn't James.

Quite abruptly Nancy leant forward and kissed her son on the cheek, after which she plastered a smile on her face and went about her hostess duties with the sort of serenely smiling look on her face one might have expected from Nancy, but which had been absent all afternoon.

The whole incident rattled Ashleigh, especially with James making his way swiftly across the room towards her with a black look still on his face. What on earth was going on with those two? She could understand that initially James wasn't pleased with his mother's having taken a returned gift from his brother to his bride on her wedding-day, especially when that same bride had once been besotted with that brother.

But surely, with her having discarded the locket, James could see that Jake was not going to be a threat to their relationship? Why couldn't he forgive and forget? But no, she thought irritably, he was a typical male, whose anger was not allowed to be so quickly discarded.

Ashleigh was initially astonished when, just as suddenly as his mother, James appeared to pull himself together and adopt a more pleasant expression. Yet as he drew closer there was no mistaking the hard glint remaining in his eyes, or the tension in his stiffly held arms and shoulders. Though, once he became aware of Ashleigh's reproachful eyes upon him, he shrugged and smiled.

'I'm afraid she's still not pleased with me,' he confessed on sitting down beside her, 'but she's agreed to play her part a bit more convincingly.'

'Play her part?' Ashleigh repeated, frowning. 'Isn't that an odd way of putting it? Your mother *loves* you, James. She wouldn't want there to be bad feeling between you. She——'

'For God's sake, don't start worrying about *her*,' he suddenly snapped. 'She'll survive.'

Ashleigh fell silent, truly shocked by his manner.

'Hell,' he muttered. 'This is even harder than I thought it'd be.'

Ashleigh stared at him. 'What...what do you mean?' she asked, totally perplexed.

He turned to lock eyes with her, his gaze penetrating and deep. 'Do you trust me, Ashleigh?' he rasped, his voice low and husky.

A dark, quivery sensation fluttered in her stomach.

'Of...of course...'

'Then don't give my mother's attitude a second thought. Take no notice of anything she says or does. Believe me when I say she isn't concerned for *your* happiness. *Or* mine. That's all you have to remember.'

'But...but...that doesn't make any sense.' Which it didn't. Nancy *adored* James. He'd always been the apple of her eye.

'I know. That's why I asked for your trust. Do I have it?' he demanded to know.

'I...'

'Do I have it?' he repeated in an urgent tone.

Ashleigh's heart started to pound and she knew that, with her answer, her fate would be sealed, irrevocably. Her mind flew to what she'd told Kate earlier that day, about not believing in destiny or one's fate being outside a person's own control. She still believed that. Her husband, in asking her for blind trust, was really testing her love for him, as well as her faith in the person he was.

There was really only one answer she could give.

'Yes,' she said firmly.

'Then just do as I ask,' came James's harsh answer.

Ashleigh was to remember later that night that she had deliberately chosen to place her future in this man's hands. So she had nobody else to blame but herself.

CHAPTER FIVE

'FANCY Kate catching my bouquet,' Ashleigh laughed as James drove down the hill away from the Hargraves home. 'You know what else? I think she and your friend, Rhys, really hit it off. They were chatting away together all evening.'

'I wouldn't be getting my hopes up about Kate and Rhys if I were you,' James returned drily. 'He's an incorrigible chatter-upper of women.'

'Oh?' Ashleigh frowned, a tinge of worry in her voice.

'And I wouldn't worry about your Kate either. If ever there was a female who can take care of herself it's that one!'

'I suppose so...'

'You don't sound convinced.'

'Kate's rather vulnerable at the moment.'

'Aren't we all?' he muttered. 'Aren't we all?'

A strained silence fell between them at this darkly cryptic remark, with James putting his foot down more solidly. The powerful car hurtled into the night, eating up the miles between Glenbrook and their destination.

Ashleigh found herself with time to ponder the not so subtle difference in James today. He was far moodier than his usual easygoing self, far more up-tight. Originally she'd put it down to wedding-day jitters, plus irritation at Jake's last-minute correspondence, not to mention his doubts over his bride's really loving him or not.

But now that the reception was over and they were off on their honeymoon Ashleigh began to wonder if there was a far more basic reason. Perhaps he was worried about tonight, about how sex between them would turn out. Was he concerned, perhaps, that she would compare his lovemaking with Jake's? And, more to the point . . . would *she*?

She honestly didn't know. All day her sexual response to James had surprised and pleased her. But it was one thing to feel a few heart flutters, quite another to experience the sort of abandon during total intimacy that she had experienced with Jake.

Not that it would overly concern *her* if they didn't achieve sexual perfection straight away. Ashleigh was a realist. She knew these things could take time. They had, even with Jake! But she had the awful feeling James would be cut to the quick if he didn't satisfy her tonight, if he thought for a moment he had failed her in bed.

Thinking about his possible disappointment and unhappiness began twisting her insides into knots. Before she could stop it a quavering sigh escaped her lips.

Hard blue eyes snapped her way. 'What's that sigh supposed to mean?' he asked in a definitely suspicious tone.

'Nothing. I . . .' Suddenly she sat up straight and blinked rapidly. 'James! What . . . what are you doing?' she gasped.

What he was doing was obvious! He was turning into a motel, a rather cheap-looking highway motel into which they were definitely *not* booked. They were supposed to be on their way to a five-star luxury hotel on the Gold Coast.

'I'm afraid this won't wait, Ashleigh,' he ground out.

Ashleigh turned to stare with wide eyes at the man sitting beside her. How determined he sounded. How...*forceful.*

She swallowed, her mind filling with all those moments today when she'd glimpsed a James she had never seen before, a James simmering with unleashed passion. Clearly he couldn't bear to wait any longer to make love to her. She found his impatience to have her in his arms both flattering and arousing, her pulse-rate accelerating into overdrive, an excited heat flushing her cheeks.

'This isn't like you, James,' she laughed softly as he braked to an abrupt halt in front of the motel office.

His sidewards glance was sardonic. 'I realise that, believe me. Wait here,' he ordered brusquely, and climbed out from behind the wheel. 'I won't be long.'

She watched James stride purposefully into the office to book in, thinking to herself that he had a very attractive walk. Funny, she had never thought that about James before. But as he came back through the door, key in hand, her eyes were drawn to his very male and undeniably impressive body, lingering on the breadth of his shoulders before slowly working her way downwards. She didn't have to wonder what he would look like naked. Mother nature had assured that, as an identical twin, he would have the same well-shaped, muscular, virile body as Jake.

A quivering started deep in her stomach and she knew beyond a doubt that nothing was going to go wrong between them. It was going to be right. *Very* right. *Exquisitely* right. Suddenly she was as anxious as he was to be in bed together, to have the right to touch his hard naked flesh at will, to lie back and accept his body into hers as many times as it would take to assuage her rapidly soaring desire.

She smiled at him when he climbed in behind the wheel, her smile the smile of a siren. It stopped him in his tracks, his eyes glittering blue pools as they locked with hers. 'You shouldn't look at me like that,' he rasped.

'Why not?' she said thickly. 'You're my husband, aren't you? I love you and want you. I'm not ashamed of that.'

His groan startled her, as did his hands, reaching out to pull her towards him, his mouth covering hers with a raw moan of passion. His kiss only lasted a few seconds, but those few seconds burnt an indelible fact in Ashleigh's brain.

This was the man she loved and wanted. Not Jake. James.

They were both gasping when he tore his mouth away, both astonished at what had transpired between them. But somehow James did not seem as happy about it as Ashleigh was. Why that was so she couldn't work out.

He muttered something unintelligible, then whirled away to restart the engine and drive the car round to the motel units behind the main building, parking in front of door number eight. Getting out straight away, he walked briskly around to open the passenger door and help her out.

Ashleigh was slightly disconcerted when his eyes refused to meet hers, also at the way he once again

turned away from her quite sharply to insert the key
in the door. Pushing it open, he waved her inside.

'But what about our luggage?' she asked, staying
where she was.

He went to say something, but just then another
car made its way around the back. Shrugging, he went
over, opened the boot and brought the two suitcases
inside, Ashleigh trailing behind with a frown on her
face but a defiant resolve in her heart. As keen as she
was for James to make love to her, she was not about
to abandon her whole dream of a truly romantic
wedding-night.

'I won't be a moment,' she said, snatching up her
suitcase and disappearing into the adjoining
bathroom. As she closed the door she had a fleeing
glimpse of James, standing open-mouthed and exasperated beside the bed.

She was more than a moment. She was a good
fifteen minutes, having a shower, powdering and per-
fuming her body, taking down and brushing out her
shoulder-length blonde waves, then finally slipping on
the ivory satin full-length nightie.

'Goodness,' she murmured to herself in the *en suite*
bathroom's vanity mirror. It hadn't looked quite *this*
sexy in the lingerie shop. But then she hadn't had her
hair down that day, and neither had her breasts
strained against the moulded bodice with nipples like
hard round pebbles jutting suggestively through the
satin.

Drawing the matching lace and satin robe up her
long arms and over her slender shoulders didn't make
the underlying nightwear any less sensuous. If anything, half covering up her full-breasted figure made
the revealing garment underneath even more tanta-

lising. She was sure that, when she walked, the overlay would flap teasingly open while the satin nightie underneath would cling to her naked stomach and thighs.

Just thinking about how James would look at her in this rig-out had Ashleigh's heart slamming madly against her ribs. But she *wanted* to send him wild with need and desire, wanted him to think of nothing but fusing his body with hers, of thrusting his hardness deep inside her already moistening flesh, of giving himself up to the pleasure she could give him.

She didn't want him to think of Jake.

He was pacing up and down across the room when she emerged, having removed nothing but his jacket and tie. He ground to a halt at the sound of the door opening, his head snapping round to glare at her. But the second his eyes raked over her provocatively clad figure his expression changed, from a black frustration to a smoulderingly stirring desire.

Hot blue eyes started on her face and hair then travelled slowly downwards, Ashleigh's skin breaking out in goose-bumps when she saw his eyes narrow on her already aching breasts.

Quite abruptly his eyes snapped back up, shocking her with the anguish in their depths.

'You don't understand, Ashleigh,' he growled, shaking his head. 'The reason I stopped here… It…'

She began undulating towards him, and any further words died in his throat. As she approached she lifted trembling hands to peel the outer robe back from her swollen breasts, letting it slip off her shoulders and flutter to the floor behind her. She kept moving, breathless but confident in her femininity, knowing that with each sinuous movement of her limbs she was ensnaring him in her web of seduction, inflaming his male need to a level that would brook no more hesitation, only action.

She drew right up to him, her lips softly parted, her head tipping back slightly as she wound her arms up around his neck. 'I don't want any explanations,' she husked, her mouth so close to his that she could feel his breath on her lips. 'I just want *you*. Right here and right now...'

Her fingers splayed up into his thick black hair as she leant into him, her breasts pressing flat against the hard wall of his chest.

Once again James surprised her, standing where he was without attempting to touch her back, frozen within a dangerously explosive tension. She could feel it in the corded muscles straining in his neck, in the way his breathing was silent and still. 'You think you know what you're doing, Ashleigh,' he muttered low in his throat. 'But you don't.'

A dark shudder raced through him. 'Hell... I wish I had the strength to deny myself this. But I haven't. It's asking too damned much!'

And, with that, his arms swept up and around her, imprisoning her against him and bending her spine back till her hair spilt free from her neck and her mouth was an open, gasping cavern. His head bent to cover that cavern with hot, ravenous lips, to fill its dark, moist depths with his tongue, to stunningly imprint upon its owner that her mouth was there primarily for his possession, to be used as he willed, to be taken and abandoned only as he ordained.

Or so it seemed. For when she struggled against such an unexpected and confusing display of male mastery—her arms retreating from his neck to push

vainly at the solid wall of his chest, her head trying
to twist from side to side—one of his hands slid up
into her hair, grasping the back of her head and
holding it firmly captive. But soon she herself was
caught up in her own pleasure, giving in to his physical
domination with a throaty moan of surrender.

She shuddered when he finally left her mouth to
trail rapid kisses down her throat, dazedly aware she
should be appalled by his semi-violence, but con-
ceding she wasn't at all. Instead she thrilled to the
savage mouth that nipped and sucked at her flesh,
working its way inexorably towards her breasts and
their pointed, expectant peaks.

'James,' she groaned when she felt his hot breath
hover over one of her aching nipples.

His head jerked up and she stared at him with glazed
eyes. 'What's wrong?' she husked in bewilderment.

She could hardly think, her whole being in a world
of its own, where it was responding instinctively,
without thought, without reason.

'Nothing,' he growled.

'Then touch me,' she begged. 'Here . . .' And she
brushed a shaking hand over the throbbing tip.

'Oh, God,' he moaned aloud, and bent his mouth
to do her bidding, suckling the tender flesh right
through the nightie, drawing the whole aureole into
his mouth and rubbing the satin-covered nub over and
over with his tongue.

Never had she felt such electric pleasure, such tem-
pestuous excitement. Heat swept through her, making
her blood race, her limbs grow heavy with desire. She
closed her eyes and let the rapture spread, her lips
parting, her arms falling limply to her side.

One of his broad hands had settled in the small of her back, the other on the flat of her stomach, moving in a sensual circular motion as his mouth continued to tantalise first one breast, then the other, both bare now, the nightie having somehow been pushed off her shoulders to crumple at her waist, held up perhaps by the hand caressing her stomach.

Ashleigh became hotly conscious of that hand as it moved lower and lower... Of their own accord her legs shifted slightly apart in silent invitation for a more intimate caress. James obliged, his hand sliding between her legs, forcing the satin inwards with him, rubbing the silken material over her arousal till she moaned in utter abandonment and need.

James moved to assuage that need, peeling the nightie down over her hips to pool at her feet while he sank to his knees in front of her, licking the soft flesh of her inner thighs, gradually easing them wider and wider apart till he could move his mouth with exquisite intimacy over her.

Ashleigh caught her breath, her hands shooting up to close over his shoulders lest she fall. For those knowing lips and tongue seemed to know exactly what to do to send her mad, moving hotly over the core of her need before returning again to her most sensitive spot. When her soft moans turned to whimpering little cries he pulled her down on to the carpet with him, kissing her mouth while he freed his desire with frenzied movements.

For several excruciating seconds his head was lifted to look down at her naked arousal, his eyes glittering with satisfaction as they roved over the stark evidence of her passion. For Ashleigh was wanton in her desire for his possession, her body restless and open for him, her womanhood moist and swollen.

With an almost tortured groan he knelt between her legs, and, scooping up her buttocks, impaled her with a single powerful thrust.

Ashleigh gasped, her back arching up from the floor, her arms reaching out for him to come to her in a lover's embrace. He sank down upon her with a jagged moan, gathering her tight against him.

'Oh, my darling, my only love,' he rasped, then began surging into her with a powerful, passionate rhythm. She gasped at the speed with which she found herself on the brink, then moaned as she tumbled headlong into an ecstatic release, the fierceness of her contractions hurtling James into an equally explosive climax that left him shaking uncontrollably.

Ashleigh clasped his trembling body close to her, totally unmindful of the potent seed he'd just spilt deep inside her. She certainly wasn't thinking of how she'd deliberately chosen to have her wedding-day right at her most fertile time of the month so that she might conceive straight away. All she wanted at that moment was to keep her husband's body fused with hers, to wrap her arms and legs tight around him, to kiss his sweat-covered neck, to tell him how much she loved him.

His shirt had come loose from the waistband of his trousers during their torrid mating, and she slipped her hands up underneath with a contented sigh to rove across bare flesh. But, when her fingers encountered the strangest ridges and dips in the skin on his back, she froze. James did not have scars on *his* back. It was smooth and clear and hairless. At least, it *had* been a week ago when they had gone swimming in the pool at his home.

My God! Exactly what *had* happened last night? Had he been in some sort of accident?

'James,' she whispered, her voice shaking, her whole insides shaking. 'What have you done to your back?'

She felt him stiffen, felt his shuddering sigh.

'Nothing,' he muttered. 'It's the same back I've had for years.'

Slowly he withdrew from her, easing himself back to sit on his heels and adjust his clothes. 'You see, Leigh,' he went on, raking her pale face with bleak blue eyes, 'the fact is . . . I'm not James.'

CHAPTER SIX

ASHLEIGH came as close to fainting at that moment as she had ever done in her life. All the blood drained from her face and for a few black moments her world tilted on its axis.

But the crisis passed, and when it did her first reaction was a desperate denial.

'Don't be ridiculous! Of course you're James. I mean... what are you trying to say?' she laughed shakily, sitting up and snatching the satin nightie from the carpet near by and somehow dragging it over her nude body. 'That you're *Jake*? If this is your idea of a sick joke, James, then...'

His hands shot out to grab her upper arms, his blue eyes steely as he leant over her. 'I *am* Jake. Look at me, Leigh. Really look at me. You know the difference. You've always known the difference. You didn't today because I was where you and everyone expected *James* to be, dressed in James's clothes, my hair cut exactly like James's, acting like James.'

He made a scoffing sound. 'Well... maybe not acting *entirely* like James. Believe me, Leigh, when I say you wouldn't want me acting like him tonight.'

'Stop calling me that,' she screamed at him. 'Stop saying you're Jake. You're not! You can't be! It's impossible! Besides, I... I *hate* Jake! I...'

Her high-pitched hysterical outburst was terminated abruptly and effectively by his right hand's covering her mouth and pushing her, none too gently, flat on her back on to the carpet.

'Shut up, for God's sake, or we'll have the motel manager knocking at our door. Look, I'm sorry for how things turned out here tonight. I was going to tell you the truth earlier but, God damn it, Leigh, you've only yourself to blame. You virtually seduced me. *Me* . . . *Jake* . . . not James. For, even if you didn't recognise me on a conscious level, your body did subconsciously. It recognised me and responded to me, right from the first moment it set eyes on me in that park. Tell yourself you hate me all you like, Leigh, but deep down you know you don't!'

Once again her face paled, her eyes widening with horror as the truth refused to be denied.

Jake hadn't sent a letter home . . . He'd come in person . . .

It had been Jake looking at her with such inflammatory desire during the ceremony . . . Jake who'd evoked that mad response when he'd kissed her in the car . . . Jake who'd just made devastatingly rapturous love to her . . .

She stared up at him, appalled.

His hand lifted from her mouth and he sat back on his heels. 'I see you've finally accepted the facts.'

Confusion and anguish sent her hand careering across his face, slapping it hard. 'You bastard!' she cried brokenly, and then she slapped him again. 'I thought you were James. I would never have let you touch me if I'd known it was you!' She began hitting out wildly with both hands, across his face, his shoulders, his chest.

He grabbed both her wrists and ground them slowly back down on the carpet above her head, both their chests heaving as he pressed down flat on top of her. 'Is that so?' he bit out, blue eyes flashing with a very male anger. 'Well, you know who I am *now*, don't you? I'm Jake. Not James. Let's see how you respond *this* time, shall we?'

'No, Jake, *don't*,' she choked out. But even as his mouth took possession of hers she was quivering with an instant and breathless excitement.

Afterwards she wept, totally shattered by the moans of ecstasy still echoing in her ears.

'Oh, Leigh, darling, don't cry,' he murmured softly, holding her naked body close to his now equally naked body.

She almost surrendered to this unexpected and disarming tenderness, almost let it wash away the bitter shame she was feeling.

But just in time she recalled what had just happened, how he had ruthlessly exploited his knowledge of her body and its sexual weaknesses, how, when she'd been at her most aroused, he'd coerced from her an erotic intimacy she'd once given freely.

'Let me go, you ... you ... bastard!'

She reefed out of his arms and, scrambling to her feet, dashed into the bathroom, slamming and locking the door behind her. The sight of her reflection in the vanity mirror almost made her sick. She couldn't help staring at her puffy red lips, at her still hard nipples, at the red marks his possessive hands had made all over her flesh.

Shivers ran up and down her spine as she hugged herself in disbelief. This wasn't happening to her, she thought dazedly. It was a nightmare, and very, very soon she was going to wake up.

'Leigh?' Jake called out through the door. 'Are you all right? Answer me, Leigh!'

Groaning, she dashed into the shower, snapping on the water, unmindful that it was cold to begin with. She washed herself feverishly, trying to get every trace of him from her body. But she couldn't erase the memory of her ultimate surrender to what he wanted. Why, she agonised, had Jake always been able to command such total submission from her? Why?

And what of James? she worried. Where was he? What had Jake done to him last night to force him to let him take his place today?

Thinking about James's predicament had the effect of making Ashleigh pull herself together. For there was more than *her* well-being at stake here. Besides, she couldn't go back in time, couldn't wipe out what Jake had made her do. What she *could* do was find out exactly what had happened where James was concerned, then make decisions from there.

By the time Ashleigh emerged from the bathroom, her nakedness covered by a large towel, she looked fully composed. Her cold gaze swept over Jake where he was sitting quietly on the side of the bed, his trousers and shirt back on, though the shirt buttons were not done up. He looked up at her, a frighteningly hard glint in his eyes.

'Can we talk now?' he asked, getting slowly to his feet. '*Properly*?'

'By all means,' Ashleigh returned frostily. 'I'm more than eager to know how you managed to bring off this despicable charade. Just how many people were in on it, besides your sidekick Mr Stevenson?'

Jake's sigh carried exasperation. 'Look, Leigh, I——'

'Just give me the bare facts, please,' she snapped. 'Nothing else.'

His eyes narrowed. 'Very well. My mother was aware of the situation. As, of course, was James and his best man.'

'*Nancy* knew?' Ashleigh gasped. 'And she . . . let you get away with it?'

A rather bitter smile creased Jake's mouth. 'Mother was only too glad to go along with my suggestions, once I pointed out the alternative.'

'I can't imagine what you could have said or done to force her to go along with such a preposterous and disgraceful idea!'

Ashleigh swayed on unsteady feet as she recalled Nancy's visit before the wedding ceremony, at how dreadfully upset the poor woman had been. Her heart went out to the lady, to what she'd felt then, to what she must be feeling now. How a son could put his mother through such an ordeal she had no idea.

She took a few ragged steps towards him, her face pained. 'How . . . how could you do such a thing, Jake?' she rasped. 'To your mother? To me? And *why*? You don't love me. You *never* really loved me!'

And then it came to her. His return had nothing to do with love, but possession. She'd once been his, body and soul, and, while he'd been able to stand her moving on to some unknown man, he hadn't been able to bear her marrying his brother, in James enjoying the fruits—so to speak—of what he had sown.

'Oh, my God,' she groaned. 'What have you done with James? You . . . you've really hurt him, haven't you?'

Jake's eyes grew scornful at her concern for his brother. 'James is fine. At this very moment he is on his way to Europe in the company of his best man.'

She gaped, totally thrown by why James would meekly go off and let Jake pretend to marry her in his stead. 'But *why* did he let you take his place? *Why*?' she groaned, and shook her head in agitation. 'This is all madness. I...I can't take it in...'

'Peter Reynolds is James's lover,' Jake stated flatly.

Ashleigh froze, her mouth dropping open, her head whirling with what Jake had just said.

'James was marrying you as a cover to ensure his social respectability,' he went on. '*And* to have the child he always wanted.'

Ashleigh staggered over to slump down on the side of the bed. She could not speak. She felt nothing but shock and sheer disbelief.

Jake walked over and sat down beside her, picking up her chilled, lifeless hands, covering and warming them with his own. 'I'm sorry to tell you such upsetting news so bluntly, but is there a nice way for news like that? The only comfort I can give you is that he loves you as much as he is capable of loving a woman. I suppose he thought he would be able to successfully consummate the marriage. He told me he kissed you a couple of times and had been aroused enough by them. To be honest, I don't think James is truly gay. He just met the wrong man at the wrong time in his life.'

Stricken, Ashleigh searched Jake's eyes, hoping to see that he was lying. But she could see he wasn't.

'The invitation to your wedding only reached me three days ago,' he explained. 'I was on a type of holiday in the hills, you see, and the letter went all around the giddy-goat in Thailand before reaching me. I've never been so shocked in all my life. Or more upset. I've sacrificed my love for you twice, Leigh, for what I imagined noble reasons. But I could not stand by and see you marry my brother. Surely you can understand that . . . ?'

Ashleigh blinked. She wasn't understanding very much at the moment. Her mind was back on what Jake had just said.

'What . . . what do you mean, you sacrificed your love for me . . . twice . . . ?'

But already a suspicion was forming in her mind that startled and dismayed her.

Those beautiful blue eyes clouded for a moment as though some dark memory had leapt from the past to inflict a special kind of torment.

'I wasn't guilty, Leigh,' he rasped. 'Either of trafficking or possessing drugs. The heroin was included in my luggage by a very clever ruse. I told you I was guilty so you would go away, so you would forget me, so you wouldn't waste your lovely young life pining for a man who was facing life imprisonment in a prison system that knew no such thing as parole or mercy . . .'

A wave of emotion swelled in Ashleigh's heart as she thought of Jake in that filthy prison, making such a noble, heart-rending sacrifice. 'Oh, Jake,' she cried in genuine pity.

'How was I to know that a twist of fate would eventually set me free?' he went on in a thickened voice. 'Or that when I rushed home, hopeful you might still love me, I would once again be waylaid through treachery?'

'*Treachery*?'

'Yes. My parents'. They didn't believe me when I told them I wasn't guilty, you see. They said I had blackened their name, shamed the family. They said I wasn't wanted around Glenbrook.' His laugh was cynical. 'I rather expected my mother to react that way. She'd always been more concerned over what other people thought and said than what her children felt. But Dad really disappointed me. He didn't want me around either. When I asked about you he told me you were engaged to a medical student and that if I cared about you at all I'd go right away and leave you alone.'

'But... but I *wasn't*!'

'I know that now, Leigh. At the time I was shattered. And torn. I didn't know what to do. One part of me couldn't believe you had forgotten me. I longed to see you, to take you in my arms, to force you to love me. But common sense and decency demanded that if you were going to marry another man I should stay away. But I needed someone else to look me in the face and tell me you didn't care about me any more, someone I could implicitly trust. I went to Brisbane to speak to James, to the address where I was told he was spending the weekend with a friend. Mr Reynolds, as it turned out. It didn't take me long to see which way the land lay there. Naturally, I was shocked, but I tried to be open-minded about it, for James's sake. When I asked him about you and he confirmed what Dad had told me it never occurred to me he could be lying.'

'But *why* did he lie? It's not as though we were having anything to do with each other back then.'

'He obviously wanted me to leave Glenbrook too, because I knew his secret. He was worried I would stay if I thought there was a chance for me with you.'

'Oh, Jake ... Do you realise what I thought when I'd heard you'd come home and hadn't even come to see me? Do you have any idea how I felt?'

He drew her into his arms and held her there, her face pressed against his chest. 'I hope you were devastated,' he groaned. 'I hope you wanted to kill me!'

She wrenched away from him and stood up, grey eyes wide with bewilderment. 'But why would you want that?'

'Because it would mean you still loved me as much as I loved you,' he growled passionately. And, getting to his feet, he tried to embrace her again.

But she resisted, her heart and mind racing with a thousand tumbling, mixed-up thoughts. 'Is that what we felt for each other, Jake? Love?'

Clearly he was startled by her querying their relationship. 'Of course ... What else?'

She shook her head in genuine dismay. 'I think there are many names one could call what we felt for each other, what we *still* feel for each other. There's an animal chemistry between us, Jake. It burns whenever we get close enough to each other to touch. But is it love?'

'Of course it is, damn it!'

'Was it love that kept you awake nights in that prison, Jake? Was it love tonight when you saw me in that satin nightie? Was it love that had to prove its power a second time, making me do things I didn't really feel comfortable with after all these years?'

Jake grimaced at the memory. 'I'm not proud of that, Leigh. My only excuse is that I was beyond reason, beyond control. I needed you to show me that nothing had changed between us, to bring to life all the things I dreamed about all these long, lonely years without you.'

Ashleigh sucked in a breath. 'Are you saying, Jake, that there hasn't been any other woman since you got out of prison?'

A slash of guilty red burnt momentarily in his cheeks. 'No, dammit, I'm not saying that,' he ground out. 'Hell, Ashleigh, I thought you were lost to me. I thought . . . For pity's sake, what do you honestly expect? I'm a normal man. Occasionally I've needed a woman in my bed. But that doesn't mean I loved any of them as I loved you, as I *still* love you. Stop trying to make out our feelings are only sexual, damn you!'

'And damn you too, Jake,' she countered fiercely. 'For thinking this was the way to handle the situation with James, for having the arrogance to take his place without telling me, for making love to me here tonight without revealing your identity first, for playing with my life and my feelings as though you're some sort of god who knows best!

'You *don't* know best,' she raved on, whirling away to pace angrily across the room, her hand clutching the towel so that it wouldn't fall. 'You never did!' She spun round to face him from the safety of distance. 'In the first place, you should never have gone on that rotten holiday without me. Then, after you were imprisoned, you should have given me the right to pine for you if I *chose*, to wait for you if I *chose*. Then, when you were released, you should have come to see me, fiancé or no, and once again given me the right to choose my own fate.

'Damn it, Jake!' she cried in real emotional distress. 'I'm not some mindless puppet. I'm an intelligent woman with, I hope, a certain degree of courage and character. Why couldn't you have treated me like one?'

Jake's teeth clenched hard in his jaw. 'Right. Well, to answer your first accusation, that holiday wasn't my idea. It was my Aunt Aggie's. You know she was my only adult confidante in those days. When I told her I wanted to marry you she thought the same as you—that our relationship was just sex. She made me a bargain. Said if I went away for a little while and still wanted to marry you when I came back she would give us some money to get started, to support us while we went through university. But I was not to tell you that. This was to see how *you* felt too after we'd been separated for a while.'

He lifted his chin with an unrepentant air and walked slowly towards her. 'Well, we've been separated over ten years, Leigh, and it hasn't made a scrap of difference to how I feel about you, or you for me. You love me, woman. Stop denying it.'

He took hold of her shoulders and looked down into her eyes. 'As for the rest of your accusations... The truth is, I took James's place today with the best of intentions, thinking I was saving everyone's feelings, yours included. What do you think would have happened in a small town like this if I'd revealed the truth to you last night and the wedding was called off at the last minute? The speculation and gossip would have been horrendous. This way gives us time to work something out for everyone's benefit. Oh, and, by the way, the wedding wasn't a legal union.

The celebrant was an actor Rhys employed for the event.'

Ashleigh was truly taken aback. 'An actor?' she gasped. 'But how...why...I mean...'

'He was an innocent enough accomplice,' Jake explained dismissively. 'Rhys told him you and I had been married secretly just before we found out our family had already planned a grand social occasion, and that we didn't want to disappoint them. He was warned to keep his mouth firmly shut, but the idiot almost let the cat right out of the bag at the signing—remember?—till Rhys stepped in.'

'But...but...the certificate...'

'A cheap photostat copy. I've already torn it up. Believe me, Leigh, when I say I didn't enjoy going through that charade of a marriage. You must know that I would have given my eye-teeth to marry you properly and publicly like that. Pretending to be James at your side was excruciatingly difficult. My only concession to my pride was having the celebrant read out John James instead of James John. Hardly anyone knows John is my real name and I knew they'd all think it was just a silly mistake, if they noticed at all. You were the only possible person who'd catch on, but oddly enough you didn't seem to be listening the first time Johnson said it. You were away in another world. Then the second time...'

'I thought it was just human error,' she finished wearily.

'Look, I know I deceived you, but at least I didn't break any laws.'

Ashleigh stiffened and stepped back from his hold. 'Maybe not in a legal sense, but there are moral laws, surely? Just how long had you intended waiting, Jake, before you told me the truth?'

A slash of guilty red coloured his high cheekbones again.

Understanding shocked her. He'd been going to keep it going as long as he could, at least for the duration of their wedding-night. 'That's what you were arguing with your mother about, wasn't it?' she accused shakily. 'The extent to which you were planning on taking the deception. My God, you don't have a conscience any more, do you?'

'I wish to hell I didn't!' Jake shot back at her. 'God dammit, the only reason I pulled in here was because my stupid conscience got the better of me. I was finally going to tell you the whole horrible truth—even if it meant you'd then hate me—but when you came out of that bathroom, looking so bloody beautiful, I couldn't resist you. Sure, I was a little rough that second time and I'm sorry for that. But I'm not sorry for making love to the woman I love. Not one iota. So shoot me down with words, Leigh. Tell me I'm a savage. A barbarian. Call me any names you like. They'll fit. But while you're calling me names have a look at this and think about who and what turned me into such an animal.'

And, stripping off his shirt, he spun round and showed her what his captors had done to him.

Ashleigh could have cried. She lifted trembling fingers to touch his beautiful skin, criss-crossed with the ugly scars of a savage bamboo flogging. And her heart went out to him. What must he have been through, a young, innocent man, wrongly accused and imprisoned for something he didn't do? How on earth could she stay angry with him, faced with such a heart-rending sight?

Impossible.

Which was exactly what Jake intended, she realised when he swung around and took her in his arms again.

'Leigh, darling,' he urged persuasively, 'come away with me ... back to Thailand ... I have a house there on one of the beaches ... You can practise medicine in the villages near by ... They're in desperate need of doctors there ... You won't want for anything, I assure you. I've——'

'*No*,' she cried out, appalled at how tempted she was to just fall in with his wishes. '*No!*'

She pushed away from him, clutching the towel defensively in front of her. 'My God, Jake, you ask too much! You've always asked too much. I'm not an infatuated teenager any more, you know. I won't come running when you click your fingers. Besides, even if I did still love you—which I'm not at all sure I do!—I can't just drop everything in my life and go off with you like that. I have responsibilities here in Glenbrook. My family depends on me. I have patients here, friends. My *life* is here. You might be able to bum around on some far away beach in a grass hut for the rest of your life, but that's not how I want to live my life. I ... I ...'

She broke off, flustered by the slow, ironic smile that was pulling at his lips.

'And what do you think you're smiling at?' she threw at him.

'At my lovely Leigh. So grown up now. So liberated. So wrong ...'

'I am *not* wrong!'

'Oh, yes, you are, my darling. About so many things. We belong together. We've always belonged together. Fate has decreed it so.'

'I don't believe in fate!'

'Don't you?' Again he smiled that infuriating smile. 'Well, maybe it takes being released from a hell-hole by some incredible miracle to make one believe in such romantic notions. But I don't mind you not believing in fate. I'm quite prepared to trust to your intelligence. And your love for me. I'm sure you'll finally come to the same conclusion I came to this afternoon, Ashleigh O'Neil.'

'Which is what?' she snapped.

'Which is that you're going to become my real wife in the end, come hell or high water.' His smile suddenly faded, replaced by an expression of thin-lipped determination. 'Now go and get dressed. We're going back to Glenbrook, where you can begin seeing for yourself that you're not wanted and loved and needed there as much as I want and love and need you!'

CHAPTER SEVEN

'So! You decided to bring her back, did you?' was
Nancy Hargraves's scowled remark when she opened
the front door in her dressing-gown. 'I presume she
knows who you really are.' She turned a perceptive
eye towards Ashleigh, who tried not to colour guiltily,
but failed.

Jake's mother gave her a derisive look. 'Well, nothing's changed where you and Jake are concerned,
I see,' she bit out. 'You were always his little puppy-
dog, running along behind him, licking at his heels.
I suppose you even believe all his protestations of
innocence over that drug business. Yes, *you* would.
But then sex does have a way of making certain women
blind to certain men. I'll bet you couldn't wait to get
into bed with him once you'd found out the truth,
could you?'

She looked quite ugly in her contempt. 'God! You
make me sick, Ashleigh O'Neil. You probably only
agreed to marry James so you could close your eyes
every night and pretend he was Jake!'

'Have you heard enough, Leigh?' Jake said coldly,
but placing a surprisingly warm arm around her by
now shivering body.

'Y...yes,' she stammered, stunned by Nancy's
vicious attack.

'Let's go, then.'

'You can't take James's car!' his mother screamed
after them.

Jake whirled. 'Just try and stop me, Mother. You're damned lucky that you and your precious James are getting off this easily. I could have pulled the plug on his little scheme with a very loud pop today. But I didn't. One of the reasons I went through with that fiasco of a marriage was to save James's reputation, as well as your miserable social position in this town. But somehow I don't think you'll be quite so generous with *Ashleigh's* reputation, will you? I can hear you now, after we're gone ...

' "You've no idea what happened on poor James's honeymoon," ' Jake mimicked in Nancy's best plum-in-the-mouth voice. ' "Ashleigh ran into Jake again and you wouldn't believe it! The wretched creature ran off with him. The poor boy is just devastated. I don't think he'll ever marry again ..." '

'Close, am I, Mother?' he taunted.

Nancy lifted her patrician nose. 'James is not really gay. He's been led astray, that's all, by a wicked, wicked man. I have to protect him till he's himself again.'

'You know what, Mother?' Jake said wearily. 'I actually agree with you. And who knows? Maybe, in time, he'll get rid of that corrupting creep and eventually meet a girl like my Leigh and fall in love.'

Suddenly Nancy's icy control cracked. 'Do you think so, Jake?' she choked out. 'Do you really?'

Both Ashleigh and Jake looked at each other in amazement when Nancy burst into tears, her slender, almost frail body racked with heart-rending sobs.

Ashleigh's soft womanly heart was moved, and she stepped forward to take the distressed woman in her arms. 'There, there, Nancy,' she soothed, hugging her and patting her on the back. 'James will be all right.

Either way he's a good man, and I love him dearly, just as you do, just as his brother does. We all want to protect him from hurt, don't we, Jake?'

Jake looked at her and sighed. 'I guess so, but not at your expense, Leigh.'

'Then why don't the three of us go inside and think of some way out of this mess? Glenbrook is our home, Jake. We want the right to be able to come here occasionally and visit, without undue scandal and gossip.'

His eyes narrowed to stare at her. 'Come back, Leigh? That suggests leaving in the first place. Does that mean . . . you *are* going to come with me?'

If Ashleigh had ever had any doubt about her love for Jake it vanished at that moment. To see him looking at her like that. So hopeful . . . so tense . . . so vulnerable . . .

This was not the same arrogant young blood she'd once known. This was a sensitive human being, who'd been to hell and back and somehow survived. But not without a great deal of damage. He was so right when he said he needed her. She could see it in his strained face, and in the way he wasn't breathing while he waited for her answer.

'Of course, Jake,' she whispered, a lump in her throat. 'You were right all along. I love you. And I want to be your wife, wherever that takes me . . .'

They stared at each other over the bowed head of his weeping mother, and neither needed to say a thing. It was all there, in the intense relief in his eyes, and the glistening love in hers.

'I hope we can come up with a damned good solution for all this mess, then,' he said in an emotion-charged voice. 'Because I want everything to be right for you, my darling. You deserve it.'

Kate stared at all three of them across the large kitchen table. 'I still don't believe it!' she exclaimed. 'When the telephone rang in the middle of the night I was sure there'd been some terrible accident. I would never have dreamt...' She darted another wide-eyed glance Jake's way, then shook her head. 'I should have known,' she muttered under her breath. 'So damned masterful... Not like James at all...'

'You weren't the only one who was fooled,' Ashleigh said, throwing an accusing though indulgent look Jake's way.

'Really?' Kate speculated. 'When did you—er...?'

Her voice trailed away when Ashleigh looked daggers at her.

'Yes, well... best I don't ask that, I think. Just as well I moved out of home and into the small flat above my salon,' she went on blithely, 'or I'd have had to explain to my mother why you were dragging me out in the middle of the night of your wedding, Ashleigh. Come to think of it, why *have* you? I mean, I'm glad you told me the rather astonishing truth about everything, and I think Jake's switching with James is rather romantic in a weird sort of way, but what can I do to help?'

'I want you to make sure the whole town knows the truth. No, not about James,' she quickly amended, hearing the gasp of shock from Nancy, 'but about Jake's having taken his brother's place at the wedding. You can act as if the families and close friends were all in on it, but didn't say anything at the last moment for fear of causing an uproar among the more elderly guests. Relay all this confidentially to some selected customers of your salon, adding that James and I were already having doubts about our marriage and that when Jake arrived home for the wedding I realised he was still the man for me. It probably won't occur to anyone to question how we got a licence so quickly, but if they do just say we told the authorities a mistake was made with the names...'

When Kate looked totally perplexed James explained to her about how Jake was another form of John and that he and James actually had the same names, only reversed.

'Goodness!' she exclaimed. 'Then when the celebrant said John James at the ceremony he really meant it. It wasn't just a boo-boo?'

'No boo-boo,' Jake confirmed. 'I wasn't about to promise to love, honour and cherish my darling Leigh here in another man's name.'

Kate looked very impressed.

'Then after you've spread all that around, Kate,' Ashleigh continued, 'you'd better also add that James decided he was still in love with some girl he'd been seeing in Brisbane last year and was going off to try and win her back.'

'Goodness, Leigh, how inventive you've become over the years,' Jake said with some amusement in his voice.

'Not at all, Jake,' Kate denied drily. 'She's as disgustingly practical as always. Believe me, this is her idea of forging her own destiny.'

'Sounds good to me,' he grinned. 'As long as I'm in there somewhere, she can forge away all she likes.'

'Be quiet, the both of you,' Ashleigh reprimanded. 'I'm thinking... Yes, and it might not be a bad idea to also let drop some "hush-hush" news about how Jake was wrongly convicted all those years ago and that was the real reason why the Thai government eventually released him. No one will bother to check, and if you tell everyone it's supposed to be a secret it'll get around like wildfire.'

'I'll tell Mrs Brown. She has her hair done on Monday.' Kate's eyes glittered with relish at the task. 'Oh, and Maisie Harrison. She's coming in on Tuesday and has just been elected president of the local ladies' guild. Don't worry. There won't be a soul in town who won't know everything within a day or two.'

'Now, Nancy...' Ashleigh turned to the woman sitting next to her. Jake's mother was still very pale, though she had pulled herself together once she'd known Kate was on her way over. 'You'll have to ring my father in the morning and get him over here on a house call. Say you feel ill. That way, when you tell him the truth about James and Jake and everything, he won't be able to tell anyone because of his having to keep your confidence. I'll write a letter as well that you can give him, explaining my feelings for Jake and that I've gone off with him. I think he'll be understanding.'

Privately Ashleigh knew her father wouldn't be too broken up over his daughter's leaving Glenbrook, other than how he and his partner would be inconvenienced till Stuart joined the practice next year. In her letter she would suggest he hire a woman locum to fill in, warning him that if he didn't watch out a smart woman doctor would set up practice in Glenbrook and steal half his patients.

'But where will you and Jake go?' Kate asked.

Ashleigh looked at Jake. 'Darling? Where are we going?' she smiled at him, and when he smiled back an incredible sensation of bonding wrapped tentacles around her heart. He was so right. They did belong together. How could she ever have doubted it? Here in Glenbrook or out the back of Bourke or over in a small village in Thailand in an old grass hut. It didn't matter, as long as they were together.

'To Brisbane first, I think,' he said. 'I'll ring Rhys— he's staying at the Glenbrook Hotel. He'll drive us to Brisbane Airport, where we can see about booking tickets to Thailand. Have you got a current passport?'

'Yes.' Ashleigh tactfully declined mentioning that part of her honeymoon had been arranged for Hawaii. 'It's in my black handbag in the car.'

'Good, then there's no reason why we can't fly out to Bangkok straight away. My home is not far from there. Oh, and, by the way, it's far from a grass hut. It's quite grand, in fact. You see, Aunt Aggie left me all her money when she died, didn't you know?'

Ashleigh was taken aback. 'No,' she confessed. 'I didn't.'

'Neither did I!' Kate pronounced, sounding affronted that a piece of interesting gossip had somehow eluded her.

'I wrote to her when I got out of prison, telling her the whole truth. The old dear must have felt sorry for me and what I'd been through, and made me her heir. Six months later she was gone, and suddenly all my financial worries were over. Not only that, but I was also recently paid a packet for the film rights to a book of mine that's about to go on the stands in America. I'm loaded, my girl. Do you honestly think

I'd expect you to rough it out in the wild somewhere? Not that I'm not flattered that you were prepared to.'

'Rhys told me that he was going to make a movie in Thailand,' Kate said with a frown. 'But I didn't make any connection with you, Jake.'

'Just as well,' Jake returned with feeling. 'As it is, I told Rhys not to talk about Thailand, but that man can't stop gabbling on about his damned movies.'

'You know he said if I ever wanted a job with his company as a hairdresser on set he'd be only too happy to oblige. You know what? I think I'll take him up on it.'

'What kind of book, Jake?' Ashleigh asked, a well of emotion filling her heart. He'd always said he'd be a great author one day. How proud of him she felt!

'A fictionalised version of my experiences in Thailand. Not all bad, either. It's a great country, you know, despite everything it put me through. Not that I can really blame the authorities. The man responsible for my imprisonment was damnably clever.'

'Yes, I'd like to know more about that,' his mother joined in. 'How *could* heroin get to be in your luggage without your knowing?'

If there was still a truculent note in her voice Jake was man enough to ignore it. He gave a nonchalant shrug. 'It was a simple yet clever ruse,' he explained. 'There was this fellow Australian named Doug, staying in the same hotel in Bangkok. He was always reading, great, thick tomes in hardback. He'd been wading through one on the day before our flight home, raving on about how great it was, even to showing me a particular passage he found very moving. I politely read it, not thinking much of it myself, but not saying so.'

Jake's laugh was rueful. 'Little did I know that this was just to reassure me it was a real book with real contents. When he complained the next day that he couldn't fit it into his luggage, and that he really wanted to read the rest when he got back to Australia, I let him stash it in mine; unbeknown to me the middle section was hollowed out and stuffed with heroin. Just enough, unfortunately, to upgrade my crime from possession to trafficking. Naturally, when I was picked up at the airport he conveniently disappeared, with my not even knowing his full name.'

'But didn't your lawyers try to trace him?' Ashleigh asked.

'They said there was little point, since I had no independent witness to any of this. It would just be my word against his.'

Nancy was beginning to look guilty. 'That still sounds negligent to me,' she muttered. 'They should have tried, the same as your father and I should have tried to find better lawyers for you, Jake. I . . . I'm sorry, son. We . . . we let you down . . .'

'It's all right, Mother. We all make mistakes in life, and we all have expectations of people that cannot sometimes be met. I was a difficult, selfish, rebellious young man back then. I can see that now. But I have matured and mellowed, I hope, even to trying to understand and forgive James. He only did what he did where Leigh was concerned because he was trying to live up to other people's expectations of him. Tell him when you see him, Mother, that you will love him, no matter what he is or does. That's very important. If you don't there's no hope for him. No hope at all.'

Nancy was not about to concede she had failed her favourite son in any way whatsoever. She stiffened, then stood up, proud and straight. 'I have a very good relationship with James. We love and trust each other. He...he didn't tell me about his...problem, because he knew it was just a phase he was going through. I'm sure he'll be fine once I can get him away from that wicked man.' She turned to face Ashleigh. 'I will try to explain all this to your father in the morning. Leave your letter here, on the table, and I'll give it to him. But, for now, I...I must go to bed. I'm very, very tired.'

Ashleigh also got to her feet. 'I'll walk up with you, Nancy. Jake...perhaps you could ring Rhys while I'm gone.'

'Right away.'

The two women did not speak as they walked side by side up the stairs. They stopped outside Nancy's bedroom door. 'Don't worry about Jake and me, Nancy,' she said in parting. 'We'll be fine...'

Nancy gave her a rueful look. 'Oh, I can see that. You and Jake were somehow meant to be, Ashleigh. He was your destiny.'

'Maybe, Nancy. Maybe...'

Ashleigh turned away with an ironic expression on her face. Destiny had nothing to do with it, she still firmly believed. One made choices in life. Tonight she had *chosen* to spend the rest of her life with Jake.

She walked briskly along the corridor and turned into the bedroom at the top of the stairs, where she retrieved the locket from under the bed and the chain from the chest of drawers. Clutching it tightly in her hand, she made her way downstairs, where Jake was just hanging up the telephone in the foyer.

'Rhys is on his way,' he said, his eyes searching her face as she joined him. 'Are you sure, Leigh? I'm not rushing you, am I?'

'Of course you're rushing me,' she laughed. 'But no matter.' She moved into his arms and raised her face for him to kiss her.

He did so, gently and reverently. 'I really love you. You must know that. It's not just sex.'

'I know,' she admitted at last, and, taking his hand, pressed the locket back in it.

'What's this?'

'I'm giving you my heart again,' she said softly. 'But not on loan this time. This is for keeps.'

He stared down at the delicate locket and thought of all the long, lonely nights he had held it to his own heart and cried for the girl who'd once given it to him. Well, there would be no more lonely nights, no more despair. He would gather this lovely, loving woman to his heart and treasure her till his dying days.

'I'll give it to our first daughter,' he said in a thickened tone. 'And when she's old enough I'll tell her the story behind it.'

Ashleigh linked arms with him and they started walking slowly back to the kitchen, where Kate was sure to be waiting impatiently for them. 'How many children would you like, Jake?' she asked softly.

'Lots.'

'That's good. Because if I've done my sums right expect the first in about nine months' time.'

When she looked up at him, expecting a measure of shock, Jake was smiling wryly down at her.

'Jake Hargraves!' she gasped. 'You *knew* I might get pregnant tonight, didn't you?'

'Aye,' he agreed with mock contrition. 'That I did. James let the cat out of the bag when I—er—questioned him about how far things had gone between you two.'

'But why...I mean...why didn't you say something?'

'I thought I'd best keep an ace up my sleeve, in case you decided we weren't quite right for each other. I rather thought a wee babe might change your mind.'

'Why, you sneaky, rotten...'

'My God, you two aren't fighting already, are you?' Kate groaned from the kitchen doorway.

'Who? Us?' Jake scooped an arm around Ashleigh's waist and pulled her close to his side. 'Never!'

'Certainly not,' Ashleigh giggled, seeing the funny side of it.

Kate eyed them both suspiciously. 'I hope not. People make their own luck in life, isn't that what you always say, Ashleigh?'

'Oh, definitely.'

'In that case,' she rushed forward, an anxious look on her face, 'would you have a spare room for me in Thailand if I came over for a while after I find a buyer for my salon? I think I'll take Rhys up on his offer.'

The front doorbell rang, and Jake stepped over to open it.

Rhys stood there, an equally anxious look on his face. 'All right, give me the bad news. She sent you packing once she found out, didn't she? I did tell you, Jake, this wasn't the way to handle it. Women don't like to be deceived, you know. They...'

He gaped into silence when Ashleigh walked forward and slipped a loving arm through Jake's.

'Now, Rhys, don't be so melodramatic. I'm not angry with Jake at all. I adore him and we're going to Thailand together to live and have babies while Jake writes and I doctor. We have only one further favour to ask of you.'

His mouth flapped open, but no words came out.

'Of both of you, actually,' she went on, her glance encompassing Kate as well. 'Would you two be our witnesses again when we really, truly get married, *legally* next time?'

'Well, of course,' Rhys agreed, still rather bemused by the turn of events.

'But only if you uphold all the traditions,' Kate inserted sternly. 'White dress and all the trimmings. I don't believe in any of those register office jobs.'

Ashleigh grinned. 'All right, Miss Tradition. But you'll have to come up with a different "something borrowed" for me. That locket just won't do any more. It's been "returned to sender".' And she looked lovingly up at Jake.

'Returned to...' Kate frowned. 'But I thought Nancy had... I mean... Ashleigh O'Neil!' she wailed. 'You've been keeping secrets from me!'

'I wonder why,' she laughed, and, smiling, went up on tiptoe to kiss the man she loved.

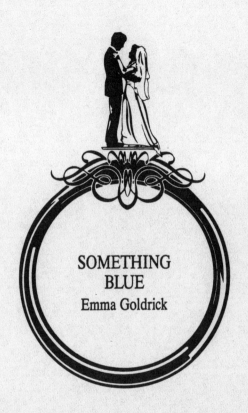

SOMETHING BLUE
Emma Goldrick

CHAPTER ONE

THE dirt road swung upward, around a cluster of maple trees, and out on to the flat meadow that was the boundary between Marne Tilson's small farm and the larger Smith acres, up at the top of the hill. Beyond the hill, the road meandered across the mountains into New York. Below her, the town of Peterboro clung to the shadows of the valley. The hot July sunshine made Marne's breathing difficult, and perspiration ran down her oval freckled face and off the tip of her sharp little nose. At five feet eight, Marne was a walker of no mean skill. She had tied her straw-blonde hair back at the base of her neck, to clear the deck, so to speak.

Miccimuc brook chattered in the far corner of the meadow, birthed by a natural spring, and then wandered east towards the city. The spring was surrounded by a grove of willows, pines and oaks, almost concealing a shady resting place for country children. On the county map the Miccimuc was called a river. Even the long-gone tribe of Mohicans would have laughed at that. The spring was also the daily gathering point of half the birds in the county.

There was something moving in the shadows. Marne caught her breath, vaulted over the low dry-stone wall, and took a couple of trotting steps into the shade.

Her ancient grey cat, Morgan, came up beside her as if this were a two-cat race, and sputtered a high-pitched *meoow* at her. Marne pulled herself to a full stop. 'Of course,' she muttered, 'why should we be in any hurry? Just because his niece Becky called, all excited, to tell me that Rob was home and wanted to meet me? Am I as big a fool as I seem to be? Four years since our divorce became final, he wants to meet me? Four years since I've seen him.' She slowed to a walk, twisting gently on the balls of her feet so that her dress swung back and forth, and her hips as well. She came to a halt at the edge of the wood, her grey-green eyes studying the shadows.

He was sitting on the edge of the granite rock that they had used for so many years as a meeting place. His fishing line was in the water, the little red and white bobbin bouncing in the rush of the current. He leaned forward and came up into a crouch, all the thin bones of him apparent to view. Marne's heart skipped a beat. He had always had this effect on her; a gangly half-fed man a few inches taller than herself. Warm brown hair that she loved to caress. A thin face that was marvellously fluid, expressing his every thought. Rob Smith. She had once been Mrs Rob Smith. The sharpness of remembrance bit into her heart.

Marne came to a full stop, nervously brushing down her simple sundress, checking the angle of her shoulder-straps. Somehow she had to make him see she was not the *kid* he once had called her. One more deep breath to settle her nerves. 'Oh, is that you, Rob?' Her usually sweet contralto seemed to squeak, even to her own ears.

He turned his head and scanned her slowly, from heel to halter, pausing there to check what there was of her figure. 'Marne? I didn't see you coming.'

What a fool I am, she told herself. For the first time in four years he comes home. He calls, I come. How's that for enlightened disinterest, Marne Tilson?

If he says, 'Lie down here. I want to talk to you,' do I do as I'm told? Wasn't that one major reason why I divorced him, because he was a dictator? What in God's good name am I doing here?

'Hi, kid. Come sit with me for a while.' He patted the space next to him, and casually brushed it off. She cocked her head, then spread her skirts and joined him.

'It's—a surprise to find you here. Have you caught anything?'

'Did we ever?' He grinned down at her, a lop-sided full-mouthed grin. Not the most handsome man in the world, she told herself, but he'll do for the ordinary run-of-the-mill girl. Like me, for example. If I were looking for a man. Which I am definitely not! His dark brown hair lay against his head perfectly even though he'd passed the big three-oh these days.

A little whimper rose in Marne's throat. Remember the times, so many, when he would lie here with his head in my lap and I would stroke that soft hair. God! What am I doing to myself? Find something casual to talk about!

He tugged at his line, then turned back to her again with that thoughtful scan. 'It's good to see you, little bit. I had thought to come by your house, but I didn't know if I'd be welcome. My mother would only tell me that you hadn't married again. Tell me, how's your grandmother?'

'She died two years ago. I'm living alone in the old house.'

He paused reflectively. 'A wonderful lady, your grandmother.'

'Funny, she used to say the same about you. I never could understand why.'

'There's a difference between being neighbours and being married,' he said. 'You sound bitter.'

'I should be all sweetness and light?' After all those slights, and finally after the videotape that had arrived on her doorstep. The tape showing Sylvia Burroughs and Marne's husband making passionate love on a sofa in somebody's living-room. Yeah, I should be—she whipped out a handkerchief and stanched the incipient tears.

'So you called me—and here I am. What do you want, Rob?'

'Hey, it was a friendly divorce, wasn't it? Uncontested? By mutual agreement? No-fault?'

'Yes, all of that.' Because you didn't dare to appear in court after your lawyer saw my tape, Rob Smith, she thought furiously. Incompatibility, no doubt about it, and Judge Hanron had granted the no-fault decree after only five minutes of the hearing. Five minutes, to dissolve a two-year marriage.

'So why meet you here?'

'Because we always did, little bit. Halfway between, a neutral meeting ground. I didn't dare come down to the house. Too scared, I guess.'

'Scared of me? Even if I did remarry or anything, you'd be welcome. As a neighbour. It *was* a friendly divorce, wasn't it? You know that. And nothing's happened to me. I'm just the same as I always was.' And *don't* call me 'little bit'!

'I'm not sure of the friendly divorce,' he said gloomily. 'Would you believe, a just-graduated lawyer, and I didn't know about no-fault divorces.' He turned his eyes to her, searching her face. She could see pain writhing across his. 'And I still don't know why.'

'Well,' she muttered, 'it's all behind us now. I'm surprised you've come home. I haven't changed much,

Rob. You're still welcome in these parts. I don't love
you as I once foolishly did, but we can still be friends.
Friends don't change.'

'I believe you haven't. Cool, generous—and prettier
than ever, Marne. I do believe you've grown up. And
Becky tells me you're her school teacher.'

'Yes, I went back to Amherst for a teaching degree.
That's a change.'

'It must have been some struggle, working and
studying. Why wouldn't you take the money I
offered?'

'I didn't want your damn money,' she snapped. 'I
didn't want anything of yours!'

'Yes, I remember,' he said. His voice was rough
and deep and caressing, and the shivers ran up and
down her spine. And when his big warm hand dropped
on to her bare shoulder he felt her quivering.

'Independent little cuss.'

'Of course,' she mumbled. 'But not so little. Don't
call me that.' You don't know why I wanted a divorce?
Lord, there seemed to be a hundred reasons. She
shivered again. It's like the old saying, Rob. 'Wear
something old, something new, something borrowed,
and something blue.' A vow of fidelity. I did, and I
was and you weren't!

'Here, now, we can't have you shivering like that.'
He pulled her over to where her hip met his, and the
warmth brought colour to her face. They both
watched the little bobbin, moving around with the
speed of the current. Her mind ached from the
thought of it all.

'Morgan the opportunist,' he said after a time.
'She's down there waiting to see if I catch anything.'

'She's missed you, Rob. There's nobody else in the
neighbourhood who fishes here.'

'Cupboard love,' he said, chuckling. 'And you, Marne?'

'Me?'

'You. Have you missed me?'

'Well, I wasn't all that interested in fishing.' She was blushing again, and praying that the wind would manoeuvre the tree branches above her so that he couldn't see. What a stupid thing to say! Tell him that you didn't follow him around all those years just because he was a wonderful fisherman! But her tongue was too tied down, and would not co-operate. Marne took another deep breath and lunged for another conversational bit.

'Your new wife, is she pretty?'

He turned her chin up so he could see her eyes. 'You must be the only girl in the county who doesn't know.'

'Doesn't know what?'

'Doesn't know that I never did marry again. The girl was—nice, and a lawyer too. But who wants to be married to *nice*? Yeah, she was pretty. On the outside, at least. Her father wanted the marriage, of all things, but I wasn't marrying *him*, and I *couldn't* marry her.'

'Why not?' Softly spoken, but with a tremolo, as if she was afraid to know the answer to her question.

'I'm not sure I can answer that,' he responded. His hand tightened on her shoulder, almost painfully. 'When you've had the best it's hard to accept second-best.'

His meaning went right over her head. 'Well, then, you had a lucky break,' Marne said indignantly. 'There are lots of women in the world who'd jump at the idea of marrying you.'

'Great. Just what I need. Name two.' He looked as if he meant it, his face all solemn, his voice coaxing, and those little devil-spots dancing in his dark eyes.

And now you're backed into a corner, Marne yelled at herself, if you really are hunting the man. He's changed in some way. Some almost indefinable way. He's not the big, overgrown, rash boy he used to be. He's—lord, I don't know, do I? Speak up. Say a name or two. The county is overrun with willing spinsters. But her mind closed down, and she could not get the right words out. Or any words, for that matter. Because, she told herself, the truth is that nobody could love Rob Smith except Marne Tilson.

'Cat got your tongue?'

'No, I was—thinking.'

'Names just don't pop up into your mind, I suppose.' And this time the sparkle was gone from his eyes, and the cheer from his cold, hard voice.

But, having committed herself, Marne was totally unable to skate off the thin ice, no matter how much she wanted to.

'It sure would be nice to come home and find a woman waiting for me,' he mused.

'Is that why you came home?'

'I—more or less. I wanted to talk to you and—damn you, cat, get away from there!'

Morgan, leaning dangerously over the water as Rob's fishing line dipped underwater, had swiped at the bobbin and the little fish suspended below it, and had fallen ingloriously into the stream.

The water was cold. Winter or summer, it was cold. Morgan screamed in rage, threshed around between the line and the bank, and squalled some more. The fish, hardly bigger than a goldfish, wiggled off the hook and was gone. Rob Smith was up and off the

rock before Marne could gear herself up to move. He
yelled too, as his shoes filled with the cold water. With
one big hand he flipped the cat out of the water and
a good five feet up the bank. And then, overbal-
anced, he lost his footing on the slippery rocks of the
bed of the spring, teetered, and fell over.

The water in the middle of the pool came up to his
armpits. Startled again, Marne stared, and then
giggled. He was such a big man, and so pompous
when he wanted to be, and the water came up to his—
but of course, he's sitting down!

Morgan, still complaining, came over to her
shoulder, seeking sympathy. She spared a hand to
scratch behind the cat's ears. And out in the middle
of the stream Rob stood up, legs apart, hands on hips,
glaring.

'Funny, is it?' Years ago, had this sort of thing
happened, Marne would have giggled, and then started
running before he caught up to her. He was a great
believer in killing the messenger, she remembered. But
that was years ago. Lord knew what he'd do today.
She swallowed the giggle and backed off up to the
crest of the rock as he stomped out of the water.

'Funny?'

'Well, not exactly,' she temporised. He stretched a
hand out in her direction, and, without thinking, she
offered help. His hand was big and strong and—
tempting? Somehow she didn't remember it being like
that. So her guard was down as he gave a yank and
she sailed by him head first and plunged into the pond.

Where the pool came only up to his mid-chest as
he sat there, on Marne it was over her head. She came
up, sputtering indignantly, only to be snatched up out
of the water and conveyed effortlessly to dry land.

'You'll have to believe me, I really didn't intend to do that,' Rob said, Marne managed to get the hair out of her eyes and looked up at him. That devilish twinkle that she knew so well was sparking in his dark eyes. Nowhere could she find a smidgen of remorse. Nowhere.

'And I'm supposed to believe that? You might put me down!'

'When I'm good and ready,' he returned, losing the twinkle and transferring into a brooding presence bent over her. She wiggled half-heartedly. He let her slip slowly through his arms until her feet touched ground, and then backed away a step or two.

'My lord, I've been blind for years!'

'What?' A hesitant question. There was something in his eyes now that she had never seen before. Some hunting animal had taken over the gentle character of the boy she knew too well. And those feral eyes were travelling up and down her figure as if he had never seen it before.

Troubled, Marne looked down at herself. Her thin cotton dress was soaked, cling to her at every crevice and around every curve. Under the dress, because it was such a hot day, she wore nothing. Everything except her conscience was on display.

'Well, who have we here?' he murmured softly. 'Marne Tilson, all grown up?'

'I—yes,' she stammered. 'Whom. That's all of me there is.'

'What I see is what I get?'

'What the devil are you talking about, Rob Smith?' She stamped her foot indignantly and instantly regretted it. Granite rocks were the bones of the earth, and her foot complained at the abuse.

He reached out for her and drew her back into his arms, and for a moment they both dripped over each other. 'Here,' he offered gently, and before she could react he had pulled off his wet shirt and was towelling her hair.

One could hardly say he was drying her. His shirt was as wet as she. But he was doing something—something that warmed her, that sent little *frissons* down her spine and back again. She opened her eyes and looked up at him. Yes, there was no doubt, this was the Rob Smith she had known and—hated? No doubt at all. She groaned and dived back against his bare chest again. This was the man, but not the man. Or she was not the woman she had been, and, being unable to settle the difference, she took refuge in tears.

'Hey, none of that, little bit.'

'Don't you call me that,' she said, emphasising each word. 'I'm not a little bit. And I'm certainly not *your* little bit! Turn me loose before I——'

'Set your cat on me?' He laughed gently, but with her head against his chest it sounded like a roar. Filled with impotent rage, she finally remembered the pointed toes of her shoes, and swung one of them into his ankle.

He yelled, and danced around in a circle on one leg. 'Dammit, woman, don't do that,' he snapped. Marne managed to break away, and then added a step or two to the distance between them.

'Sweet little bit hell,' he muttered. 'More like a wild cat, lady.'

He moved towards her threateningly, but she was unable to move. With water still dripping off her dress, feet apart, ready for flight, she found herself unable to command her muscles to movement.

'What are you going to do?' A question asked in her quavering voice, a voice touched with considerable fear.

'First I'm going to take you out into the sunshine to dry off.' He offered her a nasty little stage-door leer. 'And then you'll find out.'

His arms were around her, pulling her against the steel of his chest, binding her helplessly to him by strength and hypnotism. She struggled weakly, to no avail, as her prison closed around her, and then his face blotted out the sun as he took dead aim at her lips and moved to contact.

It was not what she had expected. Just a touch of a kiss, and then when he moved away a sort of electric *snap*, as if lightning were flashing between them. She stopped struggling. His lips roved, down to her earlobes, back to her chin, around the base of her neck, across her bare shoulders, and gently down into the declivity between her breasts.

'Marne, Marne,' she heard him whisper. 'Why have I been such a damned blind fool?'

It's time, she told herself. Time to break out of this daze. Time to do *something* to escape the trap. But it required all her attention to find the right words. Every time his lips moved to a new target she lost control all over again.

It was Morgan who saved her. The old cat, neither willing nor able to share the limelight, grumbled at her a time or two, and then unfolded her claws halfway and took a free-swinging swat at Marne's ankle.

The sharp little pain was just enough. 'No,' she muttered as Rob's lips came down again. She managed to free one hand, but only had the strength to shove a finger between his lips and his target. He stopped.

'No?' As disbelieving as one could ever find in the male kingdom.

'No,' she repeated, now fully in control. 'I'm not your dinner. And I'm surely not your appetiser. Just because you need a woman, and I happen to be the only one within ten miles, I don't expect——'

'Boy, how far wrong can you be, woman?' he said as he held her out at arm's length. 'Listen up, Marne. We've been friends a long time?'

'Yes,' she said hesitantly, 'with some exceptions. I can't swear that it's all been peaches and cream.'

'But you'd be willing to do me a favour?'

'That all depends. What favour? How long?'

'About six months would do it,' he returned cautiously. 'Would you?'

'Would I what?'

He set her aside and paced back and forth for a moment. 'Marne, you know how hard it is to make it big in law these days. The woods are full of lawyers. I've been with a large firm down in Washington for three years now. And I'm not really getting anyplace.' He left it there.

Gurgling water and chirping birds took over. The engines of a high-flying plane broke the natural cycle of sound. Marne looked up at him. There was a do-or-die expression on his face. The wind fingered her hair, still heavy with wetness, and loaded with pine scent. Her dress, pressed against her by the same wind, outlined her lithe little figure. She shivered against the coolness of it. It *had* to be the wind against her wet dress. It couldn't be anything else, could it?

'There's a "but" in it, isn't there?' she asked softly.

He nodded his head.

'Well,' she said, sighing, 'lay it on me and then we'll see.'

His breath ran out of him in a massive sigh, almost as if he had been holding it in all this time. 'Thank God for you, Marne,' he said.

'Yes, sure, thank God for me,' she sighed. 'What do I have to do?'

'It won't be difficult.' His tone hardly belied his statement. 'I've decided to come home and go into politics. Ma isn't growing any younger. She and Becky both need someone to look after them. My brother Bill is well settled in Worcester. Our present sheriff, who is seventy years old, said that he won't run again in the September primary. So *I've* decided to run.'

'But...' She laid a hand over his mouth to stop him from talking. It was such a familiar thing to do that she gave it no thought for the moment. 'But— people say that the whole county government is as crooked as a snake's belly.'

He was smiling as he looked at her. 'That's why I want to run,' he said. 'A new broom sweeps clean, and all that sort of thing.'

'People say,' she continued in a half-whisper, 'that the only reason why anybody would run for a thirty-thousand-dollar-a-year job is because there's so much patronage attached to the office.'

'Do they say that? Isn't that one of America's age-old beliefs? "To the victor belong the spoils"?'

'That's—well, *I* don't care. It's *your* reputation that might suffer.'

'Then you'll help?'

Marne nodded, not daring to speak at the moment. After a moment she said, 'Yes, I'll help. With what?'

'The only real problem,' he said, 'is that this county is about as old-fashioned as it can get. So I need to find a ... temporary wife—to display on the election platforms and at the women's clubs and——'

Deep silence. 'Marne?'

But Marne, having fought the good fight, lost control of her speeding little world. Oxygen was hard to come by. She collapsed, and if he hadn't grabbed her just in time she would have fallen into the brook again.

CHAPTER TWO

MARNE awoke the next morning in some sort of daze. She knew exactly where and what she was, but couldn't quite figure out the why of it all. Her head felt as if it were a balloon, and her nose was all stuffed up. Damn man, she thought, throwing me in the pool. Now I'll have a summer cold for the rest of the year! The sun was shining, mountain-high, through the dusty windowpanes in her bedroom. And someone knocked on her door.

Hers was an old ranch-style home, built all on one floor because Great-Grandpa had hardly been able to climb stairs. 'Come in. Don't stand out there abusing my door,' she yelled. She felt the need to shout, but her ears hurt the minute she did. The hinge on the screen door sounded off, footsteps pattered across her living-room, and Becky walked into her bedroom.

'My goodness!' The little girl came over and jumped up on to the foot of the bed. Her long blonde almost-white hair fell behind her back to her hips. The old mattress bounced; Marne moaned.

'I have a cold in my nose and an ache in my head. And it's none of your darn business,' Marne snapped. 'That—damn uncle of yours. He ought to be horse-whipped! Hand me that tissue box.'

'He came home late too,' Becky said primly. 'And he's been roaming around the house like a black bear. Even Ma can't stand him. She went out to do the eggs. I thought I'd just run over here and—you're not really mad at me, Marne?'

307

'No, I'm not mad at you, love,' Marne returned. 'I've only contracted the biggest cold in the county. I haven't had a bit to drink. But I can just see your uncle laying it on. Bolstering his courage, was he?'

'I just don't know what to make of it,' Becky said. 'There's something going on in our house, and I just don't know what it is!'

'Well, you can't always guess right, Sherlock Holmes. Of course we weren't drinking together. You know darn well I haven't touched a drop in seven years. No, I came straight home after he pushed me into the—I came straight home.'

'And you were mad as a wet hen? Or just wet?' A speculative pause by a very sharp little lady. 'He was, too. Soaking wet. Claimed you pushed him into the brook.' The attentive little head cocked itself slightly and Becky peered into her eyes.

'Well, not the first time,' Marne admitted cautiously. 'What a fine fellow you have for an uncle. Picking on a nice—person—like me. Throwing me in the water and all, and then——'

'And then?' The sharp little eyes dug deeper into hers. Marne took a deep breath. The only thing she knew for sure about Becky was that everything the child heard was immediately re-broadcast throughout the town. Up hill and down dale, so to speak.

'And then nothing,' Marne said stiffly. 'Did your uncle send you over to spy on me this morning?'

'Nope. He was just getting dressed when I left the house. But I'm sure he will be along soon. The only thing he said to Ma last night was that he had hope. Well, "it's a good idea, and there's a little hope" was what he said.' The child came to a stop. 'Why, you don't even have no nightgown on, Marne.' Another silence. 'Hope for what?'

'How would I know?' Marne said desperately. 'And if your uncle comes over here this mornng I'll probably kill him. Now, if you would kindly get out of my bedroom I could get dressed!'

'Marne?' The little girl hesitated, showing a trace of tears in her eyes. 'Did you ever think of getting married again?'

'Yes, I've thought about it from time to time,' Marne admitted. 'There were one or two men in the area—but that didn't work out.'

'Oh, no!' The child's face fell. 'No, you can't marry nobody else. You gotta marry Rob again. I need an aunt, Marne, and you were the nicest aunt a girl ever had and that's why you can't marry nobody else.' All said ruefully and in a rush as she slid off the bed. 'I'll wait on the porch for you?'

'No, I don't think so,' Marne told the child regretfully. 'I have my exercises to do, and then I've got a day full of heavy thinking. You'd better run along home, love. I'll see you tomorrow, shall I? And I'm pleased, love, that I was such a successful aunt. Who knows? Some day a fine girl might come down the Pike and marry your uncle and be the best aunt in the world for you. Scoot now.'

'Nobody's gonna do that. Unless it's you, Marne. And if I ever see anyone else coming down the Pike and looking at Rob I'll kill her. Or set a snake in her bed! Are you gonna do your exercises before you get dressed?'

'Yes, I am,' Marne said. 'Don't I always? What have you been doing, peeking in my windows?'

'Not me,' Becky defended herself stoutly. 'But there are those who would, you know. All right, all right, I'm going. Maybe you'll feel better tomorrow!'

Marne watched the stiff little back march straight
out of the door and down the steps. 'It's hardly
possible that I'll feel better in the next month. Get
up,' she ordered herself, and managed to get a bare
foot on the floor. 'What a child. I wonder what it
would be like to be her mother?' She stood up to look
out of the window, but Becky was already at the curve
in the path. Marne shrugged her shoulders, and began
the slow stretching exercises that made up the first
five minutes of her morning ritual, so that she could
hardly follow Becky any further.

That little miss came to a stop in the middle of the
path as her favourite uncle came along. He was
smiling; in fact he was looking almost human. The
little posy of wild flowers in his hand gave away his
intentions.

Becky looked her uncle over very carefully, biting
on her lip. 'I did something wrong?' he asked.

'No, everything's just fine. I was thinking. Marne's
doing her exercises. She says for you to just come
right in.' Little Becky was two hundred feet further
away, a very self-satisfied smile on her face, when she
heard the initial wild scream of anger from the house
behind her. Her uncle Rob, she reminded herself, was
always the slow one, and needed help.

'Look,' Rob said in his best placating voice. 'I swear
my little niece said I was to just walk right in. Need
some help with that towel?'

'You come within two feet of me, Mr Smith, and
they'll be scraping you off the wall.' The only thing
Marne could find when Rob Smith walked into the
house in the midst of her nude aerobic exercises was
the small hand towel that she normally kept over the
kitchen sink. Marne was a good-sized girl; the towel

was no match for her. And the more she tugged at the towel the wider that grin on his face became.

'What are you grinning at? You look like an expectant baboon!' The words exploded out of her from an empty mind. Every thought had evaporated in that moment when his hand had settled on her bare shoulder.

'Thank you,' he said mildly. 'But if you want my advice I recommend you pull the towel a little lower. There's a great deal of you uncovered in that direction.'

'Yes, I'll bet there is,' she snarled. 'And if I move the towel a little lower I'll be on display even— oh—— Hell! Look, Mr Smith, why don't you just go out on the porch while I finish dressing? Isn't that a reasonable idea?'

'Not from the male point of view,' he said, chuckling. 'There's always a certain amount of viewing that improves the world. Now, Marne—your towel is slipping!'

'I'm going to bash you to a fare-thee-well,' she muttered as she abandoned the towel. 'I want to show you something else I've learned.'

'No, now, don't slap my face,' he said, chuckling. Marne moved forward, trying not to slap his face, but to get a good hold on him, and throw him over her shoulder in the manner of instruction in her martial-arts class.

Unfortunately, when Marne took that martial arts course she had received an 'A' for enthusiasm, and an 'F' for co-ordination. In this case she stamped her foot to get a good purchase on the kitchen linoleum, and forgot that she had just waxed that floor the day before. Her foot moved out from under her, and she slid across the room like a bowling ball, with Rob the pin. Together they rumbled across the kitchen and smashed against the wall, Marne on top.

'Well, now,' Rob said as he gathered up this armful of nude woman sitting on top of him, 'look what I have here!'

'Don't you dare laugh!' Marne could hardly move. Just how, she asked herself, did Lady Godiva maintain her cool?

'I wouldn't dare laugh,' he said. She struggled against his 'helping hand', wiggling for all she was worth. But finally she broke free, scrambled across the floor and ran for her room. When she came back out, wearing her old robe, he was still sitting on the floor against the wall, holding the back of his head.

'Help me up?' He was a true penitent, and looked contrite enough, and she could hardly forget that once she had loved him. So she walked over, helped him up, and, walking in a three-legged parade, they moved out on to the porch, where he sank gratefully on to the swing.

'Better?' she asked.

'I guess. I bumped my head on the wall.'

'I hope that teaches you a darn lesson. I know Tae kwon do.'

He held up a hand in surrender. 'Which you just happened to study while I've been gone?'

'That's right. Oh, dear. You *did* hurt your head! I'll bring you an ice-pack.'

'Yeah,' he muttered. 'Ice-pack.' And then he managed a little smile. 'You know something, Marne?' She cocked her head at him. 'Bruises and ice-pack and all, it was worth it!'

'I'll bet it was.' His eyes followed her as she walked slowly back into her bedroom. Something gentle, she told herself as she thumbed through her meagre wardrobe. Something demure? But the only thing she could come up with was one of her teaching uniforms. Well, not exactly a uniform, just one of several look-alike black skirts and white blouses which fitted loosely, contained plenty of pockets for pencils and notes, and did nothing to stir up the male teachers. But she did add a little mascara, a touch of purple eyeshadow, and a gloss of pale Temptation for her lips. When she came back outside he was almost himself, up on his feet, with a hand on the banister to balance, looking down into the valley and the city below. She almost forgot the ice-pack, and had to go back for it.

'Ah, you're ready,' he commented. 'I remember that. Always on time, you were.'

And if that's all you remember about me, Marne fumed to herself, you hardly know a single thing about me! He leaned on the rail, then marched back to the swing.

'How about it?' he asked. 'Have you given any thought to our marrying?'

'Just to do you a favour?'

'Just to do me a favour.'

'Why don't we just *say* we've been remarried, and act it out from there?' she suggested. 'You were always a great actor. I'm sure I could keep up. It would be simple.'

'It would be simple,' he acknowledged, 'but if the word got out I'd be thrown out of the election campaign. People will vote for many strange people, Marne, but they won't vote for a proven liar. Besides, my mother would know, and I'd hate to have her down at the church praying for us every day. I couldn't stand it.'

'That's a big load you're placing on my shoulders,' she told him. 'I don't know. If we had another wedding ceremony we'd be lying to God. That's a terrible responsibility.'

'That too. But there are millions of people who get married without love.'

'Perhaps. And without consummation? I couldn't allow that.'

'You drive a hard bargain,' he groaned, but she could see it was artificial. 'You don't believe in recreational sex?'

'No, I don't. And let me tell you one more thing, Rob Smith. If you get me tied up in just one more lie or deceit, I'm out of here. No arguments, no explanations, I'm just gone!'

He shook his head, gently because it still ached. 'You *do* drive a hard bargain,' he said dolefully.

'There are always more women in the valley you could take up with.'

'No. That won't do. I have to have you and your name. After all, your grandfather and father were the finest doctors in the county. Everybody knew Doc Tilson. Well, how about it?'

'I have to think,' she said, and walked back into the kitchen.

'Take your time,' he called after her.

Marne slumped at the kitchen table and rested her head between her hands. What to do? Make a summary of all those things that went wrong in their first marriage? Or admit without question that she still loved him, and probably would for the rest of her life, no matter *what* he did? And in the meantime, being married again would allow her to be close to him, to snap up any crumbs he might cast in her direction. And—what the devil am I doing?

From outside she heard him call to her cat. 'Come sit with me, Morgan?'

Marne's anger sputtered to a stop. Her hands stilled. Her blouse was only half buttoned, but she ignored it. Her mind was busy again.

What's the matter with me? she asked herself. I don't like the man. I didn't like him when he was a teasing damn boy, and now he's grown bigger and there's more of him for me not to like. So why am I all over shivers when he touches me, and why am I debating this silly proposal?

Why? I've been kissed by practically every male of my age in the town during the past four years, and never had such a response as I get from Rob. So he kissed me—on my nose, no less—and I'm already turned on up to the halfway point. If he *really* kissed me, what would it be like?

'Don't be too long in there,' he called from out on the porch. 'Morgan's getting restless. Your porch swing needs a coat of paint.'

Paint—paint, Marne raged to herself. I'm going to get dressed again, enough to knock your eye out, Rob Smith, and then I'm going to come out there and paint all over you, you rotten, scheming—neighbour. And *that* seemed like such a practical thing to do that she went ahead and did it.

The fashions had changed, of course, but from her early seventeens she resurrected a pair of boys' trousers, with silver buckles just under the knees, a plain boyish shirt tucked into the waistband, and a leather belt with a large silver buckle.

Rob was waiting for her on the porch. He patted the swing next to him as an invitation. Remembering the scene by the stone just one day earlier, which had ended up with her being thrown into the pool, Marne shook her head at him, folded her hands behind her, and kept her distance.

'My, aren't we charming?' He stood up, still cuddling Morgan in one arm.

'Yes, we are, aren't we?' she shot back. She reached up and undid the top button of the shirt. Rob's eyes followed her fingers as if glued to them.

'And while you're at it please stop trying to seduce my cat. She's a good old cat, and we care for each other.'

'I have no intention of seducing your cat,' he said as he leaned over and dropped Morgan to the floor. The cat protested momentarily, then sneered at them both and stalked off. 'I'm saving all my poor talents to seduce the cat's owner.'

'Don't think you can talk me into anything with that smooth talk,' she snapped.

'Why are you blushing, Marne?'

'None of your business. Why ever did you come back here after all those years? We've all just about gotten you out of our hair.'

'I told you yesterday,' he said softly. 'I came to see how you had grown up.'

Marne stirred uneasily. He made it sound so simple, so truthful, that she almost believed, even if she knew he was lying. It took an effort for her to respond. 'Now that's a crock of worms, Robert Smith. You probably didn't even remember my name until your mother reminded you!' It was a shot in the dark, but she scored a hit, and now it was his turn to blush. Not in her manner. Marne's skin was ivory; when she blushed it turned red. His skin was always a dark tan; his blush merely turned his face darker than normal. He laughed, trying unsuccessfully to brush it off.

'You never used to be such a sceptic,' he drawled.

'Sucker, you mean.'

'Never that. Look, Marne, I need you. At least sit down with me and talk it out.'

'Talk,' she charged him. 'Just talk.' And then, because all her interior had always been marshmallow, she gestured towards the door. 'Come into the kitchen. I'll make some coffee—and I'll listen. Maybe I misheard you yesterday. Coming?'

'I wouldn't miss it for all the tea in China,' he said as he took control of the door and shepherded her inside. 'I've been to China,' he continued as she ground the beans and set the pot to steep. 'Fine place. But all the tea is really in India. Ever been to India, Marne? We could go—together—after the election.'

He sat down at the table without invitation. She slapped a mug down in front of him and reached for the pot. 'You know darn well I've never been out of Massachusetts,' she grumbled as she poured the steaming liquid. He hitched his chair an inch or two away from the steam—just in case, Marne told herself, and was unable to restrain a giggle. The big brave man!

'Well?' She poured her own cup a little more daintily, stirred in a sugar cube, and sat down opposite him. He looked so—familiar, there across the table from her. So—masculine and dependable. And if I keep thinking about him along those lines he'll have me dancing the hula in his bedroom almost any day now, she thought. 'Well?' she repeated.

'It's a detailed story,' he said. He was watching her like a hawk, while his two hands cherished his coffee-mug.

'So the quicker you begin, the sooner you'll end,' she said primly.

'Hey,' he said, protesting. 'But, if that's the way it's to be, you'll get it, bare bones and all.' He readjusted his chair, took a nervous sip of his black coffee, and told her the entire story.

'There's one born every minute,' Marne said. He looked up at her, scowling. 'P.T. Barnum,' she added. '"There's a sucker born every minute." So now you're going to tell me that you need money to keep the wolf from your mother's door——'

'And Becky's too,' he added. 'You like Becky.'

'Damn you, that's blackmail!'

'Well, I never said it would be easy.'

'I like your mother, too.'

'That's good. She likes you.'

'And if you get this—political office?'

'County sheriff.' His eyes lit up and he smacked his lips as if already tasting the victory. 'The election will be tough, but there's no incumbent. I think everything will work out fine. Especially with your name up on the banners. People still remember the Tilson name. Your father was the finest doctor the county ever had.'

'My name on the advertising?'

'You bet. Local boy marries local girl. It'll be a cakewalk. Takes a little time, of course, but we can do it. You and I.'

'Takes a little time? You and I?' A pregnant pause. 'You said in six months, yesterday.' Her eyes challenged him.

'I was only guessing. Perhaps six months will do it. I can only try.' His big dark eyes gave her one of his patented trust-me looks. Marne remembered vaguely how many times she had looked into those eyes and dived in head first. His mother in trouble? Becky? Six months?

'We are going to let everybody think we're still married?'

'Oh, no. We'll have to have another ceremony. Nothing fancy, of course. Just a little get-together at my place.'

'Now just slow down,' she snapped. 'This is going to be a fake marriage, of course?'

'Well—of course,' he agreed. His eyes lit up at the obvious surrender. 'A marriage of convenience, so to speak. But there has to be a wedding and all that. It has to be a well-constructed farce, right?'

'No hanky-panky,' she snapped.

'No—— Oh. There has to be a certain amount of hugging and kissing,' he insisted.

'But it all ends just outside the bedroom door,' she insisted.

'Marne, I guarantee that this wedding will be just what you want it to be. Is that satisfactory?'

Marne slammed her chair back and paced up and down the room. Morgan called to be let in. Marne opened the screen door and then let it slam shut behind her cat. My cat has good taste, she told herself. What shall I do, Morgan?

Her cat marched straight across the room, sniffed at the bottom of Rob's trousers, then vaulted up into his lap, curled herself up, and closed her eyes. It seemed to be some sort of omen.

'I can't believe I'm even listening to this,' she said softly. 'Nobody with any sense would enter into this kind of proposal. You want me to—to marry you just so you can present a false appearance to the voters?'

'I'd not be doing anything that any other politician wouldn't do,' he said, aggrieved. 'It isn't as if I were planning to rob the state treasury, you know. Like most politicians, I expect to be honest most of the time.'

'But I don't even like you,' Marne wailed. 'I can't forget the thousand and one things that led to our divorce! They left me with a bad taste in my mouth.'

'I think that's an advantage,' he said. 'If you don't like me there's no possible reason why the marriage would turn into something permanent. Besides, it will be a change for you—get you out of the boredom of school teaching, and make some money on the side. I'll pay you for your services, of course.'

'Who?' Marne snapped. 'Who told you about my being bored with school teaching? Who? Oh, God, that rotten little blabbermouth niece of yours.'

'That's right.' He nodded sagely; there was a Cheshire-cat smile on his face.

I really ought to hit him, Marne told herself. Give him a good bash right across that Roman nose of his, and roll him down the hill into the lake. But—there ought to be *some* adventure in a girl's life. The whole story sounds as if it's fresh out of a fairy-tale, but what else is there? Another summer of odd jobs, then back to the school again? Lord, what wonderful choices I have! Remember when I used to like him? Maybe if I worked at it we might come to that again. So flip a coin. Morgan likes him. Becky loves him— most of the people I know thoroughly approve of him. So why shouldn't I take a six-month chance on him?

'You don't need to pay me,' she sighed. 'I wouldn't take your money as alimony, and . . .' A long, gusty sigh. 'All right. I'll give it a try.' Said softly as she watched her cat's head bob up and down. And then, much louder, 'If it doesn't work out the way you say, I'm going to get a quick annulment and leave you holding the baby. You hear, Rob Smith?'

'Oh, I hear,' he said. There was a very large self-satisfied smile on his face. 'Now we'd better go up the hill and tell my mother. She told me at breakfast that you were too sensible to fall for a story like mine.'

The Smith house was a good half-mile up the hill. Bigger than Marne's, it was a typical rambling New England farmhouse, with additions at odd corners, and a look of smartness and new paint about it. Rob's mother Mabel waited at the door. Becky hid behind her, clutching at her hand. Mrs Smith was a roly-poly widow of fifty-five, who had watched over Marne from a distance until after her grandmother died, and then moved more actively into her guardianship.

'Don't ever tell me,' Mabel Smith said as she raised both hands up beside her cheeks in astonishment. 'She agreed?'

'Of course,' her younger son said. 'Did you ever have a doubt about my powers of persuasion?'

'More than once,' his widowed mother returned sarcastically. 'Are you sure he didn't just sweet-talk you into this, Marne?'

'I—well, I guess he did,' Marne said reflectively. 'But isn't that always the way?' Mrs Smith led the way into the parlour and raised the curtains. Marne paid it all no mind; it was the sort of thing one did in old New England houses. The parlour was always reserved for formal functions—weddings, funerals, the curate's formal house calls. And in between times the curtains were kept lowered to keep the rugs and furnishings from fading.

'Set yourself down.' Mrs Smith gestured towards the couch. 'And you two,' turning to her orphaned grandchild. 'Get out to the kitchen and make some coffee. Marne and I have some talking to do.'

'Now, then,' the older woman bustled for a moment, sat down in the chair opposite, and gave a sigh, 'I had always hoped——' she said. 'But then that shark swam up and tried to swallow him and—well, no matter. You really mean to go through with it all, Marne?'

It was almost as if she were holding the escape hatch open for Marne to have one last chance to get out of it.

'I—said I would,' Marne said, almost whispering. 'I'm a little frightened by it all, but I'll just grit my teeth and go through with it. You would rather I didn't? What shark was that?'

'Lord, child. You're just what the man needs. A farm girl who'll keep him in line. As for the shark, she was a lovely lady who used to live in these parts.'

'Not exactly a farm girl. Peterboro has almost seventy-five-thousand residents. I only wish...' Marne said. 'I can't remember. It was all so sweet and romantic, and then everything fell to pieces. I was too angry to think, and too young to know, and so I dropped him like a hot coal. Poor Rob. And now he feels that he did nothing wrong—and I don't have the courage to tell him.'

'There's no hurry,' Mother Smith replied with her warmest smile. 'You'll have years of time together to sort everything out. The wedding is certainly not going to be so quick that——'

'Hey, are you two already talking wedding?' Rob Smith interrupted as he walked into the room carrying a tray of coffee. Becky pranced behind him, carrying sugar and milk.

'Yes,' his mother replied, smiling. 'The bride's family always takes care of the wedding, but Marne doesn't have a family. So it's up to us to help her out. I thought perhaps—September?'

'Ha!' Her son set the tray down carefully and poured the drinks. As he handed out the mugs he continued. 'The election is in November,' he said. 'I need to have Marne aboard for the campaign. How about—a week from Tuesday?'

'Good lord,' his mother sighed. 'This isn't going to be something conducted by a justice of the peace? It takes a little time to get a wedding together.'

'I'm going to be the bridesmaid,' Becky said.

'Hush. We have some important things to settle. Bridesmaids can wait. Marne, what do you have to say to that? A wedding a week on Tuesday?'

Marne looked at them all, staring back at her as if she knew what was going on. 'A week on Tuesday, or two weeks, or a month? I don't care. I haven't the slightest idea how it should come about. Grandma took charge of everything when we—the first time. I just sort of stood around, trying to look important.'

'Then that's settled,' Rob chimed in.

'At that rate we'd better have the ceremony at home,' his mother said.

'And the Reverend Mr Hunter could perform it,' Rob added. 'He's retired now, and wishes he wasn't. A nice wedding service would be just the thing to get his mind out of the doldrums.'

'And I can be the bridesmaid,' Becky repeated anxiously.

'And Betsy Willard to play the organ,' Mrs Smith inserted.

'If it's working,' Rob said. 'I'll get it overhauled.'

'And we'll hire a caterer for afters,' Mrs Smith said. 'Parties are great, but I'm tired of doing all that clearing up afterward.'

The Smiths looked at each other and smiled. Everything seemed to be working out just right.

'But—but what do *I* do?' Marne whispered. The room fell silent.

'Oh, my,' Mrs Smith said as she leaned forward to take one of Marne's hands.

'All you have to do is look beautiful,' Rob said as he took the other. 'Look beautiful, be on time——'

'And we must get you a wedding gown.' That from Mrs Smith.

'I—really can't afford it,' Marne said. There was a little trickle of salt water running down from her left eye, and her nose was running.

'Not to worry,' Rob told her. 'I'll have to get a loan to finance the whole thing, and we'll just add the wedding dress on to the list. Right?'

'Right,' Becky cheered.

'That girl has a terrible cold,' Mrs Smith said. 'Bed and hot lemonade for her. What ever happened to you, my poor dear?'

'Rob threw her into the creek,' Becky commented. Every other person in the group glared at her. The child shrugged her shoulders and threw back that long blonde mane of hers.

Marne looked slowly around the little planning group. Busy planning my life away, she told herself glumly. Is this *really* going to be right? But all those smiles, and the dreams behind them, stiffened her backbone. After all, it was only for six months. What

could go wrong in six months? Plenty. She shuddered
again, not knowing whether to laugh or to cry.

'But you don't think you'd prefer to marry some
other woman, Rob?'

All the smiles disappeared. The meeting began to
look like a funeral directors' convention. It was too
much to bear. 'All right,' Marne stammered into the
silence. 'It will be fine. It will be—right!'

CHAPTER THREE

TUESDAY week came up roses. The sun popped up early and bright, and light cool winds were blowing across the Berkshires from New York State. 'God's in his heaven,' Marne Tilson told herself. 'And I've almost gotten over the sniffles. So why am I so depressed?'

'We all have those moments.' Mrs Smith was hovering at her side, making final adjustments to the three-quarter-length ivory dress. The slim gown clung to her bodice, marched down firmly to her hips, and then flared out and down to mid-calf. A high lace collar clung to her neck, with a sheer silk transparent panel that covered, but actually left on view, her shoulders and the upper curves of her breasts. Long sleeves, with pearls sewn into the cuffs, came down her slender arms to almost an inch above her wrists. Altogether a dainty thing that revealed a little and promised much.

When we first married it was in the congregational church, Marne thought. I wore my grandmother's pristine white gown, designed in the Edwardian tradition, with a trailing veil that almost blinded me. Grandpapa walked me down the aisle, and four of my high-school girlfriends served as bridesmaids. Lord knows which of us was the most shaken. The veil was a marvel; it hid the fact that I cried all the way down the aisle. Well, I won't cry this time. Not a tear!

'Are you sure you wouldn't want my mother's veil?' Marne shook her head. She wanted no more blinding veils. Both at that first ceremony, and for a year afterwards, she had been blinded by love.

'No. Just the flowers.'

Mrs Smith carefully fitted the little coronet of flowers on top of Marne's straw-blonde hair. 'It does look—fragilely delicious.'

Marne mumbled an affirmative. She knew everything and nothing. In twenty minutes all the guests would have arrived, and she would be expected to walk down the stairs, smile at everyone, and walk up to the improvised altar. Where *he* would be waiting. She could hear the splatter of conversation floating up the stairs. Women's voices, all the teachers from the elementary school where Marne had worked for three years. All punctuated by a few deep male voices. Rob and his brother Bill, who would be his best man. Mr Dixon, the school principal, who had volunteered to give her away. The Reverend Mr Josias Hunter, dressed in his best, whose once-deep voice had begun to crack after sixty years of serving the methodist church. All waiting for the *pièce de résistance*, Marne Tilson.

There was bird song echoing in at the window, and the smell of charcoal being lit for the feast to follow. In the far distance a labouring freight locomotive could be heard, working its way through the pass that led to New York State.

'Nervous?' Mrs Smith asked. There was a great deal of understanding in her voice, a touch of sympathy every time her fingers caressed the gown. 'Bridal jitters?'

'I guess so,' Marne responded. Her teeth were chattering, and an occasional shiver ran up and down her

spine. 'If I'm not, somebody up here has an awful
lot of loose bones.' Graveyard humour, she told
herself. Why? It's only a fake, this wedding, but I'm
feeling as if it was more than the real thing. Why?

'I don't know how you keep so cool,' Becky said.
The little girl, dressed in a gown to match the bride's,
although with a youthful Peter Pan collar and just
barely reaching to her knees, was idly toying with the
bridal bouquet. 'I'm scared to death!'

The little pump organ downstairs groaned a couple
of times and began a fugue completely foreign to
Marne's ear. Well, wasn't everything foreign? she
asked herself. Mrs Willard, who played at the congregational church of a Sunday, had obliged. The
organ itself was a real antique from the days when
Pioneer Valley was really a frontier.

Mrs Willard played the organ at our first wedding.
The church was packed and I hardly knew a soul. The
organ was one of those huge multi-pipe instruments
built into the rear wall of the chancel. I was terrified.
When Gramps walked me into the vestibule I could
feel the building shake from the power of that organ.
Something old—one of Grandma's garters. Something
new—a sparkling new wristband. Something borrowed? I can't remember now. Something blue—a tiny
lace handkerchief, tucked into a fold of my gown.
Lord, I was so terrified! And, as the marriage grew
older, I don't think I ever stopped being terrified!

'Just one more thing,' Mrs Smith said. 'Rob sent
you a bridal gift.'

The package was small; Marne's fingers fumbled
with the wrapping over the little jewel box. When she
opened the lid, sunlight sparkled. There was a con-
certed *ohhh*. 'But what is it?' Becky, too short to see,
crowded her way to Marne's side.

'A jewel pin,' Marne said. 'Look. A sapphire fashioned in the centre of a little butterfly.' And I'm the only one who will understand the message, Marne told herself. How could so rotten a man be such a— wonderful fellow? A blue butterfly, the sign of faith, 'something blue'. Fidelity? I wish it were! A small tear began to trace itself under her eye. It's probably only a paste sapphire, she told herself grimly. A paste fidelity stone, for a fake wedding!

'None of that, now,' Mrs Smith chided. 'Do you want to wear it?' Marne nodded, to keep from crying.

'Up here, then, child, just under this little fold. Now, have we got it all? Something old, something new, something borrowed, something blue?'

'Everything,' Marne said, sighing. 'And a sixpence in my shoe. Isn't that the way the old rhyme goes?'

'Better take it out before the dancing starts,' practical Becky added.

'Then let's mount up,' her future and former mother-in-law commanded, 'and go down and scatter a few pearls.'

'I don't understand that, neither,' Becky complained.

'That's because you don't read your Bible often enough,' her grandmother commented. 'Here we go.'

They came down the stairs in a formal little parade. Mrs Smith first, serving as conductor. Becky next, her flood of blonde hair tucked up under a sweet circlet of field flowers, the shaking bride last, her head bent as she nibbled on her lower lip and prayed everything would go well. At the foot of the stairs Mrs Smith stepped aside, looking very self-satisfied indeed. A tall distinguished white-haired man stood by Mr Dixon and smiled. Marne combed her mind. Of course. Mr Burroughs. The man who had kept

Peterboro in his political hip pocket, so to speak, for years. Mr Dixon proffered his arm to the bride, and Betsy Willard, at the organ, began to play.

Dixon could feel her shivering hand as she tried to restrain herself. He had known her all her life, both as student, confidant, and teacher in the Weldon Street Elementary School. 'Don't let it get to you,' he coaxed as the couple paused to let Becky get a head start. 'They're all friends. Keep your eye on that third row of chairs. If you decide to run for it, that's the place.'

Marne found her voice. 'I wouldn't dare,' she sighed, and the procession moved on. The big double parlour was full. In fact there were friends and youngsters out on the surrounding veranda, watching through all the open windows. The organ squeaked as one of the two boys doing the peddling missed his cue, and then it rose and drowned out the entire world. A couple of photographers were busy at their work. One of them, Marne vaguely noted, was a tall, beautiful raven-haired woman, whose name escaped her at the moment.

Marne sniffed up a couple of tears, and struggled to keep up the measured pace. *I will not cry*! Mr Dixon tightened his elbow as a sign of encouragement. The flower-drowned altar seemed to be a million miles away. The preacher, holding his Bible in one hand, was smiling. Rob was standing on the other side, smiling too. Why is it, Marne asked herself, that I just suddenly noticed—here, two steps away from marriage—what big teeth he has? Shark teeth? But before she could draw a conclusion her mind went off into a tail-spin. Mr Dixon drew her to a halt, kissed her on the cheek, and passed her hand over to Rob. And there, she told herself with a silent giggle, I've been given away. In this world of the 1990s, they're still giving girls away!

The organ wailed to a stop. Mr Hunter stepped forward. 'Dearly beloved,' he said, and those were the last words that Marne was to hear.

Somewhere in the middle of everything someone nudged her. 'I do,' she muttered. More words.

'With this ring——' and Rob was sliding a cold gold ring on her finger.

More words, and then, 'I now pronounce you man and wife.' All the sounds came to a halt. 'You may kiss the bride,' Mr Hunter prompted. Rob did. Gently, as if this fragile creature might break. It was the most chaste kiss Marne had received in the past five years. Congratulations thundered down on them from all sides. Marne Smith clung tightly to her husband's arm and prayed that she might not lose him in the crowd.

'And this is Mr Burroughs.' Rob made the introductions as they struggled though the crowd, heading for the door. 'Mr Burroughs has kindly agreed to show me the political ropes in this county.' A flashgun fired in their faces. The tall brunette behind the camera offered Marne a hungry-tiger smile. Rob seemed to have caught a frog in his throat. 'And his daughter Sylvia, who is also going to help out with publicity,' he managed to mumble. 'And now we'd better run.'

'You don't have time for a honeymoon,' Burroughs called. 'There's the American Legion caucus tomorrow night. You won't forget?'

'I won't forget,' Rob called. He tugged at Marne's arm and rushed her out of the door to where his station wagon was waiting. It was covered with

ribbons, smothered with confetti, and surrounded by
half a dozen boys, all of whom looked guilty of
something.

'Don't forget me,' Becky wailed. Marne turned to
look. The girl was still somehow carrying the bridal
bouquet. Marne gestured; Becky tossed the flowers
to her, and then backed off a step or two. At which
time Marne threw the lucky piece back towards the
crowd, but angled so that only Becky could catch it.
There was a roar from the watchers. 'Fixed,' some
woman in the back of the crowd yelled. And that was
the last thing under Marne's control for the rest of
that day.

'What's the hurry?' she yelled at Rob as he pushed
her almost head first into the car and then struggled
to start the engine.

'Custom,' he yelled back at her. 'We have to get
out of the way so they can get on with the serious
eating and drinking.' He shoved the car into gear, and
off they went, with a trail of tin cans tied to the rear
bumper, making sounds like the devil's chorus.

'Oh, lord,' Marne groaned.

'Not to worry,' her new husband said. 'Brains over
brawn every time, love.' He drove the car for another
hundred yards, down to the bend in the highway, and
stopped. Waiting for them off the side of the road
was a shiny Cadillac. 'Rented,' he observed as he
swapped their luggage into the new car, crowded her
into its regal silence, and then put his hands on her
shoulders and turned her in his direction. 'All well
done, Marne,' he said softly. 'Scared?'

'Petrified,' she reported. 'What do we do now?'

'Well, I told everyone we were going down to
Springfield for the night.'

'But we won't?'

'But we won't. We're going to spend one night in the Tilson house. We need the rest. Tomorrow starts the rat race. I want to tell you how proud of you I was. Could you spare me a kiss?'

'Just one,' she half whispered. It was a respectable sort of kiss, the kind to start off her married life, Marne thought. But then something rattled in the back of her mind, demanding attention. This is a fake wedding, Marne Tilson. And this is the beginning of the first fake night. And you'd better get up on your toes, girl. Men's promises are perhaps not the most dependable things in the world.

So by the time she had that well chewed and settled in the front of her mind they were outside the Tilson house. He carried the luggage in and set it down in the kitchen. Marne came along slowly. 'I haven't done much today,' she said, 'but I'm tired. Terribly tired.'

'Just a darn minute,' Rob said. 'I have to carry you over the threshold.'

'There's nobody to watch,' Marne protested. 'You did that the first time, and it didn't work.'

'Maybe times will be better,' he said softly as he picked her up and carried her into the kitchen. 'I had a little something sent over by the caterer for supper here tonight. And in the meantime we ought to change out of all this finery, get cooled down, and relax. Where shall I put the bags?'

Marne's head snapped up. That tired I am not, she told herself. He had that disingenuous look in his eye again. 'That's easy,' she told him stiffly. 'Put *my* bags in *my* room, and yours in my mother's room. Was there ever any question?'

He shook his head. 'No, I guess not. But a man has to try, you know.' He was whistling as he packed the luggage away. Morgan, who had not been invited to the wedding feast, came out of the kitchen and took up watch. Marne walked tiredly into her own room and shut the door. Whistling, was he? That wouldn't last long.

The flowered coronet was beginning to bother her. She unpinned it, laid it down on top of her bureau. In the heat of the summer day the little buds were already fading. Some symbolism, she told herself. The wedding's over indeed! She gave her hair a good rub. The dress came off gently; even if the wedding was a fake, the dress was not. She knew that—for however long this wedding lasted—she would treasure the dress.

And what did a country bride wear after the wedding? *Nothing*?

That's what Rob had teased her with on their honeymoon night. She had been so nervous that she would not have been able to get out of the wedding gown had he not helped. And for some time he had kept her that way.

Marne's blushes ran rampant. She had been a virgin then. Now, to avoid further wild thoughts, she climbed into jeans and a blouse, and buttoned and zipped herself up completely.

He was waiting in the living-room as she came out. 'It's been a long day,' he murmured as he led her out on to the porch and on to the swing. 'Something bothering you?'

'Not exactly bothering,' she said. Her hair had all come down by now. She brushed it gently, then started it into a braid. 'I only wondered.'

'About what?'

'About your campaign—and Mr Burroughs.'

'Well, in the first place,' he replied, 'he really knows how to go about winning an election. He's had more experience than anyone in the county in raising election money. And that's the secret to success these days.'

'Yes,' she said, so softly that he barely heard. 'And my grandmother used to say that if you turned over every rock in the county you'd find either Burroughs or one of his men hiding—or maybe both.'

'Hey, don't pre-judge the man,' Rob said. 'He's done some fine things over the past few years. And he's always been nice to me.'

'I'll bet he has.' She made a little face at him, and he laughed.

'Well, if that's the hard question, we're in for a happy life.'

'For a happy campaign,' she amended. 'But that wasn't the hardest question I can think of.'

He looked down at her expectantly. She moved an inch or two away from him, and was grateful when Morgan jumped up into her lap. It gave her fingers something to do, scratching the old cat's ears.

'Tell me something.' He nodded. She stared out down the valley, afraid to let him see her eyes. They had always been her give-away eyes, unable to keep a secret from anybody. 'This Sylvia—the camera person. Isn't that the woman that you——?' The words ran out. How did you ask a man who invited his last inamorata to the wedding?

'That I met a few years ago? That's a fair question. The answer is yes.'

'And you don't think we'll have trouble carrying off this masquerade while she's hanging around?'

'I'm sure we won't,' he answered. She snapped her head around to stare at him. He was nibbling at his lower lip. The smile had gone.

'Sure we won't? Wouldn't it be safer not to have invited her? I gather she means to work on the campaign?'

'That's your only fault,' he said, sighing. 'You're not only too curious, but you're too bright. That's two questions. The answer to both is yes. She intends to work on the campaign. Why I don't know. And we could have avoided a great deal of trouble by not inviting her.'

'That's it? No explanation?'

'Damn you, Marne.' He pounded one of his big fists on his knee. 'Don't you think the explanation is simple?'

She shook her head. Her long braid swung around her head, and Morgan took a swipe at it. 'No,' she said, 'nothing's too simple for me.'

He jumped to his feet and started to pace back and forth. The swing jumped and swayed, throwing Marne off-centre, and out of her concentration. 'Let me draw you a picture,' he snapped. 'Elections cost money. Lots of money. And Burroughs knows where it's at. He wants his daughter to help out. Period. End of discussion.'

'And Sylvia? I don't want to make any *faux pas* during the campaign. Do you have a strong feeling for her?'

'Yeah, I have a very strong feeling,' he said bitterly. 'I'd love to buy her a one-way ticket to Moscow. Come on, let's eat something!'

'The master speaks,' Marne whispered to Morgan as she got up and started for the kitchen. The cat ignored the whole situation. Somebody had said 'eat', and that was one word that Morgan thoroughly understood.

Rob stopped her at the door, using a single finger on her shoulder to do so. 'What did you say?'

'Me?' Marne's mind raced at something more than the speed limit. 'I said the swing caster squeaks. I've been meaning to oil it for months.' She could almost feel his eyes boring into her back as she walked into the house. Mark that down, she told herself as she moved. The master has big teeth. The master also has big ears! Still, that wasn't so bad. He would never smack Sylvia in the mouth. Men like Rob Smith didn't do that sort of thing. But maybe I could help?

CHAPTER FOUR

'KEEP your teeth showing, no matter what happens,' Rob said as he escorted Marne up to the doors of the Milford Arms in Terryville, almost fifty miles from home.

'Don't lecture me as if I were some dumb kid,' she returned. 'I'm all grown up. That's one of the reasons I divorced you, Rob Smith. You needn't worry that I'll keep my teeth showing. Lord, I might want to bite half a dozen of them. And the food so far is awful.'

He pulled her to a stop. 'You mean that, Marne? About—before?'

'Of course I mean it. I know I was only a kid, but you treated me as if I were ten. Public or private. I felt like a wet rag most of the time. If I had had more courage I would have kicked—er—done you some violence—but, then, I didn't know very much about men back then. You scared me whenever you raised your voice.'

'I—never noticed,' he sighed. 'One more regret to carry around in my sack.'

'Well, we were both young, Rob. And now we're not. Come on, let's face the dragons. What is this, the fourth stop of the day?'

'Yes, but the third one didn't serve food.'

'That's a relief. I've been carrying bicarbonate lozenges in my bag for the last two weeks. Oh, good grief.'

'What now?'

'Look who's at the door, waiting for us.'

'It's only Sylvia, love, with the briefing papers. You know we couldn't survive the day without these little notes she makes up for me at every stop.'

'How could I forget?' Marne sighed. 'She does all your thinking for you. I get the funny feeling that it's a Burroughs campaign, not the Smith campaign. Just so long as she sticks to briefing papers, I suppose it's all right.'

'Don't get any ideas, Marne!' He tugged her a little closer and bent down to kiss her pretty nose. 'I do all of my own thinking. Well, most of it, anyway. I could almost believe you're jealous.'

It was dark, almost eight o'clock in the evening, and a light drizzle was setting in, for which Marne was grateful. At least he couldn't see her blush. It was four weeks since their second marriage. Marne's feet hurt, and so did her heart. It was becoming more and more difficult to keep from telling him the real truth—that her earlier love was fast returning.

'C'mon,' she said quickly, heading for the stairs.

'There's a small problem,' Sylvia announced as she handed Rob a set of small cards. 'There's no room at the head table for Marne. I've put her over at the side-table with the wife of one of the local officers.'

'Marne?'

'I don't mind,' she answered. 'Just so long as I get a chance to sit down.' She followed the pair of them into the hall. They were discussing the card-file information. Marne looked around. The hall was almost at capacity. Which, she knew, was a welcome sign. At seventy-five dollars a plate, this one meeting would considerably swell the campaign coffers. Her only trouble was she didn't know a soul outside of Rob's travelling team, and it bothered her. She wanted to help, but the campaign committee had shut the door firmly in her face. She was strictly a decoration. As now.

Rob came back to her, caught her in his arms, and kissed her, a real honeymoon kiss. And the crowd loved it. So did Marne. 'How about another?' she asked as the applause rolled across the room.

'We don't have time,' Sylvia interrupted. 'We're on a tight schedule.'

'Aren't we always?' Rob said, disgusted. 'Well, there's your guide, Marne. I'll see you after the show.' And off he went, following Sylvia like a hound dog commanded to heel.

'My, he's such a handsome young man!'

Marne turned around to meet her own private welcoming committee. Two dowagers of a doubtful age, dressed in high fashion. So high that Marne furtively began to tug at her blue serge suit. It had been fourteen hours and almost a hundred miles since she had put it on back home. But a candidate's wife—she took a deep breath, and flashed her smile.

'Yes, he is,' she agreed. 'And he's all mine!' And wished it was true.

'It's good to be proud, but after we elect him sheriff you'll have to share,' her escort persisted. 'Ethel Norton, my dear. Vice-chairman of the town committee. We're so crowded that we've had to put our table over here in the back corner.'

'It doesn't matter.' Marne managed somehow to widen her smile. And besides, I've heard this speech three times today, she wanted to add, but didn't. Whether she wanted to or not, she was forced to admit that Rob was a brilliant speaker. No matter what he said, he left one with the distinct impression that things were going to shape up at the county jail if he was elected. She followed Ethel off into the corner, and sighed with relief as a white-haired gentleman held her chair for her. And it was only then that she noticed Sylvia sitting up on the dais next to her husband!

'I should have brought binoculars,' she said to Ethel, seated next to her. 'We've not seen a crowd as big as this since the campaign started.'

'You should have been up at the head table,' her neighbour returned. 'I can't understand why your campaign manager said that we should change the seating plan.'

And neither do I, Marne thought. 'I really don't mind, Ethel.'

'Well, I do. Now I have to sit way back here in the corner, and I don't hear as well as I once did. Try the chicken.'

Marne looked down at her plate. 'I think I've seen this particular chicken before,' she murmured. Ethel evidently hadn't. She dug in, eating and talking at the same time.

'Any children, Mrs Smith? A sheriff ought to have a family.'

'Rather difficult. We've only been married for four weeks. But Rob has a little niece who has taken us under her wing. And yes, we plan to have a family of four, God willing.'

'That's nice.'

'Yes, Becky is very nice.'

'I meant the chicken is nice, my dear. It's so hard to get such a large gathering properly catered for.'

'Of course,' Marne returned as she attacked the chicken. Note number six: candidates' wives are meant to be seen and not heard. Once again she tugged at her blouse, trying to get it back in order. Candidates' wives. The phrase still had a strange sound.

Candidates' wives. We'll be back home tonight, and I hope Morgan will be glad to see me.

Ethel put a hand on Marne's wrist, and pointed toward the dais. The speech-making had already begun, and Rob was introducing her. Obviously he didn't quite know where she had got to. Marne hastily scraped back her chair, stood up, and waved to the crowd. The spotlight operator obviously didn't know where she was either. The beam of his light wavered across the room twice before picking her out. And then Rob was off on his favourite subject, the laxity of discipline and care in the sheriff's department.

Marne sank back into her seat. 'That's nice,' Ethel said cheerfully. 'He has a wonderful speaking voice.'

'Amateur theatricals,' Marne returned. 'Years of amateur theatricals. He's a great actor.'

Chairs were scraping back all over the room as applause followed the speech. 'And you didn't even get to eat your chicken,' Ethel said mournfully.

'No problem,' Marne lied. 'I'm a vegetarian!'

The big limousine built up speed as they hit the highway. Marne did her best to curl up in the corner of the front seat. Rob had said not a word to her since the programme had ended. His eyes held the road as if driving was dangerous. Marne watched his arms as he drove. He had shucked his suit coat, and his short-sleeved shirt revealed the subtle play of a dozen muscles. She would have loved to cuddle up against him as she always had during their first marriage. But he looked too forbidding.

'It was a good crowd,' she offered. Silence. 'Ethel says you're bound to get elected. A sure thing.'

'Ethel. Who the hell is Ethel?'

Marne giggled. 'Mrs Ethel Norton is the vice-chairman of the town committee. Only I don't remember what town we're in.'

'Terryville,' he muttered. 'Why the hell did you go off and hide away in that back corner?'

Marne stiffened. 'I didn't just *go off*,' she stated firmly. 'I was directed. Ethel tells me that your campaign manager asked for the change. There wasn't enough room on the dais, she said.' But there was plenty of room for Sylvia Burroughs! But why should I be so damn jealous? It isn't as if this were the real thing, this marriage of ours.

'My campaign manager? Burroughs?'

'How should I know? How many managers do you have?'

'And what's that supposed to mean?'

'I don't know, do I? I'm just the little country girl that married you. What is it, Rob? Is Mr Burroughs doing all the planning *and* thinking for you? Every once in a while I have to look closely to make sure your puppet-strings aren't showing.'

The tyres on the big car squealed as he applied the brakes and drove them off on to the hard shoulder. 'Now that's a hell of a thing to say, Marne. I do my own thinking. What's eating you?'

'Eating me? Nothing's eating me.'

'That's not what Sylvia says.'

'Oh? And now you're listening to the girl who's been campaigning like mad. You know it's you she wants, Rob, not the sheriff's office.'

There was nothing urbane about this man next to her, not now. His voice had become rough as he reached across the seat and grabbed her by the shoulders. 'Well, at least she——'

'She what? Go ahead and say it.'

'She has the courtesy to defer to my judgements, rather than criticise me out of the corner of her mouth,' he snapped.

'And that's what I did? Is that the charge, Sheriff? Are you going to put the cuffs on me and take me in? I take it you have a secret informer?'

'Yes,' he groused. 'Sylvia keeps me posted.'

'And she could hear everything I had to say, with her on the dais and me in the back corner?'

'Damn it, Marne, there's nothing going right in all this.'

'Oh? I thought the campaign was going ahead great guns. There's only another two weeks before the primary election, isn't there?'

'I don't mean the campaign. To hell with the campaign. I mean between you and me!'

Marne's heart skipped a beat. Between you and me? Was there ever again to be something 'between you and me'? I want desperately to have something to go on between us, she told herself. But—but everything that goes around comes around. And here you are, playing games again with Sylvia Burroughs.

'I—don't think there is anything that ought to be going on between you and me,' she stated primly. 'After all, I'm only doing you a favour, marrying you again. Don't you remember? A fake marriage?'

'Marne——' He seemed to have got his tongue trapped between his teeth. 'You haven't ever thought to make it all real?'

'Our marriage? Not recently,' she said. 'Not since Sylvia popped up in the middle of things.' She coiled herself up on the seat again. 'I really don't want to talk about this, Rob. I really don't.'

He made a noise. Under the soft rumble of the engine, the clacking of the windscreen wipers, the patter of the rain, he made a noise. Or said something? Marne didn't dare to ask. It was almost like a groan. But that could hardly be, could it?

And then he shifted the car back into gear, and took off down the highway for home.

'Better be careful,' she challenged him bleakly. 'You wouldn't want the sheriff's patrol to give you a ticket, would you?'

She heard what he said next. It was an unrepeatable word. The last word he had to say until they pulled up in front of the house.

Rob set the handbrake and shut down the engine with a flourish. 'There. We now have a whole weekend to ourselves.'

'Good.' Marne stretched and opened the door. 'Sleep. That's what I want. Why in the name of all that's holy do we have to run around the county like a cat with its tail cut off?'

'That's the way elections are run,' he said gruffly. 'See the voter eyeball to eyeball. Press the hands. Pontificate. There are thirty-six towns and villages and cities in this county. And before the election I want to be seen in every one of them——'

'You'll make it,' she interrupted. 'Kiss the babies. Now there's a nice thought.'

'What? Kissing babies?'

'No, just babies. I like babies. Did we make enough money this time so you can buy a little radio advertising time?'

'I don't know,' he said. 'Burroughs looks after all of that side of things.'

'Burroughs, Burroughs, Burroughs,' she mocked. 'I wonder why *he* isn't running for sheriff?'

'He can't. He's running for the state senate. Come on, woman. We're here. Let's get inside before we drown.' Before she could escape he put his suit jacket around her shoulders. The instant comfort was there. Not because the night was cool, which it was, but because it was *his* coat. It smelled and breathed and lived of him. She could hear the little pulse in her ear crying Rob, Rob, Rob!

Marne stumbled up the steps in front of him, dodging the point where the gutter leaked and sprayed cold water on unwary necks. He brushed by her and fumbled with the key. The interior of the house was cold. Even in the late summer the mountain chill had set in.

'Morgan's not here.' When you had lived with a particular cat for a large part of your life, missing was noticeable.

He came in close behind her, lifting the wet coat from her shoulders immediately. 'Probably Becky kept her at the other house. Morgan never was a rain-lover, was she?'

Marne collapsed into the rocking-chair. Rob turned on one of the lamps, dropped his case, and did the same. 'Sometimes I wonder if it's worth it,' he said, sighing. 'Feet hurt?'

'You know they do,' Marne said. This *is* a throwback, she told herself as he sat down on the floor in front of her, removed her shoes, and began a gentle massage of the bottoms of her feet. Something he had done so often years ago. Something—loving.

Under the ministrations she began to let go. Her eyes grew heavy. She shifted her weight in the chair to rest one hip. His fingers moved across the bottoms of her feet. Did Cleopatra have a slave who gave foot-rubs? she asked herself just before she went to sleep.

Rob continued the massage for a moment or two after he heard that tiny whistle of breath that she always emitted just when she went to sleep. God, I'm tired, he told himself as he finally pulled himself up on to his own feet. And *is* it worth it? he asked. No, not the political office. If she ever knew what a frame-up *that* was. But how else could I get this near to her? He rubbed his hand through his thick hair, and stretched. Kissing babies? How in the world did *that* ever come up?

It had been an intermittent argument between them for the whole of their first marriage. 'You've got the law and outside interests,' she would complain. 'I want a baby.' But how could you explain to a woman of eighteen that she was too much of a baby herself? Or that a struggling law student couldn't afford the extra expense? Or the real truth—I want you to myself for a little while yet? So no baby. One more stack of fuel to put on top of our bonfire.

'But I wish,' he said softly, almost under his breath, 'I wish I really knew what put the flame to the fire!'

Marne's rocking-chair squeaked. Time to move her into her bed. Into *our* bed, he thought as he walked across to her bedroom, opened up the bed, and turned on the night-light. Another little fetish. She always needed a night-light. Not because she was afraid of the dark. She wasn't really afraid of anything. Except me?

He came back and picked her up with all the gentleness of which he was capable. She stirred, shifted her weight in his arms, and cuddled up against his chest almost as if she were purring. He could feel the warmth of her breasts pressing against him. It's worth the risk, he told himself. He kissed her again, once on the forehead, and once on that little nose.

She giggled when he put her down on the bed. Giggled, and then rolled over on to her side and pulled

her knees up against her chest. It made a problem
which he was happy to attack. Her blouse came off
with no difficulty. His fingers plucked at the buttons
cautiously, and seemed to touch on the softness of
her breast by accident. Accident, he told himself as
he went back for another taste of heaven. Yeah, accident! Not until she stirred uneasily did he give it up.

For the rest, he was out of practice, but he managed
to strip her down before he tucked her into the long
silk nightgown. One blanket was sufficient. He pulled
it up to her chin. She was smiling. For a moment Rob
Smith stood beside the bed and watched his wife
sleep—and wished he had the nerve to crawl in beside
her and make a real marriage out of all this.

Marne woke up with a smile. Morgan was lying across
her stomach, making cat-sounds. The sun was bright
in the sky. Saturday morning. A free day. There must
be an easier way to elect a sheriff than all this, she
told herself as she slipped out of bed and fumbled
into her slippers. The cat opened one eye. 'Becky's
come and gone?' Marne asked. The cat gave her a
wise nod, and began licking at her front paws. 'So
don't talk,' Marne said, and stood up.

Somebody in the front of the house was talking.
Some man. Marne's smile widened. Something nice
had happened to her in the night-time. She couldn't
remember quite what it was, but it involved Rob and
herself. Maybe it was only a dream? She took a step
or two towards the bedroom door, and then remembered how transparent her silk nightgown was. But
not how she came to be wearing it. Speculation could
be a nice thing. She shrugged her shoulders and
reached for her robe.

It wasn't Rob talking, out there in the kitchen. In fact it was three perfect strangers. Three rather large men, all of whom came to their feet as she came in.

'Do I know why you're drinking coffee in my kitchen?'

'No. I suspect not.' The speaker was the elder of the three, equipped with a fringe of white hair and a solemn expression. 'Dirk Wilson, Mrs Smith. We are—er—a part of your husband's campaign committee.'

She waved them back into their chairs. 'Oh, are you really? Strange that I've never seen you in these parts before.'

'Well—we're a part of the advance team,' Wilson said. 'May I make you known to Mr Jones and Mr Smith?' He waved a hand vaguely in the direction of his compatriots.

Marne laughed, her full-throated weekend laugh. 'That's my line, Mr—Wilson, is it? I'm the Smith around here. People call me Marne. Or is this gentleman Smyth with a "y"?'

'I—er—your husband——'

'My husband what? Absconded with the campaign treasury?' There was an instant silence in the room. All three of them looked as if she had just released one of the secrets of the space rocket!

'I said something wrong? Where *is* my husband?'

'He went into town,' Wilson said. 'There are one or two people he had to talk to, so he suggested we could do our work here. He also said he would bring back a pint of coffee ice-cream.'

Marne sat back in her chair, her eyes sparkling devilment. 'You see,' she commented. 'He's a devil, that man, but he sweeps me off my feet with coffee ice-cream. Just what work is it that you three do?'

'Surveys,' Mr Jones said firmly. 'Surveys.'

'Let me pour you a cup of coffee,' Wilson offered. All of them looked nervous. And then a car horn sounded outside, and they looked agitated.

'It's that Burroughs woman,' Jones said from his position behind the dimity kitchen curtain.

'My God,' one of the others commented. 'How bad can things get? Mrs Smith, do you suppose you could point out some place where the three of us might— work? We would hate to be seen by Miss Burroughs.'

'Me too,' Marne chuckled. 'Well, look, if it's all that serious, you could all three of you duck into the front parlour. Through there.' She watched as they hustled out. 'And be careful,' she called after them. 'My grandmother had that room stuffed to the roof with bric-a-brac.'

So they didn't care to be seen by Sylvia? Marne circled the table, picked up the used coffee-cups, and dumped them in the sink. She was in fine fettle. She loved mysteries—especially murder mysteries. And this scene had suddenly become a part of a best-seller plot. Just in time, for the raven-haired woman knocked once on the screen door and burst into the house as if it were hers by divine right.

'Well—Marne Smith.'

'I believe so. Isn't that what it says on the mailbox?'

'Always clever, Marne.' Sylvia wrinkled her nose, as if something smelled bad. 'Too bad you're not clever enough.'

'But I'm a "wannabe",' Marne said. 'I'm just as clever as I wannabe. What brings you to the Smith house? Rob isn't here.'

'I know that, silly. He's downtown, meeting with my father. He asked me to come out and pick up some papers for him. He left them in his briefcase.'

'Briefcase? Of course, it's on top of *our* bed.' A major lie that seemed to startle Burroughs. 'I'll get it for you.' Marne got up and nipped over into Rob's room. Luckily the door to *her* bedroom was closed. The briefcase was on the chair beside his bed. She swept it up and brought it out.

'Anything else? A cup of coffee?'

'No, I—well, maybe I should. We haven't talked in such a long time.'

Marne provided the service, and topped off her own mug. 'No, we haven't talked, have we, Sylvia? What would you like to talk about?'

'Oh, I don't know. How about, what happens after the election?'

'Sounds fine. You start.'

Sylvia managed a little trill of laughter that ran upscale for a full octave. 'Well, of course, after the election you won't be needed, Marne. Have you ever thought of moving to Connecticut? I hear there are plenty of teaching jobs down there—at a good pay too. I'm sure my father would be glad to give you a recommendation.'

Look at the nerve of that woman, Marne thought. Wait until after the election and then move in? 'Is this something you've planned out with Rob?'

'Of course. After the election Rob is going to join my father's little group. You know, we'll have full control of all western Massachusetts then.' The brunette offered a glacial smile as she sipped her coffee. 'But by that time Rob will need a more...elegant helpmate. Let's face it, Marne. You didn't have it all those years ago, and you don't have it now. I'm sorry that you've been sleeping with Rob. That will all have to go, you know. You wouldn't want to tie him down now, would you?'

'I don't know about that,' Marne drawled. 'You know—no, you wouldn't know. Rob is a great performer under the sheets. I might well want to tie him down. Hog-tie him, that is.'

The beauty across the table became incensed. Her ivory face flushed as she pushed back her chair. It crashed to the floor. 'Damn you, Marne Smith,' she snarled. 'There's no use you struggling. You're a dead issue. I—my dad and I—have Rob already tied up in knots. He's on our team, and when we take on a new player we take him lock, stock and barrel!'

'Third strike?' Marne mounted a smile large enough for the occasion. 'You've had two times at bat already, Sylvia, and you haven't scored. What makes you think that you can make it this time?'

The brunette dropped her mug. It crashed on the table and rolled to the floor. Sylvia was so angry that she couldn't speak. Marne pushed on.

'You know, Sylvia, I meant to ask you, did you send me a videotape some years ago?'

'I——' Whatever it was Sylvia was about to say went by the boards. There came a loud sneeze from the front parlour. 'What's that?'

'That?' Marne improvised. 'That was my cat, Morgan. When she sneezes it sounds like a fire horn. Why don't you go away, Sylvia?'

'I'll go when I'm ready!'

'You could get a heart attack that way,' Marne said. 'You're ready, lady.' And while Sylvia gabbled, Marne seized her upper arm and walked her out of the house and over to her car. 'And do me a favour, Miss Burroughs. It's hard enough for me to get along with you on campaign days; don't risk your life by coming around my home again. Got it?'

The fancy sports car spun its wheels and sped away. Morgan tramped out and sat down beside Marne. 'She didn't get it,' Marne said. Her cat waved her abbreviated tail in agreement. Mr Wilson stuck his head out though the kitchen door.

'Is the coast clear?'

'The coast is clear,' Marne said, chuckling. 'You know, I've always meant to dust that parlour, but it's been two years and I haven't gotten around to it yet.'

CHAPTER FIVE

'IT'S SEPTEMBER and that's the end of the campaign?' Marne groaned as she fitted herself into the front seat of the car. 'I've been to two breakfasts, three lunches, and two teas just today!'

'Brave girl,' Rob said as he wheeled the car out on to Main Street. 'There will be three or four promotions by radio tonight, and one TV spot on the Springfield television station, and that's it. As far as you and I are concerned, all we have to do is sit back and wait for the polls to open tomorrow morning.' One of his big hands came off the wheel and patted her knee gently. 'Good show, love.'

'Ah!' She felt like doing something silly, like barking at him, for example. Or licking his paw? Love? Instead she shifted over in the seat to be close against him, pulled her legs up on to the seat, and laid her head down on his shoulder. He blew the horn and waved at a couple of prospective voters hurrying through the cool sunshine. She wrapped both hands around his arm and held on for dear life. It felt good. Almost as good as once it had been, years ago.

At the corner of Bilt Street he paused. 'Will you look at that?' he said.

'Look at what?'

He pointed across the street, where heavy construction equipment was busy. 'They're tearing down the Odeon Theatre, that's what.'

'The old movie theatre?'

'That's the place the Peterboro Players used to rent. Back when we thought we were bound to be a success. Don't you remember?'

'Not really,' she replied. 'I remember you being gone night after night, but I never actually tied it in to the theatre. Well, I guess all the old houses are falling, aren't they?'

'Yes,' he said. 'But this one had memories. We *all* thought we'd be starring on Broadway some day.'

'And now you're going to be sheriff.' She did her best to soothe, but he didn't need it.

He laughed as he turned to her. 'Sheriffing is steady employment, love. There are lots of actors on the breadline these days.' He offered the old building a tip of his cap, and drove on down Main Street.

Tired, but not exhausted, Marne dropped into a daydream as he followed the well-worn path out Main Street, up the hill on Darcey, and then out on to the old Albany Turnpike. Things were what they had been so long ago. When I didn't know any better, she told herself. And that brought a glum little chill.

'Asleep?'

'No. Just sort of dreaming. Will your goons be at the house this afternoon?'

'My goons?'

'You know. Jones and Smith and that other guy, who've been camping out with us for the past four days?'

'Oh, them. No. They've finished up all their work. We may have to do one more round tonight, but it's nothing you would want to participate in, so you don't have to worry.'

'That sounds pretty ominous.' She moved her head just far enough so she could study his rigid jawline, his cat-like eyes—and the little furrow in his forehead that made him look so young. 'I thought maybe we might just...rest this afternoon. Becky and your mother have the cat, and if your goons are gone we could——' She stopped in midstream. What she wanted to do was not on the bill. But nervous little spasms were running up and down her spine, and she—well, she wanted to. Unless he felt that they— God, how did I ever get in such a mess?

'Yeah,' he said as the heavy car began to climb the hill. 'A little rest, a light lunch——'

'Don't say food to me for the next thirty days,' Marne interrupted. 'Why is it that so many women wanted to gawk at me? Is there some magic to being the sheriff's wife?'

'An American custom, love. They want to believe that they're electing a perfectly normal, honest fellow, with a perfectly normal, honest wife, who aren't going to go charging off into some wild misadventure. They want to touch and see and hear—and maybe even smell, for all I know. Here we are.'

Marne unwound and climbed out without waiting for him. Her grey suit—the second of her two campaign suits—was as wrinkled as she felt. 'I need a shower,' she called back to him as she disappeared into her bedroom to pick up the necessaries, and then walked over into the bathroom.

'Me too,' Rob called after her. 'Don't use up all the hot water.'

Lucky he reminded me, Marne thought. Now *that* was something he had always yelled at her about, using up all the shower water and leaving him nothing. Giggling to herself, she slipped out of her clothes and dumped them all into the hamper.

There was plenty of water. She ducked into its warm embrace and soaped to her heart's content. We used

to do it together, she thought. Especially on Saturday
afternoon. That was—why can't we do it again? We're
married. We have a licence from the Commonwealth,
and the blessings of the church. Why did I ever get
myself into this unholy mess? I should have gone into
a convent. Methodists don't have convents. What am
I blustering about. Excited, she gently massaged her
breasts with the soapy washcloth. Her reactions
increased.

She turned off the water and climbed out. Steam
covered the wall mirrors and condensed on the wash
basin. The bath towels were large and well-worn. One
more thing she had let go to the dogs during the past
few years. She wrapped herself up cosily in one of
them, and scrubbed herself dry. Leave one towel for
Rob, she admonished herself. And where did I leave
my robe? Not in the bedroom? A quick search of the
bathroom. Yes, in the bedroom.

A small smile touched her lips. The devil made easy
the paths to hell. How often she had heard that
sermon! I can't walk across the house naked to get
my robe, can I? The smile became a grin. Carefully
she fashioned her towel into a sarong and tucked it
in just over her breasts, and patted herself down. Yes,
she thought, there's more of me than there used to
be. I wonder if he really *would*—— A knock thundered on the door.

'Come on, chum, don't take all day.'

Marne skidded over to the door and partially
opened it. The warm air of the bathroom ran into the
cooler air of the kitchen, and a fine fog formed. 'I
didn't know there was a timer running,' she told him
saucily. He was leaned against the doorjamb, bal-
anced on one hand, with a towel fastened loosely
around his waist. It was the first time she had seen

so *much* of him in many a year. Her pulse began to race; surely he must see?

'I——' She fumbled for a word or two as she tried to sidle past him. Her foot came down on the cool linoleum of the kitchen, and she slipped.

Marne yelped.

'Don't worry, I've got you.' He seemed to be hardly straining as he snatched her up. 'Wouldn't do to have my wife fall——' Something snapped between them. Some electrical something that startled them both. He had snatched her up, but had missed her towel. It fluttered momentarily and then fell to the floor, catching at *his* towel as it went. As God had intended with Adam and Eve, they stood within each other's grip, stark naked.

'Oh, God.' Marne sighed as her hands went up around his neck and held on for dear life. Rob said not a word, but cuddled her close against him, moving her gently back and forth so that her nipples rubbed against his chest.

'Yes.' He was breathing heavily, as if he had just run the marathon. She wiggled against him, noting how quickly he had been aroused.

'Yes,' she whispered. It had been so long, but memory was quickly refreshed, in all its wild panoply of excitement.

'Yes,' he muttered, and carried her across the room and into her bedroom. The bed had been made up early in the morning, before they had hit the campaign trail. Somehow he managed to hold her with one arm, and used the other to strip back the blankets. She was trembling; so much so that when he gently stretched her out on the cold sheets another shiver hardly mattered.

'Don't,' she muttered.

'Don't?'

'Don't just stand there, looking,' she said.

'Oh.' The bed shook as his weight came down next to her. Instant warmth prevailed. His arm came up over her, and his fingers toyed with the lobe of her ear. 'Damn!'

'What?'

'Earrings,' he complained. 'How can I nibble an ear when you're wearing——'

'I'm a big girl,' she interrupted. 'There are plenty of other places to nibble.'

Whatever answer he made was lost as he found a spot for nibbling—the rose tip of her breast. Waves of tension swept over Marne, culminating in a rising climax as his soft tongue teased her most vulnerable spot. Nerves she had forgotten came into play as her breast hardened. His hand moved and landed on her other breast. He teased a nipple between his thumb and forefinger, all the while continuing to cherish the other.

Marne squirmed a little lower in the bed. His tongue followed. Her excited little hand swept up over the rise of his belly, toyed with his navel, ran up and down his chest. He groaned, and shifted his attention to her mouth. His tongue pursued hers; she opened her lips to welcome the invasion, moaning all the while.

Another change. His hand shifted down the hill of her breast, and gently coursed farther, until it reached her ultimate precipice and plunged over. In the darkness where her most sensitive part hid, his fingers found their goal. It was hard to suppress the little squeak as he discovered the right place, and began that most refined of all tortures.

Marne squirmed in the sheer delight of it all, wiggling slightly from side to side, and then upward, as

if she wanted to escape his terrorism, but of course
it wasn't true. She did not want to escape, only to
gain a few inches of space so that she could plunge
down hard on him. He laughed at the contact.

'Do it,' she muttered. She was bathed with perspiration, panting for breath, seared by fire. 'Do it,'
she whispered.

Not too reluctantly Rob rolled over on top of her,
took a moment to kiss the tip of her nose, and then
slid down into position between her legs. 'Do it,' she
urged hoarsely. He did it.

Time had a peculiar function. In moments like this,
time slowed almost to a crawl as he plunged into her,
as deeply as flesh would allow. And then time sped
as he pumped in and out. Marne, riding the wild beast
almost to an end, did her best to regulate her thrusts
to his, with no luck. His hands shifted from her
shoulders to under her buttocks, where his superior
strength took her into his own rhythm. For another
frantic moment they beat against each other until
finally, with a massive groan, he thrust even deeper,
and locked himself into her while his juices flowed
and mingled and brought her to an excruciating peak.
For just a moment they lay there rigid, two made into
one, and then he collapsed on top of her, utterly spent.

His weight was an apostrophe to the exercise. He
stirred once as if to withdraw. Her small hands
wrapped themselves around him and held him. 'Don't
move,' she said, sighing. His head rested just over her
shoulder, perspiration dripping from his forehead. She
wiped it away with a casual hand.

'Oh, my,' he offered. Marne laughed with the joy
of it.

'"Oh, my," is that all you have to say?'

'Yes.'

'You used to be more vocal.'

'I was younger then. Did I hurt you?'

'No, not in the slightest. It's been a long, long time. You never——'

'No, I never did. Not ever with anyone else, Marne. I didn't have the spirit for it. But you've certainly improved.'

'I spent a thousand nights, Rob, rehearsing how it had been, what I had done wrong. How I could have made it better.'

'You've certainly learned from experience.'

'No, I can't say that I did. Just at that moment—out by the bathroom door, I completely forgot everything that I'd studied!' A moment of silence as he unfettered her, and lay by her side.

'Rob?'

'I think I bit you too hard in all the excitement.'

'It is a little sore, but it'll get better. I've got two of them. Rob?'

'What?'

'When we were first married you always said a good man could do it twice without any trouble.'

'Which just goes to show you what a bloody fool I was. I could do it two or three times in those days, but not anywhere near as well as we did just then. I love you, Marne.'

'I'm glad.'

'What are you doing now?'

'Well, I thought if I encouraged it a little bit, we——'

'You're on the right track, glutton.'

'Glutton? Well, if you'd rather not do it again, all you have to do is say so.' She spoke primly, and patently falsely.

'If I want you to stop I'll tell you,' said the superior male. 'Oh, lord, now what?'

There came a knock on their front door. A thundering, smashing knock. And a voice calling. 'Marne? Granny asked me to bring Morgan back. She's nervous or something, so I——'

'Becky! No! Don't come in. We're——'

'*Your* niece. I don't know when I'd have been less glad to see her.'

'Where the devil are my trousers?'

'In your room, I suspect.' Marne, a broad grin on her face, lay back against the pillows and admired his firm male body as he frantically searched for something to cover himself.

'What are you smirking at?' he growled as he paused in the search. 'You're as badly off as I am.'

'Me? Why, Mr Smith! I'm in *my* bedroom in *my* bed, covered by *my* blanket. How can you accuse me of anything?' Her delightfully contralto laugh followed him as he abandoned his search and made a dash for his own room.

Of all the things Becky Smith, the ten-year-old busybody, would never think to do, one was to wait to be invited. As in this case. After one more carolling announcement Becky burst into the house and came directly to Marne's bedroom.

'I brung your cat,' she said as she walked through the door and dropped Morgan on the bed. 'She was sick for somethin'. I think she misses you. What are you doing in bed at four o'clock in the afternoon? Are you sick, Marne? Do you want I should call the doctor?'

The lovely green eyes grew wider as her uncle came in behind her. Rob had managed to find an old brown robe, and had slipped into it. His hair was wet.

Evidently he had detoured by the bathroom. The little girl's eyes grew wider.

'What the devil are you doing here at four in the afternoon?' her uncle lectured her. 'Can't we have any privacy at all?'

'Don't be so mean,' Marne cautioned. 'She just came to see about Morgan. Becky?' But the little girl stared as her eyes grew wider, and then she covered her mouth with both hands and ran for the door.

Her uncle started after her. 'So you brought the cat back. Now scoot.'

'I gotta tell Granny,' the child said.

'Don't you dare,' Rob yelled after her, but the child was out of the door before he could think of anything positive to do.

'Don't waste your time,' Marne told him as she sat up in the bed. His eyes shifted. She looked down to where he was focused, and pulled the blanket up. 'She'll be halfway home before you could get your trousers on!'

'But... Do you think she knows?' he stammered.

'Of course she knows. Modern education,' Marne told him. 'They teach all that stuff in the schools, Mr Smith. You should be proud that our school system does so well!'

'Well, I'd damn well prefer that they teach her reading and writing,' he muttered, 'and leave sex alone!'

'Old-fashioned,' Marne chuckled. 'The schools have so many subjects to teach that reading and writing hardly qualify any more.'

'That girl has a tongue that's hinged in the middle,' he grumbled. 'By tomorrow this little tale will be over half the county.'

'Fearful for *your* reputation?' Marne asked. 'Lord, how times have changed. I would have thought you'd be concerned about *my* reputation.'

His face looked as if he had just run into a block of cement. 'See here, Marne——' he started to say, and then the telephone rang. 'I'll get it. We have to talk, woman.'

Marne watched him go, like a Roman centurion in a hurry, with an invisible sword strapped at his side. So? We have things to talk about, do we? Well, let me tell you, Rob Smith, just make sure there's no more subterfuge going on around here. No more lies. No more video scenes with Sylvia Burroughs in the middle of them. Let's make sure, shall we? No more of that massive male domination. Partnership. Share and share alike. If you can do that, Mr Smith, we might have an excellent—superior—relationship.

Through the open door she could hear her husband at work with the telephone. 'Blown wide open, you say?' A pause for the other side of the conversation. 'They know everything now?' Another pause. 'Damn that woman. I'd like to hang her from a sour apple tree.'

Sylvia Burroughs, Marne told herself. Who else could qualify in the whole of this county? Let it be Sylvia. I *want* it to be Sylvia. If we had a guillotine I'd volunteer to pull the cord! Are you listening, lord?

'Well, there's no use crying about it,' Rob said to whomever he had on the line. 'All right. That's a go on everything. Pass the word. Everything goes immediately!' The telephone slammed back into its cradle, and in a moment Rob walked back into her bedroom.

By this time Marne had recovered her aplomb, and allowed her blanket to slip a few inches south of the crests of her breasts. But he wasn't looking this time.

'Now, shall we take up where we left off?' she proposed in the most sultry voice she could muster.

'I—we'll have to put it off for a while,' he said. She could hear the strain in his voice, the worry. 'There just isn't time,' he continued. 'I've got a fire-storm running through the middle of my business.'

'Running for sheriff requires a fire-storm?'

'No—I—you wouldn't understand, Marne. I have to go.'

'Explain to me first,' she insisted. 'I'm twenty-six years old, with a college degree and a very large curiosity bump. Election day isn't until tomorrow. I'm working on a fire-storm of my own, Mr Smith. You couldn't postpone this trouble of yours for—say—another hour or so?'

'No, I can't,' he mumbled. 'I've got to go. I have no idea what time I might get back. Why don't you—er—take a little nap or something? Curl up with a good book?'

'Yes, I'll do that,' Marne said coolly. 'A good book, that ought to take your place well enough.' He had gone next door, and made noises like a big man dressing in a hurry. When he came back in he was fully prepared to go.

'Yes,' he said anxiously. 'Find a good book. I'll be back as soon as I can. We've got a million things to talk about.'

'Yes, we have,' she said softly. 'This had better all be true, Rob. If I find another deception afloat in all this mess you can expect the fastest divorce in the county. Fool me once, shame on you. Fool me twice, shame on me.'

'There's nothing like that,' he maintained, but he had to wipe his brow, and she noticed the tell-tale jitter at his fingers.

'No, of course not,' she agreed, but there was the taste of disbelief behind the words. 'Run along, Rob. I'll be here when you get back.'

'Marne?'

'What?'

'We'll make it a real marriage. Children and all?'

'We'll see. You'd better hurry. The voters must be champing at the bit.'

'Voters? Oh—yes, the voters. Keep warm, love.' He leaned over and kissed her gently. In no way was it like his kisses of the past hour or so; still, it was a sincere and promising thing. The sort of kiss a married lady could well be glad to receive.

'Be careful,' he added, and was gone.

Marne Smith stretched out on her bed, and flexed her stiffening arms over her head. What a marvellous day this has been, she thought. Not since God invented nice days—have I had such a nice day. She squeaked in delight as she settled back to recall it all. Rapid eye movement set in before she could sum up the first scene. She turned over on her side, with a huge smile on her face, her legs drawn up into her chest. In a moment that thin little whistle could be heard. Morgan, eager for something more sustaining than conversation, heard the whistle and knew her luck had run out. Marne slept the sleep of the faithful.

CHAPTER SIX

ROB was gone for the longest time. Marne slept, awoke, made herself a scrambled-egg sandwich, and slept again. And still he didn't come. There was nothing on television. The local radio stations were busy with their pop tunes. After the fervour of the primary campaign it almost seemed as if someone had turned off the whole world.

Of course, it wasn't entirely true. Her *Morning Herald* came at seven the next morning, as usual. But it had been put to bed early the night before, and contained practically nothing—except a fervent plea for everyone to get out and vote.

Panic-stricken, Marne telephoned her mother-in-law. 'No, we haven't heard a word,' Mabel Smith reported. 'There were a couple of his men staying here, but they rushed off yesterday afternoon, and I haven't heard boo from them since. Would you like to come over and stay with me, Marne?'

'I th-think . . .' she stammered. I think I'd better get to bed and hide my head under the blankets. I think— lord, I don't know what I think.

'I think I'd better run down and vote. And then better come back here. But—he's missing. Do you think I'd better call the police? No? Well, then, I'd better get downtown and back. There's no telling when he might come back—or call. Oops, there's someone ringing my front doorbell. I'll bet it's him. G'bye, love.'

So excited was she that she missed the telephone cradle, and had to pick the instrument up off the floor. Marne dashed for the front door and threw it open.

'Rob, where——?' But it was not Rob. Two men stood on her doorstep. Two men she did not know. One carried a large camera.

'Isaac Stone,' the first man introduced himself. 'And my cameraman. We're from the *Herald*. Is it true that your husband——?' Marne waved them through, and led them to the living-room, where the reporter had a great deal to say, and left her, dazed, after a half a hundred refusals on her part to answer his questions.

'Thank God that's over,' Rob Smith said to his three companions as they pulled up in front of the house. 'Now, I intend to be hard to find. You people follow up all the charges, and don't call me unless the British threaten to burn Washington.'

'What?'

'That's a joke, George. Don't call me at all. Right?'

'Say, Rob.' A comment from the back seat, where his two accountants sat. 'I think you've got some trouble here.'

'Trouble here?' Rob looked up at the porch. Two suitcases and a raincoat sat at the top edge of the stairs. 'Oh, my God.'

'Yours or hers, Rob?'

'Shut up and get out of here, you guys. Move.'

There was a little plume of dust as the back wheels of the car sought traction in the dirt of the parking space. Rob climbed the stairs. It was close on seven o'clock in the evening of election day. And the suitcases were his own.

'Marne?' Morgan sounded off a greeting as he opened the screen door. 'Marne?' He heard the dry sob from the living-room. His legs seemed suddenly to be heavy. His mind raced. There *had* to be a solution to the problem, but what? It required no genius to know that Marne Smith had found out about his little game.

'The finest bust in the last ten years,' the district attorney had told him not more than an hour ago. But how to explain that to the girl who sat dry-eyed in the rocking-chair in front of the television set? Dry-eyed, and yet crying.

'I'm back, Marne.' She looked up at him, her face contorted, and then back at the television set.

'Marne?'

'I see. I packed your bags for you. There's no need to stay, now that the election is over.'

'Marne, I don't *want* to leave. I intend to stay, come hell or high water.' He walked over to her chair and knelt in front of her. Her foot, which had been rocking the chair, stopped. The woman acted as if she were frozen into stone. And the only thing that will melt it all is love, he told himself.

She made no resistance as he pulled her forward into his arms. No resistance, and no reaction. It was like hugging a rag doll.

'It's not going to be like last time,' he said firmly. 'I had no chance for a hearing then. This time you're going to listen.'

It must have been something in his tone of voice that activated her. She looked down at him, and a tear formed in her eye. 'There's no need to tell me anything,' she said in a whisper. 'They have it all over the tube.'

'There are things that the TV people don't know,' he said stubbornly. 'The first one is that I love you. That I've loved you all these years. That I'll *never* stop loving you, Marne.'

A startled look flashed across her face. She put both hands up to cuddle his face, and looked straight into his dark eyes. 'I wish it could be true,' she said, sighing.

'It is,' he assured her. 'It is the absolute truth.' Two more tears appeared in her grey-green eyes, and slowly dribbled down her cheek. He stopped their flow with his finger. Her infinite strength broke down, her stiff backbone collapsed, and she fell across his shoulder, crying her heart out. For five minutes he let her cry, and when the tears were gone he climbed to his feet and pulled her up after him.

'It was a job that had to be done,' he told her. 'I haven't been off lawyering for the past four years. I took a job with the Federal Bureau of Investigation—the FBI. Are you listening?'

One of her slender hands came up around his neck and locked itself into the hair at the nape fo his neck. It was the best acknowledgment he could expect. The saliva began to run in his dry-as-dust mouth. He moved his head, and his lips gently touched hers. Just a touch, but it was not refused.

'This county,' he went on, 'has been one of the most crime-ridden counties in the nation. So the director set up a political sting operation. I was to come back and run for office, working my way into the Burroughs machine all the time. You've seen some of my men—accountants, lawyers, detectives. We've amassed enough evidence to break the machine completely. Yes, I know it all constitutes a sort of lie, but it was worthwhile, don't you think? Burroughs himself is in jail. About five of his cronies got away. One of my people made a slip—to Sylvia Burroughs—would you believe that? And she blew the works yesterday afternoon.'

'I'll believe anything,' Marne whispered.

'Then—you'll listen?'

'Is there more?'

'There's always more,' he told her. 'I love you, Marne. That's why I was eager to come. I wanted you to know—the fake marriage was no part of the Bureau's scheme. I set that up for myself. And as far as I'm concerned, love, it was no fake. Everything was legal, including the fact that the groom loves the bride.'

And the bride loves the groom, Marne thought. Always has, always will. One of her hands escaped the crush, and wandered to the collar of her dress, where the little blue sapphire sparkled in that light of the lamp beside her chair. There was so much left to be explained. She slumped, and he lowered her back into the chair.

'You treated me like some kid,' she accused.

'Then? Not now. I know better. We'll go on as partners.'

'Equal?'

'Well, I don't know about that,' he said, chuckling. 'There were times when I felt pretty well put down. Would you allow me to be equal?'

A tiny flash of a grin ran across her face, and was gone. 'No more dictatorship?'

'No more.'

'You were gone so often that I hardly ever saw you at night.'

'Yeah. Crazy,' he admitted. 'It was that crazy thing about amateur theatricals. We all thought that we were the coming things in theatre arts. It took us almost a year to find out that it wasn't true.'

'But—you could have told me. I could have come with you——'

'I didn't dare tell you. You would have laughed your head off.'

'Which just goes to show you didn't know me as well as you thought. I would have come. And I wouldn't dream of laughing.' A pregnant pause.

'Nothing else,' he asked.

'Babies,' she said. 'I wanted a baby, and you——'

'And I wouldn't allow it? Because I was too selfish, Marne. Because I wanted you all to myself. Because I was just beginning to find myself in the law business, and wasn't making a great deal of money. Because I thought—that we were both too young.'

'There's one more problem,' she said. She got up from the chair like an old woman, creaking in all her joints, waving aside his offer of help. 'No, I have to do this for myself.'

When she came back she was clutching the video-tape that had haunted her for so many years. Clutching it so tightly that her fingers had turned white.

'Can I help?' he offered. She waved him off.

'Just sit there,' she said.

He took the rocking-chair. She marched over to the sofa, and the coffee-table next to it. All her VCR equipment was there. She turned it on, then inserted the tape.

'Watch,' she commanded. 'Just watch.'

The TV set warmed up just in time to catch the lead-in of the tape. For five torturous minutes the tape ran, showing shadow figures wrestling on a worn couch. Sex play, as explicit as one might ever see, ending just as he was stripping the formal gown from the girl. From Sylvia Burroughs. And the man was Rob Smith. She watched the screen in silence as the tape ran out, and then she turned to him.

'Well?'

'Not as well as you might think,' he said. But he was laughing as he said it. Not just smiles, but outright laughter.

'You think that's funny,' she snapped. 'I thought it was adultery.'

'You're not serious, Marne? I think it's funny as hell.'

'I didn't,' she mumbled. 'I thought it was as serious as hell when I got it. That's when I went down and filed for divorce.'

'You mean to tell me that we've been apart for four years because of this little piece of tape? My God, woman, you——'

'Yes, I did,' she said firmly. 'For this little piece of truth. I don't believe I've heard you deny it. It's true, isn't it? You and Sylvia Burroughs?'

'Oh, Marne!' he exclaimed as he pulled her into a hug. 'All those years over this? This is what set the fire?'

'This is it.' She turned her head to one side and rubbed it into his light sweater. He must not see me cry, she told herself. Must not!

'And if it hadn't been for this tape?'

'I would have struggled to put up with the rest of it. But this—no woman could put up with this.'

'If I could prove to you that it's not what you think?'

'Don't torture me, Rob,' she yelled at him, pounding against his chest with both little hands. 'If you could prove it wasn't true I'd . . .' And the tears doubled. He found a handkerchief and offered it. She accepted, stepping back from him, dabbing at her eyes.

If he could prove it not to be true? Marne grappled with her conscience. Of course, it *had* to be true. There it was in full colour, right in front of her eyes. But if it wasn't? How could she deny what she felt? If it was not true—— 'I still love you, Rob. I won't live with you, but I still love you. If wishes could make it all go away, it would be gone. Someone sent that to me. Brought it, not mailed it. I found it in the morning when I opened the door to get the paper.'

'Marne, Marne.' He cherished her closely, lifting her a little off her feet so her head would lie on his shoulder. 'Marne, I can prove that this is just another lie. Will you grant me the time?'

'Yes. Lord, yes,' she muttered as he gently set her aside.

'I have to go over to my mother's house,' he said. 'I want you to wait right here. Watch the television. The polls have closed. They'll be reporting the counts pretty soon. With county-wide machine ballots, we ought to know the results very soon.'

'All right.' But instead of watching the television she watched him as he went back into his room, came out, made a bathroom stop, and went out of the front door.

Morgan came to join her. The old cat tried to jump from the floor into her lap, but her time had gone for gymnastics. She considered the situation, then walked around to the side of her chair to where the sewing basket rested. Using the basket as a mid-point, she jumped—and made the distance.

Marne's hand dropped on to the cat's head as she rubbed back and forth. The cat hummed. Her stub of a tail wagged portentously. 'I don't care *what* he brings back,' Marne said. 'No matter what. I'm going to believe him. I'm going to, even if it's the biggest lie in the world. That shows you what a marshmallow *I* am.' Morgan offered a noisy agreement before settling her magnificent head and nudging for more petting.

Marne reached up with her free hand and found her sapphire gift. 'Blue for fidelity,' she murmured. 'Lord help me to believe!'

It was close to eleven o'clock before he came back. His car roared up to the front of the house, and made a squealing stop. Marne held to her chair, flashing a look to the ignored TV. And then broke out into a full smile.

'Well,' he said as he came in. 'That's a good sign.'

'What?'

'You're smiling.'

'With good reason,' she said quietly. 'What kept you?'

'I couldn't find it,' he said, shaking his head in disgust. 'My mother didn't appreciate it, so she put it away in the attic along with the other junk she's been accumulating.'

He was carrying an old plastic bag. A fumbling moment later he brought out—another videotape. 'Now it's your turn to watch.'

Marne smiled at him. Of course, she was going to watch. Even though she believed already whatever it was he wanted to tell her. 'Is the moon actually green cheese?' she asked.

'What?'

'The Moon. Cheese,' she repeated, smiling.

He paused and stared at her as if trying to read between the lines. And then, 'Yes, the moon is made out of green cheese. You believe that?'

'I believe that,' she admitted.

'Then wait till you see this,' he said, chuckling. He snapped the switch, and the tape began to roll, overriding the election TV programme. The title on the videotape was somewhat distorted. 'The Odeon Players,' it said, 'present *Murder in the Living-Room*.'

And for fifteen minutes Marne stared as an obviously amateur group of players stumbled through their lines and over the stage furniture, telling the story of a murder at Thacker Heights. Just when she was getting interested Rob stopped the tape.

'Now this,' he said, 'is the interesting part.' He set the tape in motion again. The scene shifted, through a squeaky door, into a living-room, and then, to her surprise, the identical scene rolled, the one she had kept to herself for all those years. It rolled to the point where her tape had ended, and then a few turns more. The loving couple separated, a door slammed, a gun fired off-stage, and Sylvia Burroughs fell dead on the floor.

'Well, that's enough,' Rob said as he shut down the VCR. 'I told you we have amateur dreams. We made three copies of this awful tape and mailed one of them to each of the three networks. I can't tell you the words they used when they mailed them all back. And then someone extracted this scene and sent it to you.'

'And someone did,' she said. 'And I believed it. Every lying inch of it. What a fool I was.'

He walked across the room and pulled her up out of her chair. 'No, not with all the other stuff that was going on,' he said. 'You had good reason. I was too full of ambition to look after you, and we were both too young to know better.'

'But now, Rob?'

'I want you back, to be my wife, to be my love. I can't say for sure that nothing like all that old stuff might never come up again. But I *do* say that if it does all you'll need to do is say the magic word to make it stop. If you'll have me.'

'Rumpelstiltskin,' she said.

'What?'

'Don't you remember? That's the magic word.'

She was up in his arms before she recognised what was going on. Into his arms, and out to her bedroom. Things were in good shape. She had taken some of the last twenty-four hours to strip and clean and re-shape. He lowered her to feet. She stood there smiling as he began to unbutton and unbuckle. She shivered as the last little wisp of silk fell to the floor.

'Cold?'

'Anticipation,' she stuttered.

'There's a cure for that,' he said.

'I was sure you would know of one.' Her fingers were busy as she told him. Cold, shaking fingers, struggling with strange buttons and curious zips, until they were both nude.

'Me Wolfman,' he said as he picked her up and threw her on the bed. The springs bounced her around for a moment, just long enough for him to join her. 'Me Wolfman,' he repeated.

'Let's have a little less talk and a little more action,' she commented primly. And he provided it.

Through the long night there were strange noises in the bedroom. Morgan came in twice to protest. At her age, the cat needed her sleep. All through the long night, and then silence.

He awoke with the sun in his eyes, and the thunder of the old grandfather clock sounding thirteen. Thirteen? The bed space next to him was empty. Twisted sheets, pummelled pillow, but empty. He rubbed his chin. A shave was in order. In fact, Marne probably needed medical treatment for wrestling with this gorilla. From out of the kitchen he heard voices. Female voices. Two.

He came up out of the bed like a soldier, ready to run or hide as might be. On the floor in one corner he found a pair of his trousers and a shirt, and one sock. The other was long gone. So he climbed into trousers and shirt and went stalking out into the kitchen, barefoot. The linoleum was colder than he had expected.

'G'mornin', Uncle Rob.' His niece Becky, dressed in neat, clean dungarees, a blouse, and sandals. Neatly dressed.

'Good morning, Becky.' He patted the top of her head and smiled at Marne, at the stove.

'Good morning, Marne.' She turned in his direction, a smile on her face and a lively twinkle in her eye—and a touch of white lotion rubbed liberally into her cheek.

'Combat pay,' she said. 'I demand combat pay. Eggs? Bacon?'

'What's that mean?' Becky interjected. 'Combat pay?'

'It's a game we were playing last night,' Marne said. 'A sort of Nintendo game for grown-ups. I was only teasing him.'

'I'll have eggs,' he said. 'Sunny side up. And toast. No bacon. I'm trying to cut down on my cholesterol count.'

'Great idea,' Marne said, chuckling. 'That means you have to cut out the eggs first. They're the worst things you could eat.'

'What does that mean?' Becky again.

'It means that your uncle is getting old,' Marne said solemnly. 'He has to watch his diet and all that sort of good stuff.' A pert appraisal, just for a moment, and then, 'You look tired, Rob. Didn't you get enough sleep?'

'No, I didn't,' he said sharply. 'And, after certain ears around here are removed, there'll be a reckoning.'

'What does *that* mean?' Becky asked.

'That doesn't mean a thing,' Marne returned. 'The poor old fellow is too weak to do almost anything, and he knows it. Here are your eggs, Rob. We'll use up the ones we have, and then get a substitute for them. I know that some organisation makes liquefied eggs without the yellow in them. That's the part that has the cholesterol.'

'I wish it could be quieter around here,' Rob said with his best dignity showing. 'It's—nine o'clock, and I'd like to hear the news. Which reminds me. How come that grandfather clock strikes thirteen?'

'It always does,' Becky volunteered. 'Been doing it for years.'

'Here's a local news station,' Marne said, and flipped the switch on the radio. The announcer was in full flight. 'And despite the fact that the Burroughs ticket was shot down in flames, the neophyte candidate, FBI Agent Rob Smith, won the nomination on the Democratic Party ticket. Since there were no Republican candidates who might run against him in the November elections, it would appear, barring a miracle, that Mr Smith is the new county sheriff.'

'Oh, my God,' Rob said as he burned his mouth trying to drink his coffee too fast.

'That does make a problem, doesn't it?' Marne said in her sweetest voice. 'What do we do? Move to Washington, or run in the finals?'

'I haven't any idea what the Bureau will say,' Rob said. 'I was told to *enter* the primaries, not *win* them.'

'You can't go to Washington to live,' Becky said. 'Or if you do you'll have to leave Marne here. I need her worser than you do.'

'Worser?'

'It's a holiday. Worser is a perfectly good word for holidays!'

'Please, Becky, your uncle is having a stroke.'

'I guess I'd better call Washington,' Rob said.

'How about Sylvia?' Marne said, interrupting his chain of thought.

'Sylvia? What about Sylvia.'

'You said she got away.'

'She did. Went sailing off into the sunset, via TWA airlines. And cleaned out her dad's cash box. Which is why we were able to catch him on the fly!'

'That's terrible,' Marne said. 'She was the guilty one. I wanted very much for you to catch her and send her off to gaol for fifty years.'

'What, for stuffing ballot boxes?'

'Well, no. She's the one who sent me that—tape. For which she deserves fifty years in jail. Or worse.'

'Or worser,' he asked.

'Or worser. Look, Becky, you've had your breakfast, and there are some things your uncle and I have to settle. Why don't you scoot home? They'll excuse you for skipping one day of school, but no more. Off you go.'

The little girl gave them a solemn look, and then grinned. 'I know what you're up to,' she giggled. 'You want to decide which one of you will be sheriff!'

'And isn't that a fine idea?' Rob said as he walked to the door with his arm around Marne. They watched the little girl skip up the hill, and out of sight.

'And now,' Marne said firmly, 'we have to talk about cabbages and kings and sheriffs, and things like that—in the bedroom.'

'Oh, please,' Rob begged, 'not that.' With which he swept her up in his arms and carried her right to where she wanted to go.

The burning secrets of a girl's first love

Anne Mather

Hidden in the Flame

From the million-copy bestselling romance author

She was young and rebellious, fighting the restrictions of her South American convent. He was a doctor, dedicated to the people of his war-torn country. Drawn together by a powerful attraction, nothing should have stood in her way – yet a tragic secret was to keep them apart.

Available now priced £3.99

W**O**RLDWIDE

Another Face . . .
Another Identity . . .
Another Chance . . .

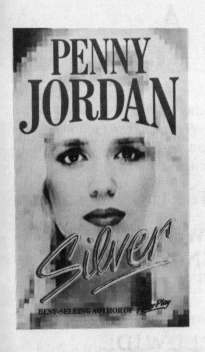

When her teenage love turns to hate, Geraldine Frances vows to even the score. After arranging her own "death", she embarks on a dramatic transformation emerging as *Silver,* a hauntingly beautiful and mysterious woman few men would be able to resist.

With a new face and a new identity, she is now ready to destroy the man responsible for her tragic past.

Silver – a life ruled by one all-consuming passion, is Penny Jordan at her very best.

W❂RLDWIDE